Advance Praise for
SWORD OF THE ALHAMBRA

"Anthony's debut novel sweeps you into a world rife with religious fanaticism and hatred. Will one man's honesty be enough to change the tides of history? Packed with bits of history, action and wit, the author presents timeless themes with a freshness and sincerity that will keep you turning pages late into the night."

- M. Murphy, Kansas

"Trained in the art of killing, Ibrahim is sure of his calling to protect the Maker's earthly paradise from "The Infidel" until he meets Santiago de Aviles, a man of morals, honor and decency thought to be nonexistent among the enemy. Can Ibrahim defeat his own prejudices and change the tides of history that are destroying his beloved world? Chock full of action and complex, appealing characters, this novel is sure to warm your heart and reach down into your very soul."

- V. Wolfe, Peru

"A moving, exhilarating and vivid read. Sword of the Alhambra takes you on a thrilling adventure as Ibrahim starts on a journey of self-discovery during a time of religious turbulence. The words written by Joseph Anthony come alive page after page to an exciting and thoughtful conclusion. This is a great book for anyone who wants to be immersed in an emotionally honest story full of history and adventure."

- J. Buol, California

"Set in 15th Century Granada, The Sword of The Alhambra is an adventure filled with romance, intrigue, and religious conflict. The story explores one man's struggle as he is caught between his loyalty to tradition and duty and his passion for the new and unknown."

- M. Ziff, California

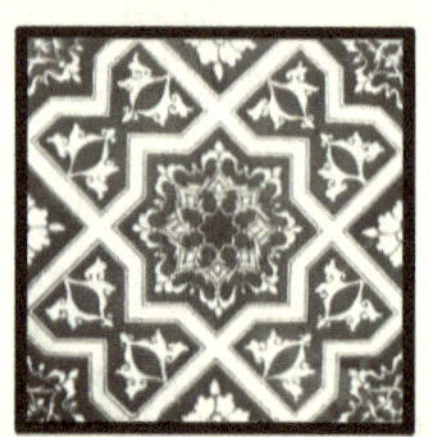

Joseph Anthony

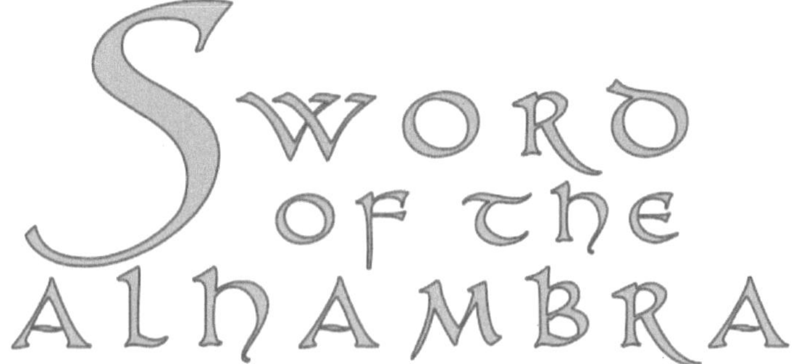

a tale of ancient spain

Azalea Art Press
Berkeley . California

ISBN: 978-0-9846977-2-4

To my lovely wife Jessica
who planned the trip to Spain
that became the genesis of this book

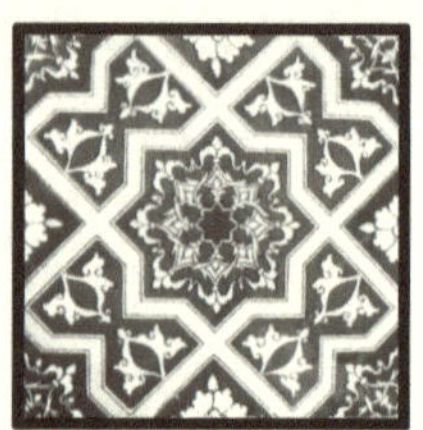

Contents

Author's Note *i*
Main Characters *ii*
Foreword *iv*

Chapter 1 1
The Dance of Sevilla

Chapter 2 5
Only God Will Conquer

Chapter 3 33
Of a Girl and a Dance

Chapter 4 39
The Triumphal Procession

Chapter 5 53
The Martyr

Chapter 6 65
Of Pomegranates

Chapter 7 72
Terror in the Night

Chapter 8 91
In the Gardens of God

Chapter 9 98
Santiago De Aviles

Chapter 10 109
Shaken Beliefs

Chapter 11 122
The Procession

Chapter 12 135
The Grey Cloaks

Chapter 13 138
Better Men

Chapter 14 153
A Sheep in Sheep's Clothing

Chapter 15 167
Upon the Ramparts

Chapter 16 170
Irem

Chapter 17 186
The Death of Jerusalem

Chapter 18 213
The Reconnaissance

Chapter 19 228
The Ambassador

Chapter 20 238
The Coming of Castile

Chapter 21 265
The Tutelary

Chapter 22 283
The Sword is Sheathed

Chapter 23 288
Only I Will Conquer

Chapter 24 301
Hijos De Espana

Chapter 25 312
Yawm Ad-Din

Acknowledgments *357*
About the Author *359*
Contact / Book Orders *360*

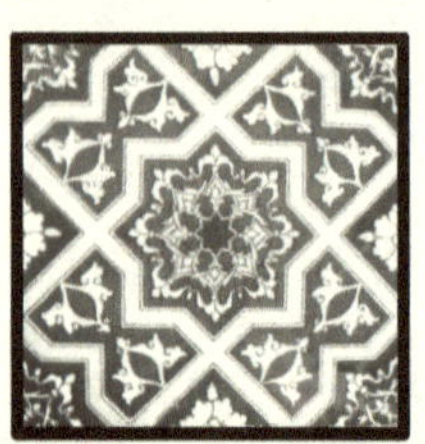

Author's Note:

In keeping with the spirit of the *convivencia* and theme of this story, quotations from the Bible, Koran and Arabic/Spanish poetry and music are not specifically cited.

Main Characters

The Muslims

Ibrahim Al-Rahim: *Capitan of cavalry. Defender of the Alhambra. Raised in Jerusalem, of Kurdish descent.*

Adnan Al Mansur: *Ibrahim's trusted lieutenant. A Berber from North Africa.*

Abdul Rahkman: *The Sultan of the kingdom of Granada.*

Osmyn: *Commander of infantry. From the Sudan.*

Yusuf: *A young soldier and native of Granada. Assigned to oversee the dungeon of the Alhambra.*

Harun*: Ibrahim's uncle from Damascus who raised him after the fall of Jerusalem.*

Exsecour: *Ibrahim's war-horse.*

The Assassins: *Cult followers of Sinan, from Syria.*

The Christians

Maria de Alicante: *A native of Granada, and seller of pomegranates in the public market.*

Rebecca de Caceres: *From Sevilla, a young lady and a dancer.*

Abran de Aviles: *A knight from a village in Castile, to the north of Granada.*

Santiago de Aviles: *Abran's brother.*

James the Priest: *Spiritual leader of the Christian populace of Granada.*

Peter: *A solitary man with a unique calling.*

Foreword

This is a story of a forgotten Spanish civilization. Remnants of the culture are still found in the music, food, dress and architecture of modern-day Spain.

A well-stocked bookstore will have few editions that teach us about the eight hundred years the Moors dominated the Iberian Peninsula and called their country, *Al-Andalus*. Between 700 A.D.-1500 A.D., while Western Europe was mired in religious superstition, intolerance, illiteracy, and forced labor, Islamic Spain was a beacon of justice, tolerance, literature, architecture, art and music.

Religious communities lived together in a spirit of peace and brotherhood unique in its day, known as the *convivencia*. (Literally the *living together*.)

While London and other cities of Europe were dark places where sewage flowed freely in the streets and disease bred as rapidly as the rats, the Islamic centers of Granada, Toledo, and Cordoba were the epitome of refinement and elegance, with paved streets, public parks, clean water, baths, and libraries.

The crowning achievement of the convivencia was the breathtaking architecture of the Alhambra. It blended man's design with a deep respect for the natural world. The result is a wonder that must be seen with one's own eyes, for it's singular magnificence goes far beyond the limitations of the written word.

After the conquest by the Catholic Monarchs of Columbus fame, Jews and Moors that did not convert to

Christianity were expelled from Spain. Arabic manuscripts were destroyed, their valuable histories and literature lost. Arabic became an outlawed language throughout the Iberian Peninsula. It is the victors that write the history and a grand civilization was forgotten.

This is a story of a mighty warrior who fought against all odds to preserve that civilization. But our story does not begin with a sword. Far from it. We begin with a girl on an outdoor patio in the city of Granada, in the shadow of the Alhambra.

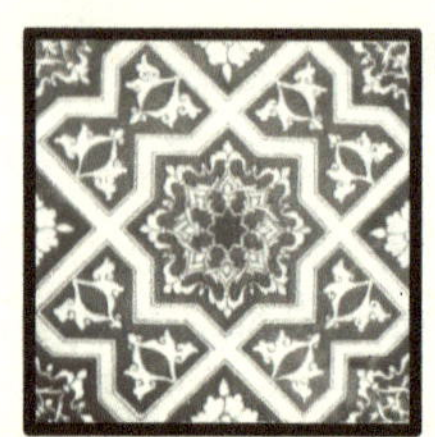

Sword of the Alhambra

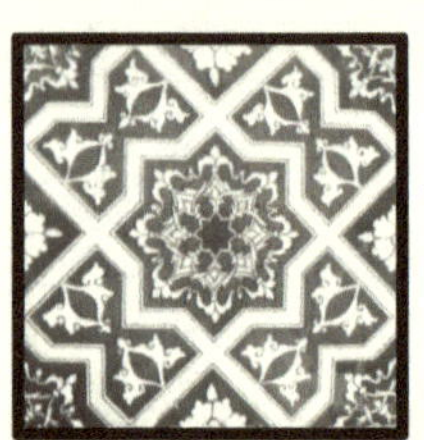

Chapter 1

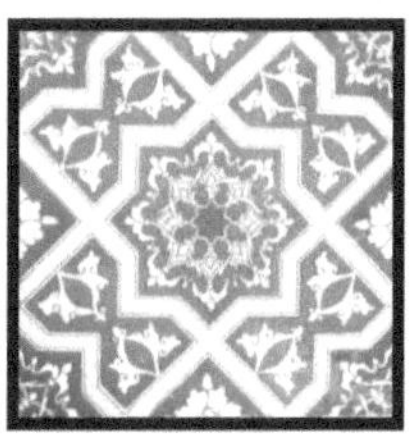

The Dance of Sevilla

In a cobblestone courtyard surrounded by white-washed walls draped in violet and blue bougainvillea, under a cobalt blue sky stood a tall slender girl. A girl in form and feature, but not a youth. She wore a simple housedress of light blue cloth that matched the hue of the bougainvillea. Her thick black hair framed her bronzed high cheekbones and flowed down to her waist. Even in the simple dress normally worn while she cared for common daily chores, she was lovely.

Her hair bounced softly as she slowly traced the steps of the inspirational dance she first witnessed in Sevilla, the dance that she now taught to the girls of Granada.

This particular dance was practiced in secret, performed by Christian girls for the benefit of their people. They danced in courtyards shielded from street view, in caves or in orchards throughout the city and Kingdom of Granada.

The girl held one hand high above her head and traced slow serpentine circles in the air with elegant fingers. At the same time, with her other hand she held the fringe of her dress up almost to her waist, and outward.

Her rhythmic movements were timed to silent music. Her almond-shaped eyes closed tight as she imagined the speeding staccato of the guitar and the clapping hands that accompanied it.

She turned in a spiral, gently tapping her feet upon the smooth cobblestones. She repeated these steps in slow, silent grace.

Since this was practice, she held herself back. She did not stamp her feet with all of her might over and over again with blurring speed, as when she was performing. As she danced, high in the minarets that sprouted like the conical tops of a branchless pines above the low skyline of Granada, the *muezzins* began their daily routine of calling the faithful to prayer, their high pitched undulating cries of praise to God filled the air.

Then the girl did a most unusual thing—while the calls of the muezzins rose and fell in pitch, the girl moved more slowly. As the calls paused between each crying refrain, she lightly tapped her feet on the cobblestones and swirled gently while she traced circular shapes in the air with her hand and fingers.

It was a strange combination, a silent dance performed to the loud calls of the muezzins. Strange as it seemed, the rhythmic cry of the muezzins complemented the rhythmic dancing motion of the girl. Two opposing forces. Blended as if by design, creating a mesmerizing form of quiet art.

Only a handful of brave souls performed this dance—those willing to chance the wrath of Islam.

The Christians of Sevilla performed the dance during the Muslims' daily prayers. The dance had a powerful meaning. It was proof that they belonged to the rightful faith of Spain and the Moors were but temporary invaders who would soon be expelled by the Lord.

As she danced in the courtyard, the girl did not entertain such grand thoughts of rebellion and change. She saw the dance and was awed by its power and grace. It made her happy. She felt like a little girl again while she danced. That little girl who was raised by a loving family, not the one in the torn blue dress alone in the muddy hut. She lived to see the joy the dance brought to others while she performed. For those reasons she brought it to Granada. For she had a vision. She wished to teach it in cities and villages, until it became the national dance of her people and gained fame throughout the Christian and Muslim world as the dance of Spain.

She practiced longer than usual today. Extra training. She wanted perfection, for more observers than normal would be at the performance.

The bulk of the Moor's army was away, rumors of another great battle beyond the snowy Sierra Nevada Mountains. Fewer troops in the city meant more Christians would take heart and come to view what could be considered a seditious event by their Muslim overlords.

Over and over again the muezzins called. Over and over again, the girl changed the pace of her dance in time to the calls, silent clapping, smiling, one final spin, head thrown back, quietly laughing, happiness flowing through her as along with her graceful movements, the prayers ended.

The innocent girl did not realize—how could she know—that her simple passion, this graceful dance, would soon affect the fates of so many and sweep her and the entire kingdom into the maelstrom.

Chapter 2

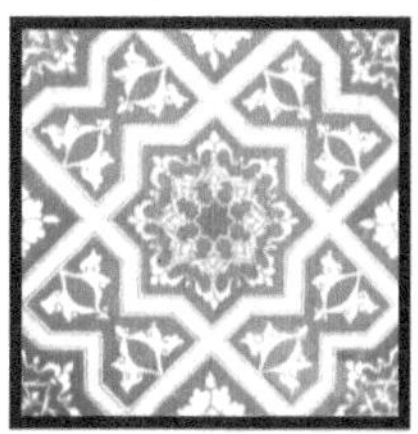

Only God Will Conquer

"Ye did not slay them.
God slew them."

At the same time the girl finished one final, joyful spin, far beyond the walls of Granada, he seethed. The anger he kept under control, as confined within borders as his neatly trimmed goatee, boiled. Outlined against the sky, on the peak of a bare ridge, he looked to be alone. But Ibrahim Al-Rahim was not alone. He stared intently at thousands of men below him, engaged in a mortal struggle for life.

He sat high in the saddle astride his charger Exsecour, a bay destrier, the same breed favored by his crusader enemies. This was the famous and likewise infamous Ibrahim Al-Rahim, commander of the Kingdom of Granada's elite horse cavalry and the Sultan's personal bodyguard.

Ibrahim wore a turban and black cloak that was clasped at his throat by a golden broach in the shape of a lyre. The cloak floated in a hot breeze that drifted across the sea, carrying with it the hard smell of the North African desert. The black face of the cloak was laced with delicate gold filigree such as adorned the walls, ceilings, arches and columns of the Alhambra. The seemingly random Arabesque lines formed words that were repeated over and over again in a continuous, never ending stream, "*Only God will conquer.*"

To Ibrahim Al-Rahim, these were more than mere words. They were his life's creed.

Ibrahim's black turban came to a sharp peak, shaped by the pointed gold helmet beneath. His almond-shaped eyes blazed fiery amber. He wore a cuirass made of overlapping gold plated leaves over his chest, which protected him from his neck to far below his waist.

He was tall for a Moor. Taller than many of the Franks, his enemies who were famed for their height.

His eyes darted back and forth, taking in the breadth and depth of a vast battlefield below.

The violent scene before him forced his mind back through the years, back to a dark and frightening time. The blurred image of a child, covered in blood, falling backwards into the abyss. Tumbling, crying out, hand thrust upwards reaching for help, grasping for a moment a tiny hand, then falling. Cries of terror in the void. Blackness.

Ibrahim's eyes watered as he jolted back to the present and the task at hand. He reminded himself to concentrate, this no time for self-pity. That would come later, where he was alone at night in his chambers, when the repressed memories of his childhood seeped into his dreams, deforming them into vicious night terrors.

His knuckles turned bright white as he clutched an eight-foot lance with its deadly triangular head of steel.

A golden bejeweled scabbard at his waist held his scimitar—a long wide blade, wickedly curved at a right angle, designed for slashing.

A hidden scabbard attached to Ibrahim's calf held a smaller curved dagger that he would use if he were swiftly de-horsed and without access to his primary weapons.

With his free hand he held fast the reins of his horse and clasped a string of simple wooden beads, tightly intertwined around his fingers. They were well worn; some of the beads were cracked in half. A stark contrast to his elegant dress and weaponry.

Unconsciously Ibrahim's fingers rubbed each bead between his thumb and forefinger as he scanned the vast struggle unfolding below, tens of thousands of men locked in violent battle.

Thousands of brightly colored banners—apricot, green and yellow, all the colors of fallen autumn leaves—fluttered in the valley floor below. On the face of each banner was written in golden filigree, one phrase, one theme repeated over and over, "*Only God will conquer.*"

The Moors carried the bright banners aloft as they rushed onward towards their enemies, an ever-shrinking circle of white-clothed Christian knights surrounded on all sides by green- and orange-clothed Islamic assailants.

These particular Christian knights, monks of the Military Orders were easily visible on the field, conspicuous by the bright red crosses emblazoned upon their chests.

A short distance away, on another sub-blasted hill, across from where Ibrahim observed the battle, the leader of all Moors, the Sultan of Granada Abdul-Rahkman, sat motionless on his horse.

He too surveyed the raging battle flowing below. At this distance the sounds of battle were like the clamor of a cyclonic wind ripping through a mountain pass. As he observed, a robed attendant handed him a silver goblet. He took a casual draught from the goblet filled with crimson colored rose water. In the pool of water, a jagged chunk of snow bobbed up and down, surrounded by a dozen shards of red and pink rose petals. It tasted cool, earthy and clean.

The Sultan wore a long flowing scarlet robe and a high round white turban. The Sultan's grey beard was very long, divided in two parts that ended in sharp points near his waist. Unlike Ibrahim, the Sultan sat astride his horse with a relaxed posture.

A group of horsemen, his commanders and ministers surrounded the Sultan. Fluttering above the group, snapping sharply in the wind were the triangular pennants bearing the half-green, half-white flag of the Kingdom of Granada, their realm that encompassed all of southern Spain and ended at the Mediterranean shore.

Directing the foot soldiers was a tall black-skinned man who sat with perfect posture on his charger to the right of the Sultan, the position of honor. He was dressed in flowing robes, a cap of silver colored steel chain mail about his head.

This was Osmyn, a most devout Muslim who hailed from the trackless deserts of the Sudan. A Bedouin by birth. Osmyn commanded the Moorish foot soldiers of Granada who at present were locked in mortal battle once again with their eternal foes from the kingdoms of Christendom.

A nervous looking young man with a narrow face and hawkish nose stood to the Sultan's left. He was an agent, an auditor sent to examine the financial operations of the Kingdom and ensure that the Caliph of Baghdad received his proper tribute.

The Sultan hated such men. Upon hearing of the auditor's arrival to the Kingdom of Granada, the Sultan disdainfully remarked, "Nothing more than a spy without hair on his chest." The Sultan was aware that this particular auditor was sent not only to inspect the books but for a covert purpose. The Caliph, indeed all of Islam's governors were increasingly concerned about the fate of Granada and its crown jewel, the pride of the Islamic world, the Alhambra.

The Sultan spoke to his retinue casually, as he emptied the goblet of rose water, and handed it back to the bowing attendant.

He said, "They never bring enough water with them, those Spaniards. Curious. This heat! Perhaps their Lord will slake their thirst? They do not respect the power of the desert as we do. Their disrespect is their undoing."

The Sultan glanced down at the young auditor, and sneered through his split grey beard. The Sultan thought to himself, *That little toad will report on everything that happens here, every move I make! Body language, hand gestures, he inspects me even now. Very well! I will provide a fine report for his master!*

The Sultan gestured toward his battle lines, to a point where a Knight Templar, mounted on a massive armor encased charger fought alone, surrounded by dozens of horsemen riding much smaller mounts and said,

"My Moors rely on light, fast horsemen, the *jinetes,* who ride the smaller North African breeds. Our tribes of North Africa are well adapted to this type of hit and run warfare. They perfected this martial technique in ancient times, before Rome dominated the Mediterranean. The riders harass the Christian knights, firing short lethal javelins . . ."

The Sultan paused, then pointed below to a unit of Moors firing their javelins in unison and said, "See there! After firing, they quickly ride away before the Christians can react. These hit-and-run tactics provoke the chivalry of Christendom. Turns them into madmen! Frustrated at not being able to close on our faster horsemen they charge heedlessly, impulsively, without support, to their doom. Templars hold the advantage over my men in the heaviness of their weapons and armor. But their tactics are predictable, arcane. A Military Monk dedicates three hours a day of training in the martial arts and they are well-practiced killing machines, but when cut off and isolated, they are easily taken down, the way a pack of wolves takes down a powerful moose, using the chaos created from greater numbers."

The Sultan paused and thought this would be an effective moment to express his faith in God. It was prudent to do so. This would add luster to the young auditor's report. The Sultan looked to heaven and cried out,

"Allah blinds them to their doom! For it is God alone that conquers!"

The Sultan glanced over to the next hill where Ibrahim Al-Rahim sat with his cavalry, waiting in still silence, the horsemen as still as stone statues for now. The Sultan sensed it. Ibrahim was about to unleash his heavy horse, rush down the hill and crush the enemy.

The Sultan said, "There is nothing more for us to observe here. Let us return to Granada, for I have many tasks to complete."

The young auditor, his report on the battle incomplete, gestured toward the battle raging below, looked up at the Sultan and objected in a frail, high-pitched voice,

"My Lord! The battle is not finished! It is not yet decided!"

The Sultan glared down at the young man and replied with disdain, "No my young friend, so recently released from his mother's breast, this battle is very much over."

The Sultan turned toward Osmyn, opened his hand, gestured and said, "The field is yours my son."

Osmyn lowered his head and replied slowly, a deep baritone, "Yes my Lord."

The Sultan tugged the reins of his horse, swinging the animal around, away from the din of battle, towards home.

From atop the adjacent hill, Ibrahim saw the Sultan swing away on his horse, returning to Granada. A silent gesture of confidence in his commanders. In total victory.

Ibrahim felt a surge of pride. Proud to have the Sultan's acceptance, proud of his friendship with the great man. Proud of his God-ordained role as defender of the faith.

Ibrahim thought about that term, *Defender of the faith? Defend against what? Enemy armies? False teachings? Sedition? Yes. The responsibility is mine! For this reason I was spared. But how many more men have to die until my responsibility is fulfilled? Will they ever stop trying to destroy us? It never ends.*

Ibrahim was frustrated. Some unknown zealot priest calls for a Crusade against the Moors. He gathers the ignorant to fight against God's kingdom on earth. The zealot tells his followers that it is God's will the Kingdom of Granada be conquered in the name of Issa the prophet. Like good obedient sheep headed happily to the slaughterhouse, they come by the thousands.

Perhaps, it is not a priest but a crazed hermit living in a cave who has a vision of a miraculous victory over the Moors. The visions always entail the same repetitive elements about a fiery cross falling down out of heaven and the enemy being devoured. Some of these seer-sayers prophesy that they will not have to fight at all! God will smite the pagan Moors with fire and mighty stones that weigh more than a man. Cast down from the heavens.

So they come again. And again. And again. Another invasion. They cross the dry mountain passes from the north and descend to Loja, spilling onto the fruitful plains below.

They march to battle slowly, noisily, without order. They are not a true army. Only rabble. They do not bear sufficient supplies. Not even water! They are certain of victory! No discipline or preparation is needed when on crusade! God will provide miraculous deliverance! Their blind faith tells them to prepare for combat would betray a lack of faith in the saving power of the Lord. Victory that was pre-ordained in heaven.

Ibrahim whispered angrily, "Stupid, fanatical sheep!"

Ibrahim was confident but uneasy. Yes, they were easily defeated. No match for his Moors. But the determination of the Christians to re-conquer the Kingdom of Granada was unquestioned. Ibrahim shifted uncomfortably on his saddle as a thought hit him. What if they found a leader, a champion, a true king to unite them and lead their limitless armies against us? Not a weak-minded priest or hermit, a true leader of men and strategist. It would happen someday. It was inevitable. Then his Moors would be hard-pressed to hold the Kingdom and the gardens of God.

Ibrahim's teeth clenched as he watched his enemy with a strange blend of hatred and fascination. The Military Monks, the Knights Templar, fought for their lives. Thoughts flashed through his mind.

Templars protect the pilgrims en-route to the holy places of Jerusalem. They kill Muslims, my people! And without mercy.

Ibrahim saw the Templar's flag. The huge half-white, half-black banner named *Beauceant.* The white portion meant fairness to those of their faith, the black portion, death to their enemies.

Military Monks were a contradiction of terms—peace and war—their headquarters in the ruins of the Temple of Jerusalem. Issa taught peace in that temple. Templars dedicated it to war.

Ibrahim focused on an individual Templar. The Military Monk charged ahead of his own infantry lines and into the Moorish lines in a thirst for blood and plunder. The Moors opened the way for the over-zealous Templar to gallop through. The trap is opened. Then the trap is closed.

The white-draped Templar, in bright armor, is surrounded by hundreds of green- and orange-clad Moors, a shining silver island in a sea of men dressed in all the colors of the forest floor in autumn. The Templar is hit by dozens of arrows that stick to but do not completely penetrate his thick steel armor. The besieged knight looks like an over-sized porcupine as he blunders about.

Inevitably the wounded and isolated Templar is dehorsed and falls on his back, seemingly immobile. The Moorish lances, swords, axes and arrows keep striking, probing for the weak spot in the armor at the base of the neck, the forearm, or the vital arteries of the inner thigh.

Borne along by the thrill of the kill, several Moors charge in. They are struck down as soon as they are in range of a razor sharp broadsword, for without warning the knight, in spite of his wounds, heavy armor and the exhaustion of battle, springs to his feet.

With one swift stroke, his sword cuts down three attackers at once.

Ibrahim swore under his breath. He and Osmyn trained their men not to be hasty in attacking a downed knight, never to get within arm stroke of that lethal broadsword.

The dexterity of the Military Monks amazed Ibrahim. As a fellow soldier, for a passing moment, he admired the strength and skill. They moved so fast, with such grace, in spite of carrying so much weight upon their backs.

As Ibrahim watched, the silver island became still, then disappeared, swallowed by the autumn floor as the Templars were overwhelmed by the onrushing Moorish tide.

As the sole Military Monk finally met death, Ibrahim thought, *A waste of a good warrior! Christendom's elite—no mercy. Very well, they attack us in the same predictable way and we will destroy them. It is God's will that we destroy them. Allah has blinded them once again. They cannot see their doom. They will meet death by our hands. By my hand. I am the vessel chosen by God to deliver destruction to the infidels. I am his instrument of judgment. His paradise and the convivencia will be secure from the infidel once again. The gardens of the Alhambra will continue to stand as a living, breathing monument to the power of the true divinity and his prophet. They are unmerciful. So we must be. If we show mercy all is lost. The convivencia, the gardens of God, my people, turned to ash. Mercy is weakness.*

Ibrahim looked beyond the spot on the battlefield where the Templars met their doom to the main battle lines. Two armies of infantrymen on foot were locked in a death struggle, swaying to and fro. Thousands of men fighting to the death. Fighting for life.

The ground where the two armies clashed looked like a massive undulating snake, bending inward, then outward. The Christians pushed the Moors back, then the Moors pushed the Christians back across the same churned patch of earth. The Christians used their superiority in armor and weapons to gain the advantage, only to be countered by the Moors' superior numbers, leadership and discipline.

Ibrahim looked to heaven. The will of Allah be done. They would not lose this day. They must not lose. There was too much at stake. The Christians could lose battle after battle, sacrifice thousands of soldiers, year after year, but if the Moors lost even once . . . The consequences were too terrible to contemplate.

Ibrahim did not commit his own heavy cavalry to the fray until he could hit the enemy at the correct moment, the moment of maximum impact. Ibrahim concentrated on the task at hand. He sensed it now. His enemy was weakening.

The Christians were finally beginning to tire and give way. All of their troops were committed to the battle. They were worn down by the myriads of Moorish troops, the lack of water, and the loss of their elite mounted knights.

Ibrahim held his horsemen back patiently, waiting, against his own will, the anger pushing him, threatening to overwhelm his emotions. He yearned more than all of the servants of Allah to ride, alone if necessary, hell bent into their lines and take vengeance. He would never stop striking them down, these infidels who wreaked havoc on his family. He would never forget, never forgive or make peace with them. He swore it! A sacred oath to Allah himself.

Now was the time.

Ibrahim glanced to his right, saw Adnan Al-Mansur, his steadfast lieutenant, always at his side. Adnan smiled through his oversized unkempt beard a stark contrast to his shiny, bald head. To men like Adnan Al-Mansur, this was not a battle of life and death that could change the course of history. It was entertainment.

For Adnan al Mansur was a Berber, a member of a unique tribe of men who navigated upon that endless ocean of sand known as the Sahara. Life in the tribes was a constant battle against the heat, lack of water, fellow tribesmen, sandstorms and bandits. To a Berber, and the other tribes that made their living on the dunes, the Touaregs and the Bedouins, warfare was as natural as eating, drinking and sleeping.

A set battle such as this? Nothing more than a day of leisure for a Berber. The Arab Moors and Berbers were allies, united in faith and purpose, against the common foe of Christendom. In spite of their alliance and common bond of faith, there was constant, underlying tension between the two unyielding races.

The Arabs looked down on the Berber as uncivilized wild men from the desert. The Berber viewed the Arabs as soft. The Berber disdained the arrogance of the cultured, learned Arab and his life of luxury. When not engaged against the crusaders, Berber and Arab had many times come to blows over their cultural divergences. However, if one were to ask an Arab, even one who disdained the very sight of a Berber, if there was any other race of man or angel that he would want at his side during mortal conflict, there would be no hesitation in the answer.

Ibrahim Al-Rahim was himself a Kurd by birth, born in the Levant in the holy city of Jerusalem itself. Therefore he was not truly a Moor. The Moor was a dark-skinned Muslim from North Africa.

Ibrahim and Adnan though very different men, were the best of friends. Adnan laughed. Ibrahim slightly annoyed asked, "Why do you laugh Adnan? Why do you find this humorous?"

Adnan responded, "Ah Ibi! Because this is an easy day! Easier than dying from thirst. Easier than enduring a blinding sandstorm that blows the brown voice of death for an entire week. If you die here, now in battle, it will quick! Perhaps painless—a silent black rush—nothing more. A death in the desert? That is pre-ordained to be a slow, painful torture from thirst or starvation."

Adnan al Mansur the Berber, laughed again as he watched the battle unfold before him as if he were watching a traveling circus or a juggling act in the plaza mayor of Granada.

"Ibi! Visitors! Let us give them a warm Granadine welcome! *Yen'aal deen ommak*!"

Ibrahim shook his head, but did not correct Adnan this time. Nor did he laugh or even smile, at Adnan's levity. Ibrahim Al-Rahim was known not to smile. Men who served with him for years remarked, "Sooner will you see the Pope pray in the direction of Mecca than you will see the Captain of the Alhambra smile."

Inevitably another soldier would object, coming to the defense of his captain and say, "If you were raised in Jerusalem, you would not be the happiest of fellows either."

All would nod their heads in solemn agreement, ending the discussion, for all Muslims knew and wept over the fate of the Holy City.

Ibrahim responded sarcastically to Adnan's unfettered enthusiasm to bloody battle, said flatly,

"Berbers. You are all the same. Barbarians."

Another man would have been insulted. Adnan laughed even harder. His large square frame quaked from a belly laugh that erupted out of his mouth, exposing every other tooth, cracked or misshapen.

"You need a barbarian in your life Ibi! I keep you from becoming like your pampered Arab . . ."

Adnan paused, turned in his saddle and pointed to the waiting cavalry, his own troops, and yelled, "Girlfriends!"

Ibrahim responded, "For the last time, I am not Arab. I am a Kurd!"

"Same damn thing!"

Mansur did not wear his armor well. His cuirass was unhinged in the back and flopped carelessly about his torso. His cone-shaped helmet was pulled back off of his head and tilted to the side. As he laughed, the helmet fell off, clanged onto the flank of the horse and slammed to the ground, rolling away, exposing his shiny, bald head to the blazing sun. Mansur did not notice. He shook his head and cried out,

"I hate armor! Its too heavy, constricting, and hot. This weight interferes with my sword stroke! I want to fight like a man! Unencumbered! Desert-style!"

Ibrahim ignored Adnan, focused on the coming charge. He heard the same protest from Adnan a hundred times. He knew that if Adnan could decide such things, he would fight every battle completely naked.

As Ibrahim Al-Rahim swiveled and looked behind him, two thousand pairs of eyes watched his every movement, yearning for the order to charge. He observed his men with a mixture of pride and true affection. They were the finest soldiers in all of Islam. He loved and respected these men, his only real brothers. The only family Allah had left to him.

Ibrahim Al-Rahim did not speak to his men before a charge. He was not given to many words or inspirational speeches to encourage his men to great deeds on the battlefield or as an inducement to charge bravely. The words of a wise Roman came to mind: "To a brave man, few words are worth many."

Brave men, well trained and motivated to defend their homeland, men of the true faith empowered by Allah, need no words of encouragement on the day of battle. Besides, it would cheapen these men and their bravery to put words to it, to explain their courage away.

The horses too sensed the coming charge. Exsecour pawed the ground and neighed, thrashing his head from side to side in anticipation. The other horses neighed and gently bucked, straining to be unleashed. Ibrahim patted Exsecour on the side of his long muscular neck and whispered softly, "Soon my brother. A bit more patience. Then I will set you free."

The men stood erect in their saddles and by impulse, grasped their lances until their knuckles turned white. They stood upon the hill, silent, barely able to hold their mounts back, outlined as dark figures framed against the clear blue sky like a black thunderhead that is sighted upon the horizon. The dark cloud drifts in slowly then covers the land. As it does, everything goes still, the wind, the call of the birds, even the chirping of the insects stops in silent anticipation of the ripping clash of thunder and the brilliant flash of light that shakes the ground.

Ibrahim raised his arm high above his head, hand opened wide, fingers splayed. Then Ibrahim closed his hand into a balled fist and thrust his arm forward.

With that one simple gesture, the storm broke open upon the earth and unleashed its full fury.

Brass horns, thin and long, began a shrill sound, accompanied by the deep bass of a thousand kettledrums, pounding out the frantic rhythm of doom.

Two thousand surged forward as one. The ground trembled, and in one practiced motion, two thousand lances swung from an upright position to level, steel triangular heads pointed menacingly forward.

The speed of the charge began at a trot, in order to maintain the strength of the horses and the cohesion of the mass. As they neared the lines of their enemies, they broke into the full gallop.

A cry arose from the cavalrymen as they poured down the slope and neared the unprotected vulnerable flank of the Christian lines. The cry started as a low murmur, then rose in pitch and fury until,

"*TAK-BIR*! *TAK-BIR*!" undulated across the battlefield, over and over again and the cry could be heard in heaven itself.

They crashed into the Christian infantry, the sound a sickening thud as lance head met flesh, horse slammed into shield and men began to fall. Dust, broken weapons and the broken bodies of men flew into the air, in a brownish-red cloud.

The shock was immediate, devastating and total.

The Christian line began to falter in cringing anticipation of the blow, broke. A levee finally overcome by the tide. The flank of the Christian army melted away. They were running now, throwing down weapons, screaming in fear, some sobbing as they ran, some wetting themselves, others vomiting from terror as they tried in vain to escape the storm of death that rained down upon them.

Ibrahim spotted a sole Templar fighting alone. Dehorsed. Surrounded by a dozen Moors who slashed at the lone man with lance and scimitar, dozens of blows glanced off his thick armor.

The Templar lashed out with his powerful broadsword, unable to come to grips with his tormentors, like a furious bear surrounded by a pack of snapping dogs. Neither side was able to gain the upper hand on their foe.

Ibrahim at full gallop, growled, hot uncontrolled rage in his heart. He dug his spurs into the flanks of Exsecour and veered off from the rest of his horsemen in a straight line towards the lone Templar, his black cloak flying behind.

Ibrahim leaned forward in the saddle, his left hand gripping the reins. The wooden beads, wrapped around his fingers. His right hand clutched the long ash lance.

The Moors who were fighting the lone Templar dispersed, running in all directions for their own safety as they saw and felt the mighty charge of Ibrahim Al-Rahim. The Templar swung his kite shaped shield forward to protect himself. Too late.

Ibrahim cried out, *"Sālīm! Sālīm! Sālīm!"* Ibrahim's lance struck the Templar in the chest. The force of the charging thousand-pound war horse combined with Ibrahim's own weight and strength delivered a blow to the thick plate armor that resisted all other attacks.

Ibrahim released the lance as it penetrated deep into the body of the Templar and exploded out his back in a spray of red droplets. The quivering lance pinned the Templar to the earth like a rag doll.

Ibrahim reined Exsecour onto his hind legs, drew his scimitar and spun, red-faced, yelling indecipherable words, curses as he peered and squinted through the dust, yearning to catch sight of the red cross upon a white field that marked another of the Knights Templar.

No more were found.

The enemy was broken. Ibrahim's cavalry pursued. It was no longer a battle, but a massacre. A few small pockets of Christians bravely turned to face the onslaught. Others crossed themselves or fell to their knees to pray their final words before being received to heavenly glory, as they were cut down.

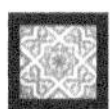

As Ibrahim's cavalry charged and destroyed the Christian lines, a lone man ran against the tide of fleeing Christian soldiers and pilgrims in a vain attempt to reach the point of battle where the massacre had reached a crescendo. What was a battle had transformed into a rout that reduced what was an army to a pathetic mob of panicked men.

This man lunged forward, as thousands flowed past him. He was sobbing, tears flowed down his face as he struggled forward. He pushed against the crush and cursed and even hit some with the flat of his sword. The mass of men running past him were hell-bent on getting as far away as possible from Ibrahim's fearsome Moorish cavalry. The lone man, running against the tide, sighted two small boys who were caught up in the fleeing stream and made his way towards them. He scooped them up into his arms, hugging the boys and cursing at them in joy and anger.

The man, prizes in hand, turned and joined the mob of men scrambling for safety.

The boys were sobbing uncontrollable fear. He heard them cry above the din.

"We are sorry *Tio* Santiago, we are sorry!"

As Santiago ran toward refuge he turned and looked anxiously over his shoulder searching for someone else, oblivious now to the panicked men thrashing about him, crashing into him. He saw something terrible. A horror that made him cry out, "No! Oh God no!"

Upon Ibrahim's battlefield the din of battle at last began to die away, fury spent, like a towering wave that slams upon the hard rocks of cliff sprays out in all directions at the peak of its fury, then subsides.

Ibrahim's cavalry drove the routed Christians in all directions into the hills.

Ibrahim galloped over to blood-splattered and grinning Adnan Al-Mansur and said, "Adnan! Order the cavalry to halt and end the slaughter."

Adnan stopped smiling. He cringed at the command and replied, "Mercy? What is this! Let's finish them!"

Ibrahim said, "No Adnan. Not mercy for our foes. My heart burns to pursue and strike them down to the very last, all the way to the gates of Rome! We must be cautious. I will not allow the cavalry to become spread out, an undisciplined mob without order, in the pursuit of their quarry. This could give the Christians an opportunity to turn on our isolated horseman and deal the same kind of blow to us that we dealt to the Templars."

Adnan nodded, began to turn his horse to ride off and give the necessary commands. As he did so, Ibrahim said, "Adnan. You are my brother. But you will never question my orders."

"Yes my Lord."

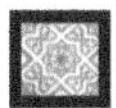

The remnants of the Christian army scampered away, disappearing over the horizon into the mountains and over the passes that lead north to safety of the Spanish Kingdom of Castile.

The defeated men were promised a *miracle*. They were rewarded with death and another unfulfilled prophecy.

An unnatural calm fell upon the battlefield as Ibrahim surveyed the scene of destruction before him. He saw a carpet of dead and wounded men, pools of blood and other fluids, parts of hands, arms and heads cast about. Ibrahim saw dark clouds on the horizon. It was always like this he thought. It always rained after a great battle. Summer or winter. It was God cleansing the earth, covering over man's sin and restoring his creation.

One of Ibrahim's men rode up to him and said excitedly, "We have captured three caballeros my lord, still with life!"

Ibrahim trotted over to the spot the soldier indicated.

Exsecour stepped fastidiously in order to avoid the bodies of the dead and injured, not wanting to soil his hooves with the scraps of battle.

Three captured knights were on their knees, held firmly in place by members of Ibrahim's cavalry.

Ibrahim dismounted and drew his scimitar as he approached. The first man, the one on the far left of the line would not last long. A red stain grew rapidly in size about his thigh; an artery had been slashed open. Already the wounded cavalier's gaze was beginning to cloud over. He looked blankly at and through Ibrahim without comprehension, barely alive.

Ibrahim stepped to the side to examine the second knight. His armor was stripped off. His entire body was covered in blood and dirt. He wet himself as Ibrahim approached, quaking with fear.

Ibrahim asked in flawless Spanish: "Are you ready to do the will of Allah? Prepared to forsake your blasphemous religion, and live?"

The knight nodded his head enthusiastically. His lips quaked as he breathed.

"Yes!"

The man agreed. But his eyes betrayed him. The eyes told Ibrahim he was lying. As soon as he was set free, he would return to the saddle and ride against Granada once more, making a mockery of his mercy. How many Moors would this one kill if allowed to live?

In the next instant, Ibrahim watched his scimitar slash at the knight's neck. Ibrahim wore a hard expression as the headless body slumped forward.

Ibrahim moved to the remaining captured cavalier. This man looked up, directly into Ibrahim's eyes. The eyes of the knight were green, unmoving and intense. This man had suffered wounds all over his body. His right arm dangled, useless at the shoulder, a wound from a slashing scimitar. He bled from the torso. His head was a mass of cuts. His red hair was matted and caked in a black combination of blood and mud. In spite of his wounds, his gaze did not falter.

Ibrahim thought to himself, *What compels you? What demons drive a man like you to raise his sword against the almighty? Against God's kingdom? Why won't you leave us in peace?*

Ibrahim observed the knight's eyes, a glare of blazing steel green. It was not the stare of a crazed martyr, one who craved the death stroke of the sword in order to receive his greater reward. Nor was his appearance a gaze of fear, or anxiety or pain. Neither was it a look of rage and defiance that some captured Military Monks expressed as they were put to death.

Ibrahim saw that this knight's armor was not as fine as the previous two. He was not a wealthy lord or prince. Neither did he wear the large crimson cross on a field of white that was the trademark of the Knights Templar, or the uniform of a man-at-arms of the Spanish order of Santiago.

Templar or not, this was a Christian knight and that made him an enemy of Allah. A foe of all that Ibrahim loved.

Ibrahim made the same offer to all captured knights. The man could choose for himself, life and truth or death and damnation.

"Are you prepared to do the will of Allah? Willing to forsake your blasphemous religion, and live? Will you swear never more to take up arms against the Kingdom of Granada?"

The wounded man continued to stare at Ibrahim with those cold green, unmoving eyes.

The knight said flatly, "This is not my fight. Not my war. I have done my duty before God and men. My work is complete. To deny my faith would be an untruth. I will not be untrue to myself or my mission at the moment of death."

Ibrahim raised his sword to execute the infidel, but paused. He had never paused before. It was not his way. He brought slashing death without hesitation. This time an invisible force stayed his hand momentarily. Why? What did the infidel mean by, "*Not my fight. Not my war?*" Strange words. Perhaps his wounds made him delirious?

Then Ibrahim sensed it. Perceived it. Came to a sudden revelation that the infidel before him was neither a fanatic nor a half-crazed follower of a prophet of doom. He was not a member of the bloodthirsty chivalry of Christendom who lived only to spill the blood of Muslims. There was a unique aspect to this knight something . . . unusual. Something special. Was it devotion? Loyalty? Not quite defiance. Not hate. Was it possible? Did Ibrahim read love and kindness in the eyes of his foe? Not possible! His enemies had no capacity for noble emotions, especially love.

This one was prepared to die if need be. Yet he did not seek death. Strange. He possessed the natural qualities of leadership, the ability to lead thousands of warriors, yet he did not lead *even* one soldier in this battle.

Ibrahim saw true nobility. There was greatness in this singular warrior that no mere man-granted title could instill.

Ibrahim offered one more time and secretly encouraged the man to take up his offer of life.

"Are you prepared to do the will of Allah? Will you forsake your blasphemous religion? Will you swear never to take up arms against Granada evermore?"

Ibrahim decided that if this knight would accept Islam he would be taken back to Granada and treated with respect. He was worthy of life. Ibrahim could not form words why this one should be spared, only that this man was worth something. Ibrahim sensed it. He felt it. A voice in the depths of his mind spoke out, barely discernible above the rage of hate, telling him to spare the knight's life. That this one, though an unbeliever, deserved life.

Ibrahim's thoughts ran wild. He questioned himself, *I wish to be just. Why won't he speak? Accept Islam and live? Are you truly just Ibrahim? Merciful? An unarmed man, on his knees before you like a slave, forced to convert in order to save his own skin? That is not a true conversion, simply a farce. You know that! A farce as untrue as your supposed justice. Still, they would not spare me! No, Ibrahim. You are wrong! This one would! He is not like the others. Not like any you have faced in the past. He is not a Templar. Speak! Save yourself, damn you!*

The man did not speak. He continued to stare into Ibrahim's eyes. No fear of death. Ibrahim shuddered, a wave of emotion slowing his hand. Ibrahim gazed upward at the dark birds circling, masses of black outlines against the darkening sky gathered for the post battle feast. He smelled the dust and spilled-blood odor of battle. He wavered. Then the anger returned, boiling red and hot, vengeance for his brothers who lay motionless in twisted mounds upon the field.

Shall I show mercy? The Christians, my enemy, know not mercy!

Ibrahim's scimitar flashed downward in a blinding, swift stroke.

Chapter 3

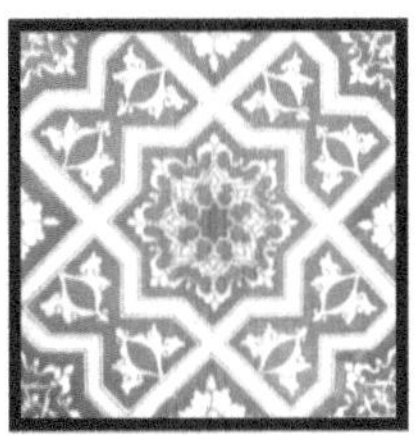

Of a Girl and a Dance

"Then young women will dance and be glad.
I will turn their mourning into gladness;
I will give them comfort and joy instead of sorrow."

The name of the girl was Rebecca de Caceres. She was not a native of Granada, but of Sevilla. She had arrived in Granada not more than a year ago.

Her thick jet-black hair, olive-colored skin, dark almond-shaped eyes, high cheekbones, portrayed Rebecca as a representative of the majority of the population of Granada, for Rebecca was a mix of Moorish and Spanish blood.

The muezzin, a holy man appointed to call the faithful to prayer, climbed the minaret of the mosque and called in all directions with a ringing melodic tone in Arabic, "Hasten to prayer."

From the tops of the minarets, that dotted the skyline of Granada came the undulating, high-pitched call.

Allah u Akbar, Allah u Akbar
(Allah is Great, Allah is Great)

Throughout the Kingdom of Granada, through the vast territory where Islam held dominated, Muslims stopped whatever they were doing and unfurled well-worn, yet impeccably clean carpets, fell to their knees and prayed in the direction of Mecca, thousands of miles to the east.

As the muezzin called, Rebecca stood on cobblestones in the middle of a courtyard filled with flowers and orange trees set in pots that circled a fountain. She loved the musical sound of the water and the sweet scent of orange blossoms.

A balcony ran along the full length of the second story of the home that circled the courtyard. Today there were many people, Christians who leaned against the railing of the balcony. When Rebecca first performed here only a handful of observers came to watch. But more and more wished to see the dance for themselves, and their numbers grew. Now the people stood shoulder to shoulder and a crowd gathered in the courtyard itself to watch.

Rebecca's brother, Fontino, began to strum softly on his guitar. It was a Spanish guitar, made of cypress and spruce, lighter in weight and smaller than a classical guitar designed to produce a sharper sound than the traditional instrument.

Rebecca wore a sleeveless red gown, rather tight on her torso, highlighting her round curves. Below her waist the dress expanded outward and ended at the bottom in several rows of delicate white lace. Her hair was pulled back and pinned with a large red rose to match her dress.

Rebecca grasped the bottom of her dress in her right hand, and holding her arm straight out, she waved the dress in a circular motion as the guitar music began.

Other girls entered the courtyard. The girls watched Rebecca's every move. They wore the same style of dress as Rebecca. All the dresses bore the same white lace fringe as Rebecca's, only the colors were distinct. One girl wore a dark blue dress, another peach colored, white, and yellow.

Rebecca swirled slowly and stomped her right foot and then her left, her head thrown back. She spun, all the while stomping her feet. Her arm rotated at the same time above her head in an elegant figure eight pattern.

"Ash-hadu al-la Ilaha ill Allah
Ash-hadu al-la Ilaha ill Allah,"
(I bear witness that there is no divinity but Allah)

The high-pitched wail of the muezzins in the minarets stopped after each refrain, pausing for an instant. In that instant, Fontino played a rapid staccato series of notes and Rebecca began to twirl faster. The muezzin's call began again. As the Arabic cry wafted over the city, the girls slowed their movements slightly. The tapping of their heels and the rapid fire of the guitar strains diminished in intensity.

"Ash-hadu anna Muhammadan Rasulullaah,"
(I bear witness that Muhammad is Allah's Messenger)

In response, Fontino slowed his playing, strumming to just a few light notes as Rebecca slowed her dancing. The muezzins paused for an instant, then Fontino began the rapid staccato anew, as Rebecca began to spin faster. The muezzins began their call to prayer anew,

"Hayya la-s-saleah - Hayya la-s-salea,"
(Hasten to the prayer, Hasten to the prayer)

This time however, Fontino did not slow the rhythm of the guitar. Instead, he maintained the staccato, fingers hitting the strings of the guitar in a flurry of movement. The music, the tapping of the feet, and the call of the muezzins blended into a tapestry of rhythm and melody.

Rebecca's feet slammed onto the cobblestone of the courtyard, faster and faster, her tight spins increasing in speed at the same time fluttering the fringe of her dress and tracing elegant patterns in the air with her arm.

"Hayya la-l-faleah - Hayya la-l-faleah,"
(Hasten to real success, Hasten to real success)

Fontino played in rhythm to the wail of the muezzins. Rebecca and her companions danced in tune with the guitar and the muezzin. Faster and faster they spun.

"Allahu Akbar, Allahu Akbar,"
(Allah is Great, Allah is Great)

All were welcome to join their instruments to the cacophony of sound and dance, whether that instrument was a guitar, an empty crate, or only bare hands clapping to the mélange of music and percussion. However, only a few had perfected the moves of the dance itself. Of those few, only one, a vision in red, set herself apart, as a true master of the dance.

Some in the crowd to clapped their hands in fast staccato rhythm to the guitar. Fontino bent over the instrument as if at labor, sweat beads formed on his forehead as he strummed ever faster.

A man on the balcony pounded in rhythm on an old orange crate, adding to the power of the percussion.

The other girls joined Rebecca in the dance, swirling in circles, sandal-shod feet slamming the cobblestones, waving the fringes of their dresses as they moved to the rhythm of the guitar.

Sweat glistened on Rebecca's cheeks. The call of the muezzin, the guitar and the rapid fire clacking of Rebecca's feet all blended together seamlessly in a powerful, mesmerizing performance.

"La Ilaha ill Allah,"
(There is no divinity but Allah)

The muezzin's call fell silent, the *Adhan* or daily prayer complete, but the dance continued. An older man, bent over with age, using a cane, stepped forward. In a soft voice so as not to be heard beyond the walls of the courtyard, he imitated the call of the muezzin. He perfected the undulating, singing cry, but instead of Arabic he spoke in Spanish,

"God of heaven please hear our prayer,
I cry when I remember time before,
We praised you in the streets without care,
When we were free before the coming of the Moor."

The performance continued. A second and then a third man began to play the guitar alongside Fontino. The girls continued to dance, shoe heels clacking on the cobblestones of the courtyard. The stomping of feet seemed to make the cobblestones tremble, but it wasn't the force of the dance that made the stones vibrate. Above the sound of music, the sound of a distant rumble. The crowd, alarmed now, began to disperse, some ran, others hid, for they realized the origin of the vibration and the distant rumble. It was the victorious return Ibrahim Al-Rahim's cavalry, roaring into the city at full gallop.

Chapter 4

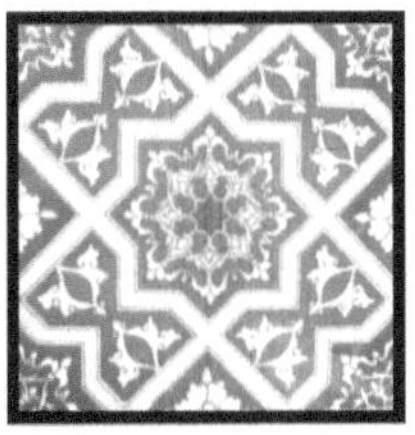

The Triumphal Procession

"Time said to Love:
That pride that you have,
I will punish you for it."

The single undulating sound of a horn from the top of the Alcazar, that unassailable red fortress of the Alhambra, carried across Granada to alert the city that Ibrahim Al-Rahim's invincible cavalry had returned from battle.

Ibrahim could sense Exsecour's excitement as they lead the cavalry to the gates of the city.

Ibrahim watched the city walls and fortifications growing larger and larger. It did not look like a fortress, with its rose-colored walls and the dense green forest surrounding it. Ibrahim whispered with a sense of awe, the words of the poet, "*A Pearl set in emeralds.*"

The impressive buildings of the fortress, which dominated the heights of Granada, looked to be a natural outgrowth of the verdant forest below.

As the cavalry reached the outer gates of Granada, the gates were thrown open to the cheers of the soldiers that lined the wall. The cavalry Ibrahim leading, galloped into the city, the horses' hooves clacked on the smooth round stones. The thundering hooves drowning out the sound of the horn.

Ibrahim gripped the reins of Exsecour in his hand. The string of beads was tightly wrapped around his fingers. He grasped a banner, blood stained and torn, that bore a crimson red cross surmounted upon a field of pure white. It was the flag of the Knights Templar.

Tradition dictated that Ibrahim Al-Rahim and his cavalry charge into Granada after a victory, as if they were taking their own city by storm. It was their version of the Roman Triumphal Procession, the victory parade held to commemorate the decisive victories of the Roman legions. In the Kingdom of Granada, the charge was done for the morale of the Moorish population within the city. It was proof that the All Powerful was with them, that the Christian kingdoms to the north could not overcome the stalwart soldiers of Allah.

They also staged the spectacle to show the Christians who lived within the city of Granada, that Islam's God had won the battle. The procession proved that the polytheistic gods of Christendom were no match for Islam's one true God.

After a battle there were the inevitable rumors. A priest would tell his followers that the Christians had at last defeated the Kingdom of Granada on the battlefield. A report would be delivered in dramatic fashion that the Moorish army was in full flight, for *Issa* himself at last had come down to earth, using divine powers to fight for his people. The dissidents would whisper that now was the time to rise against the Sultan and his oppressive army, for their own Lord would bless the uprising.

The sight of Ibrahim Al-Rahim bearing the bloody and broken Templar flag, his elite cavalry alive and well, flying through the main gate of the city quickly put all rumor to rest.

The troop charged past the open-air market on the main avenue that lead up to the gates of the Alhambra itself. The market was filled with stalls that offered the riches of southern Spain. The owners of the stalls were Muslims and Jews and Christians.

There were almonds, olives and their precious oil, wine and apricots and mountains of the red pomegranates for which Granada was famous.

Other stalls offered every color imaginable of silk cloth, incense and perfumes, ivory and ceramics, dates and figs, jewelry, spices and silver.

Each faith had a unique reaction to the thundering show of force. The Muslims cheered, arms upraised in triumph as the cavalry galloped past. The Christians looked down at the ground or pretended to be tending to their wares. The Jews looked on with indifference. Their main concern was not victory on the battlefield; it was the success of their business ventures within the kingdom. If pushed, for an opinion, the Jews would declare that they felt safer under Moorish rule than Christian. But the harsh lessons of history had taught the Jews to be hesitant to speak of politics and religion openly. Jews prospered under the religious tolerance of the *convivencia.* This would terminate if the Christians succeeded in the conquest of Granada.

As the troops clomped past the market, the cobblestone street narrowed as it wound through a neighborhood of tidy whitewashed homes with red-clay tile roofs.

While other Christians went indoors, Rebecca excitedly ran across the courtyard to the white wall topped with Bougainvillea. There was an irregularity on the face of the smooth wall, a protrusion that jutted out just enough so that Rebecca could leap onto it, hoist herself up and peer through the vines to the street on the other side.

She caught a glimpse through the green and violet vegetation as the Moors passed. This wasn't the first time she saw him. The Moor leading the troop on their victory gallop. He rode, leaning forward in the saddle, black cloak snapping behind, flashing glimpses of golden thread. She grinned as he passed and whispered, "Que Guapo," with one hand she unconsciously smoothed her hair as Ibrahim rode past her home.

She didn't notice Fontino who ran up behind her and yelled, "What are you doing? Come down from there!"

Rebecca rolled her eyes, lowered herself from the top of the wall and leapt high off the protruding brick, landing in front of Fontino.

Fontino glared at her, and said, "You shouldn't watch them! This is none of our affair!"

Rebecca shrugged and replied, "Do not worry, hermanito. No one saw me. Even if they did, what of it?"

Fontino shook his head, and said, "They will think you a spy! No Christian of Granada on honest business would watch the Moors celebrate their victory!"

Rebecca was unimpressed by his warning; she walked by him, seemingly ignoring his warning. As she passed she said, "You worry too much Fontino."

Fontino grabbed Rebecca by the elbow, squeezed, leaned in close to her face, angry now and rasped, "And you do not worry enough hermanita! You are careless. *You* are the one that should worry."

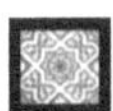

The cheering and sounds of horns carried across the city of Granada to the Sultan Abdul Rahkman, who rested on the floor on oversized tasseled pillows. He was smoking a water pipe with his ministers in the royal palace of the Alhambra.

The Sultan never tired of the magnificent view. Through the open stilted archway of the circular room he saw the gardens, pools and fountains of the Alhambra spread before him. The scene extended further over Granada proper with its brilliantly whitewashed walled buildings and terracotta-colored roofs. Beyond the city was the lush plain of the Vega, which stretched from horizon to horizon with vineyards, orchards and fields of crops. In the far distance were the perennially snow-capped Sierra Nevada Mountains that towered above all else.

The Sultan heard the pleasing sounds of running water; the song of hundreds of species of birds that found their refuge in the trees accompanied the musical sound of the flowing waters.

The living air was infused with the sweet smell of incense and the dizzying fragrance of dozens of varieties of roses, and jasmine, lavender, pine trees, lilacs, orchids, carnations, and a hundred other species of plants and flowers. The paradisiac gardens that surrounded the Alhambra disguised the fact that it was one of the stoutest fortresses in the world.

The Sultan saw far below, Ibrahim's cavalry enter the city. He stood, clapped his hands and barked out orders to his waiting slaves to prepare to welcome the Captain of the Guard.

The cavalry pounded up the steep narrow street to the entrance of the gates of the Alhambra proper. The gate entrance, shaped like a giant keyhole-rounded at the top with a large semi-circle, was topped with cheering soldiers.

Ibrahim's cavalry came to a reining stop in front of the courtyard of the Myrtle trees, the official reception area for the Sultan. It was located just below the tower of Colmares, one of the many watchtowers that lined the walls of the Alhambra. The courtyard held a long pool that mirrored the entirety of the tower of Colmares above it.

Lining this rectangular courtyard was a series of identical sandstone arches, exact replicas of the keyhole shaped main gate of the Alhambra.

Inscribed on each arch, in arabesque gold calligraphy, were the qualities of God or a simple statement, "*Only God will conquer,*" or "*God is great.*"

Ibrahim dismounted and strode into the courtyard. He saw the tower reflected perfectly in the pool. It looked as if a master artist had painted the tower onto the ground itself and the tower was floating upon a flat sea of green.

Ibrahim had seen the pool and the tower's reflection a thousand times and still the effect astonished him.

He was well aware this was the intention of the courtyard of the Myrtles—to astound and impress foreign dignitaries. To intimidate by the architecture and wisdom of Islam. The courtyard of the Myrtles never failed to achieve its intended purpose.

The Sultan stood before the mirror pool with his ministers, clad in a long scarlet robe.

Ibrahim approached the Sultan and gently laid the Templar's flag at his feet. Ibrahim bowed slightly as he presented the flag. It was not a full bow. A full bow was reserved only for the King of Heaven. Ibrahim's bow was of respect and acknowledgement of the elevated position of his Lord, and friend, the Sultan.

The Sultan spoke.

"*As salaam Alaikum*! You have done God's will, Ibrahim Al-Rahim!"

A simple sentence. No greater compliment.

Ibrahim responded, "*Wa alaikum as salaam*! It is the will of Allah, my Lord, for his is the victory. The Kingdom of Granada is secure once again for his glory."

Ending the formalities, the Sultan waved his ministers away, "Come Ibi, walk alone with me."

The Sultan walked slowly along the still reflection pool. Ibrahim, a full head taller than the Sultan, had to lean to the side, lowering himself slightly in order to hear his Lord's words clearly.

When he was sure no one but Ibrahim could hear, the Sultan inquired cautiously. "Ibi, you have heard of this Martyr movement?"

"Yes my lord. They have made much trouble in Córdoba."

The Sultan stopped, turned to face Ibrahim. "Are they coming here? Are they planning a demonstration in Granada?"

"I believe so. My informants tell me that the Martyrs intend to make a dramatic statement here in Granada. Perhaps even a procession with the cross."

The Sultan shook his head, and pursed his lip.

"We . . . YOU must handle this very carefully. I do not want an uprising. But, blasphemy against the prophet and the Quran must be dealt with. It can never be ignored."

Ibrahim said, "They will be arrested, not mistreated, and then taken to the courts for judgment."

The Sultan waved his hand dismissively at the obviousness of Ibrahim's answer. "Of course! Of course!"

He cried, "But then what? Will we execute them for blasphemy as demanded by our laws? If we do that, more of them will come to fulfill their wish of martyrdom! Then the Christian Kingdoms to the north will use the outrage among the Christians as an excuse to launch a new Crusade against us. We are powerful, yes! But make no mistake, we cannot fight a united Castile, Aragon, Navarre, Leon and God knows whom else among nations of Christendom! Meanwhile as we fight for our lives against the nations of Europe, here in Granada the Christians of the Sacramonte will rise against us, they will riot, they will attack our brothers and massacre the Jews, and then we will respond with terrible force . . ."

The Sultan paused as his voice trailed off.

Ibrahim imagined the Sultan's unspoken words: *Then, we will answer with righteous fury. We will slaughter them by the thousands until rivers of blood run through the streets of Granada. We will enslave the survivors and the convivencia will come down in a storm of death and destruction.*

Ibrahim whispered cautiously. "I wonder at times, my Lord, if destroying the Christians once and for all would not be for the best, perhaps even God's will."

The Sultan put his hand on Ibrahim's cheek and gently squeezed. "You of all people that the All Knowing has seen fit to place on this earth should know better than to speak of such things."

Ibrahim felt shame. The Sultan's rebuff was warranted. He of all people should truly know better, for he was born and raised in Jerusalem itself. The doomed city.

The city of peace that become the city of death. Still, he was a warrior, trained to kill. Ordained by Allah to kill the soldiers of Christendom, and his hatred for them burned deep in his heart.

The Sultan continued, driving home the lesson. He said, "We have accomplished something here, Ibi, unrivaled in all the earth. We have proven that we can live with the people of the book. We are living proof that Muslim, Christian and Jew can tolerate each other's presence and live in peace. But this is a fragile thing we have created, Ibi, like the wings of a butterfly. If you touch it, even slightly, it will disintegrate into dust and chaos. You cannot allow that to happen. You are the only one that can keep us from sliding into the abyss."

"Yes my Lord, I understand."

"Besides," the Sultan continued, "There are eight million Christians in Castile alone. Millions more in the Spanish Kingdoms of Leon, Navarre and Aragon, not to mention the lands of the Franks, Italians, Germans and Anglos. Oh! What I could accomplish with such numbers to command! I would march to the gates of Rome itself! In contrast, there are only three million of us in all the Kingdom of Granada, and we must include Christians in that number."

The Sultan's shoulders began to sag as from an invisible weight as he ticked off the overwhelming numbers that comprised the enemies of Islam. He continued. "We cannot, we must not give them any provocation to launch a full Crusade against us. In the Levant, there is an uneasy peace, but a peace nonetheless between the Christians and the Muslims, which makes our position here even more precarious. We, the Kingdom of Granada are the new frontline in the battle between the East and West, between the infidel and the true believers. This is where they want to fight! We cannot be responsible for losing the jewel of Islam. For such a grave sin, there can be no penance, only eternal shame."

He tugged thoughtfully on his two-pronged grey beard as he stared at the still waters of the reflecting pool. The Sultan said, "We must be cautious, for there will come a day when our diplomacy, bribes and intrigues will no longer keep the Christian Kingdoms from uniting and coming against us with overwhelming might."

The Sultan sighed, and then asked, "Another thing. I have heard talk that the Christians have sent at least one, perhaps more, highly skilled assassins to kill me. Should I be concerned about this rumor of an assassin in Granada?"

There was always such talk. Gossip spread through the market via the women gathering water at the wells. They whispered of some pending attack, conspiracy or murder. Most of such talk was nothing more than the chattel of old women and unworthy of attention.

Ibrahim answered. "I believe it to be a credible threat, my lord. Our informants in the Christian quarters of the Albacin and the Sacramonte have been told to be on the alert, and to report to me immediately if any strangers arrive in Granada. I have doubled the guard in the palace and along the walls. You should not move through the city for the time being, unless I am with you."

"Very well Ibi. Thank you."

A squadron of green parrots shot overhead, squawking loudly.

"As if I did not have enough worries to cause my beard to grey further, there is also this protest. It is some sort of dance that the Christians began in Sevilla. My ministers report that groups of girls are dancing during our daily prayers? Ah the disrespect! This dance is popping up in Córdoba like unwanted weeds in a rose bed, and in our cities and villages throughout the Kingdom of Granada."

The Sultan let out a short satiric-sounding laugh.

"I thought that the Christians were so miserable and morose! Just look at their depressing worship ceremonies, their dark churches! Compare any of their dingy buildings to the airy openness of the great mosque of Córdoba! Simply set foot in the mosque, feel the fountain cooled air upon your face and you will sense the presence of Allah! Their art and statues? They glorify torture and pain. They seem to feel closer to their gods when they are depressed. Now, out of the clear blue sky they take up dancing as a happy protest against us? A seditious method to challenge our authority! What do I do about this Ibi? I hear that they perform this dance in Granada right under our beards!"

The Sultan scratched at his forehead.

"How do we respond? Do I turn out the guard and arrest them for the "crime" of dancing of all things? Do I turn out your cavalry to chase down dancing girls? Oh what a sight that would be!"

Ibrahim too heard of this dance. He paused before responding to the Sultan as thought back to a day he was outside the walls of the courtyard close to the market.

Ibrahim entered a mosque, it was time for prayer. He unfurled his prayer rug, knelt and joined in the prayer. For a moment he thought he heard the strumming of a guitar and someone pounding on a drum in rhythm to the calls of the muezzin.

As the muezzins paused, so would the guitar. The music started again as the muezzins began the next refrain of the *Adhan.* He was near the Christian quarter, the Albacin where the sounds had emanated. He was sure that the music had its source in the seditious dance the Christians engaged in during the daily prayers.

During the five daily Islamic prayers, Granada normally fell silent as a tomb. The Jews and the Christians took pains not to disturb the Muslims during their worship. Ibrahim thought to himself, *Disrespectful Christians! They should be a taught a lesson!*

Ibrahim returned to the present and replied to the Sultan, his voice tinged with disdain, "My lord, please do not worry about a few dancing Christians. A silly dance is of no threat to our authority! It is nothing! Only a measure of the unbelievers lack of respect for the truth!"

The Sultan smiled, relieved.

"Perhaps you are correct Ibi. If that is the best scheme those troublemakers can muster against us . . ."

The Sultan inhaled deeply, his body and face relaxing, his worries calmed for now. The scent of sandalwood incense blended with the pleasing smell of roses, pine and citrus trees as he made a grand sweeping gesture towards the other side of the pool where his ministers waited patiently at attention, then pronounced dramatically, "Now I order all to drink pomegranate juice, smoke the water pipe and celebrate our victory! We will pretend that we have at last achieved a total victory over the infidels of Christendom. Of course, that is all a lie! They will come again, and we must be prepared to meet them, for this is God's fate for our tiny paradise on earth!"

The Sultan shook his head as if to dispel all worries, smiled broadly, reached up and clasped Ibrahim by the shoulders in a gesture of friendship and said, "This is not to be feared, but embraced. Trials make us stronger!"

The Sultan quoted the proverb, "Sunshine all the time makes nothing more than desert!"

Chapter 5

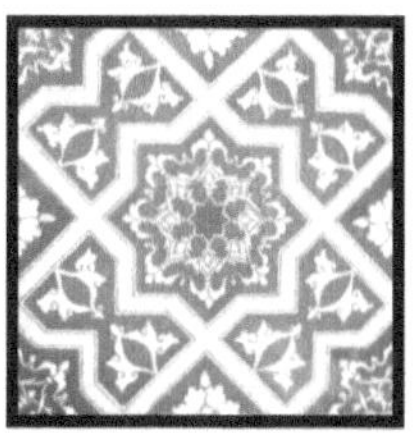

The Martyr

"Behind the funeral cart,
sobbed my mother,
She did not weep tears,
She wept blood."

Peter was a hermit, dressed in rags that years ago were clothes. He chose to live in a dark, damp cave, deep in the hills of a barren section of central Iberia. His given name was not Peter, but he chose to be known by the name of the Apostle whom the Lord called his, "Rock."

Outside of the mean cave a scrawny donkey stood guard, barely able to muster the strength to keep its head off of the ground. Peter prayed for death. The death of a martyr.

He prayed to be welcomed into the kingdom of the Lord in heaven. His reward for the sacrifice of his living flesh. He prayed for strength to follow in the steps of the Lord, and offer up his life in exchange for many.

The hermit believed one needed to suffer to prove the depth of one's faith in God. He joined the Flagellants as they marched across Europe, barely clothed, whipping their flesh until their backs were nothing more than torn bloody ribbons.

The Flagellants were practitioners of an extreme form of mortification of their flesh by whipping it with sharp instruments. One flagellant repeated the entire book of Psalms twenty times in one week, accompanying each song with a hundred lash-strokes to his back.

Other Flagellants would fall to their knees and scourge themselves, gesturing with their free hand to indicate their sin and striking themselves rhythmically to songs until their blood freely flowed.

Sometimes the blood was soaked up in rags and treated as holy relics.

The hermit became nostalgic as he remembered those holy days. Good days full of sacrifice and worship. He said out loud, "That is truly how one pleases the Maker!

Peter entered Granada on the back of his well-worn donkey. He wore only a garment of old shards of canvas that had been sown together, then re-sewn over and over. It hung like a limp rag on his bony back. His beard was long, almost to his navel, unkempt and greasy. His cheeks were sunken and his eyes bulged. Peter looked as though he had not eaten a decent meal in at least a decade.

As the poor beast shuffled slowly toward the main square, the center of Granada, Peter looked straight ahead with a blank yet purposeful stare. He did not take notice of the mid-day activity in the market as his donkey trudged along.

Peter clutched an old torn Bible, his justification for his strange actions.

He approached the main plaza of the city. The plaza itself was surrounded on all sides by two- or three-story whitewashed buildings, each a bright white home adorned with a balcony that ran the length of the building. In the middle of the plaza, a fountain gushed clear water upward nearly as high as the roofs of the surrounding buildings.

Hundreds of people swarmed through the plaza—Jews and Christians, Arabs and Berbers. There were also Numidians, skin black as night, pale skinned Franks from the north, Moorish soldiers on patrol, traders, fisherman, farmers, blacksmiths, shopkeepers, priests, mullahs and rabbis all sharing the same streets.

Peter paid no attention to the hustle and bustle of the main square. He did not know nor care to know of the rich history of the city through which he traveled. He concentrated instead on his personal mission from the Lord. He would do his part to rid Spain of the pagans who ruled it. He would make the ultimate sacrifice for the Lord and thereby prove his faith. His would be a greater sacrifice than even the flagellates were prepared to offer. A perfect sacrifice. He was proud to render such service. He slid off his donkey, stumbled, and then gained his balance. Standing erect, he raised his Bible high and shouted as loudly as his frail body could muster, "The prophet of Islam is the servant of Satan!"

At once the frenetic movement in the plaza ceased. The entire plaza became as quiet as a cemetery. It was as if thousands of people became frozen in place by an icy wind. The Jews reacted first. They scurried away from the square, ducking into alleyways back into their homes for safety, bolting the doors and windows shut.

The Muslims, mouths agape, reacted with anger.

Peter shouted once again. He summoned even more power and enthusiasm now that he had the attention of all those in the plaza.

"Yes! I curse your prophet! He is an impostor, a child of hell! Your religion is of Satan!"

Peter's voice gained volume as it echoed off the walls of the buildings of the square. Since all movement and noise had ceased, his voice resounded. He took a breath and shouted. "Your prophet is an ass who . . ."

He did not complete that sentence, for he was set upon by three Moorish soldiers who tackled him to the pavement.

One soldier stuffed a rag forcefully into Peter's mouth. Other soldiers pushed their way into the plaza, scimitars drawn, looking angrily for any bystander that may have been in league with the blasphemer.

The soldiers bound Peter's hands and feet and put a sack over his head and tied it tightly. They tossed him on a horse and quickly rushed away up the hill to the Alhambra to the *Mexuar*, where the royal tribunal met. A judge, the *Qadi*, waited to hear cases there. Carved on the tile on the entrance door to the *Mexuar* were the words:

"Enter and fear not to ask for justice, for you will find it."

They passed under the keyhole shaped archway into a passage that lead into the main room of the *Mexuar*, with their prisoner. The walls of the rectangular room were decorated with dark blue tiles in the shapes of stars and circles on a bright white tiles. Slender columns supported a second story balcony, each column a work of art in itself, carefully decorated with carvings of plants, lions, flowers and leaves, designs, and intricate arabesque calligraphy. Overlapping wooden flowers in full bloom of soft earthen colors decorated the roof.

It was in this elaborate room that the *Qadi* served.

Abruptly Ibrahim rushed in and pulled one of the arresting soldiers aside. He gripped the rotund man's shoulders and fired questions at him.

"How many martyrs were in the square?" How did the Christians react to the arrest? Was anyone in league with him?"

The soldier, trembling now, fearing he made some grave error, answered the barrage of questions as well as he could. Satisfied, Ibrahim let go of the soldier then grasped his fleshy forearm.

"It is alright, Yusuf. You have done well. You may return to your post in the dungeon."

"A question my lord?"

"Of course, Yusuf."

"I do not understand. Why do the Christians do such things?"

Ibrahim thought for a moment, stroked his goatee, then answered. "Well Yusuf. All religions have their martyrs don't they?"

Yusuf, surprised responded. "Ours as well? The one true religion?"

"Yes Yusuf. All religions. That is something you will come to learn in time. Even in the truth we have our martyrs and zealots, and they can be quite irritating to the rational. Fortunately for us, our zealots are not as extreme as this Peter whom you rightfully detained."

"Yes my Lord, thank you."

Yusuf spun on his heels and, in spite of his clumsy gait, walked smartly out of the room, glad to be returning to his quiet post in the Alhambra.

The Sultan, his ministers, Ibrahim Al-Rahim and the other arresting soldiers sat cross-legged on pillows arranged in a semi-circle in the room. Also present was the court recorder who would meticulously note every word spoken during the trial. Peter stood awkwardly in the middle of the room. The Qadi stood in front of him, dressed in the official robes of a judge, with an elegant silk turban wrapped about his head.

The soldiers removed the sack covering Peter's head. The Qadi began the proceedings.

"You stand accused of blasphemy against the prophet."

"I have spoken truth and blasphemed no one," was the terse reply. Peter swayed as he stood. He was having difficulty keeping his head upright for his thin neck was not strong enough to support the weight of his head. He looked as though he would collapse in a pile of ragged sackcloth at any second.

The Qadi continued, "There are hundreds of witnesses to the fact that you have committed a crime punishable by death." The Qadi paused to make certain that court recorder caught his next words, for these proceedings would be published for all of the Kingdom of Granada to read. All would hear of the justice of the Moors.

"You are weak from lack of food, delirious from lack of water. You have traveled a long road. There is a cell prepared for you, with food and water. We will continue with the questioning once you have eaten and regained your strength," the Qadi said to Peter kindly.

Also present in the cell but not divulged by the Qadi, was a Christian priest who would attempt to convince Peter that his course of action was not beneficial for the Christian community in Granada and would only lead to violence and bloodshed.

It had not been difficult for the Sultan to locate a priest willing to speak to Peter and convince him of his folly.

The Qadi tried to reason with Peter. He said, "Many of your fellow Christians are against this sort of display! They desire to continue to live in peace and prosperity under the umbrella of the *convivencia.* They surely do not wish to enrage us, mock the law or stir our powerful military into acts of retribution."

Peter responded, "They are weak. I am spiritual."

The Qadi shook his head and continued, "Many Christians oppose you martyrs for biblical reasons! Your actions are suicide, self-murder. Isn't that strongly condemned in the Bible? Didn't the apostle Paul counsel you Christians to, "Seek peace and pursue it?" Would your Christ approve of your martyrdom? He said, "Peace I leave with you, my peace I give unto you."

Peter was not convinced. He looked away from the Qadi in disdain and said, "Pagan! Do not lecture me on the Bible or the teachings of the Christ! It is blasphemy to mention his name here!"

The Qadi looked at the Sultan, shrugged his shoulders in frustration and tried one final time to reason with Peter. The Qadi said, "Your own people in Granada wish to live in peace. You martyrs do not bring peace, only death. Death for yourselves and for the innocents of all faiths."

Peter's eyelids fluttered as if he were about to faint.

The soldiers approached Peter, to lead him to his cell. It appeared for a moment that Peter was too weak to respond. As the soldiers grabbed his arms, he looked directly into the eyes of the Qadi. His body tensed and his voice boomed, "Your prophet is the offspring of Satan!"

All in the room gasped. They heard stories of the blasphemies of the martyrs against the Prophet, but to hear such talk with one's own ears, spoken in person with such venom was like a blast of icy-cold water that made them shudder.

As they sat in stunned amazement, Peter continued his tirade, "Your book is full of false words! Your prophet is in *Gehenna* where all false prophets are sent to be tortured and learn the true faith!"

The Qadi rapidly motioned for the soldiers to stuff a rag in Peter's mouth. But before he was gagged, Peter mustered a few more words. His voice taking on a power his weakened body should not be able to produce, he roared, "A plague upon you, your prophet and your book!"

The Qadi as appointed judge had jurisdiction over the fate of Peter. But he looked to the Sultan, for Abdul Rahkman's instructions were clear. Every measure must be taken not to allow Peter to fulfill his death wish. His execution must be avoided. There was no choice now. The law was clear.

The Sultan looked to the ground downcast. He sadly nodded his head. In response to tacit authorization the Qadi said, "You Peter, have blasphemed against the Divine Being and his prophet. You will be put to death without delay."

The soldiers bound Peter, removed him from the *Mexuar* to an isolated area of the Alcazar to be beheaded.

The Sultan ordered Granada to be "shut up." No one could enter or leave without direct permission by the Sultan himself. The Christians were put under a curfew; they were confined to their areas of the city, the Albacin and the Sacramonte. They were under strict orders to be inside their houses at dusk. No exceptions. Ibrahim's guard was sent out into the streets in groups of eight or ten, fully armed, in chain mail, as a show of force.

When Peter was arrested his forlorn donkey was left alone in the plaza of Granada.

Maria de Alicante, a small older woman who worked in the marketplace selling pomegranates, spied the poor beast and approached it.

"You dear thing." She grasped it by the muzzle and stroked it gently.

"You are like me. Old. The world has ground you down. But you still have some life left in you!" Maria led the donkey away to be cared for at her home outside the city walls.

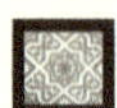

As Peter fulfilled his mission and met his demise, a ship lit upon a sandy beach at the southernmost tip of the Kingdom of Granada, not far from the massive rock of *Al-Tarik* that guarded the entrance to the Great Sea.

This was a small ship with a single mast, powered by one square canvas sail. It was a common fishing vessel, not distinct from the myriad of others that plied the rich waters of the Mediterranean. The boat's pilot chose this stretch of sand to unload his cargo instead of one of the busy ports that dotted the southern coast, for secrecy was key.

The pilot had been given a handsome sum of gold and clear directions for the temporary use of his boat. He was glad to receive the gold as payment to carry cargo that was distinct from the fish and merchandise that he usually bore.

He soon wished he carried only fish in his hold. As he learned more about his grey cargo, he came to a dreaded conclusion. He must perform this task exactly as directed, or he would meet immediate and excruciating death.

His cargo was shaped like men. But they were not men. Certainly not like any men he had encountered in many decades of sailing the Great Sea, from port to port, from Granada to Alexandria. No, these men were conjured from some kind of evil creatures. Their very presence sent a tremor up his spine. They carried about them a strange odor that added to their evil specter. The odor was not quite pleasant, nor repulsive, like the scent of a far-away forest fire, but not quite as acrid.

The pilot had heard tales, legends of wicked men who dressed only in grey and committed terrible deeds in the dark of night. Unstoppable, cruel killers. Of course he heard many such myths told in port after port—sea monsters, ships sailing off the end of the world, mermaids, and great holes that opened in the sea, swallowing entire fleets whole. Unlike most of his fellow mariners, he was not superstitious, and never gave credence to such wild tales. Now however, he knew at least one of the myths was indeed true. He shuddered as he whispered the name, "*Grey Cloaks.*"

The pilot exhaled a sigh of relief as he felt the keel of his boat slide with a sharp rasping sound into the sand and lock onto the beach. Simultaneously, five figures draped in their grey hooded robes launched themselves over the railing of the vessel and onto dry land. All five touched down at the same instant as if by practiced choreography. Rapidly, they cleared the beach and disappeared into the undergrowth.

The pilot, alongside his deck hand, leaped frantically into the waist deep water and pushed with all of their might to break the boat free of the grip of sand. The pilot pushed with such hurried force upon the bow of his boat that he felt a muscle pull in his back from the strain. A sharp pain shot up his spine. No matter, he pushed all the harder, heedless of the pain, with even more force now as he glanced over his shoulder and spotted one of the five beings staring from between the branches of one of the bushes that lined the top of the beach. Those terrible yellow eyes framed in ever-present grey, drove him on. As he hoisted himself into his boat, and the beach drifted into the distance, the pilot, laying on his back, scared and wet, looked up at the deep blue sky and muttered, "Never again. Only fish!"

Chapter 6

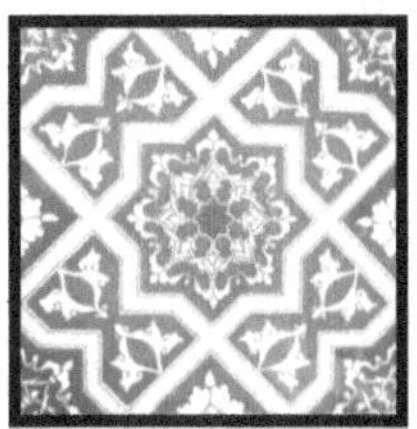

Of Pomegranates

***"Once I dreamed of the future,
an Andalusian patio. A child playing the guitar,
my wife and daughter dancing to a fast rhythm,
while I was clapping my hands."***

Ibrahim walked through the crowded open-air market. He wore a grey gown and sandals. Over the gown was his black cloak, and on his head a thick black linen, pulled back and tied neatly. Under his cloak he lightly gripped his scimitar, always ready to draw the sword if necessary. The string of wooden beads, which never left his presence, was tucked into an unseen pocket sewn onto the inside of his gown. His hand involuntarily touched the pocket every now and again, to ensure that the beads were still safely in place.

The cloudless sky was a deep, clear blue. The sun was bright, but not intense. Only warming and pleasant, even though Granada was in close proximity to the scorched deserts of North Africa, that lay just to the south.

Rich smells of sandalwood incense and flowers, punctuated by the aroma of roasting lamb, filled the air. Even though the stalls of the market were crowded with customers, the atmosphere was peaceful. Ibrahim was relieved that there were no signs of an uprising or further disturbance within the city.

Ibrahim noted a light, humorous moment as he overheard a Jewish silk merchant complain to a Christian olive oil vendor how hard it had been to get his goods into the city because of the disturbance caused by the martyr and the subsequent reaction of the Sultan.

The Jew explained that his silk came from outside of Granada from the vast mulberry orchards of the plain of the Vega and had to be transported many miles to the market. When the city was on lock-down, it was much more difficult for him and the other merchants to get their wares to market. The Jew concluded by berating the Christian.

"YOU! Tell your people to behave themselves!"

Ibrahim was relieved, for the fanaticism of Peter did not seem to be shared by the majority of the moderately inclined citizens of the city.

Ibrahim stopped in front of one of the stalls of the market. On the table was a pile of deep red pomegranates, piled high like a pyramid. Ibrahim saw protruding from behind the mound a shock of thick, grey hair that he recognized as belonging to the vendor, Maria de Alicante.

He knew that Maria was *Mozarab, a* member of a unique group of the population of the Kingdom of Granada. The *Mozarabs* were native Christians of Spain. Their descendants remained unconverted to Islam, but melded with the culture, adopting elements of Arabic language, dress and art.

Ibrahim was intrigued by the *Mozarabs* and especially Maria de Alicante. She was an infidel, but a happy *Mozarab.*

She was barely as tall as the table on which she sold her fruits, and she appeared frail. Her thin arms looked as though they did not possess the power to pick up even a single pomegranate without help. Ibrahim knew that this *Mozarab* was not as weak as she looked. He began to visit her stall and her stall alone, among the thousands of the marketplace, in spite of the raised eyebrows of the nosy denizens of the market. He knew what they whispered, "What business does the fearsome Ibrahim Al-Rahim have in the market with a *Mozarab*! And a woman!"

Maria looked up. She looked pleased and spoke in Arabic.

"Ah! My Senor Al Rahim! Are you looking for spies amongst my pomegranates again?"

Her outspokenness always took him off guard. No one spoke to him like this. He felt irritated. She always found a way to irritate him.

"Doña Maria, I only wish to buy some of your pomegranates."

Maria answered, "This amazes me! There are Moors that sell pomegranates in this market, but you always purchase them from me, an infidel!"

She spoke more kindly, as if she sensed his discomfort, but her eyes twinkled with mischief.

Ibrahim cocked his head to the side and pursed his lips. This old lady could be quite annoying.

"Your book says that the Creator makes it rain upon the righteous and the unrighteous. It is not a surprise, that even an infidel can grow a good pomegranate. After all, God is merciful."

Maria clicked her tongue with a sharp, "Tsk!" She pointed an accusing finger up at Ibrahim, who towered above her. She tried to push him, but her arm was not long enough to reach across the table. She said, "Ibi. Deep inside, you are not the terrible Christian hater that people think you are! Ibrahim Al-Rahim, the Captain of the Alhambra. Ha! I think, deep down you admire us as we persevere under your harsh rule."

Then she paused and waited for his response.

Ibrahim opened his arms dramatically as if he were pleading.

"Oh! It is a hard plight for you poor Christians to live under the rule of an enlightened Sultan who treats you better than any Christian overlord! A Christian Lord would have you making bricks out of mud, slaving away building one of his castles. The only thing we ask of you unbelievers is to pay a minimal head tax as tribute to our rule. Why, even that head tax is kept at a minimum, far less than you would pay to any landowner of Christendom! I pity you, poor Doña Maria, and your freedom to worship even in your ungodly way, without any interference from us."

Maria smiled and said, "Ibrahim. Many fear you. I like you! I truly do! Maybe I have spent too many years here out in this sun! I have known many men in my lifetime, Christians and Muslims alike. Most are false in some way or another. To be honest I don't care much for the species in general. Like I always say, 'Having faith in men is like having faith that water will remain in a sieve.'"

Ibrahim thought she was playing with him again. He said, "Do not toy with me Maria."

Maria responded. "I mean it! You are unlike any other man I have ever met. I believe you to be a dignified and honest man, true to your beliefs. You are serious but not arrogant. Blunt, but not impolite or condescending. You are Muslim, true! But I don't think that is a good reason to dislike a man. A person should not be judged solely upon the basis of the god or gods that they worship."

Ibrahim replied, "Yet you will not address me by my title as the others do."

Maria said, playful once again, "No. I do not like you *that* much. As the proverb says, "Call someone your Lord and he will sell you in the slave market!"

Ibrahim's head was spinning as he struggled to regain the upper hand, but he had had enough. He decided the best way to extricate himself was to purchase some fruit and be on his way. He said, "A dozen pomegranates please."

As he watched her reach for the pomegranates and begin to place them in a sack, something caught his attention. A man from the row of stalls behind Maria in a rust colored robe, looked directly at him. A passing glance. A glance of steel-green eyes and a crimson scar that ran from under his eye to his jawbone.

The glance lasted for no more than a second but it was enough for Ibrahim Al-Rahim to take the measure of the man. His Uncle Harun, who raised him from a young age, taught him how to read a man by watching his eyes. That the eyes gave away all.

The hairs on Ibrahim's neck stood up. That look, that quick glance. The countenance of a warrior. The glance belonged to a man skilled in the martial arts, and confident of his abilities. The man turned away and disappeared into the crowd. Ibrahim's senses heightened. He knew he had just spied the assassin that was rumored to be in Granada. The rumor was indeed true! This was without doubt the one sent by the Christian Monarchs from the north to kill his Sultan.

He had gone for his sword instinctively, drawing his scimitar almost completely out of its scabbard.

Maria must have noted the intensity in Ibrahim. She asked, "Ibrahim, are you so threatened by a poor old woman?"

Ibrahim returned his attention to Maria as the threat passed, the man blending faceless into the crowd. Sheathing his scimitar, he took a deep breath and said, "I think, Doña Maria, despite your age, you are a grave threat indeed! My sword could not hope to defeat YOU!"

She laughed, a crackling sweet sound. He took the canvas sack of pomegranates from the tiny hand of the woman. "Until next time Doña Maria."

Chapter 7

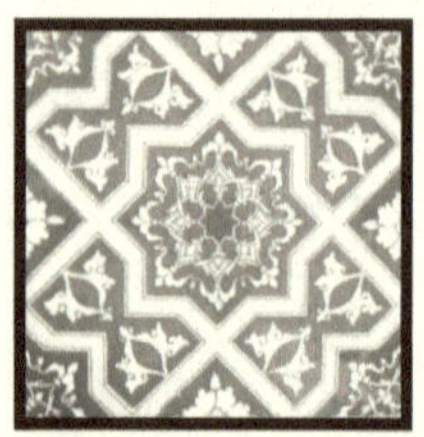

Terror in the Night

'The King of Shebab's renown was that he never lost a battle. But the King of Shebab never won a war."

It was late in the night. Ibrahim made a futile attempt at sleep. His quarters were one of the rounded corner rooms of the fortress of the Alhambra in one of the two towers of the Red Castle, the *Alcazar*. From the three open archways that led onto the balcony, Ibrahim could take in the magnificent view of all Granada and the mountains beyond. Each archway was made of polished marble; vines wrapped themselves around each column and over each archway.

His room was large as was appropriate for someone of his rank and responsibility, but not luxurious.

Hanging from a wall on pegs above his simple bed, within easy reach, were his weapons: Scimitar, the *gladius*, his heavy lance, and a pair of shorter javelins such as used by the *jinetes*. His small, curved dagger was not to be seen. That was always on his person. He slept with that weapon, still in its scabbard, on his calf. He trained himself to sleep with his hand resting on the hilt of the dagger at all times. In fact, if his hand slipped off the dagger he immediately woke up.

Next to the bed a table with a wooden chair and two well-worn books opened upon it, the Quran and the Bible. In the middle of the room was a low table. The table was covered with a dozen different maps, some spilling over the side and onto the floor. These were maps of the terrain of the Kingdom of Granada, mountain passes, invasion routes, water sources, watchtowers, rivers and hills. Larger maps of the Christian Kingdoms to the north lay on top with city centers and castles highlighted for ready reference.

Propped up against the table was a mahogany lyre with several strings curled up, like a birds nest, broken and useless.

Ibrahim could not sleep. A normal occurrence. He arose from his bed. He thought if he read perhaps sleep would come. A pair of oil lamps on the wall flickered and produced just enough illumination to allow for reading.

Shelves ran the length of thc wall. Thc shclves were filled with all sizes of scrolls and codices and loose-leaf books, in disorganized piles—the works of Tacitus and Herodotus, Suetonius and Homer. There were editions on the battle tactics of ancient Rome, Greece and Persia, next to editions of Arabic poetry. Ibrahim ran his hand along the writings contained on the shelves. His hand stopped upon an edition bearing the title, "Knights of the Temple."

Ibrahim's personal feelings about the Knights of Christendom, in particular the Templars, ranged from hatred to fascination.

The fascination began when he was a young boy in Jerusalem. He would never forget the sight. As he peered out from the ramparts of the walls looking southwest above the Jaffa gate near the tower of David, he saw them. Thousands of armored, mounted cavaliers in a line from horizon to horizon. The rising sun glinted off their armor. It appeared as if a solid wave of shining silver had arisen from the ground to the west and was slowing rolling towards the city.

The Order of the Templars itself was formed by some of those very warriors. They placed their headquarters in Jerusalem immediately after the conquest, within the confines of the ruins of the basement of the Temple built in antiquity by wise King Solomon, who dedicated the structure to the worship of Yahweh.

Ibrahim opened the volume and began to read:

The Templars' mission was the same as the other famous order of Military Monks headquartered in Jerusalem, the "Hospitallers." That mission was to provide safe passage to the thousands of religious pilgrims that undertook the perilous journey from Europe to the coasts of the Promised Land, and finally over rough roads to the city of Jerusalem itself. The roads between the coast and the holy city were hazardous affairs, for they were patrolled by brigands or Muslims who would lay in wait, then all of a sudden pounce upon defenseless pilgrims and steal their valuables. These pilgrims were highly valued targets by the highwaymen, for the pilgrims carried their entire life savings with them in order to fund their once in a lifetime pilgrimage to the holy land.

Ibrahim closed the volume and pondered that the Military Monks' stated mission was to keep the roads open and safe. But in their religious fervor they also decided that it was their holy mission to kill as many Muslims as possible, brigand or not. Each dead Muslim would please the Father and get them a bit closer to their heavenly reward.

Ibrahim removed his hand and thoughts from his books and walked out onto the balcony, passing a small mountain of soft pillows spread about the floor. The pillows were there so that he and any visiting guests could recline in comfort.

After many minutes, Ibrahim returned to his bed and tried to sleep. He fell into a light, fitful slumber.

He was having nightmares again, springing from a terror that visited him frequently, the kind of terror that only a survivor of Jerusalem could know.

He was running down a tunnel. It was dark and cramped. Black, smelly water splashed onto him as he ran as quickly as his legs would work. He frantically looked over his shoulder, as if at any second an arrow, a lance, or a broadsword would appear out of the blackness and strike him down.

He slowed his pace. Out of breath. He was tired and scared and thirsty. Ahead he heard the sound of dripping water. He ran to the sound. He cupped his hands to capture some of the water. He brought it to his lips. It was sticky. It was foul. He coughed it up, gagging and vomiting; hands on his knees, he began to wretch. What he thought was life-giving water was blood. Blood that had pooled in the street above and found its way through cracks in the pavement then dripped down into the tunnel below.

He cried out in his sleep. Outside of his chambers, in the hallway, two sentries assigned to the night watch passed.

Their task was to patrol the hallways and patios of the officers of the garrison of the Alhambra. One of the pair of soldiers was new to this duty. He heard the cry of Ibrahim Al-Rahim reverberate through the door that lead to his quarters and off the walls of the hallway. The soldier grasped his sword, alert and ready to enter Ibrahim's chamber, and fight off the threat to the Captain of the Guard of the Red Castle.

The more experienced soldier grasped his hand in a knowing way, stopping him.

"Do not worry Abdul. This happens every night. You will become accustomed to it."

The experienced soldier lowered his voice as if he were about to tell a terrible secret.

"You must understand. Ibrahim Al-Rahim was in Jerusalem as a child!"

The newer sentry was horrified. He whispered as if pleading for an evil curse to be lifted. "Oh Allah! Please be merciful."

Ibrahim's tortured dreams passed from the tunnel to a battlefield. Enemy knights were all around. He was looking into the eyes of the knight that he executed. The man who was distinct from the rest, the knight with the steel-green eyes, the man who refused his offer of mercy, the cavalier that faced certain death without fear.

It was those eyes that haunted Ibrahim now.

In his dream, the steel-green eyes detached themselves from the face of the knight and slowly came toward him. The two eyes grew larger and larger until they filled his entire line of sight. There was no escape. The eyes were coming to devour him whole. He tried to run, but his feet were cemented to the ground. He could not breathe; the eyes were on him now, filling his vision, staring accusingly into his soul.

Ibrahim cried out and sat up with a start, covered in sweat. He looked frantically around his room, dagger in hand, sweeping the space in front of him frantically to and fro with the blade. He gradually gained control of himself, the pounding of his heart slowing down.

He stood up, slipped on a luxurious red silk robe, his long hair spilling over the golden top fringe, and walked slowly toward one of the archways that lead onto his balcony.

The air smelled fresh, clean. Granada sat at thirty-five hundred feet, just high enough in elevation to receive the cool, pure breezes from the snowcapped Sierra Nevada Mountains that towered above the city and kept the hot North African winds at bay.

He breathed deeply and closed his eyes, relaxing his body and mind, pushing the horrific images away.

He could hear the soft gurgle of the fountains below. The night air was scented with the perfume of flowers. It relaxed him.

The night terrors were part of his lot in life, his discipline from Allah for the blood he had spilled. One could not take life even the life of an infidel without consequences. They too were God's creation.

Ibrahim Al-Rahim was blessed with the respect and admiration of his troops, and his Sultan. Beyond the borders of the Kingdom, Ibrahim's fame had spread through Islamic and Christian lands alike. Still, the mighty Captain of the Alhambra was haunted at night, nothing more than a scared little schoolboy. This was Allah's way to keep a great man humble. His way of touching Ibrahim's "hip socket," in the same manner the angel had touched and disabled the Jewish forefather Jacob after they had wrestled for an entire night, leaving a permanent reminder of the mortality of man. For who can contend with a divine being and not be unmarred?

As he stood, he supported himself on the balcony ledge and looked down to the open courtyard below, beyond the gardens and the smooth flowing Daro River, over the city itself. A serene view. Calming. He looked to the faraway peaks of the Sierra Nevada Mountains, their black tips framed against the night sky. Below the peaks, a stream of torches moved up and down the face of the mountains, like a procession of orange fireflies moving to and fro, or a distant constellation of burning stars in the vast expanse.

These torches belonged to the men and not a few women who made the trek to the mountains during the night to cut from their face blocks of pure, blue ice. They collected the fresh mounds of snow that would be brought to Granada in the morning. The ice and snow were a valuable commodity, especially to the Muslim population that willingly paid a hefty price to have but a slice of ice or a handful of snow with which to make delicious sherbet or to cool a vase of pomegranate juice. Some of those torches belonged to attendants of the Sultan whose nightly assignment was to collect sufficient quantities of the frozen water for use in the royal Palace and the Alhambra.

He stroked his goatee thoughtfully as he contemplated the scene. There would be no sleep tonight. He would read the Quran or the Bible until the day dawned.

As he turned from the balcony, he caught sight of a smooth, swift movement out of the corner of his eye. He had not noticed anything out of place while looking out over the city, but it was the human eye's uncanny ability to pick up movement from the corner of the eye—the peripheral vision—in low light, even if that same object could not be noticed while looking directly at it, that alerted him now.

Something moved far down the wall, several stories below, an out of place grey bump on the smooth wall of the tower. The grey bump disappeared, as it quickly passed into the tower through a window several stories below.

Ibrahim felt a rush surge through his veins. He sprang to life. He sprinted for his scimitar and ripped it off the pegs, pulling several pegs, along with bits of masonry, out of the wall in the process. He was barefoot, still wearing the red silk robe. He lunged for the door, threw it open, paused for a moment to grasp the string of wooden beads, laying on his bed, and then ran toward the circular stairway down the torch lit hall, pulling the wooden beads over his head to rest on his neck as ran.

The two soldiers guarding the hallway saw his door fling open with a loud bang and the figure of Ibrahim Al-Rahim run down the hall, barefoot, red robe and black hair flying.

One of the soldiers called out in alarm. "MY LORD?" But he was already gone. The soldiers ran after him, unsheathing their swords. Ibrahim's feet barely touched the stairs as he flew down them at breakneck speed, but quietly, making no noise at all. He reached the floor where he believed he had seen the movement. He came to an abrupt stop and slowly, without making a sound, slightly cracked open the heavy iron door.

He peered through the crack. The man in the grey cloak had his back to Ibrahim. He was clinging to the wall and silently moving down it, away from Ibrahim. Ibrahim let the door slam with a loud clang, alerting the intruder to his presence as he stepped into the hallway. The man in the cloak stopped and pressed himself even closer to the wall in a vain attempt to blend in, unnoticed.

Ibrahim said in a low, stern voice, "If you surrender yourself now, you will receive a fair trial. I swear it."

The man in the cloak stood upright and slowly turned toward Ibrahim. He moved toward the center of the hallway, and with purpose, stepped closer to Ibrahim. In the man's hand was a shortened version of the Christian broadsword, a perfect weapon for concealment—fast, deadly and quiet. This was the weapon of choice for one who does his killing in the night, silently, swiftly.

Ibrahim lifted his sword high, elbows bent, close to his body, extending his sword but not his arms, towards the assassin.

The assassin raised his sword to his face, without a word, softly kissed the blade, in preparation for combat, never taking his eyes off Ibrahim. He flicked the hood of the grey robe off of his head that was covered in red hair, causing the entire robe to fall to the floor.

He was wearing black trousers, leather sandals that muffled the footsteps, and a black lincn short-sleeved shirt. There was a scar on the man's cheek, a thick maroon streak running from under his eye to his chin. The same scar Ibrahim caught a fleeting glimpse of in the marketplace.

The assassin was shorter than Ibrahim. Lighter in weight, but similar in reach, for he too possessed long arms that ran to well below his waist.

The two sentries burst into the hallway behind Ibrahim and watched the swordsmen closing distance. Ibrahim and the assassin circled each other. One could now discern a slight limp in Ibrahim's left leg. He gently sidestepped, right foot over left, mindful of the all-important balance of weight.

They stared at each other, probing for a weakness, one professional fighter staring down the other. Looking to intimidate, probing for a momentary weakness of courage, or self-doubt.

Instead of keeping a safe space in between, both men moved quickly, the space between quickly closed. By moving closer, they could cut off a striking blow's power. This is not something that came easy, for it ran counter to the human instinct of self-preservation which screamed, "Back away!" Put distance between yourself and the killing blade! In order to quell this natural human instinct, both men had passed an untold number of hours of practice on training fields and battlefields, and learned that to preserve their lives they must not cower, and instead, launch themselves forward, without hesitation, toward a razor sharp death.

Ibrahim attacked. Not a violent direct thrust, for that would extend his arms too much, throw his weight off balance and left him exposed and vulnerable to a counter-attack.

The assassin parried the blow; Ibrahim's sword glanced off to the side. The assassin attacked, Ibrahim parried. The opponents exploded into a flurry of action.

One, two, three, four, five, times, in rapid succession, a blur of movement, attack, counterattack. Hardened Spanish steel tinged against hardened Spanish steel.

Sparks flew from the violent striking of blade on blade.

More soldiers poured into the hall, swords drawn. None interfered with the clash of the two master swordsmen.

The clash paused momentarily, the two circling each other; Ibrahim breathed hard due to the exertion of the fight. He produced an audible exhalation of breath, as a technique to control his breathing. The assassin did the same. Neither waivered.

Again to the attack! Swords clanged. Ibrahim ducked inside the defense of the assassin, leveling a blow at his face with the pommel of his sword. It struck home, smashing into the scar on the assassin's cheek. At the same instant, however the assassin perceived Ibrahim's weakness and kicked outward striking with the heel of his foot, the spot on Ibrahim's leg where the tibia had broken through so many years before, causing the ever-present limp. Pain rippled up his leg, and both fighters stumbled backwards from the blows.

Both were out of breath, trying to regain their balance. Again Ibrahim attacked, moving the sword in a series of steady, quick blows up and down and to the left and right.

The assassin pushed at the blows instead of simply trying to absorb them with his sword. He in turn, stepped forward into the blows, keeping his arms tight against his body as he deftly countered each of Ibrahim's strikes, always in perfect control of his balance.

The flat of their swords slammed into each other and locked into place, each man pushing on the other's sword, trying to force the weapon out of his hand, or throw his opponent off balance, their faces only inches apart.

With their free hands, each man frantically slapped and grabbed, in an attempt to control the other's wrist or twist his arm. It may have been a comical sight in any other setting, like two boys on a schoolyard, slapping at each other, trying to gain control.

Ibrahim made a fist and slammed it into the assassin's ribs; the assassin returned the blow, his balled fist crashing into Ibrahim's ribs in turn.

They were locked in place, each man unable to push the other's sword down. Ibrahim was clearly bigger and stronger than his opponent, he towered above the intruder, but even with this advantage he could not force the assassin down or throw him off balance. They were locked in a stalemate.

Sweat poured off each man's forehead. Each could feel the other's hard breathing. Then Ibrahim aimed a blow, kicking hard with his knee at the assassin's groin.

The assassin reacted and blocked the blow with his own upraised knee. They broke off, swords separating, then began once again to slowly circle each other, each tiring. Blood ran down the assassin's cheek from the gaping wound left by Ibrahim's sword pommel. Ibrahim too was injured. His limp had become pronounced, but he tried to hide it as he grimaced, sidestepped and tried not to put weight on his damaged leg.

More soldiers had arrived, swords in hand.

A loud yell announced that Adnan Al Mansur had entered the hallway. He screamed, "*Yen 'aal deen ommak!*"

He roughly pushed several soldiers out of his way in order to get to the front of the watching crowd, moving with purpose toward the assassin, a double-headed battle-axe in his giant hands.

Ibrahim said, without taking his eyes off the assassin.

"Mansur! No! Stand down!"

Adnan, sweat forming on his bald scalp, lowered his axe and backed away, disappointed. The assassin did not look in Mansur's direction, ignored the threat, and kept his focus fixed entirely on his deadly opponent, Ibrahim.

They closed on each other again, the distance between their bodies closing rapidly, swords flashing, clanging; the sounds of the fight reverberating off the walls of the hallway.

Ibrahim stabbed out with his scimitar, fully extending his arm and missed his target. It looked for a moment as though he had miscalculated and made a deadly mistake.

The stabbing motion put him off balance and leave his scimitar far out in front of him, arm extended too much, making him vulnerable to a counterblow. The perfect balance lost.

The assassin saw the mistake and immediately reacted, taking advantage. He slammed his broadsword down onto to Ibrahim's outstretched scimitar in a bid to knock it out of his over-extended hand, to throw Ibrahim off balance, or even shatter the scimitar, thereby leaving him defenseless. The assassin's blow was fierce; he launched the entire weight of his body into the blow, leaping up off of his feet as he slammed his broadsword downward.

However, Ibrahim's apparent miscalculation was a clever feint.

Ibrahim's appeared as though he had overreached and was now vulnerable, but the perfect balance was maintained. As the assassin's sword struck the scimitar, Ibrahim let his arm go limp.

The crushing blow of the broadsword found no resistance. It glanced off of Ibrahim's scimitar and slammed down onto the stone floor. Broken shards of stone and dust shot up into the air, as the broadsword stuck, and was held fast by the hard stone and mortar of the floor. The assassin stumbled forward a half a step, sufficient to lose the balance and weight distribution vital to defend himself from Ibrahim's next move.

Ibrahim flung his scimitar from his right hand upwards into the air, toward his waiting left hand, at the ready at eye level. He caught the scimitar mid-flight and brought his left hand down, catching the hilt of the scimitar as he slashed downward with the same blinding motion. The cutting blow sliced into the sword arm of the assassin. The assassin grunted in pain as blood spurted outward from the wound like a tiny geyser of reddish water. In the blink of an eye Ibrahim slashed again and cut the other unwounded arm of the assassin, then brought the scimitar up and thrust the tip into the assassin's neck, just millimeters from the carotid artery.

The watching soldiers gasped in awe at the dizzying speed of Ibrahim's sword, as Ibrahim pushed the tip of the scimitar lightly into the neck of the assassin, coaxing him downwards, from a standing position to his knees.

At the point where Ibrahim's sword tip sunk into the neck, he saw the vein pulsing, throbbing and pushing the skin outward.

A thin rivulet of blood ran from the tip of Ibrahim's scimitar, down the man's neck, and under his collar. His arms hung, bloodied and useless at his sides. He was breathing hard. Up and down the hall soldiers watched eagerly, waiting for the killing blow from their commander.

Ibrahim willed with all of his might to push the scimitar deep into the intruder's neck and end the life of this dangerous infidel. It was Ibrahim's assignment to keep Abdul Rahkman safe and secure. A man such as this, on such an undignified, cowardly mission, did not deserve mercy. With every fiber of his being he wanted to execute the criminal on the spot.

An invisible force stayed his hand. Ibrahim bent closer to the man and looked at his bleeding face. It was those eyes. Eyes of cold green steel, yes, it was the eyes that stayed his hand. The scar that ran from under the assassin's eyes to his chin was a mass of blood and torn flesh, but the man showed no fear, no remorse, and no pain.

The assassin grimaced, his face twisting slightly. Not due to pain from his wounds, but from the frustration of failing his mission, of being bested by this pagan unbeliever.

Ibrahim looked closer. As the soldiers and Adnan looked on, they saw their Capitan hesitate. This was not Ibrahim's way. The assassin should be dead. Executed, and on his way to some eternal place of torment. It was not to be. Ibrahim looked away from those intense green eyes, for he could not bear it no longer. He motioned to the soldiers, who were stunned at his next words. "Take him away, bind his wounds, and put him in a cell." Several soldiers leapt forward and dragged the assassin away. The rest of the observing soldiers in the hallway were confused by what they had just witnessed.

Ibrahim Al-Rahim did not spare the lives of the cavaliers of Christendom on the battlefield. Why would he spare the life of a lowly assassin trespasser? The killer engaged in a cowardly act against God?

Adnan Al Mansur approached Ibrahim and said, "You should have let me take care of that spot of camel dung. You should not be so careless with your life. I could have handled him, alone."

Ibrahim, deep in thought now, was wiping his sword to remove the blood, responded tersely, "You are no match for him, and he would have killed you, my friend."

Mansur's reply was a look of shock, as if his manhood had just been called into question. His mouth agape, he grunted in disgust.

Ibrahim continued, "He would have taken five more of my men with him before he went down."

Mansur regained his composure. The great head of the battle-axe was lying on floor; Adnan leaned forward on the shaft, and ran his hand over his baldhead thoughtfully. He was irritated with Ibrahim and asked sarcastically, "Ibi, are we now to spare the lives of assassins?"

Ibrahim looked at his old friend, ignored the provocation, and pointed to Mansur's huge double-edged battle-axe weapon. It was not the type of weapon that the Moors deployed in their armies. Ibrahim asked, "Where did you encounter that THING?"

Mansur shrugged casually. "It was the first weapon I laid my hands on in the dark of my quarters when I heard the fight. If I remember correctly, I took it from a dead Frank, long ago. He let me borrow it. He told me he had no use for it anymore!"

Ibrahim had already turned away from Mansur, ignoring the response, not saying another word, he left the hallway, opened the door that lead to the stairway, and walked up the staircase to his room, limping badly.

He returned to his room. As he opened the door, his hands began to tremble, then to shake violently. His scimitar rattled in the scabbard as he removed it and placed it on his bed.

The stress of combat caused his entire body to quake involuntarily. He sat down on the bed, and put his head in his hands. Tears began to well up in his eyes. It was a common occurrence for any warrior who engaged in intense combat to be afflicted with this condition after a battle had terminated, for the body becomes flush with energy.

In Ibrahim's case there was another factor that caused his body to react in such a way. It was those piercing steel-green eyes of the assassin, the unwavering gaze.

For the first time serving as a warrior of Allah, he felt remorse at killing. He spared the man. It did not matter. At this moment in time, sitting on his bed late at night in his quarters of the Alhambra, after besting a master swordsman in a fair fight, he felt no better than the ungodly demons that killed Jerusalem when he was child.

Chapter 8

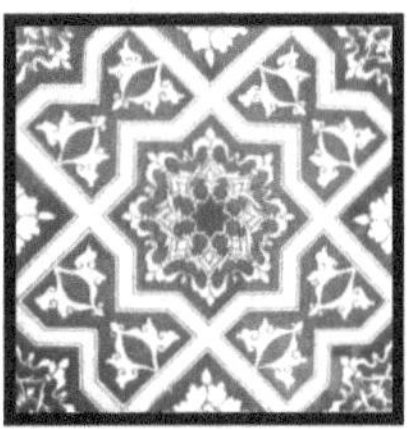

In the Gardens of God

"God sells knowledge for labor —honor for risk."

The morning after the fight Ibrahim Al-Rahim was recovering in the lush gardens of the Alhambra.

He sat on a marble bench, the lyre from his quarters lying across his lap. His injured leg rested on a wooden stool. His leg was wrapped tightly in a burlap bag filled with cooling snow from high in the Sierra Nevada Mountains.

His leg throbbed from the assassin's blow.

The assassin noticed Ibrahim's slight limp and discerned correctly that the old fracture on Ibrahim's leg was indeed a vulnerable spot.

Fortunately for Ibrahim, the original fracture had healed well. In fact the area where the fracture had occurred healed strongly, his body created a bump on the fracture of additional, reinforcing bone growth, limiting the damage from the assassin's blow.

However, strong as it had become, it was still a sensitive area. A true weakness.

A fountain bubbled in front of Ibrahim. A low fountain of black and white tiles in the shape of an eight-pointed star. A stream of water shot upward from the middle of the star. The peaceful sound relaxed Ibrahim. On the other side of the star-shaped fountain, a well-tended plot of Ibrahim's favorite flower, the red poppy alongside other flowers. Many of the species were native to Southern Spain. Others were imported from Africa, Asia or other far-away islands. There were brilliant roses, carnations, purple lupines, iris, crocus, and exotic orchids of many colors. The air was filled with a mélange of different scents as each aromatic plant and flower vied to outdo its companions.

Overhead, circling effortlessly on the air, a pair of golden eagles patrolled.

Hanging in the boughs of the trees were birdcages filled with colorful animals, some native to Granada, others acquired from all parts of the world. There were Crested Fly Catchers, Ruby-Crowned Kinglets, Whip-Poor-Wills, White-Eyed Vireos, Parakeets and Macaws, African Grey Parrots and Cockatoos. They sang out happily as well-trained servants of the Sultan fed them their breakfast.

Pink Flamingos and black-winged stilts walked free and daintily in the fountains, in contrast to the immobile Great Blue Herons.

Attendants pruned the trees and shrubs or tended to the flowers. Still others cleaned the fountains and pools using large square nets attached to long wooden poles.

The gardens of Allah were like heaven itself.

Ibrahim was strumming softly on a lyre, attempting to recreate a love song he heard played by a traveling minstrel in the main plaza of the city. Ibrahim spent many years practicing the lyre. In spite of many hours dedicated to perfecting the art, the instrument never did sound quite right to his ears. He could never perfectly recreate the notes he heard played in perfect tune in his head.

Ibrahim believed it much more difficult to be a skilled musician than a soldier. He paused his playing as that thought struck him. *You can teach any dolt how to soldier. That is why there are so many soldiers in the world. What if there were more musicians than soldiers? The world would be a better place! No real talent is needed to be a good solider, one only needs training, practice, a bit of experience, and a whip laid across the back occasionally to drive a lesson home. However, to excel as a musician,* he thought, *you either have the gift instilled by Allah at birth or you do not.*

Ibrahim did not have the gift. He grunted out loud and said, "Do not blame the Maker! I am just terrible!"

Adnan Al Mansur appeared on the lilac lined path that led back to the Alhambra proper. He looked at Ibrahim and chuckled as he said, "I came as fast as I could run to aid the camel struggling to give birth."

Ibrahim did not smile. He pursed his lips and continued to concentrate on his playing.

Mansur continued, knowing that he was irritating his friend, "Allah has blessed you with many talents Ibi, but music is NOT one of them."

Mansur laughed out loud, his untended beard shaking back and forth, pleased with himself, and then continued on his way.

Ibrahim was perturbed. Even that crazy, uncouth Berber made a correct evaluation of his musical skills.

At least it was relaxing for him to be here, in this earthly paradise, surrounded by the blissful sounds and pleasing aromas of the creation of Allah. It helped to sooth his conscience, this constant reminder of why he went to war, why he took lives in battle, why he shed blood.

He must protect *this*, not just plants and trees and birds, but what these represented. The life that was symbolized by this garden. *THAT* was an ideal worth fighting for, even if it meant killing and if need be, dying.

Soon the Sultan strolled past, surrounded by a tight knot of ministers and aides. He wore a violet-purple colored robe, the royal color. The unique and beautiful purple-colored dye derived from the Murex sea snail's shell that the Phoenicians had traded for centuries. They had built a mighty trading empire from the Levant to Tarsis on the back of the tiny sea-creature and its priceless dye.

The young auditor, recently arrived from the Caliph, was holding reams of documents and busily shuffled through the sheaves, head down, as he walked. As he consulted the papers he briefed the Sultan on import and export figures to and from the North African trading ports.

But the Sultan paid no attention to the eager young man's chattering. He stopped and bowed low over a violet rose to enjoy its perfume. He cupped the flower gently in his hand breathed in its scent and smiled.

Exasperated, the young auditor lost control of several pages of his precious records. They fluttered out of his hand and flew to the ground.

He dropped to his knees to scoop them up as he cried, "My Lord! Did you hear what I said about the silk exports to Morocco?"

The Sultan replied in a bored, even tone without turning away from the rose, refusing to give the auditor even a minimal amount of attention,

"Not a single word! Not a syllable!"

The auditor, still on his knees re-organizing the papers, began to recite the facts and figures that he diligently memorized for the benefit of the Sultan.

Still ignoring the auditor, the Sultan spied Ibrahim Al-Rahim sitting on the bench and shouted in relief, "Ah, Ibi!"

The Sultan dismissed the young man with a casual wave of his hand. "We will discuss the all-important silk exports later."

The young auditor looked dejected, the way a child looks when his favorite toy is taken away.

The Sultan approached Ibrahim who, in spite of his injured leg began to struggle to stand up, out of respect for his Lord. The Sultan stopped him, with a gentle push downward on his shoulder, and said, "Please Ibi, stay seated."

The Sultan sat and complained. "If I have to hear one more word about almond exports I am going to throw myself off the tower!" He glanced down at the lyre. "Still banging away at that thing? I must admit, Ibi you are one of the most persistent men I have ever encountered!"

The Sultan gestured to Ibrahim's leg. "How is that old war wound?"

Ibrahim responded quickly, to show his strength, embarrassed that the Sultan had pointed out the weakness. "It is well, my Lord."

The Sultan paused as he tugged on his long grey beard thoughtfully and asked, "Ibi, I do not understand what happened last night. An assassin was sent by the Christian Kingdoms to kill me in my sleep like a dog, and yet this morning, that criminal is alive and well in my dungeon, Why?"

The Sultan scowled, his brushy black eyebrows almost meeting above his beak-like nose. He looked directly at Ibrahim and said, "I have always trusted your judgment and counsel. I never question it. Now I am perplexed and I must inquire; how is it that the Captain of my personal bodyguard spares the life of an assassin lurking in my castle when he would gladly execute that same man if captured on the battlefield?"

Ibrahim was staring at the red poppies as he responded.

"My Lord, I would never allow any man to live who harbored ill will toward you, I have sworn by Allah and his prophet to protect you and this kingdom with my very life. I would be sinning against God himself if I allowed such a man to live."

The Sultan shook his head slowly.

"I know! I have full confidence in you! This is what puzzles me! Why is it that the assassin takes breath still, Ibi?"

Ibrahim turned his attention from the poppies and looked at the Sultan. "Because, my Lord," he paused, "The assassin's mission was not to kill you."

The Sultan's eyes widened, "What are you talking about," he asked.

Ibrahim continued gravely, "I wished to keep this a private matter, but now that my Lord wishes to know my motivation, I must tell you. He was here to kill . . ."

Again he paused. Then he sighed and continued with difficulty, "The assassin came here to kill *me*. But do not worry my Lord, I will see to it that justice is served. Now, I ask for your leave as it is time to begin the drills."

Chapter 9

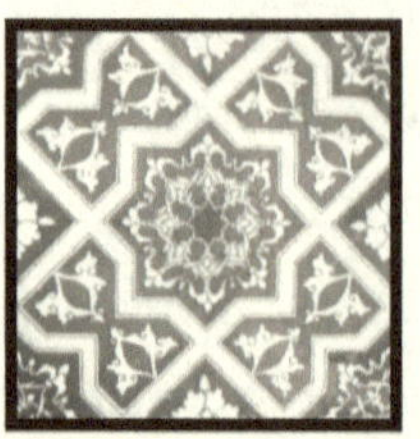

Santiago De Aviles

"I am unlucky,
Even in walking,
For the steps I take forward,
Turn back upon me".

After his conversation with the Sultan Ibrahim Al-Rahim returned to his quarters, removed the bandages from his leg and dressed for the daily afternoon battle drills. He tied his long hair tight behind his head. He dressed in the same clothing each time he directed the drills: trousers of tan linen, and a thick tan sleeveless coat of silk. The front of the coat was embroidered with gold colored tracings. His *gladius*, the Roman short sword, in its polished bronze and leather scabbard, hung on his hip. His feet were shod with heavy sandals of leather.

As he stepped onto the training field of the Alhambra, he made a concentrated effort not to limp in front of his men. He must not show weakness. He stood up to his full height and strode onto the courtyard.

A group of passing soldiers stopped to salute him and called out, "*EMIR AL RAHIM*!" Their salute was not motivated solely from duty. It was a measure of respect for a man that can only be borne from selfless deeds.

Already, all of the Alhambra, all of Granada had heard about last night's encounter with the assassin.

The story had been retold a thousand times. It was well known that Ibrahim Al-Rahim could have called upon a hundred of his warriors to dispatch the killer who slipped into the castle in the dark of the night. But no! Ibrahim took the danger upon himself, protecting his beloved men from harm. As the story was retold through the streets, the Muslims would proclaim. "Who of all of the Lords of Christendom! What Captain of the infidel would risk their hide for the sake of their men?"

The hippodrome was crowded with two thousand defenders of the Alhambra who assembled for another day of "bloodless battle," training for the next inevitable attack of the infidel's armored knights.

They stood at attention, upon the hippodrome, a vast enclosure below the Alcazar. A soldier shouted out, "Hail Ibrahim Al-Rahim! Scourge of the Christians! Hammer of Allah!" Two thousand warriors raised their fists and cheered. Ibrahim blushed. He motioned with his hand for the men to stop cheering, and quickly gave orders to start the drills.

The drills lasted for three hours and incorporated fencing skills, horsemanship, archery, classes on tactics and marching exercises. The sword drills consisted of one thousand strikes on effigies made of straw. Training with the lance entailed a seventy-two movement precision exercise.

Ibrahim studied Roman tactics and drilling techniques for preparing a legion for combat and incorporated their practices for his own elite guard.

He often told his troops, "Legion's drills were bloodless battles and their battles were nothing more than bloody drills. So it shall be with us."

The men began to drill with their scimitars. They were practicing a technique that Ibrahim had learned from his warrior-like uncle Harun. Because of their greater stature the cavaliers of Christendom had a tendency to swing high with their broadswords. The heavy armor they bore naturally limited the speed and agility of a downward thrust. His uncle Harun, taught Ibrahim to dive or roll under the high strikes of a knight and then attack their vulnerable and less armored lower body.

Ibrahim spoke to his troops, encouraging maximum effort in the dusty heat of the hippodrome,

"If the Templars can dedicate three hours out of their daily routine of drunkenness, sodomy and man-rape to drill for battle, we can find more than three hours a day!"

A total of five thousand horsemen were employed for the defense of the Alhambra.

Three thousand of that number was the *jinetes*, the famous Moorish light cavalry.

This group of two thousand was Ibrahim's carefully selected heavy cavalry. Ibrahim ensured that these men were equipped and trained like no other soldiers in the Kingdom. They bore the heaviest lances and the thickest armor. He formed them for one sole purpose—to destroy the best soldiers in Christendom—the Military Monks of the Order of the Temple.

Ibrahim, although dressed for the drills, addressed his men but did not participate today as usual, for he had another task to perform.

He turned away from the hippodrome to a small, indistinct iron door on the stone wall, opened it and descended down a narrow, twisting, darkly-lit staircase that ended at an iron gate that marked the entrance to the dungeon.

Yusuf, the guard, recognized Ibrahim Al-Rahim and threw open the gate. Yusuf was short and pudgy with a wide, friendly face. He appeared to be a man who enjoyed food and probably drink as well. He looked as if he would be right at home cooking in the kitchens of the Alhambra. In spite of his less than war-like appearance, Yusuf was a responsible young officer. He was first on the scene to arrest the martyr Peter and he carried out his assignments seriously, and viewed the dungeon as his personal domain.

Yusuf rarely received visitors of note to his dungeon and was surprised by the appearance of Ibrahim.

"My Lord!" Yusuf bowed.

"May I see the prisoner?"

"Of course! It is an honor!"

Yusuf motioned to the cell that held the dungeon's only inmate.

Ibrahim walked down a dimly-lit passageway with a high-arched ceiling. Along either side of the passageway were cells. The dungeon, a place for punishment and correction, was clean. There was no particular foul odor other than the natural mustiness of a subterranean cave.

There were no machines of torture, not even a chain or a set of shackles. It was so quiet that from time to time the crisp sounds of water gurgling or splashing from the fountains and pools overhead in the gardens would filter down through the walls.

Ibrahim made his way to a cell halfway down the passageway. Seated cross-legged on the floor behind strong iron bars was the assassin. He was not chained. A clay vessel of clean drinking water sat next to him.

The assassin's cheek, smashed by Ibrahim's pommel the night before was bound with cloth. A skillful physician had stitched the sword cuts on his arm with thread made of sheep's intestines. The thread was dried and cut as fine as human hair. Before sewing the wounds shut, the physician had cleaned the wounds with sour wine to prevent infection, and applied a poultice of herbs.

Ibrahim grabbed the bars of the cell and looked down at the assassin, who did not respond to Ibrahim's presence. Instead, he stared dispassionately at the floor.

Ibrahim felt a strange feeling as he watched the assassin, an indefinable dread that this conversation would be bitter for him.

But why should that be so? he thought.

This man was a criminal. An assassin. The most vile, dishonest work a human can engage in. A man like this was devoid of honor. Ibrahim dwelled on that, took courage and began the conversation by asking, "Did your contacts in the *Albacin* misinform you as to which floor of the tower my room is located? Or did you simply misjudge and enter on the wrong floor yourself?"

Ibrahim nodded in answer to his own question.

"Yes! You were misinformed. No question. A man of your skills does not make errors. You would not have made the mistake of entering the wrong floor and missing your target. Perhaps you should have paid them more gold for the proper information? I want to know who your informants are, so they too can be brought to justice."

The man stirred, still looking at the floor, and finally spoke, his words laced with scorn.

"Justice?"

He spat on the ground and snarled. "You know nothing of justice."

Ibrahim was not in the mood to be lectured and responded, "This from an assassin? A man without honor?"

The assassin finally looked up, Ibrahim saw the same cold, steel-green eyes that haunted his recent dreams and stole his slumber.

The assassin's hair was disheveled and the bandages covering his broken face did nothing to diminish his intensity. He said simply, "Abran De Aviles."

Ibrahim looked at the assassin quizzically. The man repeated, "Abran De Aviles."

Ibrahim, puzzled now, pulled at his goatee as he attempted to discern the intent of the assassin's words. Was the man saying his own name? Perhaps the assassin was not of sound mind?

Again, "Abran De Aviles."

Ibrahim was not in the mood to play mental games. He asked tersely. "What is the meaning of this? What are you talking about?"

Ibrahim put up a stern front, but began to fidget uncomfortably. His fingers danced nervously on the hilt of his sword.

"Abran De Aviles. Do not forget that name, Moor. He was a true knight. Noble, honest, fair and kind. It was Abran De Aviles who built the orphanage with his own hands and money. Forty children are housed and educated there. Children who would be living in an alley or at forced labor, or worse. Thanks only to his grace."

Ibrahim felt his gut twist. A Christian knight could not be capable of such noble deeds. As for helping orphans, No! Not that. It could not be true! Impossible! This man was a base assassin, unworthy of honor or trust. He was lying! Yet, the words of the proverb rang a warning in Ibrahim's head. "*Beware! Some liars tell the truth*!"

He backed away from the bars and turned to walk away and said, "I am done with you for now assassin. Be assured, I will be back, and the next visit will not be so friendly."

As Ibrahim walked away the man called out. His words reverberated off the cold stone walls. "ABRAN DE AVILES! MY BROTHER WHOM YOU MURDERED IN COLD BLOOD!"

Ibrahim stopped. He was out of sight of the assassin, closer to the exit but still within earshot. He yearned to escape the dungeon, but something caused him to pause. He turned and asked into the dimness even though he already knew the answer. He knew the answer to this question when they fought in the hallway the night before. He knew the answer but was scared to ask, "You knew him? You are his brother, then?"

The man responded, words pouring out, filling the passageway. "Yes! I am Santiago De Aviles. I watched from afar, trying to reach my brother, unable to do so, masses of men running away from the battle, I could not get through to fight by his side. He was on his knees, unarmed, defenseless. You cut him down like a dog. Do not speak to me of justice! You show no mercy. May you rot in hell for your crime!"

Ibrahim leaned against the wall of the passageway; he rested his head on the cool dark stone, just out of sight of the assassin's cell and answered meekly, "It was war. It was battle. He would have done the same to me if the roles were reversed. He would have executed my men. It was the All Powerful that slew him, not I."

"NO!" was the sharp retort from Santiago. "He would NEVER kill an unarmed man! Even a godless Moor! He was a man of honor! He would not do so even if ordered by a king! God himself!"

Ibrahim was struck. He never considered the possibility that a warrior of Christendom was capable of such high morals. They were all bloodthirsty monsters. An infidel knight was not capable of such mercy!

Yet, he knew that Santiago De Aviles told the truth. When you fight a man the way that they fought last night, staring into a man's soul as he fights for his very life, you truly learn what kind of man he is. Ibrahim could sense from Santiago's steady, green eyes that he was not a liar. He spoke truth. A rare few did, regardless of their faith, Christian, Moor or Jew. Ibrahim did not want to believe Santiago de Aviles, but he had no choice. He could not erase the intense gaze of Abran de Aviles from his mind, the steady green eyes that stunned him, caused him to hesitate, on the battlefield.

Ibrahim slowly walked down the passageway toward the door past Yusuf who stood at attention, to the spiral staircase that lead him out of the dungeon to safer ground. Far from accusation.

As he walked, Santiago screamed all the louder, enraged, shaking the bars of the cell so furiously that Ibrahim imagined the wound on his cheek opened up once more, "ABRAN DE AVILES MY BROTHER WHOM

YOU MURDERED IN COLD BLOOD!" Again and again came the cry.

"ABRAN DE AVILES MY BROTHER WHOM YOU MURDERED IN COLD BLOOD!"

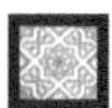

That night as Ibrahim slept in his quarters, the nightmares came again. This time the nightmares were even more real, starkly horrific. Now the steel-green eyes coming toward him dissolved into an army of children silently marching toward him, their faces expressionless. They wielded garden and farming instruments as weapons, hoes and scythes, rakes and staves, all dull and unsharpened. Ibrahim's feet were cemented into place as the children came slowly toward him. As they came closer, somehow he knew they were orphans.

They came on swinging their "weapons," closer and closer. He did not want to hurt them, but they would not halt.

He raised his sword. He cut them down as they came, one after another, a never ceasing horde of faceless, silent orphan children. His arm continued slashing as if under the control of some unseen being.

He sobbed as against his will, he struck them down. His vision blurred from the tears as he slashed left and right, children falling by the dozens, hundreds of decapitated, faceless heads piled at his feet.

He shouted at them to stop attacking him, to no avail. He begged them to stop. Still they came. He thrashed about on his bed, screaming and yelling, rocking the bed from side to side.

Outside the door one of the two sentries of the night watch sighed and whispered, “It is an uncommonly bad night.”

Chapter 10

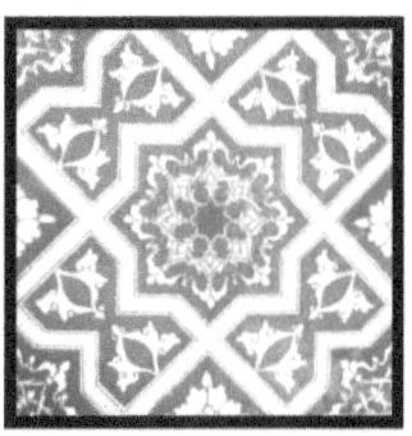

Shaken Beliefs

"Immediately the Lord stretched forth His hand, and caught him, and said unto him, O thou of little faith, wherefore didst thou doubt?"

Vital to the fragile *convivencia* were certain laws the Sultan decreed, governing how each religion could conduct its sacred worship. The Moors would not bend these laws, even for the sake of the *convivencia.* Islam as the ruling power, was the only religion unfettered in their practices.

The Christians were allowed to hold their services within the confines of their churches free from interference. They were not permitted however, to ring bells from the church towers. The Moors hated the sound of church bells. That brassy sound represented to them all that was intolerant and unrighteous about Christendom. It reminded the Moors of the crusades—terrible memories of massacre and death.

The ringing of church bells easily drowned out the call to prayer by the muezzins in their minarets. It was akin to blasphemy to ring church bells in the Kingdom of

Granada. Church bells had not sounded in the city for generations.

Another uncompromising Islamic mandate was that the Christians were prohibited to hold processions in public, or carry the cross in the street, or display that symbol in any fashion outside of one's home or outside the walls of the churches. For the Muslims, the cross was a repugnant idol. To add the abomination of a cross to a public display was beyond forgivable. This was the instrument that was used by Satan to kill one of the revered prophets, Issa himself! To venerate such a thing was repulsive, to carry it in procession in the street was worse. Blasphemy. It was outright rebellion, and an insult to Allah himself. A procession was a direct challenge to the power and sovereignty of the Moors, of their right to rule Granada.

The Alhambra itself was covered in delicate filigree writing extolling and praising the qualities of God, but there was not one image or idol to be found in the architecture of the fortress, or in any Islamic structure in the world. To Islam it was unthinkable to use images of any creation sculpted by the hands of man as an imperfect replacement for the glory of God.

This creed brought the two faiths into conflict. The Christians adored their idols formed of wood and stone. On the other hand, the Sultan was unyielding in the enforcement of the religious laws. He enforced these laws without exception, without debate. It was a black and white issue. He said,

"If you want to cause confusion, give them a choice!"

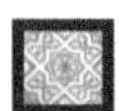

Now then, there lived in Granada a priest by the name of James. For many years he led his flock in one of the churches of the *Sacramonte*, that neighborhood on a hill directly across from the Alhambra, beyond the *Albacin*, or Christian quarter wherein lived the majority of the Christian population of the city.

James lived in one of the many caves that centuries before were dug out of the soft earth of the hillside. For decades, James worshipped in peace under Moorish rule and encouraged his flock to seek peace with their overlords. He preached that the Father would in his lifetime free his congregation from Islamic rule. They only needed to be patient and wait on his deliverance. As the years passed however, James became impatient. He wondered why the Sovereign Ruler of All Things did not act to remove the cursed Moors from Granada and allow them, the holy people, to worship freely and carry both the holy cross and virgin in sacred procession through the streets once again.

Over the decades, James' hair turned from brown to grey. He began to bend from the weight of age. Once his stride was long and sure, now he was slow and unsteady and needed the assistance of a gnarled cane hewn of oak.

As part of his sacrifice to the Lord, he forsook marriage and family in order to fully devote himself to

God's will and prepare his people for salvation. A salvation that did not come.

He questioned why God did not act to deliver his congregation. Perhaps God's inaction was due to their own spiritual inactivity? A lack of faith?

James preached and believed in salvation from Islamic rule in his lifetime, but now he doubted.

Then James heard of the dance that the girls performed during the Muslim's call to prayers each day. He was encouraged by the protest. He thought it God's will for the dance to be performed in Granada. Not only in this city, but with the speed of a brushfire fanned by the wind, the dance took hold throughout the entire Kingdom. James hoped that the recent martyrdom of Peter would have stirred the people into more activity, even open rebellion, which would in turn force the Christian kingdoms of the north to put aside their own petty squabbles, unite and destroy the Moors once and for all.

Now James planned to fire the spark of rebellion and prove to the Creator that he and his church were indeed ready to, "Stand still and see the salvation of the Lord." There spiritual inactivity would be replaced with vigorous acts of devotion.

His flock constructed a cross out of strong oak, made up of several separate pieces.

The distinct sections of oak did not appear to be anything more than tan pieces of timber used to support a balcony. When slid into place however, using a tongue and groove system, they formed a wooden cross nearly twenty feet high and ten feet across. This would be the largest cross seen in southern Spain since the days of the Visigoths, the blessed days before the Moors stormed across the water from North Africa and conquered Iberia.

On top of the wooden cross would be placed a plaque that read, "*INRI*" in reference to the words, *"Iesus Nazarenus Rex Iudaeorum"*, or "Jesus of Nazareth, King of the Jews". The very words Pontus Pilate commissioned to be placed at the top of the torture stake that killed the Christ.

The congregation would gather in the Sacramonte and with the cross in the lead, march down towards the main plaza of Granada, enter their church and place the cross in a permanent foundation that was already built for such a purpose.

James divined that now was the time to make a public statement of their commitment to the one true religion. He told his flock that the Almighty would reward their act of faith and set in motion the events that would lead to the downfall of Moorish rule. Perhaps, preached James, the Rock would rain down fire from heaven as he did during the ten destructive plagues he brought upon Egypt and erase the Moors and their invincible army in one fell swoop.

Word spread among the Christian quarter and many came to participate in the procession. Many more however, decided it would be best to, "Stand still and see the salvation of the Lord," from the safety of their own homes and shops. Still, more than three hundred of the faithful gathered, hauling the distinct pieces of the cross into the street to be fit together. They prayed on bended knee as James flicked holy water upon each one, while reciting prayers in Latin. Then as James splashed the holy water on the cross itself, he raised both arms upward in a dramatic fashion, shaking his cane.

"Brothers! Hear me! We witnessed the signs; we have read the words of the prophets together these many years. We have heard of our brothers' sacrifice! We have seen right here in Granada a brother of Christ willingly sacrifice himself for our Father's own glory. The martyrs have offered their very lives to hasten God's judgment upon these godless, pagan MOORS!" He spat as he spewed out the word. There was a murmur of agreement and nodding of heads from the gathered crowd in response. James continued, "Now it's our turn to fulfill God's will, and accept the prize of martyrdom, for the sake of his kingdom."

He ended on a dramatic note and screamed, "I say to you all, see the salvation of GOD!"

The crowd responded, "GOD'S WILL!" or "AMEN!"

The cross was set into place upon the ground, the separate members interlocked together then slammed home by men with sledge hammers who struck the four open ends of the timbers of the cross to secure the entire structure in place.

James, supported by his cane, hobbled over to the now-complete cross lying on the ground and placed the plaque bearing the letters "*INRI*" in place at the top.

The cross was raised, supported by half a dozen strong men. James led the cross and the rest of the faithful, and at a slow pace, moved off, down the main avenue of the *Sacramonte* towards the main plaza of Granada.

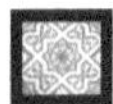

At the same time James was encouraging his flock, Ibrahim returned to the dungeon. He carried a wooden stool. His red silk slippers did not make a sound as he approached the cell that contained Santiago De Aviles.

Santiago was asleep, his disheveled red hair pressed up against the side of the cell, the bandage still covering half of his face. He sat, arms hanging straight down.

Ibrahim thought how vulnerable and weak Santiago looked. This surprised Ibrahim, for sitting in front of him, sleeping soundly, was the most skilled swordsman he ever faced, now reduced to a simple, defenseless prisoner.

Ibrahim prayed a silent prayer to Allah that he would never find himself in such a naked, disarmed and weak state, at the mercy of the infidel.

Santiago stirred. His unbandaged eye began to flutter, head rising up slowly. Ibrahim sat down on his stool. Only the iron bars divided the two men who sat, nearly at eye level just a foot away from each other.

Ibrahim spent most of the day meditating on how he would question Santiago De Aviles. He felt strangely compelled to do so. To justify his actions. He would show Santiago the error of his ways. His beloved brother, Abran De Aviles erred in judgment. It was this flawed judgment that led to his death, nothing more. After all, Ibrahim reasoned, Abran De Aviles was on a field of battle of his own free will. He was on the losing side. Of course he lost! He fought against Allah himself and as it is written: "Only God will conquer."

Abran de Aviles lost his life. He was defeated. No one was responsible or blood guilty for an error Abran himself committed. It was God's will. Ibrahim was guilty of nothing. He did not sin. Was protecting the Maker's earthly paradise somehow a crime? It was Abran de Aviles, pondered Ibrahim, who should have thought first and foremost about the safety of his wife, children and orphans under his charge. Especially the defenseless orphans who relied upon his protection and guidance. He abandoned them!

Santiago De Aviles finally looked at Ibrahim with his piercing steel-green eyes, across the space that separated the two. He looked tired. But it was not fatigue. It was the throbbing ache from his wounds. Santiago would not grimace, would never show the pain that he felt rippling through his damaged arms and face.

Ibrahim spoke with the physician that tended to his wounds. The physician described how he offered Santiago sour wine mixed with myrrh to help dull the pain. He refused the potion, then lay perfectly still as the physician used a razor-sharp needle made of bone and sewed the wounds closed. Santiago lost consciousness from the pain of the wounds, the blood loss and the pain of the surgery. He awakened here, in this cell in the belly of the Alhambra.

Ibrahim broke the silence and said, "Only a fool grabs onto the tail of a hyena. The tail is too small, he cannot hold on, he will lose his grip and then he faces the powerful jaws of the angry creature. He who attempts this is a fool and deserves to be bitten."

Santiago did not respond. Ibrahim continued, slowly stroking his neatly shaved goatee with his thumb and forefinger, confident in his line of reasoning and supreme self-righteousness.

"In the same way, any man that raises his sword against the Kingdom of Granada will be bitten."

Ibrahim paused to let the words have their desired impact. Santiago remained silent. Ibrahim, encouraged now, said, "Abran De Aviles, your brother, whom you contend was a good man, was a fool."

Santiago reacted to that. He clenched his teeth and sat upright, his face turned crimson in anger. This was the response that Ibrahim hoped to evoke from Santiago. He finished his lesson. "You have followed in his footsteps. A fool's errand, an affront against the All Powerful himself."

Satisfied, Ibrahim leaned back on the stool, and stretched his leg. It was causing him discomfort. He was about to stand up, take his stool and leave, the lesson complete for the day when Santiago De Aviles spoke, softly, not much more than a gruff whisper, "Allow me to tell YOU a story, MOOR."

Santiago dwelled on that last word with disdain and added, "There is a boy named Lucas. His father cared for the boy alone, for Lucas' mother died from pneumonia while he was young. Lucas has a younger brother named Daniel, named after their father. Lucas looked out for Daniel. He shared whatever scraps of food his impoverished father could provide with Daniel. The boys were close. Inseparable. Lucas and Daniel loved each other dearly."

Ibrahim squirmed a bit in his chair, his confidence beginning to ebb. Sharp pain shot up his injured leg.

Santiago continued. "The father came down with the cough. He was sick for weeks. Lucas did his best to tend for his father, his brother Daniel and the dirty plot of land that passed as a vegetable garden. When he wasn't busy tending to the garden or his ill father, Lucas was in the street, cleaning the shoes of travelers and passersby of mud, dirt and horse crap."

Ibrahim fidgeted noticeably on his stool.

"When my brother Abran found Lucas, he was draped across his fathers' lifeless body, his small arms embracing his father" neck. Daniel was curled up in a tiny ball in a corner of the hut, sobbing quietly. Abran put his hand on Lucas head and said, "It is alright, little one, you are now under my care and I swear by our Lord and Savior that I will protect you and your brother with my very life."

Abran raised Lucas and Daniel at the orphanage. The two boys were educated there. They were taught reading, mathematics and art. They were favorites of my brother Abran. Abran and Lucas, developed a very special bond. He would call Lucas "*mi hijito*," I never heard him address any of the other children in the orphanage that way. I only heard him use that term when speaking to his own flesh and blood."

Ibrahim felt a sudden urge to leave, to run away. He felt his stomach drop. Santiago looked directly at Ibrahim and for the first time since the conversation began, it was Ibrahim who looked away. He pretended to look down the passage toward the entrance gate where Yusuf, in charge of the dungeon, stood at attention, as if there was something important occurring that needed his direction.

Yusuf noticed his Captain staring directly at him. He stood erect and motioned to himself with his index finger as if to say, "Do you wish to speak with me, my Lord?"

Ibrahim noticed the gesture and waved the guard off.

Santiago continued, "Ten years the boys lived at the orphanage. When Abran would visit, Daniel was always the first of the children to sprint to him, leap up into his arms then climb on his head and shoulders like a squirrel, laughing in delight."

Santiago chuckled for a brief moment at the thought of the heartwarming sight, his heavy heart lightened by the memory. He voice suddenly turned to anger, he said, "When that damn crazed hermit came out of his piss hole of a cave to summon the people for a holy war against the Kingdom of Granada, Lucas and Daniel answered the call."

Ibrahim looked down at his feet. His urge to flee now replaced with a sinking feeling of shame. Santiago was about to reach the climax of his story, and drive his own lesson home; that this Moor bastard seated in front of him was not half the man that his brother Abran was. It would almost feel as satisfying to Santiago as driving a broadsword through Ibrahim's heart. Almost.

Santiago continued and said, "Abran forbade the boys to go. Two days after the hermit and his mob marched off, the boys snuck out, into the night to join them. Their flight was discovered. Abran donned his armor and rode off after Lucas and Daniel to retrieve them. Abran arrived just as the battle was joined. And how do I know all of this? I too heard that the boys ran off, and Abran had followed them, so I dressed for battle and rode hard to join them and aid in the rescue."

Santiago paused, closed his eyes. "I arrived too late. I saw, down below in the valley, the boys running wildly for their lives, your cavalry in pursuit, cutting down men from behind . . ."

He looked at Ibrahim, scowled and repeated the words in a low whisper, "Cutting down fleeing, unarmed men from behind like the brave, noble warriors that you are. Mere boys without weapons. Where is the honor in that?

Is that what your religion teaches you? It is murder! Abran charged into the melee directly toward the boys. Too far to aid, I watched as Abran drove his horse between the boys and your cavalry. He cut down three of your riders in quick succession as they bore down on the boys. In the process Abran was de-horsed. The rest of the Christian army was running pell-mell, screaming, moving as fast as their feet could carry them. Abran was quickly surrounded by the Moorish infantry and immobilized. That is how you found him, Moor. I reached the boys and carried them to safety. I watched from afar as you murdered him in cold blood. I returned to the battlefield hours later, after ensuring the boys were in safe hands. The least I could do for my noble brother was to provide him an honorable burial. I arrived on the field but the bodies were already gone, carried away or piled into mass graves. Abran De Aviles, the man who dignified so many others with his kind acts did not himself receive a dignified burial."

Ibrahim could not bear to hear any more. He shot up, and limped down the hall away from the cell of Santiago de Aviles, leaving his stool behind.

Yusuf could not help but notice that Ibrahim's limp had become more pronounced, that Ibrahim Al-Rahim looked disturbed, confused, and pale.

Ibrahim had just reached the iron gate that served as the entrance to the dungeon when a soldier, running down the narrow stairway, out of breath, nearly ran into him.

"MY LORD! You must come quickly!"

Chapter 11

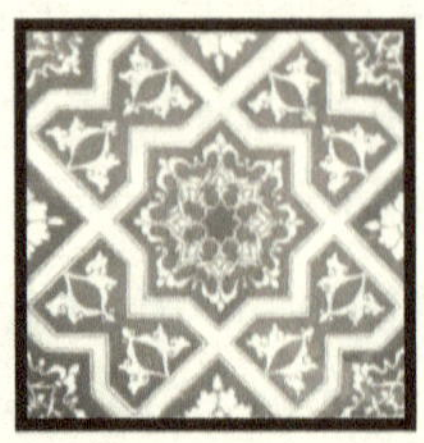

The Procession

"You shall have no other Gods before me.
You shall not make for yourself
an idol in the form of anything
in heaven above or on the earth
beneath or in the waters below."

Ibrahim's disturbed countenance immediately transformed to confident commander. Instinctively he gripped the hilt of his sword and ran, following the soldier up the narrow winding staircase and onto the training field of the Alhambra. He yelled at the back of the reporting soldier's head.

"What is it? What is going on?"

The soldier, turning his head slightly around as he ran, yelled back.

"The Christians are marching with a large wooden cross from the Sacramonte toward the city center!"

Ibrahim swore a curse in Arabic as he dashed into the full sunlight of the training field. This could be the beginning of a full-scale rebellion.

Already, his cavalrymen filled the hippodrome, donning their armor, gathering their mounts and weapons in anticipation of his orders. Squires ushered horses out of their pens. All the activity stirred up the dust, which floated like a puffy brown cloud over the field.

The training field was a blur of orderly activity.

Ibrahim barked, "Heavy lances! Full armor! We ride in three minutes!"

A pair of squires approached him from behind. An instinct learned from countless hours on the practice field told Ibrahim to hold out his arms as the squires lowered his golden cuirass over his head, working his arms into the openings, then closing the bronze clasps behind his back.

Another squire lead a prancing Exsecour with one hand and carried Ibrahim's eight-foot lance in the other, while a fourth squire lowered his golden helmet onto his head, then draped his black cloak with the gold filigree around his shoulders while clasping the golden lyre broach at his throat to hold the cloak in place.

Dust swirled around him as the squires worked. The cavalry hoisted themselves onto their mounts and stood at attention, in perfect order, the result of thousands of instances they drilled in preparation for such an emergency mobilization of the elite horse.

Exsecour sensed the excitement and pawed the ground. Ibrahim swung up onto his mount. Without a word, he spurred his horse forward. Exsecour reared back on his hind legs then shot off at a gallop. The gates of the training field burst open as Ibrahim charged through, followed by hundreds of his elite cavalry. The roar of the cavalry at full gallop was like the low rumble of distant thunder.

The ground shook.

The members of the procession and the old priest felt the thunder before they heard it. They had heard the sound before, many times, as the cavalry was called out to battle. This time however, they knew that the cavalry was not headed for the main gates of Granada and out onto the Vega beyond to join some distant conflict. The thunder was coming directly towards them.

James gimped slowly in front of the large wooden cross, his followers trailing in a clumped mass of worshippers. James thought to himself, *If only that clumsy assassin had done his job correctly! I drew it out for him, with exactness, the window that led to Al Rahim's quarters! He should have entered the window during the dead of night, when Ibrahim Al-Rahim lay sleeping soundly and done away with him!*

James shook his head in disgust. If only he himself were younger. He would take up a sword and with the help of God and the holy angels, smite Ibrahim Al-Rahim and all that came to his aid, the same way that Samson smote two hundred Philistines with the jawbone of an ass!

As they passed the whitewashed homes that lined the avenue, they heard the sound of slamming doors and shutters while citizens scrambled to get out of the street, ducked down alleyways, or disappeared through open doors that were then thrown shut and bolted.

James looked to the sky and the deep stunning color known as "Granada Blue," a shade of blue that could only be produced by the clear, cool air that ran down the peaks of the Sierra Nevada Mountains and spread over Granada like a gentle blanket. James prayed as he stared into the clear sky, "Into your hands, oh Lord, I entrust my spirit."

The distant rumble grew in intensity as Ibrahim's cavalry drew rapidly closer.

The Sultan was serious about the law. Judgment would be swift. If the Christians of Granada broke the law there would be no arrests. No trials in the Mexuar with a judge to determine cause and guilt. There would be an immediate and merciless execution.

Ibrahim rode hard. Though it was mid-day and the hour of peak activity, the streets were empty. Exsecour's hooves clacked on the cobblestones, magnified a thousand times by the clamor of his fellows.

Adnan Al Mansur rode by his side.

Ibrahim remembered his conversation with Santiago de Aviles. Now he was perturbed that for a brief moment he allowed guilt to wash over him for the death of Santiago's brother, Abran De Aviles. That feeling of guilt was replaced with hot anger. He relished the opportunity to bring down the wrath of Allah upon the heads of the infidels. He knew that the Christians had fooled him. They thrived under the *convivencia* and pretended to be at peace, enjoying its liberty, while they plotted against it! They feared the Moors. They feared him, they were his enemies. Nothing more. Ibrahim whispered, "Fear those who fear you!"

He wished, at that moment to strike down all who called Christianity their faith. As he galloped he thought, *There is no making peace with these people! They will not allow it. The end of their path is death. There is no other way. They worship death. They worship death in their churches. They pray to death, they emulate death. So be it. I, Ibrahim Al-Rahim will bring them death.*

The events of the past day had upset his balance. He questioned himself and the actions he took in the service of Allah and defense of the Kingdom. Now, riding in his saddle, his loyal friend at his side, his men behind him ready to obey his every command, his life's purpose came back clearly into view. This procession could be the beginning of a general uprising of the Christian population in the city. It must be harshly put down. The *convivencia* must be preserved no matter the cost.

The cavalry rounded a corner. Ahead, coming towards them at a slow pace was the procession; the old priest James in the lead.

Ibrahim saw the cross and raised his hand to signal a halt. His cavalry skidded to a stop. No more than a hundred yards away the Christian procession halted.

Ibrahim felt anger surge through him at the sight of the huge wooden cross and the crowd of men, women and even children. Ibrahim was incensed. What an abomination! He could not believe the utter disrespect of these people for all that was holy.

The sight of children gave him pause, but only for a moment. His duty was clear. Ibrahim shouted, "This gathering is illegal! You know the law! Disperse now!"

James and his followers were stalwart. The six men supporting the cross raised it even higher.

Ibrahim yelled again. "We will run you down! I swear it! Disperse!"

Ibrahim's sense of justice told him that he must offer the Christians the option of disbanding. He would seize the cross and burn it. However, the darker, bitter parts of his heart hoped that the old priest James would reject his order, and give Ibrahim an excuse to take his vengeance upon them. Ibrahim was eager for a fight.

James waved his cane at Ibrahim. He cried out, his voice coarse and old with age, but strong.

"This is a holy procession! You pagans must leave! We are here by divine will! It is *you* who must leave the street! *You* who must leave Spain forever!"

James' face reddened as he screamed as loud as his old windpipes would allow, he appealed to the very power of heaven.

"LEAVE SPAIN! OR GOD STRIKE YOU DOWN!"

A few members of the procession trembled, wide-eyed with terror. One young boy wet himself and ran back up the cobble stone street to the Sacramonte and safety. However, most were resolute, steady, without fear in the face of the mighty cavalry of the Alhambra, ready to die like martyrs for their beliefs.

A helmetless Adnan, his bald head shining from perspiration, leaned over in his saddle and whispered to Ibrahim.

"They will break and run. How far should we pursue them, my lord? To their caves in the Sacramonte? Do we follow them into their homes?"

Ibrahim response was automatic.

"YES! Strike them down!"

Adnan responded, "*Yen 'aal deen ommak!*"

As Ibrahim spoke, a vision exploded in his mind. Two young boys, unarmed orphans running in terror for their lives, his cavalry at full gallop in pursuit when one man, standing tall, his sword unsheathed without fear, confronting two thousand armored horsemen, shielding the fleeing children from certain death.

Without explanation, Ibrahim hesitated, then shouted, "Orders! Do not run them down from behind!"

Al Mansur looked at Ibrahim quizzically. "My Lord?"

Ibrahim responded.

"You heard me! When they break and run, DO NOT cut them down from behind!"

Adnan was disappointed. He rubbed his hand over the great scar on his bare head as he digested the unusual order, but for once, did not contest Ibrahim's order.

James the priest hobbled toward Ibrahim's cavalry, followed by a handful of his most ardent followers. Some prayed out loud, either a Hail Mary or The Lord's Prayer. They fingered rosary beads as they prayed their final prayers and prepared to enter God's celestial home. They knew their sacrifice would be for the greater good. Their example of mass martyrdom would not go unnoticed by the Christian Kingdoms to the north. This event would finally unite the Kingdoms of Iberian Christendom into a grand Crusade against the pagan Moors. There could not be a more worthy cause.

Ibrahim gave orders. "At the trot! Lances forward!"

Al Mansur turned in his saddle and called to his troops behind, "AT THE TROT! LANCES FORWARD!"

In one motion, five hundred lances, a forest of gleaming, deadly steel points, rushed downward with an audible swoosh. Spear tips pointed at the heads of the slowly advancing priest and his disciples. At the same instant the horsemen moved forward with a soft but intimidating clacking on the cobblestones, the horses began to trot. The empty space on the avenue between the two groups diminished. Each horse strained at the bridle, having been trained to jump into full gallop at the slightest nudge of heel on flank.

Exsecour thrashed his head from side to side as he trotted forward, yearning to break into a gallop.

Then something occurred that took both groups, Christian and Moor, off guard. It was unexpected and surprising. Some would later contend it was a miraculous event.

No one was on the streets save the two groups that faced each other in deadly standoff, neither side willing to yield. Windows and doors were locked down tight. The streets had been deserted in anticipation of the inevitable violence. A heavy silence lay over the city.

Then without warning a flash of color appeared from an alleyway. A dozen women spilled out into the street, midway between the two groups of religious enemies. They wore bright silk dresses, blue and green, pink and violet—long flowing gowns that ended in wide frills bordered in brilliant contrasting colors—red and black, gold and yellow.

The lead girl, Rebecca, was stunning in a sleek white silk dress that set her apart from the others. This particular dress was distinct. It did not flare into frills at the bottom, but hugged her rounded hips and tapered down her legs until it brushed the ground. The entire front of the dress was embroidered with white lace. An embroidered braid of red leather held her hair off of her face. It tumbled down onto her shoulders in a thick cascade. Her smooth olive complexion and coal black hair produced a lovely contrast to the cloud-white color of her dress. Black wooden sandals with thick heels completed the outfit.

This striking figure stood in front of the other girls, silent and fearless, free of expression, as she faced the oncoming cavalry.

Seemingly out of nowhere the notes of a guitar sounded. The tones carried across the silent city. Then a second guitar, and a third, joined in. They were the same guitar strains Ibrahim heard as he bowed for his midday prayer that day in the mosque of the market.

The girls began to move, oblivious to the mounted warriors just a few yards ahead. Rebecca gyrated as she began a steady beat of rhythmic hand clapping, the other girls following suit.

Ibrahim and his men, though not ordered to do so, had come to a full stop.

The staccato rhythm of the guitars built in emotion and fury. Then the sound of percussion provided a steady pounding beat to the music. The soft gyrations of the girls gave way to fierce stomping and graceful arm movements. They twirled, their arms moving gracefully, tracing serpentine patterns in the air. Their fingers and hands seemed detached, tracing their own circular patterns. The girls' heels pounded on the cobblestones, loud as the hooves of Ibrahim's cavalry at full gallop.

The music and the dancing rose in intensity. The guitars' staccato fired faster and faster, gathering force and momentum. The girls twirled faster in time to the music. It seemed impossible that they could keep pace so easily.

Their feet slammed into the cobblestones over and over again with speed.

Rebecca, head flung back, twisted her body. The power of the pounding caused her cheeks to ripple from the shock wave of the incessant stomping. Her feet were a blur.

In stark contrast to the whirling motion and frenetic dancing of the girls, the Moors to a man were motionless, frozen in place. They stared in wonder at the performance unfolding before them.

It wasn't the first dance they had seen. They all enjoyed the seductive and captivating belly dance—a beautiful woman, not entirely clothed, alluringly moving her body and hips as only a woman could. The belly dance was captivating to behold.

This dance was different in a striking way. It was unlike anything they had ever seen. It was beautiful and seductive, true, but it contained another element. This dance held a unique quality that Ibrahim never before attributed to a dance or to a woman. It was *powerful.*

Powerful as a cavalry charge thundering down a hill toward a frightened enemy. Powerful like a mighty rogue wave in the ocean during a storm that tosses the largest boats as if they were toys. Powerful like an earthquake that causes the stoutest of stone buildings to quiver as if constructed of straw. It was that unexpected aspect of the dance that caused Ibrahim's cavalry to come to a complete stop and sit paralyzed with awe.

The dance continued. Sweat flew from the girls' foreheads. The music and the clacking of their feet reached a thunderous crescendo. It seemed the guitar could not be played any faster and that the girls were stomping and twirling as fast as humanly possible. Then as unexpectedly as they started, the music and dancing stopped.

The girls walked slowly toward the alley from where they had come. As Rebecca walked, her chest heaving from exertion, her face wet in perspiration, she turned her head to look at him, a long steady stare. Her walk was slow, purposeful. Her silk dress clung to her body ever more tightly due to the perspiration. The dress showed the outline of her body. The tightness displayed her womanly waist, the way it curves perfectly inward, as if when the All-Knowing made the mold of a woman, he picked her up by the waist with his thumb and forefinger, causing the divine indentation unique to the female.

Their eyes met. In her gaze, a look not of defiance, but of self-confidence. Her almond-shaped eyes crowned by a thin brow and long black eyelashes, flashed.

Ibrahim felt himself shrink from her gaze.

A loud clinking sound broke his trance. He realized that the arm hoisting his lance had gone limp and the steel triangular head slammed onto the cobblestones. He turned in his saddle and saw that many of his men had unconsciously done the same with their lances.

Even Exsecour, his battle charger, was still calm as if ready to return to the stables and sleep, his fire for battle extinguished.

Ibrahim realized at that moment that the lady in white was the most stunningly beautiful woman he had ever seen.

As she disappeared from view, a mirage of grace and power, Ibrahim felt himself trying to catch his breath, as if he had just run a mile in full armor under the midday sun.

The cross had vanished, carried down a side street, supported by a half a dozen men, had found its way into the old priest James' church.

James, with a stalwart handful of followers still stood in the street, as paralyzed as Ibrahim Al-Rahim and his elite horse from the surprising spectacle that had unfolded before them. As if by some unspoken understanding, James turned and walked away.

Ibrahim and his cavalry, without being told to do so, reined their horses around and slowly trotted back to the Alhambra.

Adnan Al Mansur, the most jaded of warriors, looked shaken. He said what they were all thinking but could not quite form into words.

"What the hell just happened? What kind of wizardry was that?"

Ibrahim did not respond. Did not know what to say.

He knew one thing for certain, that without question, the mighty "Hammer of Allah," the "Scourge of Christendom," had been defeated.

His was not defeat borne from battle with the powerful armies of Christendom, nor the grand elite Templars. No! He had been undone by a small dark-haired girl and her powerful dance.

Chapter 12

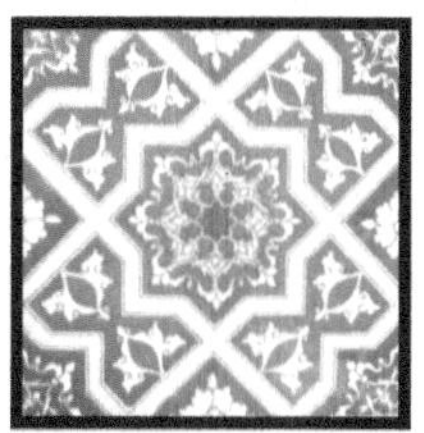

The Grey Cloaks

***"The words of the wicked
are to lie in wait for blood,
but the mouth of the upright
shall deliver them."***

Yusuf stood guard at the gate that led into the dungeon. He enjoyed his assignment. The solitude. He was young but reliable. His seniors were not impressed by his round boyish face and short stature. Still, they deemed him ready for more responsibility.

He had a visitor who announced himself without voice but with a musty, burning odor. Then Yusuf heard a low hissing voice.

"You have someone here I am interested in. I may have business with him. I wish to see him."

Yusuf, startled, spun around. In the shadows stood a man, grey cloak pulled tight around his face. Eyes of yellow. The man with yellow eyes held a white tube of paper between his thumb and forefinger. It was lit. He put it to his lips and inhaled deeply, closing his eyes.

"Who are you?" Yusuf demanded.

"You don't look like much of a soldier. Are you a guard or the pastry chef? No wonder they keep you down here, out of sight."

"I will ask you one more time. Who are you? What is your business here?"

The man was silent. He put the tube to his lips. Inhaled again and taunted. Yusuf said. "If I ring this bell, thirty men will come."

"That is a start, but you will need more men than that."

Yusuf reached for the string attached to the bell. The man put up a pale, blue veined hand and said. "That will not be necessary. I believe you know who I am."

"A Grey Cloak."

"I have heard us called that. I prefer *Fidai*."

"A *Fidai*?"

The man closed his jaundiced eyes and spoke in a trance.

"Yes. You will remember that name, boy. *Fidai*. There is a man here in custody that you wrongly label *assassin*. I will teach you about true assassins. Sinan is our leader. Praise him! Hail his divinity! He knows all events before they come to pass. At our initiation a true assassin is given a mind-opening potion of cannabis. When we awake, we have arrived in the heavenly paradise. Only then are we *Fidai*. A disciple of Sinan, completely devoted to him. In such a state we are given orders along with a dagger. Sinan says this each time, "When you return my angels shall bear you into Paradise. If you should die while carrying out the mission, even so I will send my angels to carry you back to Paradise."

We smoke hashish to maintain the ecstasy of the vision of paradise and as a reminder to accomplish our sacred missions."

Yusuf noticed four other cloaked figures lurking in the shadows, and came to the realization that they had been there the entire time.

The *Fidai* said.

"I tell you this because you should join us. You do not look like much but you are made of steel aren't you? I can discern such things. You are not a *puuup-pet*."

The assassin dwelled upon the word puppet slowly, sounding out the syllables with raspy voice *puuu-pet*. It was not simply a sinister sound, it was the blackest evil given breath.

"I deny you entrance to my dungeon."

"No matter. I now know where to find him."

The Grey Cloaks turned and disappeared into the darkness. Nothing marked their passing save several thin wisps of acrid smoke.

Chapter 13

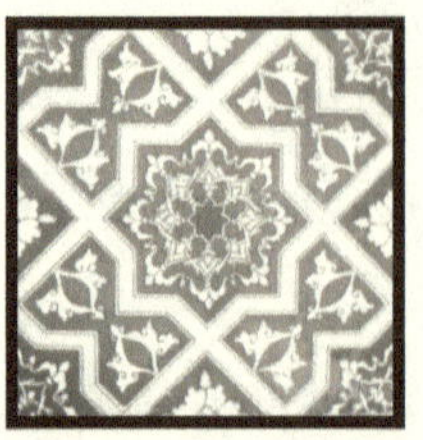

Better Men

"I don't know where,
I don't know how,
This rope got around my neck,
Without my knowing it."

They dined together, Ibrahim Al-Rahim, Adnan Al Mansur and the officers of the elite guard of the Alhambra. The men reclined on large down pillows of earthen colors in the elegant dining hall. The pillows were arranged in two long rows that faced each other with the meal placed on the floor in between.

As with many of the elegant rooms of the Alhambra, the walls of the hall were adorned with the ever-present blue and white ceramic tiles. The tiles in turn, were decorated with interconnected blue and gold geometric shapes.

The myriad tiny shapes had no beginning point and no end, a continuous flow of beauty and design. The design honored Allah the Creator who had no beginning and has no end. Some of these elaborate geometric shapes were slightly deformed intentionally by artists to show humility, for only Allah can produce true perfection.

Arched openings along the walls allowed the diners to look out upon the garden of rose bushes, myrtle trees, and fountains.

The officers reclined. Ibrahim Al-Rahim was at the head the row of pillows as thirty of his officers began the meal that was placed on the floor.

Adnan Al Mansur as lead officer was always seated to Ibrahim's right. A position of honor. Servants in clean white robes bustled about serving the delicious banquet.

They dined on succulent roast lamb with yogurt and mint sauce, plates of black and green olives, figs, toasted almonds, goat cheese, and baba ghanoush—eggplant paste mixed with sesame seeds and spices, with warm flatbread for scooping. There were pyramids of pomegranates, flagons of pomegranate juice, oranges, and sweet Damascene pears that sat on a bed of snow that had been brought down from the heights of the perennially snow-capped Sierra Nevadas.

The delightful aromas of the freshly-prepared feast filled the room.

The officers were accustomed to such a bounty for their evening meal. There were some select luxuries that only the officers of high rank enjoyed, such as the snow-cooled Damascene Pears.

However, even the common soldier of the Red Castle of the Alhambra was blessed with an abundance of food. Allah greatly blessed the fertile plain of the Vega and all of the land of the Kingdom of Granada. Therefore, the Creator's bountiful blessings should be shared by all.

Men like Adnan Al Mansur had come to Granada via the scorching deserts of North Africa. Once in God's own paradise, the desert natives were overwhelmed by the fertility of the earth and the vast fields of crops and orchards. Men who knew only the brown sand of the Sahara could not believe that the bare ground had the power to produce such verdant shades of green.

The men thanked Allah for the meal and began to feast. Adnan chomped loudly as he tore into a piece of roasted lamb, drops of fat spilling down the front of his unkempt beard. He spoke loud enough for all to hear.

"This food is fine, but all a man needs in order to live is figs . . ."

He was interrupted by a chorus of voices who completed the sentence that they had heard a hundred times.

". . . DATES AND WATER!" Raucous laughter followed.

Al Mansur did not smile. His face reddened as he tried to drive his point home.

"It is true! *Yen 'aal deen ommak!"* he declared.

One of the officers said, pointing to Mansur's fat-moistened beard.

"It's killing you to eat that lamb, right Adnan? Like ash in your mouth!"

More laughter from the men.

Adnan responded, shaking the half eaten piece of lamb at his antagonist.

"You bring that pampered Arab ass to my desert for twenty-four hours, and you will cry for your mother and beg Allah for a merciful death!"

The men goaded Adnan.

"That is why we stay here in Granada!" or, "You can keep that camel dung hole of a desert to yourself!"

Ibrahim looked over at Adnan shook his head, and said in an affectionate way, "You truly are a barbarian!"

It was Adnan's turn to laugh now, he threw back his head and roared, chunks of lamb spewing from his mouth. He slammed his fist onto the ceramic tile floor and bellowed.

"Praise be to Allah! An Arab can give no greater compliment!"

"I am not Arab. I am a Kurd!" responded Ibrahim.

"Same damn thing! *Yen'aal deen ommak!*"

The comment was a reminder why Adnan Al Mansur was one of Ibrahim's favorite people. There was no deceit with Al Mansur. No hidden agenda, only loyalty. Ibrahim heard it said that everyone has a secret motive for seeking the friendship of a powerful man. Not Adnan. He was incapable of deceit.

The officers continued to laugh. One said, "Tell us Adnan! Tell us again about your first battle!"

Some of the officers heartily agreed and others moaned in anticipation yet another version of a story they heard told many times.

Adnan grinned at Ibrahim and winked. They were both so young at the time, just teenagers. New recruits to the army of Allah. Ibrahim Al-Rahim did not care much for Adnan at the beginning. He was uncouth, unkempt and crude. But it did not take Ibrahim long to ignore Adnan's rough edges in favor of his bravery and skill in battle.

Adnan for his part did not like the soft-spoken, unemotional Ibrahim Al-Rahim. Until their first battle, they did not speak to each other much. Adnan preferred the company of his fellow tribesmen, he was not all comfortable in the company of Arabs.

Ibrahim simply did not speak much with anyone whether they be Arab or Berber.

In spite of their differences, Adnan came to respect the quiet dignity of Ibrahim. It was obvious to all, even as boys, that Ibrahim would become a commander of men.

It was many years ago, their first battle against the fearsome knights of Christendom, when Ibrahim's leg was severely injured in battle. The same leg that Santiago de Aviles had so efficiently wounded in the swordfight in the hall.

The Christian battle lines collapsed and the pair charged after the fleeing footmen, when a lance pierced Ibrahim's horse. The mortally-wounded creature toppled over on top of Ibrahim, pinning him from the waist down.

Adnan looked at the seated officers, and in a low-dramatic voice began the story.

"I saw two heavily-armored Military Monks, charging Ibrahim on foot, as he weakly struggled to get out from under that horse! He was in pain, I heard him cry out as pain shot up his broken leg. He freed himself. I was running quickly to defend him. Hacking away at the infidels.

Ibrahim was frantically searching the ground for some weapon to defend himself. He grasped a javelin head from a shaft that had been sheared in half. That is the only weapon he could reach. He sat up and cried to Allah a quick prayer, sure he was about to meet his maker.

The Military Monks sprinted toward the wounded Ibrahim. I saw him holding the javelin head tightly, pointing it forward to defend himself. One of the knights, in spite of his heavy armor, leapt with surprising agility over the horse, broadsword held high, aiming a lethal blow. I can even now clearly see the man's grimacing face as he started the downward stroke.

Ibrahim held his broken weapon in front of him in a weak attempt to block the fatal blow. Just when he was about to meet his doom . . ."

One of the seated officers interrupted and yelled, "You distracted the knight with a long boring story!" The other officers roared with laughter. Adnan stopped speaking. He stared for a long intimidating moment at the heckler, then for dramatic effect, opened his arms wide, thumped his chest and cried:

> "Then I arrived! Flying! A shadow passing over Ibrahim, screaming, "*Yen 'aal deen ommak*!" Followed by a 'whooshing' sound. My eight-foot lance struck the knight. His body turned to rubber in mid-air and collapsed on top of the dead horse like a sack of potatoes.
>
> I was over Ibrahim now, wielding my scimitar in one hand and a broadsword that I confiscated from a dead knight in the other. The remaining cavalier came straight at me! I twirled both weapons, yelled, and charged. The knight leveled a blow at me with his lethal double-headed battle axe. I somersaulted under the blade and let go of the scimitar, grasping the hilt of the broadsword with both hands. As I completed a somersault, now on my knees, I thrust upwards with the broadsword, and stood up. The sword entered the groin of the warrior and pierced deep into his bowels. The knight looked down at the sword in disbelief at my agility! Then he slumped forward.
>
> Meanwhile, Ibrahim struggled to remove the Spanish short sword tucked in his waist. With every movement he cried out in pain. I thought we were safe, but a third knight, tall as a desert palm appeared. He stood a full head taller than me! I faced him with a scimitar, and Ibrahim threw his little

javelin head at him. The knight saw the steel triangular head slicing through the air at his face, and with a swift flick of his sword, knocked it aside with ease. So once again, I had to play the role of savior.

Ibrahim finally decided to defend himself instead of having me do all the work! He flung his short sword with all his might. It rotated end over end, flashing as the burnished steel blade caught the sunlight. The knight cried out as the sword struck home and sank deep into his thigh. He was distracted for a split second, enough time to allow me to strike. The knight tried to defend himself, but it was too late.

My sword stroke found the weak point in his armor where the neck and the head meet. A fatal weakness. The knight's head soared through the air. The headless body fell sideways and crumpled to the earth.

I ran to Ibrahim, helped him to his feet, Ibrahim's arm around my shoulders for support. I guided him as he limped off the battlefield. We slowly moved off toward the tent of the physicians, and I said to Ibrahim, "HUMPH! Is it going to be like this every time? Must I risk my beautiful neck to save your pampered Arab ass? '*Yen 'aal deen ommak!*'"

"I am not an Arab. I am a Kurd!" moaned Ibrahim.

"Same damn thing!"

Adnan laughed, pleased with himself, as he concluded his tale.

Ibrahim stopped listening to the story many minutes ago, for his mind drifted off to an important order he must convey to his men. He stopped eating and said quietly,

"Men. Attention please."

Immediately, the men sat up from their reclining positions as if Ibrahim had screamed at the top of his lungs. Food was put down, drinking vessels hit the floor with an audible clink, and half-chewed food was gulped.

Adnan sat upright and folded his hefty arms over his belly, jovialness gone. All eyes were on their commander, awaiting his orders.

Ibrahim spoke softly but firmly. "I want you to pass this order along to your men. From henceforth, after a battle, all prisoners will be bound and brought to cells in Alcazar of the Alhambra. There will be no more execution of prisoners, even the Templars or the Order of Santiago."

The officer's expressions ranged from disbelief to outright shock. Some thought the order a joke, but they knew that Ibrahim did not joke about such things. They dare not laugh or even smile for fear of showing disrespect of their commander. Could this be true? They wondered silently. The Captain of the Guard of the Alhambra was ordering them NOT to execute captured monks? How could that be?

Only Adnan Al Mansur objected, for Adnan was the only one of their number who would dare question Ibrahim Al-Rahim publicly.

"What about the infidel? Will he return the favor, and spare our brothers from execution?"

Ibrahim responded slowly, calmly, "It does not matter. We are the better men. We practice the enlightened faith. We will lead by example."

Adnan shook his head and began to protest. "Ibi, this order . . ." Ibrahim cut him off. He raised his voice, a sharp rebuke, "ADNAN! ENOUGH!"

Mansur, the mighty warrior, chastened, shrank back upon his pillow. Ibrahim lowered his voice to a friendly tone, "Very well. There will be no further discussion. You have your orders. You will ensure that your men follow them."

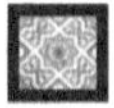

Night fell over Granada. Only the very top of the snow-capped Sierra Nevada Mountains still held onto a bit of orange light from the now invisible sun, their snowy peaks glowing against the darkening deep blue sky. A cool breeze rushed down the Sierra's slopes and into the city, purifying the air.

The day birds had fallen silent for the evening. The bats, however, awoke from their diurnal slumber and took to the air, flittering here and there in their wild aerial dance. A screeching owl, sounding its unearthly call, began the night patrol.

Ibrahim, limping badly, once again made his way to the dungeon and the cell of Santiago De Aviles. An indefinable urge propelled him. Ibrahim had to see Santiago again. As he approached the cell, he saw Santiago standing, looking out through the bars of a rough, small window, down onto the darkening streets of Granada below.

Santiago did not turn as he stated flatly, slyly,

"My Lord, you seem to have forgotten your stool."

Ibrahim sat down heavily and stretched his weak leg. He massaged the scar where the broken bone ripped through his skin many years before during the fight when Adnan came to his rescue.

Ibrahim gestured to the book that lay on the cot in Santiago's cell.

"I see that the Bible was delivered to you. Do you read it?"

Santiago turned from the window. Ibrahim saw that Santiago's bandage had been removed, his cheek a bulging mass of blue and yellow. Santiago leaned back against the stone wall,

"Yes Moor." Santiago replied. "I read the one true book."

Ibrahim chose to ignore the insult to his own holy book the Quran and asked, "Where does the Bible, or Issa, whom you call Jesus, command you to worship death?"

Santiago looked puzzled. "What are you talking about?"

"You Christians worship death! Look at your rituals, your processions, and your desire for martyrdom. You love death, you adore it. You find new and more grotesque ways to portray your savior's agonizing demise. You bow down to the instrument of his death, that horrid idol you call the cross. Your churches are dark and dank. Even your songs of praise are nothing more than sad dirges. Your prayers sound like words heard at a funeral. You people cannot get enough of death. Death, not Issa, is your God."

Santiago was not insulted. He ran his hand through his matted red hair and looked thoughtful. He had no quick retort, no sarcastic answer. He nodded his head slightly.

Ibrahim stroked his goatee, perhaps he was convincing the infidel? He continued.

"You see, Santiago, the difference between you and me is that I worship *life*. We worship life. You see life honored all around you in the Alhambra. Here we worship the creation and give credit to the Creator. Even in this place that you call a 'dungeon,' there are no torture devices, no filth. One hears the soft calming sounds of water flowing from fountains. Even in this cell, you can smell the roses, the lavender and the star jasmine. We have gone through strenuous efforts to dig only the best and deepest wells that produce the cleanest, most crystalline springs to water the city. That water is precious to us. It is God's finest element. Do you know, Santiago, that here in the Alhambra there are staircases that lead between the varying levels of terraced gardens, and that the handrails on these staircases are also aqueducts that allow the water to flow from the gardens above to the gardens and fountains below? Where in all of Christendom may you find such a simple invention borne of a love of the creation?"

Let him argue with that! thought Ibrahim.

Santiago looked at Ibrahim. He was the prisoner, disfigured and unarmed. Yet, Ibrahim felt a twinge of discomfort as Santiago smirked and said sarcastically,

"Amazing! The Moor has discovered that water flows downhill. I stand in awe of your superior intellect!"

Santiago shook his head and continued. "You who say you worship and respect the Maker's creation . . . You may protect the trees and the plants and the flowers and the birds, but you relish killing the greatest of all the Sovereign's creations. There is only one creation formed in his "image," and you thirst to destroy it. Worse, you believe you perform the Lord's will when in cold blood you destroy his most miraculous achievement!"

Ibrahim sighed audibly and replied, "This is an imperfect world, Santiago. Until Allah puts an end to war, men will die on the battlefield. It is the way of the world. It was not I that slew them, it was he. It is an unfortunate consequence, nothing more."

Santiago shook his head angrily. "Do not blame the "world" or your God for your practice of striking down unarmed men on the battlefield! Where does your God command you to commit such wickedness? Where in your holy book does your prophet command it? You may say with your lips that you love the creation, but your actions prove that you DISDAIN it. How do you rationalize love of the creation and the destruction of it? Your hatred is the only thing you respect!"

Ibrahim looked away, down the hall, losing the advantage once again. Feeling shame. He looked towards Yusuf, stationed at the iron gate that lead out of the dungeon.

Once again, Yusuf stood upright at attention. Perhaps his commander, Ibrahim Al-Rahim, was looking him over, inspecting him, or perhaps in need of his help. Yusuf could not know that Ibrahim was in need of assistance, but that no human being could provide it.

Ibrahim stood up, rubbing his leg, more painful than ever. He approached the cold iron bars of the cell, placing his face up to the black bars and whispered,

"Santiago. I have something to tell you."

Santiago leaned toward him.

"I ordered my men to stop the execution of unarmed prisoners. Prisoners will be bound, brought here and imprisoned. I intend to hold them for ransom. After all, royalty or a wealthy family member will be willing to purchase the freedom of a captive knight. Until that ransom is paid, they will be treated humanely. I swear it! The truth that I kept from men is this—I gave that order out of respect for the memory of your brother, Abran."

Ibrahim turned abruptly. He walked out of the dungeon before he saw Santiago's confusion or the tears that began to pour from Santiago's steel-green eyes.

Chapter 14

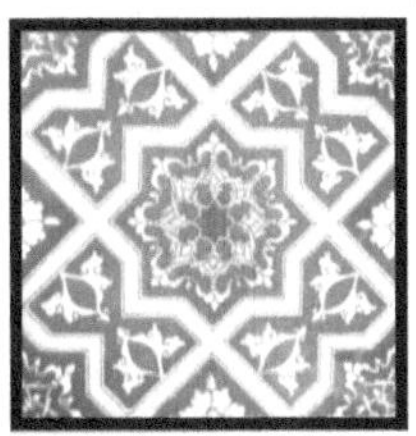

A Sheep in Sheep's Clothing

"I've seen a man live
With more than a hundred knife wounds,
Then saw him die
from a single dance."

Maria de Alicante was arranging a pyramid of pomegranates in her stall in the marketplace when she saw the mysterious figure. The market was especially busy today, she noted. The vendors were out in full force, no doubt attempting to make up for the lost sales that were the result of the Sultan's orders to 'shut up' the city in the aftermath of the martyrdom of Peter.

Men and women, entire families, passed her stall, shuffling shoulder to shoulder, laden with recently purchased products.

Noise filled the air as sellers called out prices for their wares and bargained with buyers.

Maria piled the fruit so high she could barely see over the top, but she did not miss the tall, broad-shouldered man in the dark grey cloak.

My God, who is that? she wondered as he approached her stall. The hood of the cloak concealed his face, but as he came near and peered over the top of the pomegranates she recognized the warm eyes of Ibrahim Al-Rahim.

"Ibi!" she exclaimed, "*As salaam Alaikum!* I did not recognize you in that cloak! How nice you have graced my simple stand with your glorious presence once again!" Maria chuckled.

Ibi should definitely smile more, she thought, not for the first time. *What a strikingly handsome man! If only I was thirty years younger! Stop that Maria, you old fool!*

She wagged her finger at him and teased, "People are beginning to talk! You should know that I am too old for you!"

Ibrahim shook his head and the hood slipped down around his shoulders. He pulled his long hair back, enhancing his high cheekbones and firm jaw.

"I do not involve myself with women over the age of ninety-five, Doña Maria."

Delighted, Maria laughed and tried to think of a humorous retort, when Ibrahim turned serious.

"Maria," he began, "What can you tell me about this dance that the Spaniards practice during our prayers?"

The question surprised Maria. It even frightened her. Why did he want to know? Why was he disguised in that cloak? She tried not to worry and strove to keep the conversation light. She smiled and asked, "So those girls made quite an impression on you and your men, eh?"

The details of the standoff between the elite cavalry and the old priest James had spread throughout Granada. The Christians finally had reason to gloat. Many Christians in Granada did not agree with the religious fanaticism of James the priest, or Peter the hermit, but it was still a joyous thing to hear that Ibrahim Al-Rahim and his mounted shock troops had been bested by a handful of girls and their dance.

Levity gone, Ibrahim leaned closer.

"Doña Maria, it is a dangerous thing to mock Allah and the prophet. Your own book says, 'it is a fearful thing to fall into the hands of the living God.' Many people could have died yesterday. It would have been a massacre. If they flaunt the law again, I swear to you as Allah is living, my troops will not be stopped by a few dancing girls."

Maria stopped smiling. Serious now. She pondered his words. She knew Ibrahim was a man who meant what he said. She had always trusted him. She bantered with him, never fearing for her safety no matter how much she teased, but she never forgot his terrible reputation as a warrior in battle. She realized she did not know *that* Ibrahim. But he had such kind eyes . . .

"Ibi," she said, "First you have to promise me that you will not harm those girls."

"I swear it," he said.

Could she believe him? She trusted him, but the stories she heard about his conduct in battle . . .

"Swear upon the prophet!"

"I am not in the practice of making deals with old women for the information that I require!"

Maria knew she had insulted him. Too bad. She pointed a worn finger at him and said, "You will have to torture me before you learn anything from me! That is, if you have the stomach for it! Go on your way!"

She dismissed him with a wave.

Ibrahim sighed and looked heavenward as if seeking guidance. He gave in to the old woman's demand.

"I swear, Doña Maria, upon the prophet, and the holy book, I will bring no harm to those girls."

Maria paused as she pondered whether to accept his vow. In reality, she was enjoying the moment, for once again she had beaten him in their game of wills. Although this time, she could see, it was not a game.

So Maria told Ibrahim where he could find the dancing girls during the mid-day prayers. They were at a home in the Christian quarter, not far from the market. Maria's hope was that Ibrahim could somehow avert bloodshed in the city, for she and her fellow *Mozarabs* did not support the fanatic Christians. While Maria did not think the dance an expression of that fanaticism, she knew it could be a focal point of further tensions. She believed Ibrahim Al-Rahim to be a reasonable man. His enemies would beg to differ, but he of all men of Granada had the authority to keep the peace and the *convivencia* intact.

When she had told him the location of the dance, Ibrahim simply said, "Thank you, Doña Maria."

He pulled the hood over his head, ducked away, and slipped into the crowd.

Breathless and a bit shaky from the encounter, Maria watched as Ibrahim disappeared from view and she prayed all would go well. She hoped she had not been an old fool, and that the information he had drawn from her would not lead to more trouble.

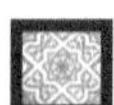

Ibrahim walked past whitewashed walls of homes that lined the street. Every home had its own courtyard and flower garden. The plants of the gardens grew high, topping the walls, and creeping down to the street. He could hear on the opposite side of each wall fountains gurgling happily.

Ibrahim passed bright violet bougainvillea, dark blue morning glory, vines of ivy, star jasmine, lavender and citron.

He entered through a door into the courtyard that Maria indicated. A large crowd had gathered in the courtyard and the balcony overhead. More people were filtering in from the street. Ibrahim joined them and entered, his identity concealed from the throng.

He found a spot next to a column that supported the overhead balcony and waited for the prayers to begin. He felt strange not preparing to offer his own mid-day prayer. It was not his custom to miss a prayer. He would compensate for the lack by offering a "double prayer," on his knees while facing Mecca, when the muezzins called the faithful to prayer later in the afternoon.

A young man with a guitar appeared and was joined by three more musicians. They sat on empty wooden fruit crates and tuned their guitars. The fountain bubbled in the center of the courtyard, the pleasant sound of flowing water drowned out by the playing of guitars that filled the courtyard, as the observers maintained absolute silence.

Then the girl he saw in the street entered the courtyard, followed by ten others. Each girl wore a brilliantly-colored silk dress. They stopped in the middle of the courtyard, the most beautiful girl, the one who stopped his horsemen cold, in front.

Her dress was of sleek, shiny purple silk that clung tightly to her lithe frame. The dark color of the dress was in stunning contrast to her smooth bronze skin. The dress had a wide slit up the front to just above her knee, slightly exposing her long shapely legs. Her feet were shod with low cut black leather boots, with a thick wooden heel. Her black hair was loose and fell around her shoulders. In her hair she wore a bright purple flower that perfectly matched her dress. Round purple and gold earrings dangled from her ears. She looked sweet and serious at the same time. Her dark almond-shaped eyes were intense. She held her arm out in front, bent at the elbow, fingers in an elegant display, while she held her right arm above her head, her index finger pointing straight up, her other fingers pointing out or down toward the floor. She looked like a marble statue of a goddess of mythic lore.

For this particular performance the girls tried something new. They had driven nails into the heels of their shoes to create an even higher pitched clicking as they stamped on the cobblestones.

The silence was broken by the call of the muezzins perched atop the minarets throughout Granada:

"Allah u Akbar, Allah u Akbar,"
(Allah is Great, Allah is Great)

The instant the call paused, the guitars began to play in fast, staccato rhythm. The statue came to life. She stamped on the ground and placed her hands on her hips. She moved quickly right and left, with great agility. Her glances became more fierce and fiery as she clapped her hands in between the calls to prayer. The other girls imitated her every move.

Then came the final refrain:

"La Ilaha ill Allah,"
(There is no divinity but Allah.)

The muezzins fell silent, the Adhan complete, but the explosive dance continued. Ibrahim was mesmerized by the dance and most of all, by the beautiful girl in purple.

The sharp sound from the girls' stamping was even louder than previous performances due to the nails they had driven into their heels. The prayers had ended, but the music and dancing continued.

An old man, bent from age, began to imitate the call of the Islamic muezzins in a strong voice that no doubt carried over the walls. He perfected the undulating, singing cry. It took nearly a full minute for the old man to sing out the verses as he drew out each syllable.

I made a fire in the hills,
The wind came and blew it out,
Where there was fire,
Ashes always remain.

As the spectacle unfolded before him, Ibrahim was oblivious to the music, the verse, or the girls, save one. He watched her. He could not remove his eyes from the beauty dancing in the purple dress, a vision of grace and power. His reverie was rudely interrupted when his brain began to register the verses of the old man's song:

You will return from the desert
whence you came,
A ship that will soon leave the shore,
It is the will of God,
To end the rule of the Moor.

Shocked, feeling as though a bright light pierced his eyes, Ibrahim realized that the dance, the music, the timing with the prayers of the muezzins, were dangerous expressions of Christian rebellion against Islamic authority. Not a rebellion carried out with sword and spear, but with music and dance. These Spaniards indeed mocked the prophet and the sacred rituals. There could be no doubt. They were inciting the Christians to resist Islamic rule in hopes that their deities would intervene and destroy

Moorish rule once and for all. Ibrahim knew their hope was in vain. Wasn't it?

He knew no good could come of this. He looked around at the crowd, at least three hundred strong. In a week there could be three thousand people crammed into the streets and onto the rooftops to watch the defiant display.

At last, he understood. The greatest danger to the *convivencia* was not the martyrs, or an army of Christendom's chivalry, or an unlawful procession of the cross. NO! It was this! This simple but overwhelming display of power that could signal the end of Islamic rule in Spain. He had dismissed the threat, even been disdainful. It was only a dance, performed by women no less! Now he knew better. He underestimated its power and influence.

As he pondered, he did not realize that the girl's movements had brought her purposely close to him. She turned her head and looked directly into his eyes. He turned away, so as not to be recognized. Finally, the dance ended. The people began to filter out, returning to the drab duties of their daily lives.

As Ibrahim headed to the door he felt a firm tap on his back. It was not threatening. He turned slowly. Yes, it was the girl. She stood before him, hands on her hips. Tiny beads of perspiration glistened on her forehead, her dark hair beautifully out of place from the exertions of the dance. Now that she was so close to him he knew how lovely she truly was.

She swept the hair from her forehead and said directly, "My Lord! You are a clumsy spy!"

Ibrahim was disarmed by her beauty and directness. He was also disturbed that his carefully chosen disguise had not concealed his identity.

"Do not look so surprised! Your height, your gait, and your bearing give you away, my Lord Ibrahim Al-Rahim!"

The courtyard was now almost empty. At the mention of the name of the fearful General of the Alhambra, the remaining handful of attendees hustled out the door as quickly as possible.

Ibrahim removed his hood, no need to conceal his identity. He towered over her, yet the girl was not intimidated by his commanding presence. He asked, "What is your name?"

"Rebecca De Caceres. I am from Sevilla. I live here with my brother Fontino."

Fontino had in fact been watching the exchange between his sister and Ibrahim from the safety of the shadow of a doorway. He exhaled audibly at the sound of his name being declared to Ibrahim.

It was Ibrahim's turn to be direct. "What is the purpose of this dance?"

"It is art to us. It reminds some that one day, Spain will be returned to the Spanish."

On hearing that reply, Fontino disappeared from the doorway and toward the inner security of the home, whispering as he did so, "*Callate mujer insensata*!"

Rebecca continued. "I do not care for such symbols. I dance because I love the art, the performance. It is the most beautiful thing I have ever seen. It is the dance of our people. I teach it in Granada. I will teach it throughout Iberia in both Moorish and Christian lands. We will open schools. We will teach the dance and music and this dance will become, it has already become our national dance. It is our soul. One day you too, will join us in our performances!

Ibrahim let out a sarcastic, "HA! Your dance mocks us! It shows disrespect for our faith. Why would we join a base dance of the infidel?"

"For this reason," Rebecca responded, moving up close to Ibrahim now. "You cannot deny its beauty, can you? You cannot dismiss its power. All who witness it are mesmerized. That is not a weakness, for you cannot help yourself. This dance is the life breath of our mother, *Espana.* You and I, all of us in Granada, we are all beholden to her. We are all sons and daughters of her, we do her bidding. You are powerless against her."

"No. You are naïve. My duty, my allegiance is only to my Father. I am beholden only to Him and His purpose."

Rebecca, her lithe body brushing against Ibrahim's, placed her hand lightly on his shoulder. She looked up at him. "Ah, my Lord. Maria is right about you. You are a sincere and honest man. But you are the one who is being naïve."

"You've been talking to Maria de Alicante! Don't listen to that old woman! Her senses were lost years before you were even born!"

Rebecca laughed at him. "*Ojala* the adversaries you face upon the battlefield are never as wise as Maria de Alicante!"

Ibrahim said accusingly. "You dance because you want the attention and admiration of the people."

"No, I don't!" Rebecca looked down at the ground, then up at Ibrahim and grinned, "Well, maybe a little."

He attempted to warn her, his voice dropping ominously. "This is not a game. Your dance could be considered blasphemy against God and his prophet. There are those among us who consider the dance a direct threat to our rule."

Rebecca ran her long elegant fingers through her hair, smiled and said softly, "I am of no threat to you."

"I believe, girl, that you are a most formidable threat that I have underestimated."

Rebecca laughed, a gentle, feminine sound. Ibrahim's attempt to be stern, to put on an air of authority, to intimidate the girl, was not successful.

"Your actions yesterday in the street could be viewed as subversive, even blasphemous." He questioned slyly, "Perhaps, you were in league with the priest and his illegal procession?"

At this Rebecca threw back her head back and laughed heartily, her thick black hair flying in all directions, exposing her long aquiline neck. "Ha! That crazy old man! No, Ibrahim! I am not one of his followers."

Ibrahim rolled his eyes in frustration, and gritted his teeth. He muttered.

"This is serious, girl. You could have been killed yesterday. If this continues, there will be bloodshed. Next time my cavalry will not hesitate."

His words were intense, but the tone of his voice was not. He tried to be commanding, to talk to her as if he were giving her an order that must be obeyed, but his thoughts were expressed as a plea of concern for her very safety.

Rebecca replied playfully, "I do not think Ibrahim, that you are the sort that would run a girl through with a lance."

Now Ibrahim's anger flashed, his patience at an end. He yelled at her, coming close to her face, towering over her. "GIRL! You have no idea what I am capable of! You MUST STOP THIS DANCE!"

Rebecca's eyes widened. She backed away from the eruption of a warrior's temper. She spun on her heel and ran across the courtyard into a doorway and disappeared from view.

Ibrahim, alone in the courtyard, questioned. Would he really kill these girls if ordered to? Of course not, how could he? If it was the will of Allah? Would he uphold the law? Would he sacrifice these girls to keep the *convivencia* intact? What if he was forced to take drastic action against those who propagated the dance? Would he do it? Would he be forced to do it, to protect the peace and the greater good?

He thought of that fateful day in Jerusalem when he was but a child. He thought of Santiago de Aviles and Rebecca, and Abran De Aviles, the orphans, his Lord the Sultan . . . He left the courtyard loaded down with more questions and no answers.

Chapter 15

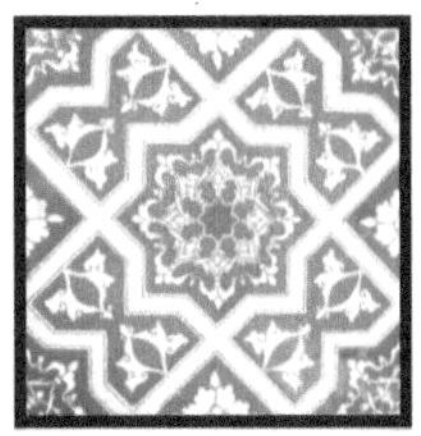

Upon the Ramparts

***"If the watchman sees the sword coming
and does not blow the trumpet
and the people are not warned,
and a sword comes, his blood I will require
from the watchman's hand."***

A single shrill horn sounded. An alarm. The warning of pending invasion. Ibrahim ran, leaping two steps at a time in his rush to reach the ramparts of the *Alcazar*, the most fortified section of the Alhambra. Already several of his officers peered out over the top of the wall, across the city of Granada, past the Vega and beyond. On the horizon, black smoke in dense columns was climbing into the sky.

The smoke signals were generated by ever-vigilant watchmen posted upon the peaks. The warnings were conveyed across the Kingdom of Granada from the very border of the Christian Kingdoms to the north.

The smoke was accompanied by more specific information passed from station to station using a series of signal flags. The signals reached the relay station at the top of the Alhambra.

A well-trained signalman waved and dipped a flag to convey the messages. The signalman had access to a mass of different flags of different colors and designs. Each flag conveyed a special meaning. The flags of red, orange, white and blue were surmounted with shapes of triangles, circles, squares or other geometric shapes.

The movement of a flag conveyed, acknowledged or requested information. Next to the signalman an interpreter read out the meaning of the signals as another soldier meticulously noted the information by writing it down on a scroll.

Ibrahim was well versed in the language of the flag signals. Now, as he read the signals, he sighed, and murmured, "Here they come again."

The interpreter called out in a loud, excited voice the meaning of each dip and sway of each flag's movement.

"An army of Christendom will cross the northern border within days."

Flags were dipped, raised and exchanged for other flags, the interpreter continued.

"Heavy armored cavalry, at least three thousand strong, many Templars and Order of Santiago!" More information was called out. "Fifty thousand infantry, archers, and pike men, formed into road column, tight formation, professional in appearance, well-armed, marching at an even pace. Baggage train to the rear."

Ibrahim too was reading the flags, he said, "No rabble led by a hermit this time!"

Ibrahim would ride out himself to survey this newest threat to the existence of the Kingdom of Granada. They would observe the enemy on the march and formulate a strategy.

For now, the information conveyed by the signal flags proved that this was a well-organized, well-funded, and well-supplied expedition.

The "large baggage train" to the rear revealed that careful planning had gone into the formation of this army. Perhaps they planned to have sufficient food, water, weapons, and medical supplies, even gold and silver to pay the men and keep the army on the march. Probably a king, or several kings of the Christian lands to the north sponsored this latest threat.

Yusuf was there. As a newer enlistment he was not well versed in the significance of the whirling flags.

He said,

"My Lord Ibrahim! How many have come this time?"

"How many, Yusuf?" He repeated the question. "How many?"

Ibrahim watched the furious snapping of flags, the interpreters struggling to keep pace with the flow of information and numbers represented by the flags. Ibrahim could see the columns of smoke rising from watch fires far on the horizon and after a long while softly responded.

"*All* of them."

Chapter 16

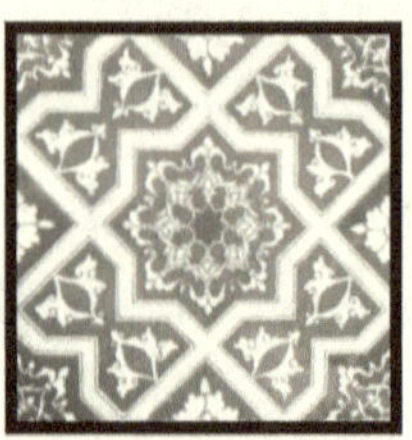

Irem

"Then they said, "Come, let us build ourselves a city, and a tower with its top in the heavens, and let us make a name for ourselves, lest we be scattered abroad upon the face of the whole earth."

Before setting out to scout the enemy army, a journey of several days, Ibrahim wished to speak with Rebecca one more time. He thought it was logical to try to convince her to stop the dance of protest before it was stopped by force. He reasoned that he must speak with her because it was his duty to keep peace in Granada. He would not admit it. He fought to push aside his burning desire to see her again. To think of any excuse to visit her one more time.

As he donned his plain charcoal grey cloak, he heard a knock at the door of his quarters. When he opened the door he was surprised to see the Sultan.

He declared, "My Lord! *Marhabbah*!

The Sultan answered in kind. "*Marhabbteen*." It was unusual for the Sultan to visit Ibrahim's quarters. More unusual still, the Sultan had come alone. This was a visit the Sultan wished to keep private.

"May I enter?" asked the Sultan.

"Of course, My Lord!"

Ibrahim apologized for the Spartan furnishings of his quarters. He felt embarrassed that he had nothing to offer the Sultan, not tea or a water pipe, or even a plate of dates or figs.

As the Sultan entered, Ibrahim stuttered.

"I, I am sorry My Lord, I have nothing to offer you."

The Sultan cut him off abruptly.

"Please Ibi, relax. This will not take long."

The Sultan walked to one of the open arches that overlooked the city. He gazed out over the ruddy clay roofs, his hands clasped behind his back. His long flowing golden robe brushed against the tile of the room as he walked. As he looked out, he took a long deep breath and exhaled slowly. A cool breeze ruffled his long grey beard. His robe fluttered gently. "Do you smell the pines, Ibi?" he asked. "We are blessed to live in this place. Don't you agree?" Before Ibrahim could respond, the Sultan continued, "It is a protected, precious garden. Designed by the finger of Allah. How you ever noted, Ibi, how even the sun has mercy on and blesses Granada? The sunlight is never too strong, it never burns."

Ibrahim watched as the Sultan examined the sunlight falling upon the back of his hand. He moved his fingers in a serpentine motion, and continued.

"It is a light touch, not more than a kiss upon the skin. Yet, just a few miles to the south, across a narrow stretch of water, the sun blazes without mercy, taking its vengeance upon man and beast."

Ibrahim sat down on one of the thick, soft floor pillows and crossed his legs as he listened respectfully to the Sultan, like a pupil receiving instruction from his master.

To Ibrahim, the Sultan sounded sad.

"The garden of *Irem.* You recall the legend don't you Ibi? A legend similar to the one the Christians tell in their book of Genesis, a legend passed from generation to generation beginning with the prophet Moses."

Ibrahim nodded acknowledgement. He learned the tale of Irem when he was a young child, as did all Muslim children.

The Sultan spoke in a faraway voice as if he were alone in the room. "That far-famed garden, a miracle of the desert, Irem only appears today at certain times to travelers in the Sahara. It takes form as a beautiful vision of towers and palaces and gardens spilling over the walls in a rainbow of flowers."

The Sultan continued speaking as if he was reminding himself of the legend. "It is said that the country was governed by King Shedad, the son of Ad, a great-grandson of famous old Noah himself, who built the original city and christened it "Irem." When he saw how magnificent was the design and the grandeur, his heart became puffed up with pride. Shedad was determined to create a paradise that would exceed even heaven itself. He decided to build a main tower in Irem that would reach all the way up through the heavens to the very presence of the All Powerful himself. The Addities would be equal to the mighty one himself in fame and grandeur. But Allah was angered, and brought a plague. His curse fell upon Shedad because of his arrogance. He and his subjects disappeared from the face of the earth. His city and palace were put under a never-ending spell, which hides the beauty of Irem from the sight of humans. However they are seen every once and again, to remind men of his sinful state. I have heard of Berbers, or Touaregs crossing the track-less sands in their caravans, speak of a mirage that seemed to rise out of the desert dunes and become a glorious city, unspeakable in beauty and grandeur."

The Sultan turned his attention to Ibrahim as if he had just recalled that there was someone else in the room.

"Ibi! Irem is not a legend. It has been re-created, and it does exist!"

He pointed to the floor emphatically with the index fingers of both hands. "THIS! HERE! The garden of Irem. This Alhambra, and the city of Granada! Irem is no longer a mystical story to be passed from one generation to the next around campfires in the desert. It lives, breathes and exists at the southern extremity of Spain!"

Seemingly spent, Abdul Rahkman sat down heavily on one of the large forest green floor cushions next to Ibrahim. He stroked his beard and continued.

"I feel a terrible change is coming to our blessed garden, Ibi. I feel it in my blood; it robs me of sleep at night. It is the same feeling one has when you know your enemy is nigh, even if you have not laid eyes upon him yet, you feel his presence, you feel the tension in the air. He is about to strike. Can you feel it Ibi?"

"Yes my Lord, I do."

The fate of Irem, of the Kingdom of Granada, hangs in the balance. We are in grave danger."

Ibrahim nodded respectfully but did not respond. He began to feel uneasy, unsure of why the Sultan was telling his this.

"Remember when we walked in the court of the myrtle trees alongside the reflecting pool after the battle, and you suggested that perhaps it would be for the best if we massacred the Christians once and for all? You made that statement as if it were inevitable, a terrible thing that must be done for the sake of peace."

The Sultan came back to the present.

Ibrahim looked down at the cool white tile and nodded. He felt the shame well up inside again.

"Is that truly your desire?"

Ibrahim looked at the Sultan, who was examining him closely.

"I have thought of it, My Lord, many times in the past, I felt that drastic measures must be taken against the Christians. Now, however . . ."

Ibrahim paused. A rush of images flooded his mind. The faces of Abran and Santiago, a multitude of orphans, and the strongest image of all, Rebecca, in a purple dress, dancing, laughing, spinning with angel-like grace. He measured his next words carefully.

"Now, I am uncertain as to the best way to preserve the peace, to protect the *convivencia*, my Lord."

"Ibi, you know I rely upon you above all others. All the rest of them," he waved his hand in disdain, "They look out for their own self-interests, they look to curry favors from me. Some spy on me. They are building their own empires, and they are not to be completely trusted. Oh Ibi, the intrigue! The wheels of conspiracy are turning fast now!"

The Sultan stroked his beard. "But you! You are a man without hidden motive, incapable of deceit. I have trusted you implicitly, without question. Your only impulse has been to please your Father and fulfill your duty."

Ibrahim felt embarrassed at the praise. He knew that something was coming. He looked away and responded sheepishly.

"Thank you my Lord."

"Lately, however, your judgment has become of concern to me." He sighed, then stated directly,

"You do not seem yourself. You look tired, Ibi. You look distracted. I need you now, more than ever. You allow an assassin to live in a cell here in the castle. You order your men to be merciful to captive cavaliers, those demons in human form whose very will is bent on our destruction! Finally, you allow yourself to be distracted from your duty by a dance, of all things, Ibi? A *dance?*"

Ibrahim remained silent. He was uncomfortable. His leg ached. He readjusted himself on his cushion, but felt no relief.

The Sultan went on relentlessly, "We are confronted outside of Granada by a professional army of Christendom. Inside the city, the Christians are becoming bolder, more subversive. The incident with the martyr, the procession, the cross, led by that damn priest James, this dance that mocks our faith . . . We cannot allow these dangers to continue unabated. There is concern among the other rulers of Islam that events here are spinning out of control. They say we have not been firm enough with the Christians. So I ask you. Ibrahim, are you prepared to do your duty? To carry out *anything* that I ask of you in order to protect the Kingdom of Granada and the *convivencia*, even if the order is shall we say, distasteful?"

Ibrahim nodded and answered with force, "Of course my Lord! I will always fulfill my duty to God and you, without question!"

The Sultan seemed relieved to hear this confirmation. He stood up. Ibrahim, out of respect did the same.

"Thank you Ibi, for listening. I know I can still trust you. Do not disappoint me."

Among the mélange of wonderful scents that drifted into his quarters from the gardens below, Ibrahim detected a new one. It was a sweet, yet acrid odor. He could not identify it at first. Then it came to him. *Hashish.*

Ibrahim's first thought was that whomever was smoking the hashish had best not be a member of any of the Moorish troops that were posted to the city, and if the smoker was one of his men, Ibrahim would find the scoundrel and lay the whip across his back personally.

Then the hair on the back of his neck stood up. He knew without having to investigate, innately, the hashish smoker was not a member of the royal garrison. Not one his men.

His instincts told him that the smoker was no native of Granada or even a casual traveler passing through the Kingdom. He almost breathed the words out loud with awe, unwilling to give voice to the name. A chill went up his spine.

The old man of the mountains. Sinan. Grey Cloaks. Fidai.

Ibrahim knew that Sinan loaned out his fanatical *Fidai* for a hefty price in gold to handle any unpleasant tasks.

Ibrahim always thought, perhaps naively so, that Abdul Rahkman, *his* Sultan, was morally superior to other rulers who weakly turned to the assassins, the Grey Cloaks to do their dirty work.

As he left the Sultan stopped and looked directly at Ibrahim. Placing his hand on his shoulder he said coldly, "I believe that soon I will ask more of you than I have in the past. You must prepare you heart and mind now to carry out my orders and protect the Kingdom of Granada. If you cannot fulfill the tasks I ask of you, I will have to call upon other means."

"Yes my Lord, I believe I understand."

Ibrahim did not understand. What type of "distasteful orders" would the Sultan give him? What "tasks," did Abdul Rahkman have in mind for Ibrahim to "fulfill?" And why were the Grey Cloaks in Granada?

That night was another of torturous nightmares for Ibrahim. The lack of a good deep night's sleep was beginning to affect him. He had dark circles under his eyes. His hurt leg was worse than ever, and the limp was beginning to affect his balance and stride, a dangerous condition for a warrior.

At mid-day, Ibrahim donned his grey cloak and set off to the home of Rebecca and Fontino.

As he turned the corner that led to the courtyard where the subversive dance was to be held, he saw dozens of people awaiting entry into the courtyard. Others had set up makeshift ladders consisting of a long pole or a piece of lumber and had climbed up the whitewashed wall that looked onto the courtyard. They sat among the vines and flowers of pink and violet bougainvillea that crowned the top of the courtyard wall and spilled over the side in a lovely avalanche of flowers.

There were hundreds of Christians and *Mozarabs* in the crowd and more and more poured in. Ibrahim estimated at least five hundred were in attendance. He gazed upward to the neighboring homes on either side of the courtyard and across the street, their walls too were full of observers.

Quite an audience, thought Ibrahim.

The afternoon call to prayers began. Then came the first stanzas of rapid-fire guitar notes, followed by the stamping rhythm of the girls. Ibrahim was not able to witness for himself the performance, for the crowd overflowed into the street and he was unable to enter the courtyard proper.

Ibrahim could discern, however, from his years of experience of listening to and counting enemy numbers and troop movements that the number of participants in the dance had doubled. He thought it amusing that the clacking of the girls' nail reinforced heels on the pavement sounded like heavy cavalry at a quick trot. Above the rhythmic din of stamping feet, he could discern the individual dancing of Rebecca herself. The interpretation of her dance was fired with an additional measure of strength and precision.

He closed his eyes and could picture her clearly. In his mind's eye, she was dancing alone, on a stage, brilliant in a blue silk dress against a black backdrop, twirling. Elegant.

He was stirred by the music and the sounds of the dance. At the same time he felt a deep unease. This dance mocked everything that was sacred in his belief system. He should not enjoy the dance. He should not enjoy *her.* He should be outraged.

He was not.

A new feeling welled up into this heart, a strange feeling that took him by surprise. It was an emotion he had not felt since he was a boy, tumbling down the sewer, fleeing for his life from a red-faced, drunken, screaming Templar. It was fear. He feared for the safety of Rebecca. He feared for her life. He could foresee that this subversive movement would terminate in bloodshed, and her death.

Of this, he had no doubt.

It was inevitable.

For either the Muslim citizens of Granada would react with violence to the blasphemy, or the Christians of Granada, emboldened to rebel against their Islamic overlords would take up the sword in full revolt, or Ibrahim's troops would be called out to put down the dance and disperse the crowd. The Jews, as always, would be caught in the middle of the conflict and massacred.

Mansur and the cavalry would not be stopped again by the power of the dance. There would be no hesitation this time. Lives would be lost.

He thought about the Christians of Granada. They would be emboldened to consider these dances of protest as the final in a grand array of signs that marked the "Time of the end." They will rise against us. He saw it all happening. Vivid images in his mind.

All through the Sacramonte the Christians were speaking in wondrous tones about the, "miracle of the cross." Thanks to divine providence, the cross had been carried through a forest of Moorish lances by the old priest James into its holy resting place. They would embellish the tale. They would speak of how the Divine One "blinded" the great Ibrahim Al-Rahim and his elite guard so that the priest passed right through their midst, unhurt, untouched, the way Moses lead his people unharmed by Pharaoh's chariots through the heart of the Red Sea.

He shook his head and leaned backwards against the courtyard wall. The bougainvillea flowers and vines cushioned his head through the hood of his cloak.

The coming violence unfolded before him like a stage play. Each actor was already in his predetermined position, lines memorized and practiced. They stood in place motionless, awaiting the curtain to rise and the cue given to spring into action. The actors: the Sultan, the Grey Cloaks, Santiago and Rebecca, the advancing Spaniards, Adnan Al Mansur, Maria . . . He asked himself grimly. "And you Ibi? What will be your role in the deadly drama? This is the question you must answer! What will be your final act?"

Ibrahim was so deep in thought that he did not notice that the dance had ended and most of the crowd had filed out of the courtyard.

He did notice however, on the other side of the cobblestone street, a man dressed in a fine flowing purple robe fringed in gold colored thread. On his head was an oversized circular turban, like a large white tangerine. The man's fingers were adorned with rich gold, ruby and sapphire rings. He was pointing one sapphire-encrusted finger accusingly at a group of people—Christians and *Mozarabs* who had just attended the dance.

The man, upright and proud in bearing, was an Imam.

Ibrahim, though devout himself, was never comfortable in the presence of an Imam. He found them to be pompous and self-righteous. They were self-appointed enforcers of Islamic law and tradition. They believed in a rigid application of theocratic law without exception.

Ibrahim viewed them as a detached group from the real world, separated from the everyday needs of the soldiers who battled for the very survival of the Kingdom of Granada, or those who struggled to earn enough on a daily basis to feed their children.

Ibrahim found it odd, even hypocritical, that these learned men who did not work, did not raise children, did not run a business, or fight in battles, were somehow qualified to judge others in matters of child-rearing, work, business and warfare. As if divine wisdom was the fruitage borne from a lack of experience in life, and a poor work ethic. Yet, here they stood, as the judge and jury of all, enforcing the law down to the letter. Ibrahim was reminded of the Scripture: "And you experts in the law, woe to you, because you load people down with burdens they can hardly carry, and you yourselves will not lift one finger to help them."

Ibrahim tuned into the conversation and the condescending words of the Imam who was arguing with the group of men. "This is blasphemy! You mock our holy prayers! Never has such a vile thing occurred since Allah gave breath to our forefathers in the garden!"

Ibrahim thought to himself that if the dance was the most "vile" thing that the Imam had witnessed, then Ibrahim should forcibly make the Imam ride alongside his cavalry in the upcoming battle against the Spaniards. The Imam would probably wet himself in horror and scream like a girl as he witnessed for the first time in his cloistered existence what occurs on a real battlefield, far outside his sheltered world. Ibrahim enjoyed that thought.

The Imam raised his voice and shook his finger with fury, "Sinners! The Just One will punish you for your foul, wicked deeds!"

He raised his arms heavenward in a dramatic display of holy piety. "Allah! You who can see a black ant walk on a black stone on a black night, do not leave these sinners unpunished, these infidels who dare to mock you with their unholy, worldly acts!"

The group, toward whom the Imam directed his tirade, had by this time melted away. One man stayed. Ibrahim recognized him from the market as a vendor of olives and the sumptuous oil that is derived from the fruit. The oil was the one constant ingredient on every table and in every kitchen in the Kingdom Of Granada whether that kitchen belong to Moor, Christian, Jew, or *Mozarab*. The vendor fired a verbal Parthian shot at the Imam.

"Your day of judgment is at hand, MOOR!"

It was the manner the man said the words that caught Ibrahim's attention. The olive oil vendor was proclaiming more than words of religious fanaticism. The man made his prediction with an air of confidence, as if it had already occurred. In the olive vendor's mind there was no doubt—the kingdom of Granada would fall, and it would fall *soon.*

Ibrahim contemplated the man's statement, rife with meaning and warning. The thought hit him like a stinging slap to his cheek; they were planning something, these Christians in Granada. They were organizing, preparing. Surely the foundation for their plans had already been laid.

They were planning something dramatic. Perhaps they were in league with the army of Spaniards that was on the northern border. He could see it. Messengers dressed in black, during the blackest part of the night, slipping over the walls, unseen, a clandestine river flowing with messages, orders and information between the army of Spaniards and their allies within Granada.

Ibrahim would double the guard on the outer walls of the city. It would slow, but not staunch the current of intelligence flowing in and out of Granada. The open trade that the Kingdom carried on with North Africa and the other Islamic lands, the lands of Europe and the Spanish kingdoms of Castile, Aragon, Leon and Navarre made certain that an open flow of trade would continue even in wartime. A portion of that trade would always include that of espionage, as spies plied their wares for heavenly reward and earthly profit.

Ibrahim too, had his trustworthy espionage network. He determined to order his spies to heightened activity and put inactive operatives back to work.

These were the logical steps that Ibrahim would take to fulfill his duty to Allah and the Sultan. He must protect the Kingdom. Yet, in his heart, Ibrahim Al-Rahim knew that these actions were not sufficient to avoid bloodshed. There would be violence right here in his city, and the fight would come up to and over the walls of the Alhambra and the gardens of Allah.

Chapter 17

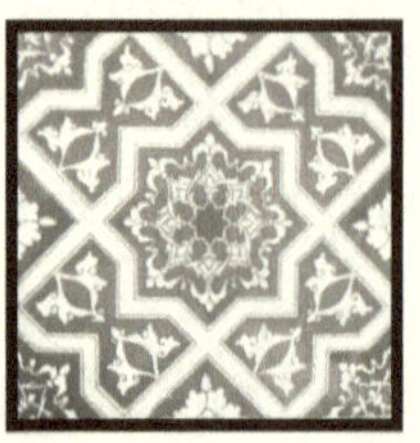

The Death of Jerusalem

"If my heart
Had a little glass window,
you could look in and see
it weeping drops of blood."

Ibrahim, limping painfully, finally entered the now empty courtyard.

Rebecca was alone. She sat on a chair next to the fountain that adorned the center of the courtyard, sipping fine red wine made from the grapes that grew plentifully in the Rioja region of Spain. She took a long drink of the dry, black wine from a wide-mouthed goblet of rosewood.

Her glistening hair was plastered with perspiration to her bronzed forehead. She sat, legs slightly apart, still breathing heavily from the exertion of the dance. Her silken dress was opened all the way down to her navel. Her breasts heaved from the deep breaths of air she inhaled.

She saw Ibrahim limping into the courtyard and said between breaths, "I looked for you in the crowd. I hoped that you would come."

Ibrahim approached her. "It appears you have a sufficient number of admirers here in the city. Why would you care about the presence of one broken down old Moor?"

Rebecca laughed. To Ibrahim her laugh was like the sound of a pure clear fountain of the Alhambra, or the wind as it fills the lofty branches of a grove of pine trees, sweet and pure.

"Not just *any Moor*, but Ibrahim Al-Rahim, Capitan of the Sultan's personal bodyguard, the Scourge of Christendom!"

Ibrahim felt his face flush as she noted but a few of his titles. At that moment, he preferred not to be reminded of his martial reputation. She lifted the goblet to her lips and took another deep draft of the wine. As she swallowed, Ibrahim could not help but notice her long slender neck. A drop of wine rolled down her chin. She casually wiped it away, then asked abruptly,

"Ibrahim, why do you hate us so?"

"Hate whom?" He asked, surprised.

"US! You know what I mean, Christians! Why do you hate us?"

Ibrahim thought for a moment, and then said softly. "I do not hate YOU."

"You may not hate me, but you hate my faith. You hate those who represent my faith. You hate my people."

"Not all. My mother was a Christian."

"What? How is that possible? You are a *muladi*?"

"No I am a Kurd!"

"You were born of a Christian mother and a Muslim father! That makes you a *muladi*!"

"Please don't mock me."

Ibrahim sat down on the cool pavement of the courtyard at her feet. He looked up at her for a long while before he spoke.

Rebecca looked down at the fiery amber eyes, the manicured goatee and high strong cheekbones. Rebecca noted sadness in his eyes, softness and a vulnerability that was the antithesis of the ferocious reputation of Ibrahim Al-Rahim.

Ibrahim pulled at his goatee as he thought about his response. He had hate in his heart. He nurtured the hatred, fanned it, fed on it, for it was of use to him in battle. It made him strong. Recently however, he began to question whether a true servant of Allah should be motivated solely by hatred toward others who were created in God's image, even if they were infidels.

He said. "Allow me to tell you of the death of Jerusalem. Perhaps then you will understand."

She nodded. Ibrahim began his story:

> "My mother Anna was indeed a devout Coptic Christian from the Nile river delta. Hard to believe, I know! She was from Alexandria. Her father, Thomas, my grandfather was a bishop in the Coptic Church. He lived and practiced his faith in Egypt, but would take many perilous journeys up the Nile through the Sudan and in-

to the mountains of Ethiopia, preaching as he traveled, converting the tribal negro peoples who scratched out a meager existence in the God-scorned lands that line the Nile until one reached the more hospitable climes of the mountainous region of Ethiopia where the Nile herself is born.

Thomas was a historian and delighted in the thought of following in the tracks of Herodotus and the Roman expeditions sent by the emperor Nero to discover the sources of the Nile.

Once at his destination he held services deep in the mountains, in the churches that dot the Ethiopian highlands that have been cut out of the living rock itself, some say by ancient Jews, sons of Jacob, perhaps even by wise King Solomon himself.

Thomas brought my mother along on these journeys, even though she was a child. He felt it vital for her education to travel outside of the comfortable confines of a large populated city and out into the "true world." The stories my mother would recount of these journeys!

I sat motionless and fascinated for hours as my mother, Anna, spoke of crocodiles as long as a barge that plied the waters of the Nile, the awe-inspiring roar of the hippopotamus, and tales of the wild, naked tribesmen who painted themselves with red clay and would welcome warmly all travelers, and just as quickly, kill them in cold blood.

She spoke in reverent tones of the life-giving Nile, flowing like a long dark blue necklace of sapphire through the death-dealing desert, the river, a gift from the Creator that boiled with fish and gave life to all who lived near her banks.

Upon returning from one of these trips, she met a man, a Kurd from Iraq, who hailed from where the mighty Euphrates and Tigris rivers join hands, from where all life on earth originated long ago.

The man was to become my father. He was Musa, traveling with a caravan, destined for Alexandria. He presented himself as a writer and a poet who made a living doing neither! He would joke that his writings and poetry were not famous—yet! He would laughingly tell us that in the future, when the tastes of more advanced peoples became more refined, they would erect statues to the genius of "Musa the Wise," the greatest of all the writers of antiquity.

My grandfather, Thomas the bishop, brought my mother along to meet a caravan entering Alexandria. Thomas was planning another expedition to Ethiopia and wished to be well-stocked with writing supplies in order to journal the daily events of the trip for posterity and to re-supply the Coptic Churches of Ethiopia in the high mountains where they lacked such writing materials.

Musa earned his keep, as a salesman of vellum sheets and papyrus scrolls or other writing material that he sold in the large cities.

Alexandria, due to its fame for the immense, well-stocked library, attracted an army of would-be and actual writers, historians and poets. The Jews were especially prolific writers and the large Jewish populace of Alexandria was one of his best sources for business.

The Jews meticulously put to paper or scroll their genealogies and family histories and wise words of their rabbis. They keep track of such histories in order to identify the family line of the Messiah when he finally arrives to save them.

The Christians too, especially the sect of the Essenes, were engrossed in the never-ending labor of copying and re-copying the Bible and translating the holy book into other languages than Latin, to make the word accessible to all peoples of the world.

The Essenes are so exact in their task that if just one slight error is encountered on a copied page, the entire page, sometimes representing days of hard work was put to the fire and started anew. The accuracy and the purity of the original sacred manuscripts must be maintained, to ensure that the Bible survives through the ages exactly as the All Knowing dictated.

Musa would arrive with the caravans, after many weeks of travel, a half dozen of his camels laden with his writing materials. Word spread through the scholarly circles of Alexandria that he was arriving with his wares.

His clients were historians, rabbis and priests, Imams, wholesalers and shop-keepers. He always sold his entire stock, right there, on the side of the road before he could even enter the main marketplace of Alexandria.

Musa was a bit older than Anna. Family members remembered that it was a true example of love at first sight. My father, tall, dignified in bearing, broad shouldered and strong, dusty from the caravan trail, looked like a prince from a fairytale to Anna. To Musa, she appeared as one of Job's daughters, or perhaps King David's Abishag, the most beautiful girl in the entire kingdom.

After their initial encounter, Musa appeared at Anna's door to offer her an azure blue-quilled pen, a valuable and honorable gift. My grandfather, Thomas was less than delighted to see that a Kurdish Muslim had turned the focus of his affections upon his only daughter.

Weeks passed, but Musa was undeterred. He found many clandestine methods to shower Anna with affection, in spite of the constant vigilance of my grandfather. A scrap of vellum with a love poem, left in the crook of a tree, or under a rock, a secret nighttime conversation in hushed whispers though the ventilation grate of Anna's room.

My grandfather Thomas, not wholly unaware of these proceedings, determined to take Anna on his forthcoming expedition and remove her from the attentions of my father.

He surmised that the time and space between Musa and Anna would cool their emotions and reason would prevail. A Copt and a Muslim joined in mutual affection? Who had ever heard of such a thing? Such a bonding could not meet with success!

In spite of her protestations, she set off for the upper Nile and the mountains of Ethiopia as her father commanded. Anna desired to run off with Musa, leave Alexandria and live far away.

But she would not.

She would not disgrace her father this way, or bring ill repute to her family's good name. That was the solution of cowards. Of the weak. There would be no running. Instead, one day, while drifting up the Nile through the desolate country of the Sudanese Negro, she confronted her father.

It was a battle of wills for the ages. She stood in front of her father, on the deck of the boat as it bobbed up and down in the Nile River, in a courageous yet respectful way and informed him that upon returning from the voyage she would marry Musa. There would be no secret marital rendezvous. It would be done in full daylight, honorably, for all of Alexandria to witness. They would not run off to a far distant land together in order to escape the scorn of either the Coptic Christians or the Muslims.

Well, Thomas was distressed at the news. His initial reaction was anger and threat. While launching insults at Musa and his pagan god-dishonoring religion, he implored Anna to consider her reputation as well as his. What kind of future would she have chained to the side of a chauvinistic Muslim? How would he treat her! Worse, her very eternal life could be imperiled by the constant exposure to the Muslim's blasphemous teachings and ways! Anna stood firm, on that boat on the Nile, as resolute and unbowed as the timeless desert that surrounded them.

His anger flew, then expended itself. He finally declared, "I cannot stop you from this foolish course. But I will not support it. This unequal yoking with an unbeliever will not have my blessing!" Thomas quoted the Bible. "For what mixing has the darkness with the light?"

Rebecca, engrossed in the tale, interrupted Ibrahim and exclaimed,

"What did they do, Ibrahim? Your mother was courageous and tough! I like her! Did Thomas finally relent?"

Ibrahim almost chuckled at her enthusiasm. He said:

"Well, Thomas was vexed by Anna's plans. What caused him greater frustration was that he truly liked and even admired Musa, though he would never admit this to Anna. He knew Musa to be an honorable, educated man who would take good care of his daughter in all aspects, except for the all-important spiritual facet of her life.

Upon return, many months later, Anna met up with Musa in Alexandria. He was waiting as planned, in front of the family home for her arrival.

Musa stayed in Alexandria, did not return with the caravan to Iraq. He was determined to wait for Anna for years if necessary, as the forefather Jacob waited, and labored for years for Rebecca. Musa was prepared to search her out in the dark mountains of Ethiopia, if need be.

Thomas ignored him.

Anna ran to him and jumped into his arms. Thomas' designs to break the bond between them had failed.

They determined not to settle in Alexandria for the sake of Thomas, his reputation, and the unavoidable friction their union would cause in the Coptic community of which Thomas was an important leader. It would be wise to raise a family in a more peaceful setting.

They choose in Alexandria's stead Jerusalem. The "City of Peace." They did not know at the time it was an ill-fated choice. The Holy City held many advantage for Musa and Anna. It was located at equal distance between Musa's native Iraq and Anna's native Alexandria. Communication with each other's family would be a simple matter. Jerusalem was close to, or directly on top of most of the east and westward bound caravan routes. The trade and communication of the entire known world passed from Egypt and Africa through Jerusalem to Asia Minor, Europe and the Middle East.

Musa could continue plying his products without a pause. He could even hire out camel drivers in his name to take his vellum and papyrus to and from Egypt without being physically present personally to conduct business.

Our life in Jerusalem was uneventful for many years. I was six when the Crusaders arrived in the Levant. Pope Urban went to great lengths to fire the Franks, and all of Europe with religious fervor.

Oh that the Franks burn in the fires of hell!

They determined to take Jerusalem, and in their greed, all the holy land from the Muslims.

I was the middle child. My older brother was eight and my younger sister four."

Rebecca interrupted and asked, "What were their names, Ibi? Your brother and your sister?"

"Oh Rebecca, I cannot." Ibrahim paused, his eyes began to fill with tears . . . "I simply cannot say their names. It causes me too much pain. I am sorry."

Rebecca took his hand and said. "It is alright, Ibrahim. I understand. Please continue."

Ibrahim composed himself and continued.

> "Musa allowed my mother to teach us the Bible within the home. Outside of the home, we children would accompany my father to the mosque and join him in the daily prayers. I read from and loved both of the Holy books. My mother continued as a Coptic Christian, taught us their ways. She never converted to Islam.
>
> We lived a quiet, happy life there. I was too young to truly understand how sacred and coveted the city of Jerusalem was. How the three great faiths all laid holy claim to it."

Ibrahim paused, a new thought came to him, he repeated the words, "The three great faiths." Then added, breaking away from his tale as a thought struck him. He said:

> "What devious machination! The dark one ensured that the three great faiths would zealously desire the same city to be theirs alone! That same exact patch of earth on the top of the mountain within Jerusalem itself

would be considered worthy of such conflict, division and bloodshed.

To me, Jerusalem was nothing more than a happy place of play, full of mysterious narrow streets to explore, and exotic travelers and pilgrims from all over the known world. I wish now, that I understood and spent more time in those holy, historical places that fill Jerusalem like nowhere else in the world.

The Crusader army came across the Bosporus, and into Asia Minor, taking Antioch, and then marching into the Promised Land. I remember the feeling of anxiety, the tenseness that was felt in the city due to the oncoming Crusaders.

My father told us that most Crusaders were "rabble," simple thieves out to loot and steal from those who resided in the Promised Land. He swore we would be safe for the Crusaders did not have proper siege equipment, or enough men to breach the stout walls of Jerusalem.

When they arrived, I ran to the ramparts of Jerusalem and beheld the sight; a waving forest of red and blue banners, pendants and flags. The horizon filled as far as the eye could see with armed men and mounted knights.

In the forefront of the host, a large wooden cross. The Crusaders thought it the same wooden instrument used to kill Jesus himself, the "True Cross." Crusader legend said that any army that marched with this particular cross, the True Cross, going before it, could not be defeated in battle.

The defenders who lined the wall of Jerusalem were many, including my father who took up the sword to defend the city. At first the siege went badly for the Crusaders. They suffered from the lack of food and especially their lack of water.

As my father noted correctly, the Crusaders did not have siege equipment to breach the walls. It seemed that the Divine Warrior was fighting against the infidel. They would die of thirst in front of the unbreached walls of the holy city.

We heard a relief army was in route, volunteers from Persia and Arabia flocking to the call to defend Jerusalem from the Crusaders, a vast number that would crush the Crusaders between their mass and the walls of Jerusalem.

I went to school as normal. My mother cooked, cleaned and taught us the Bible as if there was not an army outside the walls seeking our destruction. My father was not present often, as he spent much time on the ramparts, guarding the city.

Although Musa, as a Muslim, cared about the fate of the city, Musa was on the wall to protect his beloved Anna, and to protect his three children. Musa would gladly die if it meant that his family would survive the siege.

The siege turned in favor of the Crusaders. They found a solution to their lack of proper siege equipment. They received help from the Genoese sailors of Italy. The Genoese dismantled the timbers of their sailing ships, hauled them overland to the walls of Jerusalem, and with these stout timbers, constructed siege towers high enough to breach the walls.

I remember, vividly, my father, stooping down on one knee and hugging me, for the enemy siege towers were now positioned at the top of the walls of the city. Musa was on his way to defend the walls; the final assault on Jerusalem was about to begin.

His last words to me were. "Ibi. Always show others honor and respect. They will in turn respect and honor you. I do not know what Allah has destined, but I know with all my heart, you will be a great and good man. Since birth, you were bound for greatness."

Ibrahim paused, grasped Rebecca's hand tighter and said, "Rebecca. Each day I think of those words. I wonder if my parents are proud of me. I always thought they were. Now I am not sure."

Rebecca smiled and said, "There are those who call you a "great man." Others call you things I will not repeat! For my part I see in you something better than greatness. I see before me a "good man." Tell me, what happened to your family?"

Ibrahim took a deep breath and continued.

"Musa rushed out the door sword in hand. Horns blew all over the city, kettle-drums pounding, calling the men to arms. Men were running by our home, shouting. My father ran out the door to join them. That was the last time I saw him.

With the siege towers provided by the Genoese the Crusaders broke into Jerusalem and overwhelmed the defenders. It brings me slight comfort to imagine that my father, when they finally struck him down, was surrounded on all sides by dead crusaders who died by his hand.

The Crusaders piled into the city in a furious orgy of killing and rape. They struck down all before them, men women and children.

The Jews huddled for protection inside their synagogue. The synagogue was near our home. The Crusaders set it alight and all inside, hundreds of people were burned alive. We heard the terrible sounds of screaming from the tortuous pain of the heat and flame. I did not know that human beings were capable of such screams. Unearthly. Inhuman. Above the screams we heard the Crusaders outside of the synagogue, laughing, singing and dancing joyfully.

"Christ, We Adore Thee!"

Muslims sought shelter in the Al-Aqsa Mosque, the Dome of the Rock. They were slaughtered.

The Crusaders waded ankle deep through the blood of the dead.

More than ten thousand people were butchered in the Mosque alone. Most of my schoolmates died there. No one was left alive, neither women nor children were spared.

We huddled together in the main room of our home as we heard the slaughter reach full fury outside. The end of the world had arrived. My mother dressed us in the typical clothing of the Coptic Christians. My mother placed her copy of the Bible open and in front of us on the floor. Surely the Crusaders would spare us, a family of Christians. She was praying to Issa loudly, in Latin, whom you call Jesus, when a knight kicked down the front door. I remember him as if he were here, right now, standing in front of us. A tall Frank. He filled the entire doorway, blocking out the sun light like some giant demon god, armored from head to foot. He held a blood-drenched broadsword. His tunic was red with bloodstains and chunks of tissue, hair and other human matter, so much debris of dead humans that the crimson cross he bore on his chest was obscured. His dress was exactly the same as that of the soon to be formed Templars. I know that he became one of them. Now in my dreams, that Templar haunts me.

My mother spoke to him calmly in Latin, his native language, and explained that she and her family were Coptic Christians, neither Muslims nor Jews.

Her pleadings fell on deaf ears. He thrust the sword into my dear mother's stomach. She fell to the side, groaning in pain, pleading with the knight in Latin to spare her family.

My older brother, enraged, flew at the warrior who struck him down, cleaving him open from shoulder to waist. As he did so, my mother, lying on the ground, blood pouring from the wound in her stomach, reached out for a metal grate that ran along the bottom of the wall of the room. With a painful heave, she set the grate free, exposing a black space on the other side. She commanded me, her voice failing as she died. "Ibi! Take your sister, go!"

She pointed to the black space where the grate had been removed. She thrust something into my hands, her wooden rosary beads. My mother always had the beads on her person. She prayed with them, carried them while she purchased food at the market, and even slept with the beads entwined around her fingers. These were the last words she uttered as she passed, "Remember me Ibi. Remember that I love you . . . I will see you . . . ," her voice stopped, and I saw her eyes glaze over.

I grabbed my sister and scrambled for the opening. The knight was distracted for a moment for he was rummaging through a trunk where my father kept gold coins and other valuables.

He turned and bellowed, "Where do you two rats think you are going?"

I tumbled down the hole, still holding my sister's tiny hand. I pulled her toward me, toward the dark hole and safety, but she would not budge.

The knight had grasped her by the ankle and was pulling her back into the room. She was screaming in terror, "Ibi! Help me! Help me!"

Her hair was flying in all directions as she frantically struggled to break the grip of her attacker. I held onto her arm and pulled with all of my might. She kept screaming, tears pouring from her eyes. Then I heard a sickening thud, the sound of sword penetrating flesh, and her arm that I was holding onto so tightly went limp. I fell backwards, letting go of her. Her body was yanked back through the opening into the room where my mother and older brother already lay dead.

Suddenly, like a nightmare from hell, the opening was filled with the red-faced, blood streaked face of the "Templar." His eyes burned with blood lust, Satan himself had taken human form and was hunting me.

The knight roared in his blood lust, "Come here you demon rat! Damn you!"

He thrust his sword into the opening, frantically slicing the air just inches in front of my face. The sword clanged, causing sparks on either side of the opening. I backed away as fast as I could. The next thing I remember, I was falling into a deep, dark void.

I landed hard on my back. The landing knocked the wind out of me. There was very little light. It was a tunnel of some sort. There was a bit of water in the tunnel. The water

> sloshed up to my ankles as I groped along the wall, looking for an exit. I half walked, half stumbled, sobbing in grief, falling down, getting back up, moving forward, and cursing myself for not saving my younger sister from death or defending my family from that wicked cavalier."

Ibrahim paused his story, looked up toward the sky and uttered, "Hmmm. That is strange. Yes, very strange."

Rebecca said, "What Ibi? What is strange?"

He looked at Rebecca and said, "I don't think . . . Yes, I am certain I have not told anyone about my sister's death until this very moment."

Rebecca smiled, eyes swollen with tears.

Ibrahim continued and said:

> "I believe I landed in Hezekiah's tunnel, the very water tunnel that was carved by the King to bring fresh water into Jerusalem during the siege of Jerusalem by the Assyrians. As the tunnel brought water to besieged Hebrews in the time of Hezekiah, too it would be my salvation. I heard overhead, through the rock, the piercing, horrible sounds of the massacre that continued on unabated.
>
> I remember vividly the sound of dripping water. I headed in that direction, hoping that it would lead me to an exit. The dripping water was directly ahead of me. I moved quickly towards it. I was thirsty and

cupped my hands to take a drink. I tasted the water. It was salty, thick and bitter, I spat it out and wretched as I realized that the trickle of water was in fact blood that found its way from the street above, through the cracks and crevices and into the water tunnel.

I fell to my knees and cried, defeated. I don't know how long I sat there, but I perceived a slight draught of fresh air. I followed the smell of fresh air to a slit in the ceiling where a sliver of light burst forth. I pressed myself through the opening and out, once again into the daylight, at some unknown point below the city walls on the side of a steep cliff. I tumbled out down the sandy cliffside into the Kidron Valley below.

I looked up at the walls of Jerusalem that topped the cliff I had just exited. Smoke and flame filled the air above the city. I could hear men and woman screaming in horror and pain. The air was heavy with the smell of burning timbers, hair and flesh. A line of bedraggled people passed me by.

They were Jews, Orthodox Christians, and Muslims, old men, children, women and a handful of younger men. They were grouped together and walking slowly northward, heads down, clothes in tatters. Many were injured, some were burned. They were newly-minted orphans, widows and widowers. One of them told me they were heading north, to Muslim held Damascus, safely outside of the reach of the bloodthirsty Crusaders.

I joined them. This is how I came to my uncle Harun in the city of Damascus. Harun searched for me among the hundreds of stragglers that filtered into the city. Harun prayed that my family survived the massacre. He prayed that Allah spare the children, an unfulfilled hope that the Crusaders not put the children of Jerusalem to the sword.

Harun took me in and raised me as one of his own. Before Jerusalem was besieged, my father sent a large sum of funds to Harun in order to care for us three children in case something happened to him and my mother.

Uncle Harun ensured that my education continued. Part of that education included classes in swordsmanship and archery, taught by him, or experienced warriors that he hired as tutors. We spent many hours, outside of Damascus, in the olive groves, at swordplay and archery, for Harun was more warlike than his brother, my father, Musa.

Musa had a certain skill with the sword that came to him naturally. A mandatory talent for one who traveled across the desert in a caravan, out in the open, easy prey for marauders or Bedouin tribesmen who hold to the belief that any possessions that pass through their territory belongs to them. Out of necessity Musa was adept at self-defense. He was especially skilled with the bow. He could launch a flurry of razor sharp arrows from the back of a camel hump at full gallop. However, for my father this was not something that he considered an impressive accomplishment. To Musa, his skill with the bow paled in importance to his skill with the quill and vellum script. A necessary evil, nothing more.

Harun was altogether different. He enjoyed weaponry and warfare. He lived for it. In the olive groves, while practicing archery, Harun would have me throw a walnut high into the air. He would let loose an arrow and hit the walnut squarely, blowing it into dust, time and time again. He taught me how to shoot arrows with such precision.

Harun had a reputation for his ferocity in the skirmishes that occurred between the tribes and clans of families who inhabited the region. These skirmishes were fought over a well, a flock of sheep or a grove of olives.

Harun was forced to live inside the city of Damascus instead of the countryside due to a 'blood feud' that raged with another clan. Harun was responsible for the deaths of not a few members of the rival clan. The dead men's relatives, in turn, searched for my uncle in order to satisfy the blood feud.

One night as I sat on the floor of our home, rubbing the wooden beads that my mother had thrust into my hand right before her death, Harun entered the room and noticed the beads. He approached me, put his large strong hand on my head and said, "Keep those with you always, Ibi. They will make you strong in battle. Remember! With the infidel there can be no peace. They will not stop until all Muslims meet the same fate as our family. Never forget that. Never forget Jerusalem."

I nodded my agreement and through tear-filled eyes, and a burning hate in my heart, I promised my uncle.

"I swear upon my family and the King of Heaven himself, I will never make peace with Christendom. Never. I will kill them without mercy, until the day all breath has left my lungs."

"Well said, my boy!"

Ibrahim paused for a long moment, overwhelmed by the memory.

"It was true in my life what the wise man says, "What is learned in youth is carved in stone." Ibrahim realized that he had been talking for a long time. It was not his custom to speak so much, for he believed, "Wisdom was lost in a multitude of words." Yet he could not help himself, he felt a strange urge to tell Rebecca everything.

He snapped back into the present. While he told the tale she had reached out and lightly held his hand, she held it still. She had moved closer to him and was looking at him, no space between their bodies, fully attentive to his story.

Ibrahim saw that she had tears in her eyes, and other tears had already fallen, leaving her cheeks wet. Rebecca looked at him, sadness in her eyes. She said,

"I am truly sorry. It's not fair that a child watches as his family die. Executed because of their religion? How can men be capable of such things?"

Her words and the tone of her voice struck Ibrahim. He felt her compassion.

He looked at the softness in her eyes and replied,

"Oh my dear girl. Men are capable of such terrible things."

She was moved by the tale of his personal tragedy. No one had expressed such compassion before. There was only a handful who he entrusted to tell the entire story of the massacre of his family in Jerusalem. Adnan knew the story, as did the Sultan.

Adnan's reaction to the tale was predictable.

"I will gladly help you kill them all! What are we waiting for! Let us start right now! *Yen 'aal deen ommak!*"

Others reacted with quiet nods of understanding. Many of them too had lost family and friends in the never-ending conflict between the two faiths, between east and west.

But never had he heard such words of sympathy. It was unexpected. A new emotion. A woman's touch. He was caught off-guard.

Ibrahim felt an urge to say more to Rebecca, to explain why he warred against Christendom. To justify the hatred that boiled inside of him.

He concluded:

> "Is it the will of Allah for me to destroy the knights of Christendom when I en-

> counter them on the field of battle? Yes! I must kill! I justify the blood on my sword by reasoning, how many Muslim families, how many children have I spared the pain of my personal nightmare? A thousand? Ten thousand? Then a contrary voice chimes in. Is it my conscience? The voice condemns me, how many orphans have I created? A thousand? Ten thousand? I too am an orphan. I know the pain of losing ones' parents to death and war. Is it truly the will of Allah that I fill the world with fatherless children? My father dreamed of being a famous poet and author. He wanted to leave something of value in the world. Is my destiny, my legacy, to leave nothing more than rows of freshly hewn graves? Is that the kind of life my mother Anna wanted for me?"

He fell silent. Rebecca said sympathetically, "The Lord still has a purpose for you, Ibrahim. Perhaps you will have a chance to live a life of peace. One day the pain of your childhood will ease, and the anger will be gone.

Then Ibrahim Al-Rahim did a most impulsive and unplanned thing. He kissed her. A light gentle kiss upon her lips. The fine wine still lingered. A pleasing taste of currants and tannins. He held her. She felt soft, but firm like a cotton bale warmed by the sun.

She started to pull away from his grasp, a physical objection to the kiss, but stopped. She looked up at him, into his eyes and returned the kiss. Rebecca's body relaxed as she melted into him, sharing the soft moment.

Ibrahim stopped the kiss, shook his head and said, "No. This is not possible. It cannot be!"

Ibrahim tried to back away but Rebecca would not let him go. She said, "Lower your defenses, Ibi, and open your heart to me."

Ibrahim said, "My heart? You do not want to see what is in my heart. It is filled with hatred, Rebecca, and if you touched my heart, it would poison you."

Ibrahim broke free from her grasp and left her standing alone in the courtyard.

Chapter 18

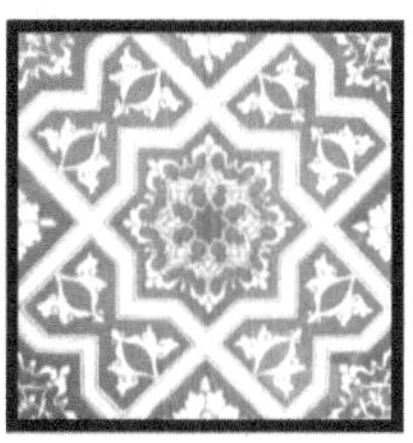

The Reconnaissance

"Destruction cometh;
and they shall seek peace,
and there shall be none."

A small number of horsemen rode out together, through the gates of Granada, beyond the lush Vega, and over the passes of the Sierra Nevada. They carried no banners, no pennants, and were lightly armed. They comprised an expedition designed for speed and stealth, not pitched battle. From a distance the riders appeared as common folk, travelers or merchants bunched together for safety, or partners in enterprise. Upon closer inspection however, in spite of a lack of elegant clothing, shining armor and colorful banners flapping in the wind, one could see that the riders carried themselves with the impressive bearing of warriors.

Each rider bore the air of self-confidence and bravery about them. They could have been mistaken for members of a royal house, out for a jaunt in the open country air. Even their horses moved with a regal bearing, at a steady constant gate.

Ibrahim Al-Rahim rode alongside Adnan Al Mansur, upon Exsecour. Ibrahim put on his charger an old, well-worn saddle and a plain, torn blanket. Exsecour objected to the worn-out accessories with neighing and kicking as if it were beneath his dignity to be decked out like a common draft-horse, instead of the decorations of a mount preparing for battle.

Included in the scouting party was Osmyn, the talented general in command of the Sultan's infantry. He was a true "Moor," the very essence of the word. He was tall, strong and broad shouldered, skin as black as coal.

Their reconnaissance mission was to evaluate the army from Castile that recently crossed the northern border into the Kingdom of Granada. The commanders wished to view the invaders with their own eyes, and to make an evaluation as to how grave a threat they posed. With this eye-witness observation, they could prepare their plans for an attack.

Ibrahim knew from the information conveyed by the signal flags that this army was not composed of untrained rabble on a fanatical mission of martyrdom. He prayed that the number of true professional soldiers and mounted men-at-arms would be few. He hoped too, that this army like all the others before them, was hastily cobbled together, without sufficient supplies, especially the most vital of all supplies to a marching army, water. If the army did indeed lack the water necessary to keep man and horse hydrated, they would have to march from water source to water source. This meant that Ibrahim and Osmyn could track their every move and counter them accordingly.

Ibrahim and Osmyn discussed a plan to dig in on a good piece of high ground on or near a well.

The Castilians would have to attack the Moors on ground not of their choosing. The Castilians would attack, or choose to march on toward the next water source. Their army would begin to die of thirst. Out in the open, in the heat, marching in the dust, they would be easy pickings for Ibrahim's well-watered and rested cavalry.

The scouts would observe the enemy, plot their probable line of march, and prepare the counter-attack. This was an exercise they had performed together on many occasions. They knew this would not be the last outing. They would be called upon to make many more of these rides.

Al Mansur rode alongside Ibrahim as they trotted through a fragrant citrus grove. Adnan looked forward to these missions outside of the city. He was delighted to hear of the coming of Castile. He relished sitting around the cook fires at night, drinking wine and telling stories with his fellow warriors. These journeys reminded Al Mansur of his childhood, growing up in the trackless sands of the desert, sleeping under the stars.

"This is good Ibi! I love to get out of that stinking city and into the open air! Thank Allah that the Spaniards hate us so much."

"Granada does not stink, Adnan," replied Ibrahim.

"Surely it does! All cities stink! Granada stinks less than most, I will concede, but all cities are rotten."

Ibrahim was not in the mood to engage Adnan about the disadvantages and odors associated with city life. Ibrahim did not wish to argue the point. His mind was consumed with more important issues.

As they trotted regally down the road, they passed the villa of Maria de Alicante. Standing guard was the donkey she rescued from the plaza. It looked better. Its flesh more full, the ribs not as pronounced. The old woman was in front of her clay-colored home, bent over, tending to her herb garden. They passed. She straightened up and pressed both of her hands into the small of her back. She wore a wide-brimmed straw hat and a simple sky-blue housedress with two pockets in the front. The pockets held a pair of scissors and a small hand-rake.

Maria glanced up at the riders from beneath the brim of her wide straw hat. She frowned and threw up a cautious wave. She looked worried, even upset, at the sight of the soldiers. She called out cautiously.

"Hello Ibi! Out for a pleasant ride in the country I see."

Ibrahim grunted in response, shaking his head, irritated at being discovered once again. He did not acknowledge her. He was embarrassed that she called to him using the familiar diminutive of his name in front of the other officers of the army of Granada. He said to Adnan,

"By the prophet, we MUST become more skilled at disguising ourselves!"

After many minutes, Al Mansur noticed that Ibrahim was silent, his gaze, distant. Al Mansur knew this happened to Ibrahim from time to time. Ibrahim would begin to meditate on a thought and shut out everything around him, as if he were suddenly transported out of body to a far off land where no one could reach him. This bothered Al Mansur. Why be silent when there was so much to talk about, laugh about, and mock in the world?

Al Mansur leaned over in his saddle and with his arm jostled Ibrahim. "Awake from the trance, Ibi! Return to us!"

Ibrahim, scowling, slowly acknowledged Al Mansur. "What? What words of wisdom does the Berber wish to share that demand immediate attention?"

"The top of that mountain over there!" Adnan gestured to a far-away peak, then rubbed the wide crimson scar on his bald head. "It looks like a woman's breast with a hard nipple on the top."

Adnan exploded in laughter, as if he just said the most amusing thing in the history of mankind.

"Do you ever think about anything else but women, Adnan?"

"As the wise man says, 'Even a one-eyed man will wink at a beautiful woman,' you don't think *enough* about women Ibi! I am beginning to fear that your obsession with the Templars is tempting you to imitate them, boy lovers and man humpers that they are!"

"Strong talk from a man whose people are known only for their ability to 'ride' camels."

Adnan stopped laughing, feigned surprise.

"Ah! Not bad, Ibi! You are improving! You are learning the proper way to insult a man! My fine influence is at work upon you!"

Ibrahim repeated, making reference to Adnan's most recent proverb. "One-eyed man . . . Really? How does a barbarian think up such things?"

"The wisdom of the desert my friend, the wisdom of the desert," Adnan cast a playful glance at Ibrahim. "An Arab cannot understand such wisdom."

"I am NOT AN ARAB!"

Adnan was happy that his words had the desired effect upon his friend. He continued as if giving a lecture to a classroom.

"Now a Bedouin, thieves though they are, every last mother's son of them, can understand the wisdom of the desert, but an Arab? An Arab is too far removed from the sand. His senses have been dulled by sensuous pleasures."

Lesson concluded, they rode on. Adnan's tone became more serious.

"Ibi. Listen. Seriously, you are more distracted than usual lately, what is going on in that gourd of yours?"

Al Mansur was adept at toying with Ibrahim. One moment joking and sarcastic, and in the next, serious and concerned. It was his way.

Ibrahim was confidant that his friend would never divulge his private affairs to another man's ears. In spite of Adnan's rough exterior, speech, and general lack of formal education or manners, Ibrahim knew he could turn to his friend for straight, honest advice. Ibrahim thought of the saying, never truer than in the case of his friend, Adnan, "Ask the experienced rather than the learned!"

So Ibrahim decided to confide in Adnan. Ibrahim asked, "Adnan. What do you think about getting involved with a Christian girl?"

"What do you mean, involved? Passing an evening of pleasure with the girl? I must say Ibi, you are becoming more of a man by the day! 'The sinning is the best part of repentance!' Let me tell you, those girls from Christendom. They aren't like our boring, sheltered, covered from head-to-toe innocents! I mean the things they are willing to do . . . "

Ibrahim cut him off.

"No Adnan! I am not talking about that! I mean, taking a Christian girl as a wife."

Adnan thought for a second, rubbing the scar on his head, then said.

"Well Ibi, marriage is like a fort, those who are in want out, and those who are out want in! As for taking a Christian wife, well, it is not unheard of. But a man in your position? That would be a problem. You could not bring her into the Alhambra, nor could you live outside of the Alhambra in the Sacramonte. Yes, it would be unacceptable. What will you do? Raise a litter of *Muladies*? The poor things! They are half Arab and half Christian. What the hell are they? They don't even know! Look how confused you are! One parent Christian, the other Muslim! Why would you want to do that to a child?"

It would be a long, hot day in the saddle with little to do, so Ibrahim decided to entertain himself for a brief moment.

"Let me guess. You hate *Muladies* too?"

"Hate is too strong a word, Ibi. I don't dislike them anymore than I dislike all other races of mankind."

Adnan smiled. "But I really do HATE Arabs! *Yen 'aal deen ommak!*"

Ibrahim did not fall for the bait this time, instead asked, "Sudanese?"

Adnan grunted, "No. Too tall."

"Franks?"

Adnan spat on the ground, "Transparent white skin with smooth, unshaved faces? They are like hairless, pink cats, Ugh!"

"Egyptians?"

"Too short."

Ibrahim paused, pulled back on the reins, stopped Exsecour and asked.

"Berbers? Hmmmmm?"

"Well. There was this round Berber girl straight from the desert. I was sweet on her! Her hips were good for birthing. But she did not return my affections. In fact she married an Arab. So yes! Berbers that aren't me, make the list too!"

Ibrahim got Exsecour going with a gentle clicking then returned to a more serious matter and asked, "What if I left Granada? I could live in Alexandria or Damascus. I could pick up my father's trade and travel the caravan routes."

Adnan reached over and grabbed the reins of Ibrahim's horse, bringing it to a stop. He looked at Ibrahim with an expression that bordered on panic. Eyes wide, he objected. "What? Do not dwell on that! Don't even consider it! You will not leave me in Granada alone, to deal with those lily-assed Arabs all by myself! Besides, you cannot live the rest of your days selling paper to the Jews. That would kill you quicker than a spear through your heart. The next time you have such warm feelings for an infidel girl, take those wooden beads you have, run them through your fingers, and remember what Allah put you on this earth to do!"

Adnan let go of Ibrahim's horse and with an evil grin challenged, "Which girl? That dancer in the white silk dress who stopped us in the street?"

Ibrahim shook his head in disbelief. "How did you know that?"

"I saw the way you looked at her, Ibi. You think you are so sly, that no one knows what you are up to, what is going on inside of that head of yours. It was so obvious a blind man could see it! It was so obvious that the Pope, sitting on his fat ass in faraway Rome took notice, sat up in his throne and said, "My! Ibrahim has been taken by that dancing girl!" The Pope was so taken aback that he forgot to sell his daughter as a prostitute for the night as is his custom!"

"No Adnan, he would never forget to do *that*!"

Adnan continued, "I must admit, I do admire your taste. She is captivating. I have never seen a girl move like that. That dance, it was unlike anything I have ever witnessed, a beautiful thing to behold."

As the sun began its descent over the Alpujarra Mountains to the west, they made camp. That night they sat around the fire, telling stories, jokes and fables. Adnan passed around a clay vessel with a handle, full of red wine. Most of the men drank from it. The vessel was passed to the devout Osmyn, who, without drinking, passed it to Ibrahim.

The Quran outlawed the use of alcoholic beverages, and Ibrahim obeyed the law of prophet. He did not drink wine, even though it was plentiful in Granada. The Christians in the Sacramonte, the *Mozarabs* and even the Jews drank the fruit of the vine daily. The Kingdom of Granada produced a seemingly limitless supply of grapes, and wine was plentiful.

The Christian Kingdoms that shared the Iberian Peninsula also grew the vines in abundance. The weather and the soil of the entire peninsula were perfect for growing grapes. Still, Ibrahim adhered to the law. He felt it his duty to lead by example. He was aware that some Muslims, even some of his own elite cavalry imbibed from time to time. What his men did on their time was their business, as long as they did not attempt to perform their martial duties under the influence of wine, Ibrahim did not interfere.

This time, however when it was passed to him, Ibrahim grasped the vessel, and to everyone's astonishment took a deep draft. Then he wiped his mouth and passed pass the clay vessel on.

Beyond the light of the campfire, a sentry who patrolled the darkness beyond the firelight called out a warning. With that, the captains of the Alhambra leapt to their feet and drew swords. They heard a scuffle in the bushes. The sharp bray of a donkey. The sentry appeared. He had captured an intruder. The sentry held the arms of the intruder fast and roughly shoved the person to the ground. He placed his knee on the intruder's back and pulled back the hood to reveal the stranger's identity. A shock of grey hair appeared.

Ibrahim sheathed his sword and ran to Maria de Alicante. He kneeled down and spoke to the sentry. "Thank you for your vigilance. I will take care of this."

The sentry stood and bowed low, clutching at a bloody wound on his forearm. He said, "Be cautious of the old woman's donkey. It is a foul tempered beast."

He retreated into the shadows to bind his wound.

The old woman got up, brushed herself off. Her face was creased with worry.

"Ibi. I have to talk to you. You must do something for me! That is why I came."

Ibrahim touched her shoulder and said, "Dammit, woman! What are you doing sneaking up on us in the middle of the night! This is no place for you!"

"Ibrahim. We have to talk alone."

She grabbed him by the arm and tried to pull him away from the rest of the men so they could speak in private.

Adnan strode forward. Chuckled.

"Are you certain you want to be alone with her, my Lord? It is my duty to protect you! This one might be dangerous!"

Ibrahim missed the humor. "Yes Adnan, it is alright."

The men began to laugh, a raucous, hoarse laughter. Ibrahim, annoyed, ignored the mocking and moved away with Maria.

She said. "I need you to do something for me. I need you to promise me! Promise me as if I were your own dear Anna!"

Ibrahim was struck. He questioned. "How do you know the name of my mother? I have not spoken of her!"

Maria ignored the questions. Tears glistened in her eyes as she continued.

"You have to promise me you will stay away from her!"

"What are you talking about Maria? Stay away from whom?"

"*Tsk*. You know! She is good, Ibi! You know that. She is pure. She is selfless. She doesn't dance to defy you!

She dances because she loves to make people happy. To make them smile. To forget their worries if only for a few moments. I am wracked with guilt. I can't sleep at night from the worry. It is my fault! I told you where to find her!"

"I will not promise you I will never see her again!"

"You must!" Maria grabbed his tunic and pulled him forward with desperate strength, until her face was close to his.

She pleaded. "Death follows you, Ibrahim. It is always with you, waiting for its next victim. You will be the death of her. She is light, and you will extinguish the light. Please, please leave her be."

Adnan and Osmyn approached. Osmyn interrupted, "We cannot allow this woman to return to Granada and report our absence to the spies in the city. What shall we do with her?"

Adnan said excitedly.

"Make her cook! Yes! Make the woman our cook until we return to the city!"

Osmyn raised an eyebrow. A good idea. Maria glared at Adnan. "I am not a slave! I will not cook for you, you bald-headed brute!"

Adnan said. "Oh! I like this one! She reminds me of a good Berber woman! We should keep her! Make her cook!"

"Leave me be! I will not tell a soul you are here."

Osmyn approached Maria, came up close. "How do we know that? Will you swear it?"

"No. I will not swear it. But I will give you my word as Maria de Alicante. I will tell no one that I saw you here."

Osmyn took a moment to examine Maria's face. Reading her eyes, he pronounced, "She speaks truth. You may go in peace, and take that contemptible ass with you."

Maria countered. "He is a gentle beast, just a bit protective."

Adnan whispered under his breath. "Damn. We should keep her. I'll bet she is a fine cook."

Ibrahim helped Maria to mount the donkey. Even though she was mounted, Ibrahim towered above her. He said, "Maria. I promise you I will let no harm befall her."

Maria turned the donkey and headed off into the darkness. She parted with the words.

"You promise? Ibrahim you do not control everything! You are not God. You cannot guarantee anyone's safety!

As Maria began her journey back to Granada, James the priest was sleeping.

He fell asleep at a table within the cave that was his home in the Sacramonte. He was tired. It had been a busy day. Busier than normal. Secret communiqués borne by messengers entered his cave and been sent out all day long. There was much to plan, much to do.

James fell asleep in a contented mood. More content than he had felt for years. Finally the Lord's will would be done. After all these long years of repression from the Moors and silence from God—a true test of his faith—he would have his reward. He would live to see it! He drifted off thinking, *We have them now! By God, we have them! At long last! They have no idea of the wrath we will bring upon them! We will catch the wily Ibrahim Al-Rahim by surprise!*

James was hunched over the table, sleeping soundly when a noise awoke him. He lifted his head up slowly and in a half-conscious state, smelled a foul odor. He didn't know what it was, only that it permeated the room.

Then he identified the odor and thought, *hashish!*

A strong hand pushed him roughly down onto his opened Bible. He heard a voice, sinister and raspy.

"You have been a most troublesome puuup-pet, haven't you?"

The light from the cave's solitary candle allowed James a glimpse of jaundiced eyes looking into his. James, fully awake now, eyes wide in fear said, "Oh no. Please. Not now. Please."

He tried to cry out but a pair of hands clutched his throat. He heard a thud, felt a sharp pain, then all went black.

Chapter 19

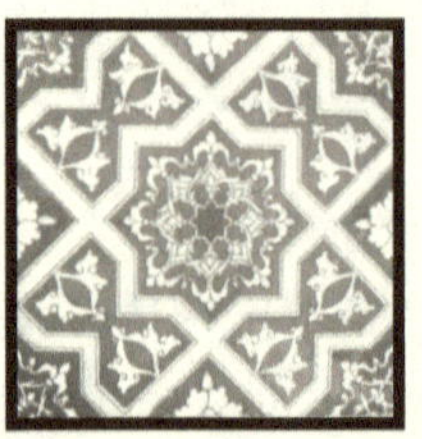

The Ambassador

"Don't pride over your wealth or beauty,
one will be gone in a night,
and the other with a fever."

In Granada, the same night that the captains of the Alhambra were exchanging tales and wine around a campfire, the Sultan Abdul Rahkman welcomed a visitor to the Alhambra. The Sultan strode, upright and dignified, through the Courtyard of the Lions to meet the delegation sent from the Caliphate of Baghdad.

Abdul Rahkman was dressed in his finest clothing, a gold flowing robe with purple embroidery that mimicked the arabesque geometric shapes that covered the Alhambra's walls, ceilings, fountains, and floors. The robe trailed behind him for several feet and made a soft sound like a slight breeze passing through the pines as he walked. He wore golden slippers with pointed toes that looked to be far too large for his feet. On his head was a royal blue turban. On his fingers, many rings of gold, silver and precious stones. His long, grey two-pointed beard was neatly trimmed and it waved gently to and fro as he walked.

Behind him trailed a small army of counselors, Imams and wise men, each splendidly dressed, following the Sultan at a respectful distance.

The entourage passed the fountain for which the courtyard was named. In the center was a large alabaster basin supported by twelve marble lions in white marble. Each lion stood regally at attention and faced outward.

The fountain was out of place when compared to the stilted arches, gold, green and blue arabesque tracings that beautified the arches and walls of the courtyard. It was not formed by the same hands that created the Alhambra. The fountain was a gift from the Jewish populace of the Kingdom of Granada. Each of the twelve lions represented the 12 tribes of the nation of Israel. The fountain and the lions had its model in the Fountain of the Temple of Solomon.

It was presented to the rulers of the Alhambra as a symbol of the *convivencia*, the unique peace that allowed the Jews to finally live in tranquility within the borders of the Kingdom.

Lining the courtyard on either side was Ibrahim's elite cavalry as the ceremonial guard, still as statues, dressed in ceremonial robes and turbans, wickedly curved, gleaming scimitars drawn and resting upright on the chest of each man.

They were on duty, unaware that their commander was far away on a secret mission.

Some of the guards were tall, slender, black skinned warriors from the Sudan. Others, short and stocky Berbers from North Africa. Some were olive-skinned natives of the Kingdom of Granada itself, and some, with blond hair and skin as white as snow, were converts to Islam who hailed from European lands far to the north.

The Sultan led his reception committee between the guards to the entryway to meet an equally elegantly-dressed man, also accompanied by a small army of counselors, Imams and scribes. The two groups met in the middle of the entryway under a domed roof.

The visitor approached. He touched his head and then his chest as he bowed low.

"*As salaam Alaikum,* Abdul Rahkman! Lord of Al-Andalus, protector of the Kingdom of Granada, and regent of the gardens of the Alhambra!"

The Sultan smiled, nodded his head in acknowledgment and replied warmly, "*Wa Alaikum as salaam*! The Ambassador of the Caliph of Baghdad is welcome here."

The men embraced.

Porters and servants seemed to appear from nowhere and descended upon the visiting delegation with silver trays holding silver goblets filled with orange sherbet in rose water and pomegranate juice.

The members of the visiting delegation drank the cool refreshments and were lead to their quarters leaving the Sultan and the Ambassador alone. A night breeze filled the entryway, causing the robes of both men to lift of the ground and flutter slightly.

The Sultan was no longer smiling. He knew this was not a casual visit from the Caliph of Baghdad's most trusted and senior diplomat.

The Sultan asked, "I know your journey has been long and dangerous. Why does the Caliph risk his most trusted counselor on a mission to the far end of the Islamic world?"

The Ambassador replied, "My dear, wise Sultan, you whose Kingdom, of all the Kingdoms of Islam, is most at threat from the infidel, I have a word for you from the Caliph. The same message arrives from the Sultans and Satraps whose lands I passed and ports I called upon in my journey westward. Their words are written on scrolls that my Imams have under their protection in their baggage. We will read their words together."

The Sultan tugged at his beard, twirling one of the two points in his hands. He pressed, "Most trusted counselor and loyal servant of the Caliph, I have many matters that I must attend to. Surely you are aware that the Castilians are coming, that there is unrest in the Christian quarter here in Granada. I have many preparations to carc for, therefore, I pray that you will tell me now, what is this "word" of which you speak."

The Ambassador looked beyond the Sultan to the fountain. "Ah! The courtyard of the lions! Lovely, simply lovely. The fountain a gift from the Jews correct?"

"Yes, Ambassador. In the lands of Christendom, Jews are forbidden to employ Christians as servants, to serve as doctors to Christians, to sell food items, or clothing. The Pope decreed that Jews be marked as an inferior race. They must wear a circular patch of yellow felt on their clothing.

Here in Granada, by contrast, the Jews live under the protection of the *convivencia* without restriction, without fear of a state or church sponsored pogrom.

My own personal physician is a Jew! He is quite good, I assure you! Many of my counselors are Jewish. Here the Jews worship freely in their synagogues. It is little wonder then, that as a symbol of their appreciation, the Jewish population gave us such a gift as this fountain."

The Ambassador listened carefully them responded, "Ah yes. The *convivencia*." He bit his lip and continued,

"Your tolerance. That is why I was sent. The Caliph and the Lords of the Islamic lands between Granada and the rising of the sun are anxious about the fate of the Kingdom. This blessed place that contains the gardens of Allah, his expression of heaven on earth itself. This kingdom is the battlefront, the frontline, and the testing ground between Islam and Christendom, between the holy ones of Allah and the Infidel, the contest between monotheism and polytheism. In the Levant and Israel there is a fragile peace between the Crusader Kingdoms and our lands. Europe and the Pope in Rome look elsewhere to carry on their war against us, to incite their people to Crusade. Their fury is aimed here, at Southern Spain, here in the Kingdom of Granada. This is where the east and the west are destined to collide. The great question will be decided here. Even now, from throughout

Europe, knights and pilgrims are arriving to the Christian Kingdoms of Spain. They have one sole purpose. They are Volunteers in the "Holy-Struggle," to expel us from the Iberian Peninsula and from all of Europe. We are a stain to them. A tiny footprint of Islam in all of Europe. We must be prepared as never before to face new hordes of clean shaven, vile blasphemers."

The Ambassador paused, and took another sip of the pomegranate juice from the silver goblet. Then he continued.

"The Islamic world is worried, my dear Sultan Al Rahkman. I have written petitions from the Lords of Islam and the Caliph himself. It appears that at this critical moment in our struggle against the infidel, the Kingdom of Granada is weakened . . ."

The Sultan, irritated, took umbrage at the word "weakened," and interrupted. "Weakened? This is mindless gossip such as told by old women gathered at a well! This Kingdom is not weak! We have annihilated every army of Christendom that has been raised against us in the past; we will do so in the future, *Inshallah!* My army can whip any force from any kingdom of Christendom or Islam! With the blessing of Allah, who protects this kingdom, we are strong!"

The Ambassador raised his hand in a gesture of calm. "Please, Sultan, hear me out. I do not infer that your military has lost its potency. Why, the entire world marvels at the exploits of your army. Schoolchildren in Baghdad are told tales of Osmyn and Ibrahim Al-Rahim, the orphan survivor of the rape of Jerusalem who has become the "Scourge of Christendom," no; to this I do not refer. As you know, Sultan, there are other ways that a Kingdom may soften, then fall from the *inside.* A Kingdom with an invincible army can be defeated. When Rome fell, her legions were still strong! Do not forget our own recent past here in Iberia. Not long ago we held the entire Peninsula, from the rock of Tarik all the way to the land of the Franks. All Spain was under our rule. Now we are reduced to this southern portion of land, barely a thumbprint on the mass of the European continent."

The Ambassador took another deep draught of the cool, pure pomegranate juice, closed his eyes to savor it then continued.

"The Caliph has heard of disquieting events here in Granada that could result in Allah retaining his blessing from your kingdom. Without his favor, all is lost. To be direct: Your Kingdom is *too* tolerant. Your soldiers are given to drinking wine, Muslims freely marry Christians, giving birth to children that are not devout in their faith of the prophet. The believing women wear only head scarves that do not cover their entire face. A Burka is not to be seen in this city as our tradition dictates. Too, Christian martyrs appear with more and more frequency, unchecked, the unholy sects that produce them, unpunished. Finally, and most disturbing are these unsettling reports about a Christian dance, a dance that the infidel women perform for the purpose of mocking our prayers, our prophet and our book, all in broad daylight in the shadow of the Alhambra! The Caliph worries that the proximity of the Kingdom of Granada to the wicked, god-dishonoring Kingdoms of Christendom has weakened the true faith. The letters I carry from Islamic rulers throughout the known world ask if you, you who are charged with the care of the Kingdom of Granada have taken appropriate measures to counter these threats to our faith. If not, what will you, if anything to return Granada to the path of righteousness? If you are unable, or unwilling, to correct these dangers and take charge of the situation, then the Lords of Islam are prepared to call for Jihad and muster the faithful to come to this place and restore spiritual order."

The Ambassador stopped to allow the Sultan to digest his words then added, more as a personal plea than an order from the Caliphate: "My dear Sultan. We must do all that is necessary to protect the jewel of Islam. Our people throughout the world and generations to come could not bear the loss of this precious place to the infidel. *I* could not bear it. Such a disaster would cause the hearts of our people to cry out in sorrow for a thousand generations."

While the Sultan pondered his words, the Ambassador, out of respect for the Sultan, stood patiently in the entryway of the court of the Lions. He could see the marble fountain over the shoulder of the Sultan. The air smelled like freshly cut roses with an undertone of jasmine. Then the Ambassador caught a new scent. Something he had not smelled in a very long time, and prayed never to smell again. A scent that made his mind flash to a flood of memories from his most dangerous diplomatic mission. The Ambassador did not expect to return from that mission with his limbs intact or at all.

He was to deliver a message. A warning from the Caliph of Baghdad to Sinan deep in the wild mountains of Syria.

The Ambassador remembered those eyes. Sinan's small eyes. Pools of pure black. No whites at all. Sinan held up the roll containing the message from the Caliph and without unrolling it begun to read its contents, word for word, observing even the punctuation perfectly as if it were a poem memorized from childhood.

Sinan gave a hand signal to two of his *Fidai* high on a tower. At the fleeting signal from their leader, the pair, without the slightest hesitation, leapt off the tower and to their death. A shiver went up his spine as he put a name to the odor . . . hashish. *The Grey Cloaks.*

The Ambassador looked uncomfortable now, visibly shaken by the wafting aroma of the burning herb. The Ambassador, composing himself, asked, "Did you know my Lord Sultan, that Sinan's *Fidai* attempted twice to kill Prince Saladin himself? Imagine that! The Great Saladin! The *Fidai* nearly succeeded in their mission, wounding Saladin during one of the attempts. On the third attempt, instead of killing Saladin, the Assassins left a calling card of a dagger and hot cakes on Saladin's pillow in his sleeping quarters inside his royal tent. This unnerved Saladin to the point of obsession for his personal safety!"

The Sultan replied, "Yes. I know of the feats of the *Fidai*, the Grey Cloaks. Why do you make mention of them now?"

"No reason in particular," the Ambassador lied. "Only the ramblings of a tired traveler."

The Ambassador would include his observations in his report to the Caliph. He would write the report tonight, then send it on a fast ship speeding eastward across the vast expanse of the Mediterranean Sea.

Perhaps, after all, the old Sultan Rahkman was prepared to take the drastic steps needed to rectify the spiritual decay in the Kingdom of Granada, cleanse it, and a wasteful jihad against a fellow Islamic Kingdom would not be necessary.

Chapter 20

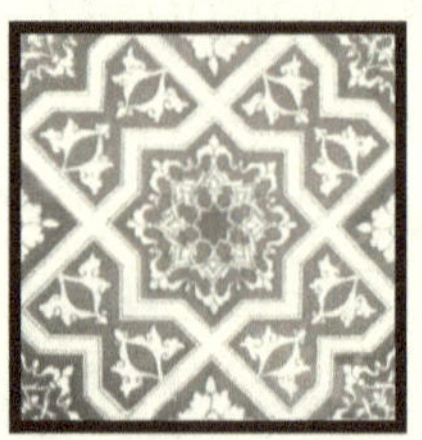

The Coming of Castile

"When one goes in search of water, be certain to bring water."

The Captains of the Kingdom of Granada neared the end of their observation mission. They approached the crown of a small hill, dismounted and climbed to the crest. When they reached the crest, the men lay down and peered to the valley floor below.

Their view was unobstructed by trees, for the valley lay in the path of a rain shadow, making it a bare, dry place. Ibrahim and the others produced long, looking glasses to magnify the scene that unfurled before them.

They spotted a slow roiling cloud of brown dust on the horizon, several miles away, drifting through the ripples of invisible heat that radiated off the cracked, bare ground. The dust cloud was not so dense as to obscure the army that marched at a relaxed pace and filled the valley floor. The column itself was eight men wide and miles in length. They marched in perfect order, unhurried and disciplined, their pennants and banners of blue, red, white, yellow and gold flapping overhead like wild unruly birds of prey.

Several of the dark blue flags were overlaid with a gold *Fleur-de Lys.* Others were white and surmounted with the red cross of Saint George.

The Moors on the crest of the hill spent many minutes observing the invaders in grave silence. Next to Ibrahim a scribe lay prone, writing in a book of loose-leaf vellum bound with silk string. An officer, looking through a glass, counted off the numbers of the enemy forces and dictated the sums to the scribe who made careful notes of each type of unit, how many men comprised each unit, and from where each unit hailed.

Ibrahim, Adnan, Osmyn and the others made their own calculations and observations. It was Osmyn who spoke first, his voice an elegant, deep baritone. He spoke slowly, clearly enunciating each individual word. "They probably mustered in Toledo. Do you see the swordsmen and mounted knights marching under the dark blue flag and gold fleur-de-lys of the Franks? And the archers march under the red cross of St. George, banner of the king of England. They are professional soldiers all. Christendom has put aside their hatred of each other and united to throw us out of Spain."

Ibrahim agreed with Osmyn's assessment. He said, "As the proverb reads, 'My brother and I against my cousin. My cousin and I against a stranger.'"

At the very front of the formation, far out in front of the knights Templar and the order of Santiago rode a single rider on a massive black horse bearing a huge yellow flag surmounted with the fanciful image of a blood-red lion standing on its hind legs, thrashing the air aggressively with its huge front paws.

This flag was the symbol and banner of the powerful Spanish Kingdom of Castile, the leading kingdom of Spanish Christendom. It was the king of Castile who sponsored and was in command of this crusade to reconquer the Kingdom of Granada from the Moors once and for all.

Behind the King of Castile was a vanguard of shining, armored knights and lords. Each group hoisted its own particular battle flag. Conspicuous among the thousands of soldiers in the van were the Military Monks of the order of Santiago, who with their squires counted a thousand lances. The Order's flag was a field of white with a purple cross-like image. The flag was immense, the size of a sail, easily seen from the top of the hill.

Adnan noted, "It appears that all of Santiago have dressed up and come to the dance."

The Order of Santiago was a sworn enemy of the Kingdom of Granada. Its primary mission was to provide security for pilgrims traveling to and from the tomb of the apostle St. James, believed at the time to have been in Compostela. It was the largest pilgrimage center in Iberia, if not all of Latin Christendom. The other sworn purpose for these Military Monks was to kill Muslims and reconquer Spain for the glory of God. They referred to their patron saint as Santiago "El Matamoros," or "Moor Killer," for the Order believed that the apostle had personally come down from heaven during battle to kill the Moors and would continue to do so until the Moors were expelled from Spain.

The Knights Templar too rode in the van with their banner *Beauceant*, surmounted by a Cross of St. George. Each individual Knight Templar in turn bore a long, thin white pendant decorated with the crimson Red Cross of the Templars, sign of the almighty presence of Jesus Christ himself in glory as a risen God, this Christ who is the holy cornerstone of the temple itself. Each knight wore over his armor the long white tunic that bore the crimson red cross.

Mixed amongst the standards of the Military Monks were the banners bearing the crests of rich and powerful lords and knights. These knights did not belong to any particular religious order; they were wealthy landowners who took up sword for their king. Each knight or lord was accompanied by a knot of half a dozen or more mounted squires.

Toward the rear of the marching column was another group of Military Monks. They too were Templars, but from Portugal. Their banners bore a double red cross surmounted on a field of white.

The invading army rode slowly at ease, confident in their massed power, guarding the wagon train that contained the vital supplies needed to keep the army alive.

The wagons came in hundreds, each piled high with barrels of foodstuffs for man and horse- cooking oil, wine, rum, flour, wheat, dried meats, and water. Some wagons were mobile blacksmiths, others piled high with bandages in large bundles and casks of herbs used for poultices and other medical supplies.

Others carried lumber and carpentry tools for the construction of siege towers and tunnels for undermining walled fortifications. The rest of the wagons, escorted even more closely by knights, carried gold, silver, and jewels for payment of the men and mercenaries who marched in the army, and for bribes and other expenses they would incur.

Marching in between the elite, mounted Knights that guarded the front and the rear of the column were tens of thousands of men in assorted units-archers and cross bowmen, pike men and swordsmen.

Adnan noted. "Look at those pike-men marching! Their pikes stand up, straight as trees, no swaying as they march. The mark of true professionals."

Ibrahim knew his cavalry would have to face those lethal pointed spears in battle. He would have to be cautious. A well-trained pike man was pure poison to a charging cavalryman. A handful of pike-men were enough to break the momentum of a charge and turn the tide of battle. In this army of Castile, there were more than a handful of pike men, for the King of Castile had recruited thousands of them.

Ibrahim added. "They are not rabble, for they are a true *army* . . . too bad for us. The sheer numbers of mounted knights! I doubt such a number has been collected since the first Crusade. My own heavy horse will be sorely outnumbered."

The men continued to watch and evaluate. Each began to form a strategy to counter the invaders. Finally Osmyn spoke, giving voice to exactly what each of them had been thinking. "It has been very hot of late."

Granada stayed at a pleasant temperature year round thanks to the snow-capped Sierra Nevada that defended it against the hot winds that blew northward from the Sahara desert, across the narrow waters of the Mediterranean and into Iberia.

The mountains did their job well, keeping the heat of Africa at bay. However, once or twice a year, the Dark Continent gathered its strength and resolve and blew northward, a powerful dry front that not even the mighty Sierra Nevada could hold back. The hot, dead air was devoid of all moisture. The scorching winds of Northern Africa dried the skin and made one's hair brittle.

The Moors would use this yearly change in the climate to their advantage.

Osmyn continued to speak in a low, clear voice. "They will cross the Guadalquivir and obtain water. Then they will march toward the springs near Moclin, deep in the Kingdom of Granada, to replenish their water supply before they begin their assault on our city. It is at the springs we will engage them. We cannot stand up to them face to face in the open field-their knights and pike men would destroy us, their numbers are too many."

Ibrahim nodded in agreement. "It is a good plan. Such a host, with so many horses, will be in need of much water. By the time they reach Moclin, they will be very thirsty indeed."

Al Mansur noted, "Some of those wagons in the rear guard carry water. But I tell you from experience, once again, they do not carry enough for so many men and horse. The Spaniards always underestimate the amount of water they need to keep an army alive. The Spaniards have not spent enough time in a desert to learn that lesson. Let me tell you; all that is needed to survive in the desert is figs . . ."

He did not finish his thought, for the normally stoic Osmyn interrupted him brusquely. "Adnan, stop!"

"Yes my Lord, sorry my Lord," was the sheepish reply.

They lay still for many minutes, observing, and counting. Each man pondered his role in the defense of their homeland.

Osmyn broke the silence. "Of one thing I am concerned, brothers. Moclin is deep within our country, and only a day's hard ride from the gates of the Alhambra. We are allowing the Castilians to venture close to their goal. Closer than they have ever come in the past. This makes me uneasy. Perhaps we should engage them out here, far from Granada."

Ibrahim countered and said, "The deeper they enter the trap, the harder it will shut upon them! When we break them, they will be far away from any sanctuary, too far for any to escape our grasp."

Ibrahim lowered his glass and gave orders to Adnan Al-Mansur. "I give you command of the *jinetes.* You will use the *jinetes* to harass the infidels as they march toward Moclin. Get at their baggage train. If you can destroy those wagons that carry the water, they will become demoralized. If you can provoke the knights that guard the water wagons to charge you, better for us. You will isolate them with your lighter, faster horses, then cut them to pieces. Target your missiles on their pike men, take out as many as you can. In other words Adnan, await my signal, you have my permission to wreak havoc on them."

Adnan smiled broadly. "Thank you, my Lord! It is a delight to carry out your every command!"

Ibrahim continued. "When the enemy reaches the springs at Moclin, you are to disengage, ride to Osmyn and protect the flank of his infantry or be held in the reserve for a counter-attack, you will go wherever Osmyn decides you are most needed.

His next words were directed at Osmyn, "I will stay in Granada for now with the heavy horse. We need them to keep order in the city, for I fear the Christians are scheming mischief. I will stay in the Alhambra for now to keep order. When the army of Castile approaches you at Moclin, I will ride out from Granada. I will time my approach so that we arrive on the battlefield after you have engaged the Spaniards. I will fall upon their flank and destroy them with the heavy horse."

Osmyn nodded his agreement and added, "Our army has been mustered and is already on the march. I will lead them with all haste to Moclin. We will have two full days to dig trenches around the springs and construct a wall of pointed stakes to defend them. The springs are on a hill; we will have the high ground. We will have the advantage. They will arrive tired, hot and thirsty. My men will be well rested, the horses well watered, we will rain down arrows and rocks upon them from above. They will have to attack us on that ground to acquire the springs or die of thirst. This will make their attacks desperate, they will lack discipline as thirst drives them to madness."

Osmyn paused, then continued in a sinister tone, "We will slaughter them all. We must destroy them to a man. A complete victory here, against the best they can muster against us, will discourage the Franks and other Christian nations from aiding Castile in the future. Finally, we can destroy the Military Monks once and for all."

Osmyn stated this in a matter-of-fact way. He did not raise his voice, did not gesture. His voice was not tinged with emotion. He was convinced this was the manner that Allah destined for the battle to occur. That is how it would happen. He knew it. It was already complete and counted as a great victory for Islam. Of this he was certain.

The men could see the power of their enemy. They also knew that the Sultan sent out the alarm, by fast horse and sailing vessel, throughout southern Spain and North Africa, calling the faithful to defend the jewel of Allah.

The faithful were answering the call. Militia was on the move throughout the Kingdom of Granada. The highways, trails, and mountain passes were choked with marching soldiers coming to their aid.

All along the dry coasts of North Africa they were piling into sailing vessels, volunteers and professionals alike, horsemen on their light African mounts, nomads mounted upon their camels, coming by the thousands.

When Castile mustered into battle lines in front of the springs of Moclin, the Moors could count upwards of one hundred thousand spears to counter them.

Adnan turned to crawl down the hill, keeping out of sight of the host below, to his horse to carry out Ibrahim's orders. Ibrahim grabbed him by one of his beefy forearms.

"Adnan. If you capture any of them, my orders still stand. Are we clear? Repeat it!"

Adnan nodded his head obediently and said, "Yes my Lord. We will not execute any captured knights."

Adnan added with a smile. "No matter how much they deserve it!"

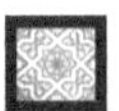

The column of marching Castilians and their allies came to a sudden halt in their slow march on Granada. Before them appeared a large solitary tent. Flying high above the tent was the flag of the Kingdom of Granada, a silk banner, half white and half green. In front of the tent, planted in the ground, a solid white pennant flapped in the wind. The sign of truce.

A horseman from the Castilian army galloped forward on a black charger. He and his horse wore armor, silver shining and strong, made by the finest blacksmiths that could be found in Castile. Behind him galloped a contingent of cavaliers heading for the tent.

The man on the black charger reached the tent first. Though attired in heavy armor, he nimbly slid from the saddle and lightly hit the ground before his horse came to a complete stop. He did not draw his sword as he threw back forcefully the flap of the tent and entered.

Inside Osmyn and Ibi stood at respectful attention.

Osmyn was dressed in his usual white robe. The top of his pointed helmet poked through his white turban.

Ibrahim was also simply dressed in his black cloak clasped by the golden lyre and a long turban. The loose end of the turban ran over his shoulder and down to the floor. Under his cloak, intertwined around his fingers he held the string of wooden prayer beads and grasped the hilt of his scimitar.

In contrast, the man who entered the tent wore a coat of mail under the tunic that made him look twice the size that he actually was. Even his legs and feet were wrapped in silver burnished steel. His shield bore the emblem of the yellow cross and blood red lion. His heavy broadsword, four feet in length, rested in its scabbard.

He wore a heavy rectangular helmet for full protection in battle that left two round slits as the only openings in the steel encasing. His long robe was emblazoned with a yellow cross, and his tunic was surmounted with the fanciful image of the blood-red male lion standing on its hind legs and attacking the air.

The man slowly lifted off his helmet, unveiling a wide face and a full black beard. His large eyes were brown and clear. Finely made mail, myriads of tiny intertwined ringlets covered his head and ran down the back of his neck.

The man was tall as and appeared wider, than Osmyn or Ibrahim, as they were not as heavily armored; in any case the King of Castile was powerfully built, and of greater proportion and weight than the two Muslim commanders. The King carried himself with an air of stern nobility and pride. His powerful presence filled the tent.

Osmyn spoke, the deep dignified baritone, "The Sultan of the Kingdom of Granada, his eminence Lord Abdul Rahkman, apologizes that he could not come here to meet you. He has many pressing matters to attend to in Granada. My Lord Rahkman prays that the distinguished and honorable King of Castile will not view his absence as an affront to his honor."

The King's stern expression changed, and he smiled. But his smile did not cause Ibrahim to lower his guard. Ibrahim grasped the hilt of his scimitar tightly and remembered the proverb: *"When you see the fangs of the lion, do not think the lion is smiling!"*

The king opened his arms wide and declared, as if addressing two old friends many years unseen said,

"Tell your Sultan that he does me the greatest honor by welcoming me to his lands with his two most powerful war-lords! My God, there are so few true warriors left in this world! I am forced to spend my days with men like these . . . " The King pointed backwards with his thumb toward the Templars who were entering the tent.

He looked at Osmyn. "You must be the great Lion of the Desert, Osmyn, and captain of infantry."

Then he looked at Ibrahim. "And you! Ibrahim Al-Rahim, I presume!"

Ibrahim, head cocked slightly to the side, gave a half-nod of confirmation.

The King of Spain was pleased, he declared, "AH! The legendary Sword of the Alhambra! The bane of the Templars!" The King touched his forehead, his chest, and added a slight bow as he said in perfect Arabic,

"*As salaam Alaikum*!"

Ibrahim replied as a courtesy, "*Walaikum as Salam.*"

The King continued, "In my lands, parents reprimand their children and say if they do not behave, Osmyn will come in the black of night and abscond them to the deep deserts of Africa, never to be seen again, or Ibrahim Al-Rahim will carry them away to imprisonment at the very top of the Red Castle, to be forever tormented with the grand views through the iron bars of a cell of Granada of the gardens of the Alhambra, and the Sierra Nevada mountains."

The King laughed heartily, throwing his heavy arms wide again. "The fame of your exploits precedes you!"

Ibrahim motioned with his hand. An attendant came forward, a two-handled silver goblet in hand. The attendant knelt as he presented the goblet with arms raised high above his head—a gesture of respect to the King of Castile.

The King took the goblet. He did not call for his cupbearer; he did not smell or inspect the crimson liquid inside the vessel. He lifted it to his lips immediately and took a deep draught of the rose water, cooled with the small pieces of snow that bobbed within. The King drained the entire goblet. As he drank with gusto, streams of the red water seeped out from the side of his mouth and beaded on his dark beard. He finished, closed his eyes and sighed in delight. "Thank you! That was wonderful! Especially after a hot day in the saddle! I see that the legendary hospitality of the Moors is not exaggerated!"

Behind him, more well-armed men filled the tent. They removed their helmets and stared at the two Moors standing before them.

Some of these men looked with disdain upon Osmyn and Ibrahim, gripping their hilts tightly. Others, eyes wide with surprise at their first close-up view of a soldier of Islam. These knights knew of the terrible reputation of the two Moors that stood by themselves, alone in the tent, confronted with a steel wall of Christendom's finest soldiers.

Osmyn opened his arms and said with elegance, "The King of Castile is welcome in the Kingdom of Granada; we pray that his stay here will be a peaceful one, Inshallah."

The King bowed slightly and began in Latin. "*Data venia*! My sojourn will be peaceful if your Sultan agrees to return this country to its rightful owners."

Ibrahim countered, "There have been many owners of this land. The Visigoths have long since been forgotten, as have the Romans before them, the Carthaginians and the Celts. We are by divine providence the rightful owners of this land, from the Rock of Tariq to the border of Castile."

The King replied cheerily, "Well then! I fear that my journey here will not be a peaceful one."

Osmyn glanced at Ibrahim, who nodded his silent agreement at Osmyn's next words, "Very well. If you return to Castile now, the Sultan guarantees that not a single Islamic soldier will molest you. As a special consideration, he has arranged payment to be made, for expenses incurred during this enterprise. This payment will be delivered once you cross the border and arrive with the blessing of the Merciful One, in your home country. Too, we wish to provide food-stuffs and water for the King and his men to help them in their peaceful journey back to their lands."

The King bit his bottom lip as he considered the offer of the Sultan. Then he smiled again and said, "You may advise your Sultan that I will accept his offer of payment. Yes! It is generous! However, I will take payment for my expenses when I enter the courtyard of the Lions of the Alhambra and he becomes my honored prisoner!"

Ibrahim knew that this exercise was a waste of time, but it was the way of kings, an expected courtesy. At least Ibrahim could evaluate the King of Spain, as he stood close, no more than the distance of a short sword stroke. What Ibrahim saw in the Spaniard's eyes was a proud, intelligent, and confident leader. He bore a yellow cross on his tunic and on his shield, but he was not a religious fanatic. He did not undertake this invasion for the sake of the Pope in Rome, or to please God. He would not make the mortal mistake of blundering into battle expecting to be delivered by the hand of an angel as so many fools had done who came before him.

It occurred to Ibrahim that this King was much worse than a fanatic or a Crusader. He was out to make a name for himself, to be known as the sovereign who finally broke the back of Islamic rule in Spain and united the Iberian Peninsula under his banner.

That meant this King was meticulous in his planning. He had prepared the invasion well, every contingency was considered. He gathered a force from many kingdoms that did not care for each other, to unite and fight a common foe. To accomplish such a feat would require a great deal of skill and diplomacy.

His allies from the Kingdoms of Christendom obviously thought that this king had a sound plan for the conquest of the Kingdom of Granada, a very sound plan, or they would not have committed their own irreplaceable professional troops to the effort.

What else had this King prepared in advance? What designs did he create to catch the Moors by surprise? Ibrahim sensed that his troops would be hard pressed to turn back this latest invasion by Christendom. This was finally, the charismatic leader he feared would one day come.

A young Templar entered the tent and strode forward wide-eyed, menacing, moving with purpose straight toward Ibrahim. Ibrahim saw the hate in the young man's eyes, a new recruit to the order, full of religious zeal and fervor, eager to wet his blade in Moorish blood.

Ibrahim tensed, ready to spring, and thought, *"Come to me boy! You and I will die under this tent, and you will lose your King."*

Ibrahim reasoned it was a fair trade, his life for the life of a king. Ibrahim considered the situation logically as if he were negotiating for a bag of pomegranates, making a deal, not contemplating the end of his life. Ibrahim weighed the bargain in his mind and thought it fair. The words of the proverb came to mind, *"Make your bargain, before beginning to plow."*

This King of Castile was a man to be reckoned with, a true threat to Granada. If he were to die, right now, the enemy army would be led by lesser men, or would dissolve into the petty squabbling between lords and foreign contingents that always sapped the strength of the Spanish Kingdoms. Lesser men would accept the bribes of the Sultan! Yes, a fair trade of lives indeed!

The young knight was in the midst of drawing his sword as he strode with deadly purpose past the King of Castile. He did not take another step. A large mail covered hand slammed onto his chest with such force that the man's feet came out from under him and he fell hard to the floor on his back, his head striking the ground with an audible, *crack*.

The King of Castile, his jovialness gone, planted his armored foot onto the young knight's neck, twisted his heel and growled, "We do not violate a flag of truce, Templar! Did they not teach you the meaning of honor at the monastery?"

Ibrahim relaxed his grip on the hilt of his sword. He heard the disdain in the King's voice as he growled the word "*Templar.*" There was the proof. This King was no religious fanatic. He was not influenced by the dictates of the Church of Rome.

The Templar got off the floor, clutched his chest, and walked out of the tent. There was no further incident.

Osmyn concluded the negotiations. He touched his forehead, then his chest as he bowed and stated, "I regret that we have nothing more to discuss."

The King replied, "As do I," then added in perfect Arabic, "*Ilaa-liqaa*!"

The King said, almost as an afterthought, "The next time we meet, it shall be upon the field of battle, with honor."

Osmyn replied, "It shall be so my Lord, I believe we will meet, and I look forward to the encounter."

The King of Castile turned sharply on his heels and strode out of the tent.

Ibrahim and Osmyn rode away at a gallop as the army of Castile resumed their march toward the heart of the Kingdom of Granada.

Ibrahim carried the green and white banner of the Kingdom of Granada. As he rode, he grasped *Exsecour* by his thick brown mane, leaned forward and spoke into his ear, "You are going to be angry with me that you missed this, my brother!"

As he galloped, he lowered the flag until it nearly dragged on the ground. That was the signal that Adnan Al Mansur prayed he would see. The negotiations failed.

The army of Castile marched past a low treeless hill as Ibrahim Al-Rahim gave the signal. Ibrahim heard a soft peal of thunder from over the mountains. The sound of thunder grew louder and more constant, but the exact direction of the thunder could not be discerned.

The King of Castile, on his black charger galloped full bore down the line of marching men, shouting orders as he rode, for he knew from the thunderous roar in the distance that violence was about to break upon his army.

The column of men broke into small square formations. The pike-men ran out along either flank of the column and positioned themselves as a thin line of razor sharp defense against the coming attack. The king sent additional pike-men running double-time to take positions around the wagon train, to form a protective circle of spears around the vital supplies that meant death to his army if lost. The knights slammed shut their helmets, protecting their faces, and drew swords, their mounts pawing the ground in anticipation of the coming action.

From the crest of the hill burst a mass of horsemen. It was Ibrahim's *jinetes* under the direct command of Adnan Al-Mansur. Adnan rode far in front of a thousand horsemen, shirtless, without helmet or armor, screaming, "*Yen 'aal deen ommak*!" He twirled his scimitar in the air as he charged like a demon flying out of hell toward the pike men protecting the wagon train.

The very sight of this madman, who appeared like a nightmare from a legend of the Old Testament, caused the pike-men in his line of ride to tremble.

The pike-men braced themselves as the horsemen closed the distance in what seemed like seconds. Just as the thousand flying horsemen, screaming, "*Allah Ak-Bar*" at full throttle were about to hit the pikes that would rip into and kill their mounts, they turned in unison to the right and to the left. As they turned, they launched a cloud of spears and arrows. Whizzing, whining, razor sharp projectiles fired at point blank range caused dozens of the pike-men to fall in unison as if on cue, leaving wide gaps in the circle of protective steel around the wagon train.

This was the type of warfare the Moors practiced on the hippodrome of the Alhambra daily. These horsemen grew up on the hard pan of the Sahara. From the time they could walk, they learned this type of mounted attack. This time however instead of puncturing an effigy-like figure made of hay on a hippodrome, their weapons struck home against bone and flesh.

The *jinetes* continued to ride up and down the Castilian lines, launching spears and firing arrows with incredible accuracy from the saddle, a highly concentrated rain of death.

Adnan led a wedge formed of several hundred *jinetes* into the breach left by the fallen pike-men, in an attack on the now vulnerable wagon train. The team of horses of two wagons each filled with hundreds of barrels of water panicked and slammed into each other, the cargo tipped over and slammed into the ground, shattered wooden barrels emptying their precious cargo onto the dry earth. The attackers leapt onto the wagons and overcame their drivers. With a harsh whip they galloped the wagons toward the crest and over the hill from whence the attack had come.

Adnan was everywhere, his scimitar striking down upon the heads of the Castilian troops and wagon drivers.

Ibrahim stood up in the stirrups. He leaned forward, silently urging his cavalry on as if he could command them with his very thoughts.

Exsecour, eager for battle pawed at the ground, lurching forward. It took all of Ibrahim's strength to hold him back.

The cavaliers in charge of protecting the wagon train charged in a frantic counter-attack, headlong, toward the *jinetes.* Adnan gave a signal and the *jinetes* turned and rode at a full gallop in apparent retreat toward the hill. More than a score of Templars and Santiago followed, in full pursuit, eager to wreak vengeance upon the pagans who dared attack in the open during full daylight.

The *jinetes* rode hard, closely pursued by the knights, up and over the crest of the hill and the knights followed, and disappeared from Ibrahim's sight.

There was the sound of steel upon steel, men screaming, and horses neighing. Clouds of dust arose from behind the hill. Then silence. Not a sound. Stillness. The quiet that falls upon the land after a violent thunderstorm.

Over the crest of the hill a single horse galloped toward the Castilian lines. The horse was in a panic. It wore a mantle with the crimson cross of a Templar.

The mantle was covered in blood. A pike man grabbed its reins and pulled it to a stop, whispering quiet words of consolation. After the lone horse of the Templar, nothing, not a soul appeared. As if the cavaliers that charged after Adnan's *jinetes* had fallen into a deep, black void and disappeared without a trace.

The attack, so rapid in its execution, lasted no more than the time it takes to peel and eat an orange.

The King was shaken by the sudden furious attack. How easy for the Moors to disrupt his entire army and cause loss. He knew of the sudden swift attacks of the Moors. But to experience the fury and speed of the attack in person . . . He stood up tall in his saddle, projecting only confidence, as he ordered the army, spread out and disorganized, back into a cohesive column. The dead were collected and the march continued.

Ibrahim watched the attack unfold from the safety of a hill far in front of the Castilians. Ibrahim smiled in silent pride for his *jinetes* and for the leadership of his loyal friend Adnan Al-Mansur. It was a brief attack, just a pin-prick against the mighty army, but as it is written, "Even a mosquito can make the lion's eye bleed."

Ibrahim thought to himself, as if he addressed the Spanish King directly, "*That is but a taste of the hell we will bring down upon you! The attack you experienced—imagine the effect on the morale of your troops when it occurs not just once, but three times a day, even at night! You will never know from which direction we will hit you! Before this is done, you will pray to your to your false gods for a swift, merciful death.*"

Osmyn rode up to and alongside Ibrahim and said, "Well done! Your cavalry has never been better!"

Osmyn turned his horse and prepared to part ways. Osmyn was headed toward Moclin to command the Moorish defense on the high ground around the coveted springs, Ibrahim would return to Granada to look to its security, and then ride to aid Osmyn at the most opportune time.

Osmyn, tall in the saddle, a beautiful rider, leaned over, grasped Ibrahim by the shoulder and said, "Ibi! I will see you in Moclin! Do not be late!"
With that, he spurred his horse to a full gallop, trailing a long cloud of dust, his lieutenants riding through the plume, attempting to keep pace with their commander.

Ibrahim rode alone at a moderate speed south towards Granada. Exsecour loped along, enjoying the pace. Thoughts raced through Ibrahim's head, the exact wording of the commands he would give to his commanders, the timing of the coming charge at Moclin, the defense of Granada if it became necessary. He rode for hours without realizing how much time had passed.

Then he saw far ahead, slowly making its way down the face of a mountain on the far side of an arid, dusty valley, what appeared to be a snake. It was miles long, moving down the mountain face, descending into the valley below. A gleaming meandering mass punctuated by earthen colors of green and orange. He stopped momentarily to admire the scene. It was the army of the Kingdom of Granada marching toward Moclin.

Ibrahim shook his head in amazement and thought. *When Osmyn decides to move, by god he moves fast! What organization and efficiency! An entire army massed and moving in such a short amount of time!*

Ibrahim continued on and met the first units of the army of the Kingdom of Granada. These were tall, black Bedouins from the Sudan, fervent believers in the prophet. Some were kinsmen of Osmyn. These men worshipped Osmyn as if he were the prophet himself, full of pride that one of their own, from the far distant deserts of Africa, would rise to command the army of Allah on the Iberian Peninsula.

Each was dressed in similar fashion to Osmyn-white cloak, turban wrapped around their steel helmets. The tip of the helmet pointed up through the white turban the way a bare mountain peak rises above the clouds. They marched in serious silence, in perfect unison and order, under long poles surmounted by green banners.

He passed tan skinned men, natives of Iberia, eager to defend their homeland, dressed in rust-orange cloaks. Long scimitars draped on their sides, circular shields strapped to their backs. Their morale was high and they cheered as Ibrahim rode past. He acknowledged them in turn with a nod and a raised fist.

Some of the units sang songs of praise to Allah as they marched, others marched in silence.

The army reflected the multi-cultured ethnicity of the Kingdom of Granada: blond converts from Europe, *Mozarabs*, Berbers, and Arab archers from the Levant, even Christian militia who would rather fight against their own religion and die. Better to die than be crushed under the rigid rule of a Spanish Monarch and his corrupt minions.

He passed the Jewish militia, their long curls sprouting out from underneath their helmets. The Jewish population of Granada had much to lose if Christendom imposed its rule. They were not only fighting to protect their homes or to defend their faith. They of all peoples had no other choice. The rule of a monarch of Christendom would bring, sooner or later, at least exile or a sure death sentence upon them and their families.

Ibrahim fed on their enthusiasm and strength. His self-doubt and unease began to ebb. To lead these magnificent men! That was the Divine One's purpose for him, to defend this Kingdom to his final breath.

At that moment, as he passed the army in their thousands, his life's purpose came back into focus, clear to him once again. Abran de Aviles, Santiago and even Rebecca began to drift out of his mind like a heavy fog burned off by the heat of the sun.

The men cheered him, thousands of them, raising spear and scimitar aloft in salute. He cheered back, urging them on. He recognized many of the men. He reached down to grasp their upraised hands as they passed. He shouted words of encouragement and commendation.

Before Ibrahim could react, Exsecour broke into a full gallop, head held high, pounding along. The horse reveled in the attention given to his rider.

Ibrahim unsheathed his sword and twirled it above his head, standing up in the stirrups, cheering on the passing battalions of Islamic troops. Exsecour glistened in sweat. Ibrahim became hoarse from his full-throated cheering.

Finally, he found himself alone again, on the road that was churned and broken up by thousands of pairs of marching feet. The terrain began to change as he neared Granada. The dry hard pan of the north gave way to green fields of grass punctuated by knots of poppies, orchards, pine and juniper trees. A squadron of swallows flew over the road performing their unique aerial maneuvers, while up high in the air a golden eagle scanned the land below.

The snow-capped Sierra Nevada came into view, keeping watch over the Vega and the city of Granada. Ibrahim could feel the cool, pine-scented air again, drifting over the orchards. He took a deep, cleansing breath as he sighted far in the distance, gleaming in the falling sunlight, the Alhambra, its Red Castle towering above the white walls of Granada like a lighthouse, calling a sailor home to safety from a stormy sea.

Ibrahim entered the Alhambra to the welcoming cheers of the soldiers that guarded the wall. He had returned home. The only true home he had ever known.

Chapter 21

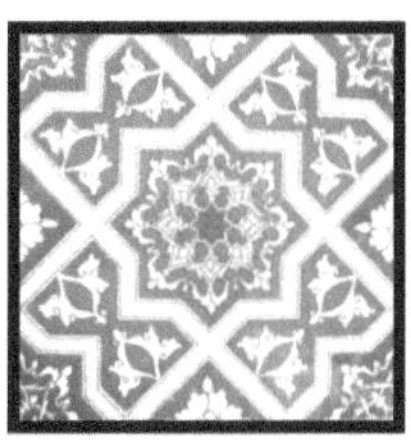

The Tutelary

"You shall serve not serve any but Allah and you shall do good to your parents, and to the orphans, and the needy . . ."

Ibrahim found himself, once again, sitting on the little wooden stool in front of the still captive, Santiago de Aviles. The two men looked at each other for a long moment, taking measure, in silence.

Santiago's steely green stare sliced through Ibrahim. The intensity of his eyes never diminished. Ibrahim thought that if Santiago spoke of a subject as mundane and docile as tending to a rose bush, it would seem to his listener that he was preparing to ride to war.

Santiago broke the silence with the words, "Have you seen, Ibrahim, how a cow reacts when it sees its fellows slaughtered? Have you noted the look of panic in the beast's eyes because it knows it is next to die? It bellows and stamps and tries to escape, to no avail. Its doom approaches. I pity the poor animal, for its simple desire is only to live, the same desire of all living things, a blade of grass. When I slaughter an animal, I ensure that it dies quickly and without pain. I do not prolong the beast's agony. Yet, here you have me locked away, my fate is sealed, and you will not grant me the mercy that is given to a poor unreasoning animal. It is a most exquisite torture."

Ibrahim did not respond to Santiago's statement. Instead he asked, "Were you and Abran always close as brothers?"

Santiago looked perplexed. He was quiet, then finally answered, "Not when we were young, but as the years passed, yes, we became close friends."

Ibrahim continued, "Tell me about that, and tell me more about your Abran."

Santiago ventured a suspicious, "Why do you, of all people want to know?"

"I want to know how a man like Abran evokes such loyalty that others would willingly die for him."

Santiago did not respond for a long minute. Only the faint, faraway sounds of fountains interrupted the silence in the dungeon. Eventually, Ibrahim got up to leave, then Santiago began, "My parents always favored Abran. He was the first born, smarter and stronger than I. He was born with a kind disposition that drew people to him. Even at a young age his strength of character shone through. And he always won!"

Santiago laughed out loud, remembering, "That bastard! I could never beat him at anything! Even in games of chance. Chance always favored him. Never me!" He laughed, then winced and put his hand to the long scarlet scar that ran from his eye to his chin.

Santiago continued:

"I was jealous of Abran, jealous of the attention he received from my parents and from everyone in our village. I became aggressive with him and my parents as well. I picked fights with Abran for no good reason. He whipped me every time. I bested many others though, in spite of my short stature. I became known in the region for my short temper and eagerness to court trouble.

When I was seventeen, my parents ordered me to leave. They were exasperated with me and the reproach that I heaped upon my family's good name. I spent the next few years on the road, earning a meager living as a hired sword hand. I was nothing more than a thug, paid to assist other thugs to collect payments on overdue loans. Eventually, I found myself in Asturica in the employ of the local Bishop, a fat mound of a man, who fancied himself a warlord with his very own private army.

This "army" was nothing more than a collection of the flotsam and jetsam of humanity like myself, none us worth a damn. I spent the next several years fighting for wages against other warlords, or bullying the locals, in a constant state of drunkenness. People feared me and at seventeen years of age I drank that up as if it were a magic tonic. It felt good to see people, fully grown men, cower before me. Mine was a life devoid of any meaning. The kind of life that I thought I wanted. Then, my life changed unexpectedly. One day that fat barrel of lard ordered me to perform a task, an unspeakable assignment that changed me forever."

Santiago paused, the hard memory difficult for him to express.

Ibrahim said, "Please continue. I want to know."

"There was a pretty young girl who lived in the mud huts that surrounded the fat man's palatial residence. The girl's parents died a quick death at the hands of highwaymen on the outskirts of the Bishop's pitiful kingdom. She had no other siblings or family to speak of. The Bishop commanded me to "go get her," and bring her to his chambers. Without hesitation, without contemplating my master's evil intentions, I strapped on my sword and went down the hill to the shanty to fulfill the Bishop's wish. I remember kicking in the door of the hut, sword in hand, as if I were to fight a gang of men. The little girl, no more than ten years old, was sitting on the cold dirt floor in the middle of the hut. She was disheveled and dirty, clothed in a torn light-blue dress. She looked up at me with wide dark eyes. Her long black eyelashes fluttered in surprise. But there was no fear in her eyes at the sight of an intruder with a sword barging into her home. She did not cry out.

She did not shudder in terror. No, in her eyes was a look of resignation. Of defeat.

She knew that with her parents dead, she had no control over her fate. No doubt her parents were dispatched by the Bishop so he could have her without any interference. I could tell, in that defeated look that she lost hope and knew no one would come to her aid. She knew that she had no advocate, no protector, that she was helpless. I could see all of this in her eyes! She was sure that even the Lord himself forsaken her. Left her to be thrown to the wolves like a dying, diseased animal. I have never seen such hopelessness.

I remember looking at the upraised sword in my hand, then at the sad girl, then at the pitiful mud-walled hut that was once a home to this poor family. For the first time in my life through my drunken haze, I realized what it was to feel shame, true disgust. Revulsion. What tool of evil did I allow myself to become? Not even an animal preys upon the defenseless for a perverted motive.

Is there any act that a human being can commit viler than taking advantage of an orphan girl?"

Ibrahim, completely engrossed in the tale, leapt off the stool as he blurted out an answer to the rhetorical question, "NO! There is no fit punishment devised by god or man that is sufficient for such wickedness!"

Santiago said:

"I agree. I would have none of it. I stood there for a good long while, my head hung down in shame and nausea, that was, for once, not a side effect of the wine. I had a sudden urge to fall upon my sword and end the sickness I felt twisting in my gut.

I approached the girl. She shrank back before me. I sheathed my sword and told her I was here to help, not harm her. I bent down and handed the girl a fistful of gold coins. I told her how to reach the village where my parents dwelled, to tell them that Santiago sent her. I was unsure the girl understood my instructions, or that she would survive a journey to my village, many days travel from that place.

The girl leapt up and wrapped her tiny arms around my neck. She did not say a word as tears filled her eyes, but in those eyes I saw a glimmer of hope.

In that instant I felt something that I never felt before. As I held that tiny soul, stroking her back, delivering silent comfort, I could feel the sharp ends of the bones of her spine protruding through her shabby, torn dress, I discovered what it was to be a *protector*. A tutelary. It was a pleasant and new emotion that welled up inside of me. For the first time in my life, instead of acting as aggressor, the bully, the taker of life, I was the protector of it.

The girl left the hut, and I crumpled down in the dirt for what seemed like hours, pondering and praying. This was my first conversation with my Heavenly Father for many, many years.

I told the Lord that if he did indeed exist and was truly a God of love, that he would use just the smallest sliver of his power to ensure that the innocent girl arrived safely to the village where my family resides. If he saved her, I would devote my life to a worthy cause. I became fully sober for the first time in years.

I was in a trance-like state, and only vaguely remember the thud of the door of the hut being thrown open and the sharp pain of something striking my head. Then all went black.

When I awoke, I discovered that the Bishop chained me in a filthy cell in his dungeon. That crap hole was not like this cell I am in now. It was a *real* dungeon, a foul smelling, black place of torture and misery.
My head throbbed from the club strike. The blow was administered by one of the two powerful men that the Bishop employed as his personal bodyguard. They were Norsemen; broad as doorways and a head taller than any tall man I have ever met. They were the fiercest warriors I ever encountered. I saw them in action on behalf of the Bishop. During battle they worked themselves into a demonic frenzy, so wild and animalistic that many times our enemies would not fight, but panic and flee.

As my blurred vision cleared, I realized a man was standing on the other side of the bars of my cell.

I thought at first it was one of the Norsemen. But instead of the blond hair, I saw a shock of red, neatly combed and pulled back. I saw bright green eyes and a ruddy colored beard. My visitor wore a long thick velvet green cloak clasped at the neck with a golden broach in the shape of a lyre. He stood, feet apart, hands on his hips, looking down at me with the expression of a firm but kind schoolmaster. He spoke kindly and it sounded to my ringing ears as if an angel had come down out of heaven to console me. "Brother, can you hear me?"

I could not help but respond irreverently. "I almost forgot how ugly you are!"

Abran laughed as he reached out and clutched the bars of my cell. "HA! It appears your talent of irritating people extends far beyond our family and village!"

Ibrahim interrupted Santiago and said in a playful tone, "Abran was right about you! You have a rare talent for making both Christians and Moors angry!"

Santiago grinned, then continued with his story:

"Behind Abran, the two Norsemen entered the dungeon and glared down at me. They were behind Abran and towered over him. I felt the urge to warn Abran to be careful and whispered softly in Spanish, for I knew that the two wild men from the North did not understand the language. "*Ten cuidado con las montanas detras de ti.*"

Abran did not respond to my warning, did not change his expression or his posture. He seemed at ease, but I could sense he was on his guard.

The Bishop entered the dungeon. I could hear his heavy, plodding steps as he came into view, his round frame outlined in the torchlight of the dimly lit dungeon hall. He was clutching greedily in his pudgy, sausage-like fingers a purple velvet bag.

The Bishop grunted. He gestured towards me and said in his raspy, vile voice, "A touching reunion to be sure. I am deeply moved, but this piece of trash has cost me dearly!"

Abran did not turn his head to acknowledge the Bishop. Still keeping his eyes on me, he responded with force, "You have your money. You have been more than compensated for any loss caused by Santiago."

I objected, and told Abran, "You should not have wasted your money. My life is not worth the price of a sparrow."

Abran responded, warmth in his voice, quoting the Christ. "Not a sparrow falls to earth unnoticed by our loving Creator. How much more are you worth? The very hairs of your head are numbered."

The Bishop leaned on the slime-covered wall of the dungeon, tired from the exertion of walking down the hall to my cell. He spoke as a man accustomed to having his every desire fulfilled without question, however wicked that desire may be.

"I believe it is the Lord's will that this man be executed to atone for his sinful ways. Perhaps the Lord will be kind and allow his soul eternal rest. It would be a merciful thing for us to extend such a kindness to him."

Abran responded, "I ask you, good Bishop, to honor our contract. You have your gold. I will take my brother, and we will be on our way."

The Bishop grunted, "Oh! Do not you worry! I will keep this gold. It belongs to me!" He pursed his bloated, cratered lips and sounded a quick, sharp whistle. I heard that signal many times in the past. It was his order to strike. I was about to call out a warning to Abran, but it was not necessary.

Abran did the most peculiar thing. Instead of unsheathing his sword to fight off the two Norsemen who stood guard behind him, his hand shot up to the lyre-shaped broach that held his cloak in place. The broach burst open, releasing the cloak. He twirled, fast as a cyclone, and the cloak flew off his shoulders and shot into the air towards the Norsemen as they raised their battle axes.

It is human instinct to dodge any rapidly approaching object, even one as harmless as a large piece of colored cloth. The Norsemen, fearless as they were, did what was natural. They ducked. I watched as Abran pierced the flying cloak from behind. The razor-sharpened piece of flat steel reflected the glow of the torchlight on its polished surface as it

> struck one of the Norsemen square in the chest as he tried to duck below the cloak.
>
> I watched Abran drive the blade home, without seeing the target but sensing where the man was on the other side of the flying cloak. Abran's timing was flawless, his blade burst through the cloak, deep into the Norseman's heart. He withdrew his blade, spun and in the same motion plunged it into the abdomen of the second Norsemen as the man slapped the cloak down with his battle-axe, in a vain attempt to remove the obstruction of his view. The cloak fell harmlessly to the floor."

Ibrahim impressed, interjected, "A brilliant tactic! Though outnumbered, he achieved victory by deception. He out-thought them!"

Santiago agreed, "Like I said. He ALWAYS won!" Santiago continued:

> "The Bishop's bodyguards lay motionless at Abran's feet. Abran said casually as if he were offering advice to the two dead Norsemen.
>
> "Too big. Too slow."
>
> The Bishop turned to run but tripped over his feet, falling to the floor, the velvet bag of gold spilling in the process. Abran was on him in and instant. He raised the Bishop to his feet, and with one of his powerful hands clutched his fleshly neck, his fingers disap-

pearing into the mass of fat as he lifted the Bishop and slammed him into the wall.

That terrified piece of garbage wrapped in human skin wet himself. His arrogance evaporated in an instant. Abran put his face close to him and muttered, "I took a vow never to strike down an unarmed man."

The Bishop seemed to relax. He struggled to speak, as Abran's clamp on his neck was strong.

He squeaked, "Yes! It would not be wise to harm a man of God. It is written that the Lord will take vengeance. Yes! I will honor our contract. Take your brother and go."

Abran growled, "Good. I will take my brother. I will take the gold."

At that, Abran thrust his sword deep into the fat man's belly, so deep that the fat crept out and covered the very hilt of his sword. The Bishop gasped in surprise and pain, as Abran declared, "And I will take one more thing, your life!"

Then Abran said to the dying man, "It would be an affront against the Just One himself if I were to allow so vile a being to continue to exist and exploit others to satisfy his vile desires. Your day of reckoning has arrived. 'If you oppress those below you, you will not be safe from the punishment of the one who is above you.'

The Bishop's round body went limp. Abran released his grip and pulled out his sword as the body slunk to the floor. Abran looked down and said simply, in a disgusted tone, "A man of God should know better."

Abran acted quickly. He grabbed the ring of keys that hung from the Bishop's waist and flung my cell open. He was not breathing heavily, not perspiring, he was calm, as if he had just awoken from a nap. The exertion of the quick fight did not tax him in the least. He embraced me, smiled and said, "That little girl, the one you saved, she is safe and under our family's care."

I could not speak. My body went limp and I began to sob uncontrollably, my entire body pulsing and shuddering, cleansing itself, renewing itself. Abran held me for a long time, there in the cell, as I wept."

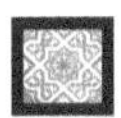

"We rode together, once again, as brothers united. We returned to the land where I was born. My home was a village that was gifted to my legendary ancestor in recognition of his deeds while serving as a legionnaire under the command of the first and greatest Caesar."

Ibrahim, surprised, asked, "Your family was Roman? You are of Roman descent?"

"Yes! Well not exactly. I will tell you how my family came to Spain some other time." Santiago repeated, "Some other time . . . huh."

Santiago shook his head and said. "That is if I have any time left."

Neither man spoke as they pondered Santiago's fate.

Ibrahim massaged his aching leg. The more Santiago spoke, the more his leg hurt.

At the same instant, Santiago rubbed his cheek. They looked at each other and paused. Both men attempting to relieve wounds.

Santiago smiled, the irony not lost on him, then said:

> "Abran gave me a fine green velvet cloak like the one that he used to defeat the Norsemen. He gave me the purple velvet bag full of gold coins. This was my re-purchase price. On the road he spent many hours telling me of the comings and goings of our family and of others who lived in our village, names of people that I once knew, that I had not heard for many years. It was pleasing to hear about our relatives, childhood playmates, or the old schoolmaster. It was as if I was reacquainted with old friends, long gone. Abran did not scold me, did not preach to me about my many sins and how I wasted my life and in the process brought reproach upon our family's excellent name. It was not his way, to remind men of their faults and sins, to make men feel guilty for their wayward course.
>
> Abran told me about the girl in the torn blue dress, how she arrived, miraculously, in the dead of night to the village, unharmed.

She followed my instructions to the letter. Abran thought it something of a miracle that the girl arrived at all. Then he told me something unexpected, something that caught me completely by surprise. At first I thought he was joking with me when he stated, "Santiago! You have inspired me! Thanks to you, I am going to begin a project when we return to the village. It is all because of you! Well done!"

Inspired? How could I possibly inspire my noble older brother by my mean works? Cautiously I inquired as to the meaning of his words. I prepared for a response of biting sarcasm or rebuke.

"That defenseless orphan girl you saved, Santiago. How many more are there like her in this world? The small ones, innocent, without an advocate, without a defender, easy prey for walking excrement like your dear Bishop. Our family has the means to help them, to aid them. I have decided that I will use our money to house, protect and educate these little ones. We will open a home for them, a place where they will be secure. I have pledged my sword to protect and defend them, until the death, and I intend to keep that pledge, come what may."

We rode on in silence. I did not know what to say. We reached a rise in the road. At the top of the rise was a crossroads. One road led east toward the lofty Pyrenees and the land of the Franks. One led south, toward Castile and Madrid. Another ran south and east toward Navarre and beyond to the coast, ending at the port of the city of the Barcas. Still another led due west toward Portugal. At the top of the rise, I could see to the north, the view of our home village and the fertile valley where it rested peacefully. Abran slowed his mount and turned toward me. He said simply, "This is where I leave you, my brother."

Reaching out he clasped my arm and said to me these words. I will never forget those words. They are indelibly printed forever upon my mind, "I grant you life. Do with it what you will. My prayer is that henceforth you will use it wisely, so that one day, when you go the way of all mankind, men will say they were the better for knowing you."

With that he spurred his horse to a gallop and rode off, down the rise, toward the village, eager to start upon his mission. I sat there for hours, looking down each road, pondering my life's course and the strange turn of events that lead me to that spot. The bag of gold coins was sufficient to start a new life somewhere, but where?

I thought about riding to the coast, to the city of the Barcas, paying passage for a ship heading anywhere, it did not matter, perhaps to the Crusader Kingdoms where my sword could be put to good use.

But of all the roads before me, there was only one that I could choose. One that I *must* choose. That road had already been chosen for me, undeservedly so, for some unknown reason, perhaps by the Sovereign himself.

My brother's words were running circles in my mind as I spurred my horse and headed down the rise, toward the village where I was born, where I resolved to live the rest of my days, a life with purpose, my sword used in the defense of the defenseless."

Ibrahim said softly, "Yes. A worthy life indeed. A worthy cause. How long ago was that?"

"It's been twelve years since I stood at the crossroads. The years hence were spent in operating the orphanage. We received much assistance. Our village rallied around our noble venture, and made it their own cause. The orphanage became the pride of the region, more beloved than any grey, gargoyle-adorned church. There was never a lack of help, materially, physically and spiritually to care for the children. The villagers began to informally call the home "*El Refugio*," and the name stuck.

A kindly older nun, Sister Elaine, a principled and wise woman, heard about our home and offered to take care of the day-to-day operations and teach classes. Through her guidance we taught the children language, history, mathematics, and skills to help them later in life, like agriculture and smithing.

Abran and I became skilled at seeking out the newly orphaned or rescuing children from enslavement to cruel masters, many

> times at sword point. We had many, many adventures. Many wicked people became our sworn enemies; many more good people became friends and allies.
>
> We became adept at finding distant relatives or people of good will to care for the children. The child whom I met in the hut, who was the inspiration for all that we accomplished, was placed with distant relatives, a good Christian family of means, who cared for her as if she were a princess of the royal family of Castile. I think about that girl every day, how I saved her life. In reality, she saved mine, in every possible way a soul can be saved."

Santiago sighed, tears filling his eyes. Ibrahim realized Santiago had nothing more to say. Ibrahim sat stoically, but his eyes too, glistened and he did not attempt to wipe away the tears that rolled down his cheek. He cared not if he looked vulnerable.

Without another word Ibrahim stood up, turned and limped slowly down the hall past the ever-present Yusuf, up the winding staircase that led to the Alhambra above. His head bowed low as if he were retreating in defeat from a crushing loss on the field of battle.

Chapter 22

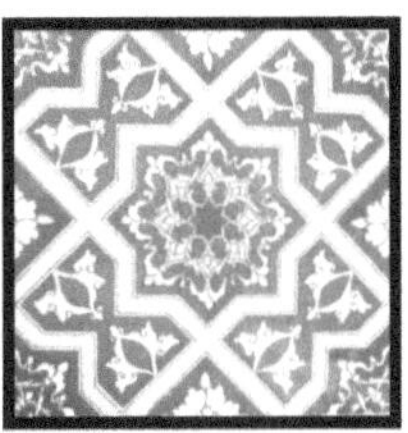

The Sword is Sheathed

"Yea, everything is vain,
except GOD alone,
and every pleasant thing
must one day vanish away!"

Ibrahim returned to his quarters. The hour was late. He stood on his balcony until dawn, gazing out upon the tiled rooftops of Granada. A chill night breeze whipped his hair, and cloak lifting it over his head, whipping his hair in all directions slapping at his face and even into his eyes. He was deep in meditative thought and prayer.

He spoke with Allah that in the soft moonlight, the way one speaks with an old friend about his deepest thoughts and fears. He prayed, using the personal name of God, in order to address the Father as a friend. His mother Anna taught him in the Bible that God did indeed have a personal name that one should use when addressing him in prayer.

He alternately praised the Divine One, asked for forgiveness, questioned him angrily and, ultimately, decided what his course must be. Like Santiago at the crossroads above the village, there was a road he now must take. It was clear to him. His life had to change.

He opened his palm, the wooden string of beads spilling out over his fingers. He brought them up to his lips, and softly kissed them.

He said in a whisper. "You are avenged. I can do nothing more."

He held the beads to his lips for a long moment, then said, "I will live the life that you raised me to live, and I pray that I will finally make you proud."

Ibrahim returned to his room. Skilled carpenters of the Alhambra replaced the pegs that he ripped out of the wall in his rush to grab his scimitar the night he fought Santiago. An entire section of sandstone was removed and a new piece set into place, along with stronger iron pegs to hold his weapon horizontally. The new sandstone's color was slightly different from its neighbors. It was smoother, lighter in color without a blemish, cleaner. Ibrahim slowly, reverently, lifted his sword and placed it up on the pegs.

He stared at the scimitar, the weapon used to end the lives of countless men, now in its permanent resting place. He held onto each end, one hand on the hilt, the other, lightly holding the sharpened tip of the scimitar, hesitant to let go.

The smooth steel surface reflected the candlelight and even the rays of the moon that filtered into the quarters. The scimitar appeared soft and gentle, as if it was rendered harmless by the curing light of the moon.

Ibrahim saw the faces of men reflected in its surface, hundreds of men he had slain upon countless battlefields over many years. He saw the faces of the three knights who tried to strike him down when he was pinned under his horse and rescued by Adnan Al-Mansur.

The faces drifted across the surface of the scimitar, as clouds pass across the moon. One after another the faces appeared. His memory opened up and remembered, each one. He saw faces twisted in pain, flaring in rage, or bearing the pitiful expression of terror and panic.

One face though, was constant. It filled the entire surface, in the background, as the others passed along. Steel-green eyes that penetrated into Ibrahim's marrow. They glared without a hint of fear or hatred. Resolute, determined, and honorable. The other faces would fade one day from his memory, but this one would stay with him forever, until death, perhaps even beyond, haunting his dreams as eternal punishment. He was full of regret as he peered back at the gaze that burned him like a hot iron brand.

He had spilled too much blood! He could never live in perfect peace. But he would try, and thereby honor the life of that honorable man whom he had slain.

Finally, after much hesitation, as if saying goodbye to an old friend, he let loose his grip on the scimitar. He unstrapped the gladius and set it upon its pegs on the wall. Finally he removed the small curved dagger that he kept strapped to his calf at all times, even during slumber, for ready use in case his two primary weapons were not accessible to him in the midst of battle.

Then he stepped back and looked at where his weapons were mounted peacefully on the wall. He took a deep breath and exhaled forcibly, at last relieved of his burden. Then, impulsively, Ibrahim ran out of the room. There was somewhere he must go. Something he must do.

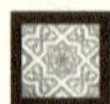

He was at Rebecca's door. He stood there, doing nothing for a long time. Hand balled into a fist, inches away from the door. Eyes closed. Gathering courage. He knocked hard. She opened. His heart leaped at the sight of her.

He told her. "I dwell in the very gardens of heaven, yet I've never seen anything as beautiful."

He grabbed her, pulled her close, almost suffocating. A ferocious kiss. Ibrahim wrapped his arms around her waist. The kiss grew in intensity as Rebecca bent backwards, forming a lovely arch, accepting him. Indeed she had dreamed of this since their first tender kiss in the courtyard.

Her hand rubbed the back of his head, kneading his hair. She wrapped her leg around the small of his back.

Ibrahim inhaled, catching his breath, drinking in her smell. Scent of wildflowers.

The world disappeared. Only the two of them existed. Nothing else mattered in that moment. Nothing else had meaning.

Ibrahim slid the straps of her dress off her shoulders as he pushed her out of the doorway into the privacy of the courtyard. He gasped.

"Is anyone here?"

"No. We are alone.

"Praise be to God."

He lifted her off her feet. Powerful hands. Kissed her again. A deep, soulful connection. He carried her across the courtyard. They disappeared into a darkened doorway and out of view.

Chapter 23

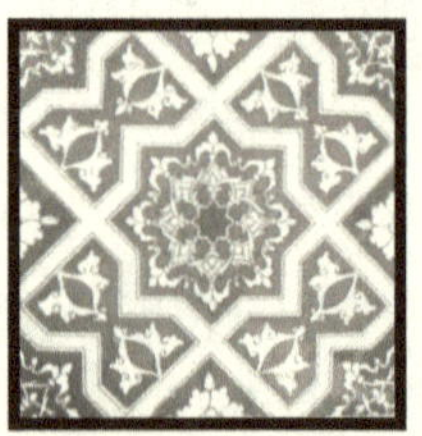

Only I Will Conquer

"An army of sheep led by a lion would defeat an army of lions led by a sheep."

The sun made its presence known across the Kingdom of Granada, unseen but slowly lighting the sky to the east.

The air was stale, the cool breeze of the night before a distant memory. It promised to be a hot still day as the desert of North Africa exerted its dominance over Southern Spain. High above, a brown haze dimmed the rising sun. The hard smell of the desert foretold the coming heat. The stillness of the air caused even the myriads of birds that normally dominate the sky above Granada to sit still in their nests silently, as if afraid to venture out into the unfamiliar atmosphere that surrounded them. Above the Sierra Nevada a few slight puffs of clouds were rapidly forming, gaining shape and purpose.

Many miles away from Granada, Adnan crept slowly forward upon his thick forearms toward the hillock that overlooked the camp of the sleeping enemy. On either side of him were thousands of his fellow soldiers, many belonging to his own light cavalry. Thousands more had been loaned to him by Osmyn, who approved of the bold plan.

It was Adnan who suggested that they take advantage of the sleeping Castilians and open the battle with a surprise attack at sunrise. The confusion and alarm the attack would cause in the Castilian camp would allow Osmyn to sally forth from the protection of the fortifications into a headlong charge down the slope with every man available. He would sweep the Spaniards from the field within the hour. Ibrahim's mighty heavy cavalry would not be needed to apply the final blow to the enemy army.

They spent most of the night crouched on all fours, staying low, stalking their prey like silent wolves. None wore armor and carried only *one* sword or spear. There would be no accidental pinging of metal to alert their unsuspecting enemies.

They covered their spear points and scimitars with red ochre to dim the shiny sharp metal with dark reddish dye.

Adnan Al-Mansur went one step further. He slathered himself in a thick coat of the red ochre from bald head to stumpy toe, showing only the whites of his eyes. He chose to wear a simple loincloth as his battle uniform. He intended to instill terror into any enemy soldiers that came across his path. He would appear like some unholy demon newly raised from the underworld bent on the destruction of humanity.

He would play that part well.

His light horses, the *jinetes*, fast upon their small desert mounts hit the Castilian army again and again always at unexpected times from unexpected directions. The King of Spain was forced to move the entire baggage train and its vital water reserves to the center of the marching column, protected by mounted men-at-arms and pikemen several rows deep, thereby slowing the speed of his march.

Adnan's raids left hundreds of their number, including dozens of knights of note, dead upon the hard ground. He relished the fact that the Castilians granted him a nickname in the aftermath of his hit and run strikes upon their column. They anointed him, "*El Calvo de La Muerte*," or the Bald Death.

The Castilians and their allies spent this night in unrestrained revelry. It was one of those countless Christian holy days, which to the Muslims were nothing more than blasphemy. Another excuse for the infidel to lose their minds with drink and carry on shamelessly.

Because of their revelry Adnan knew they would be slow to wake, slow to take up the sword. He would punish them for their negligence.

The Castilians advanced towards Moclin exactly as the captains of the Kingdom of Granada had foreseen. But when the King of Spain was within sight of the town and the vital life-giving springs that bubbled forth from the dusty ground, the view of the springs was obscured by a forest. Not of trees, but a forest of flags, pinions and pennants in colors of apricot and green, white and orange, peach and yellow, protected by a circumvallation of pointed stakes, trenches, and sharpened wooden and iron spikes driven into the ground that would penetrate any foot or hoof that lighted upon them.

The Moors were dug in deep around the springs.

The Castilians set up their camp on the plain, within full view of the Moors, below the town and springs.

The left flank to the east of the Castilian camp was protected by the chain of low brown hills that Adnan and his thousands were slowly skulking up behind, sight unseen.

The Castilians seemed unsure of their next movement. They could see from their camp on the flat plain that the fortifications constructed by the Moors were formidable. They were populated with thousands of troops of high morale, placed there to defend their homeland, families and faith. Still, the Castilians needed those springs for their very survival. They must have water. All day long, the Castilians heard a constant thrumming from the Moors' camp. The sounds of a thousand kettledrums, the unceasing rumble of doom.

Osmyn, observing from the springs, did not intend to grant the Castilians time to mull over their plans. He would engage the enemy and destroy them on the plains before the town.

Adnan finally reached the crown of one of the round hills. He motioned for the mass behind him to be still. The thousands of eager soldiers stopped crawling and lay flat, motionless upon the ground.

In the increasing light it was possible to make out only the tops of the tents of the Lords of Castile. Adnan honed in on the largest of the tents. Above it flew the battle flag of the King of Spain. That tent was his objective. Adnan would strike down the enemy king in the initial attack, and take the heart of the enemy.

Adnan heard Spanish being softly spoken by sentries below the crest of the hill. He could smell the newly-stoked cook fires, preparing roasted meat for the morning breakfast.

Adnan slowly stood upright. He motioned for the rest of the men to stand and ready their weapons. Behind him and alongside, thousands of dark figures rose to their full height.

Adnan yearned to scream a bloody war cry and charge down the hill at full speed, but he must restrain himself so as not to alarm the Castilians. He started at a trot, then broke into a sprint. He swung the scimitar above his head as a signal to the rest of his men. Now was the moment to bring the quiet rush of death upon an unsuspecting sleeping enemy.

The tide of dark figures broke upon the camp of the Castilians. As Adnan ran toward the pavilion of the King of Spain, his men split off in all directions. Spread out before them were mounds upon the ground. Sleeping soldiers. The Moors thrust spear and sword into these mounds. The only sound was the thrusting of metal weapons into the defenseless enemy. The swooshing sound was repeated thousands of times in the half minute it took Adnan to reach the King's tent.

Adnan raised his scimitar and brought it down, ripping a huge gash in the fabric. He leapt into the void, followed by dozens of his men.

Adnan slashed at the nearest man, in full armor, with all of his might. A high-pitched clanging sound was followed by a thud as the full set of armor hit the ground.

The armor was empty.

Adnan ran through the tent frantically slashing at curtains to attack any unseen enemy hidden in ambush.

The Moors met in the middle of the empty grand tent, practically bumping into each other. The inspection of the King's quarters was complete. One of the soldiers shrugged his shoulders as if to ask in confusion, "What is going on here?"

Adnan walked out of the great tent. In the light of the morning sun he saw that the mounds his men ran through with sword and spear were nothing more than clumps of straw in the form of sleeping men.

Adnan heard the faint sound of galloping horses in the distance as the few hundred remaining Spanish soldiers took to flight. They were left behind to demonstrate and make the Moors believe that tens of thousands were camped here.

Adnan kicked at one of the mounds in frustration, sending a spray of straw high into the air. Enraged, he cursed, "*Yen 'aal deen ommak*!"

His rage soon gave way to a feeling of helplessness. Granada would face the hordes of Castile practically alone. Ibrahim was there with the two thousand heavy cavalry, but against such a multitude . . .

Adnan's head slumped as he thought about his good friend, truly his only friend, the man whom he considered closer than a brother, fighting against impossible odds. He saw his friend dying before the gates of Granada, surrounded by dozens of Military Monks.

Adnan would get his horsemen moving right away, of course. A furious rush to save Granada. But would they arrive in time to save the city and the Lord's kingdom on earth?

Adnan looked up the valley to the fortifications of Moclin. Osmyn was already moving his troops with haste to leave Moclin for the defense of Granada. Osmyn stood on top of the highest of the fortifications just above the springs. His robe flowed in the hot morning breeze. His arms were moving up and down frantically as he barked hurried orders to his army. He looked to Adnan like a conductor directing an orchestra of tens of thousands.

In response, battle flags were moving out of the fortifications as Osmyn rushed his troops out of Moclin in order to save the Kingdom of Granada.

Adnan thought, *If we move quickly we may be able to blunt the Castilians before it is too late. Or perhaps the King of*

Spain will not move as quickly as he should and we will get to Granada before him . . .

Adnan knew this was wishful thinking. This King would not make a mistake. Others might, but not this one. The King would not pause or delay, would not allow the Muslims an opportunity to save Granada.

Adnan whispered to Ibrahim Al-Rahim as if he was saying farewell. "I am sorry, my friend, I have betrayed you, I will not be there to save you this time."

One of Adnan's lieutenants, who was also his first cousin Andraos, ran up to him and said excitedly, "My Lord Mansur! Look! Look at the battle flag of the King of Castile!"

Adnan looked up at the battle flag atop the tent that was so recently vacated by the King of Spain. The flag was the King's banner, a field of yellow surmounted by the blood-red lion standing upon its hind legs and thrashing the air with its front paws.

But this flag was unlike the other battle flags of the King of Castile. There was something written across the face of this particular flag. It was penned in the same style of arabesque filigree that covered the columns, walls and ceiling of the Alhambra. In flawless Arabic, the writing so precise, it looked as though it was lifted from one of the columns of the Alhambra itself and placed neatly upon its face.

The writing that covered the Alhambra extolled the virtues of Allah and often declared, "Only God will conquer." Throughout the Islamic world, the battle flags bore the same words written in bold gold arabesque: "Only God will conquer." And now this flag of the infidel King of Spain proclaimed, "*ONLY I WILL CONQUER.*"

Andraos gasped in horror. "My Lord! The blasphemy! He mocks us and he mocks Allah!"

Adnan sighed. "Yes, Cousin. The King of Castile mocks our God and us. Worse, that flag was made not yesterday or last night but many months ago while he was preparing for the invasion and *Reconquista* of the Kingdom of Granada."

Adnan rubbed his bald head, unintentionally covering his hand in red ochre, as he pondered the strategy of the King of Castile. He said, "You see Cousin, we have been played for fools! This is his game. He has been toying with us all along. He anticipated our grand plans months ago. He has been in complete control of the situation from the moment he crossed our borders with his army."

Adnan pointed to the flag, flapping in the wind, mocking them, and said, "We have been arrogant, stupid, boastful and overconfident."

Adnan quoted the wise man, "Had the monkey seen its ass, it wouldn't have danced! Now Andraos, take that thing down and burn it. Do it quickly before the men see what is written upon it and lose heart."

Ibrahim felt happy. A sensation he had not felt for many years. He was yet unaware of the deception of the King of Spain and the mortal danger to the Alhambra.

Instead, he was in the market. From the cobblestone street he could clearly see the graying crown of Maria de Alicante's head bobbing up and down as she moved about her pomegranate stall. He watched her for a long time. He felt a twinge of envy as he observed her go about her simple daily duty. She was a straightforward woman. Her life was simple and uncomplicated. Not because she was a simpleton, no not at all, it was because she had CHOSEN to live a simple, uncluttered life. Her days were not weighed down by the demands and guilt of organized religion, or the expectations and opinions of others. Still, he mused, she was a woman of profound faith, in her own style. She certainly believed in Issa, the God of the Christians and their book, but she discovered her own path, her own way of worship.

In fact, at that moment she was handing over several large pomegranates to one of the local beggars, a mute who could only communicate with grunts and crude hand gestures. She did this sort of thing often. He knew it was an important part of her faith and that she truly believed the words of the proverb, "Whoever is generous to the poor lends to the lord, and he will repay him for his deed."

She was, he realized, of all people that he knew, rich or poor, Muslim or Christian, the freest and most unfettered of all. He needed to speak with her, needed her wisdom at this moment. He approached her stand. She looked up at him. He grinned for once, and nodded respectfully to her. She did not respond. Was she teasing again? Ibrahim said playfully, "You have a customer, Doña Maria!"

Still she refused to respond. Instead, she kept herself busy arranging her pomegranates into a neat pyramidal stack. She would not look up. Finally she spoke, sadness in her voice. "Did you have to kill him? He was an old man."

Her words caught Ibrahim off guard.

"Of whom do you refer, Maria?" he asked.

Maria finally looked up and glared at him accusingly. "You know! I did not like him much either, always blathering on about the end of the world and God's wrath. He was bombastic, arrogant and annoying, but he was also a frail old man."

Her voice rose in anger as she pounded a closed fist into her palm. "AN OLD MAN! My god, Ibrahim! It is not fair. He was defenseless! How could you do such a thing?"

Ibrahim stunned, shook his head vigorously and cried, "MARIA! What are you talking about?"

She cried even louder than he, her gravelly voice carrying across the market. People stopped to stare at the confrontation.

"The old priest James! People have always told me about terrible things that you have done on the battlefield, but I did not believe them! I defended you! I told them that you are a good man, not capable of such evil! I was wrong!"

Ibrahim leaned toward her, over the pomegranates, knocking several of them to the ground in his effort to defend himself against her accusation. "I did not harm that man!"

Maria ignored his protest. She continued, "They say he was killed at his table, murdered the night before I saw you and your friends heading out on your jaunt to the countryside. They say he was killed silently by one who is an expert with a sword. The men who know of such things say there is only one man in Granada with the skill to kill with such stealth and precision, unseen. I know his procession with the cross was an embarrassment to you and the Sultan and against your laws, but you did not have to kill him like a coward while he slept in his bed! What is next? Will you kill Rebecca too?"

At the mention of Rebecca, Ibrahim felt his face grow hot. He said. "Maria, I swear to you, I did not touch him! I did not know that he was dead until this very moment!"

He held up his hands to her, imploring.

Maria was unyielding. She shook her head sadly. "It is said that someone wearing a grey cloak was seen sneaking out of James cave. A grey cloak just like yours! Go away Ibrahim. In the end, you are no different than the rest. I do not wish to speak with you again. Never come back here."

She returned to stacking her pomegranates.

Ibrahim hesitated then turned and limped slowly back to the Alhambra, his head down. This was truly the first he had heard of the murder of the priest. He would look into it. He was bothered by the unjust act. Who would do such a thing? Who would order it?

The answer struck him immediately.

Chapter 24

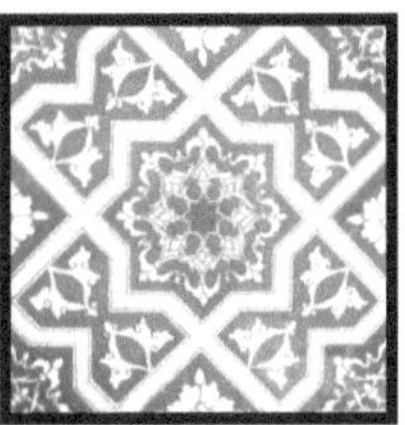

Hijos De Espana

"Seek counsel of him who makes you weep, not of him who makes you laugh."

Ibrahim appeared in the low light of the dungeon of the Alhambra. Yusuf stiffened and saluted.

"My Lord!"

Ibrahim nodded toward Yusuf. "How goes it with you, Yusuf? How goes it with our solitary guest?"

"All is well my Lord. The assassin has not caused disturbance. However, he has been employed at a most unusual work."

"What work is that?"

Yusuf continued, "The prisoner has spent many hours using a shard of stone to carve letters, names upon the wall of his cell. I thought to stop him, but it is of no harm."

"Names of what, Yusuf?"

"Names of people, my Lord."

Ibrahim walked down the hall, hands clasped behind his back towards the cell of Santiago De Aviles. The dungeon was dimly lit by several oil lanterns that hung from the center of the arched, smooth ceiling that rose above the main corridor.

Santiago was looking out the small barred window that was cut into the reddish rock to allow fresh air to flow inward. Ibrahim saw him inhale, no doubt enjoying the individual scents in the mélange that flowed like a river into the cell. Juniper and jasmine, the earthy scent of oak and rose, and cedar incense that arose from an unseen wick.

Ibrahim squinted to get a better look through the bars and saw delicately carved into the grey stone wall of the cell, names. Names set in neat straight lines. The lines combined into straight vertical columns. Ibrahim saw at least a dozen vertical columns, each column containing twenty names or more. Most of the names were Spanish and Arabic, masculine and feminine names. There were other names that he identified as German and French, Flemish and Hebrew, Italian and Greek. Ibrahim thought that Santiago must have spent entire nights without sleep in order to place so many names upon stone.

As Ibrahim focused on the individual names, his stomach began to twist as he divined to whom these names belonged.

Santiago continued breathing deeply of the clean fresh air. At first he did not acknowledge Ibrahim's presence, then he turned.

Ibrahim saw that Santiago's wound closed and was healing well, though his cheek was still swollen red. Santiago, eyes closed, whispered, "Have you come to finish it my Lord?"

Ibrahim shook his head. He could not look Santiago in the eye. The remorse he felt! "No, Santiago. I am not here for that purpose. You will not die at my hand or by my word. This I swear before Allah."

Santiago's green eyes were sharp and clear as ever. He said, "One day soon, perhaps even today, they will tell you, nay, they will demand my execution. You cannot deny this. What will you do on that day, Ibi?"

Ibrahim was surprised to hear Santiago address him as "Ibi," the diminutive of his name that only his friends employed, or in the case of Maria De Alicante, employed primarily to annoy him. Ibrahim sighed and responded, "That will be a most interesting day indeed, Santiago, and I fear it is coming, soon."

Ibrahim questioned. "Even when it comes, you will not fear. A man like you does not fear death, do you?"

"No, Ibi. I do not. Death is easy. It comes to all. The manner of death that awaits men like us is quick, there will be no suffering. There is nothing to fear. It will be a blessing, at last, released from a life of guilt and regret. Besides, I have died a hundred deaths. A thousand deaths. The death of my body will be the easiest death of all. Finally, freedom."

A heavy silence fell between the two men. Ibrahim stroked his goatee and said, "I too welcome it, Santiago. I wish for it. I pray for it."

"It will come soon enough, Ibi."

Santiago approached the bars, grasped them tightly, putting his face near them and asked, "If it is the will of your Lord, Allah, to kill Christians, but you wish death, how will you serve your Master from the grave?"

Ibrahim answered. "I am no longer certain about God's plans for me, or his purpose for the Kingdom."

Ibrahim did not wish to ask about the carvings on the wall. He must ask, but did not want to. He fought the question with all of his being. He knew the answer would be the end of him. He knew the answer before he even asked it. The words came pouring out against his will.

"The names, Santiago. Who are they?"

Santiago glanced at the wall that contained the carefully written names. He looked serious, proud. "Those names, Ibi," Santiago took a deep breath as tears filled his eyes, his voice cracking. "Those are the names of all of the children who have walked through the doors of "El Refugio." They were the lost ones whom we saved. The condemned ones that Abran and I redeemed. This wall is my headstone, my final testament, and my epitaph. The sum total of every good thing I achieved with my miserable, worthless life."

Ibrahim stared at the wall for many minutes, picking out individual names, imagining each child, where they were now, what it was like for them to be accepted into the bosom of a loving family. A refuge. He knew the terror, firsthand, of losing one's family in a brutal instant.

Without realizing it, his face pressed up against the

bars of the cell as he strained to read each individual child's name.

Santiago stepped back.

Ibrahim whispered through the bars, "This may not yet be your headstone. You may live to see your little ones, your children, again."

Santiago laughed. "Ha! I am done! Thanks to you! But do not worry! I go my way in peace. It is long overdue. It is inevitable. As the wise man says, 'Death is a camel that sleeps in everyone's house.' "

I should have been dead long ago! You by contrast Ibi, are not at peace! You do not go quietly! There is turmoil, a storm, deep inside, am I correct?"

Ibrahim said nothing only continued to stare at the names etched on the wall.

"Now I will tell you what causes of you anguish! You, Ibrahim Al-Rahim the scourge of the Christians, the hammer of Allah, you are no longer simply a Moor."

Ibrahim grunted in objection. "You mock me, Santiago."

"NO! Far from it! It is a great compliment! I want to hate you. I did hate you. I wished your death more than all else. Now you are transforming into something more than a man who is marked by the blind fanaticism of his religion. I put you on the course! Who was it that truly won the swordfight? Eh? You, this transformation. A struggle deep within you, but your resistance is to no avail. Once you come to that realization, you too will go your way, as I will and finally be at peace."

"What is this realization of which you speak?"

"That you Ibi, are not an Arab, or a Moor, you are what I am, what my ancestors were and what my brother was, an "*Hijo de Espana*," a true son of Spain."

"Spain is my enemy, I do not live for her. I do not fight for her!"

"Oh, but you do! Call your Kingdom by any other name, Granada, Al-Andalus, it does not matter, for this is Spain!" Santiago smiled and continued, "This occurs to all that come here, to this place. There is a mystic element at work in this land! The people, the conflict, and the music that transforms the soul. The dance that stopped you and your cavalry in its tracks—it is not a dance created to oppose your people. It is simply the magic that rises from the soil of *Espana* and overtakes the mind and heart."

Shocked, Ibrahim protested. "How do you know about that confrontation in the street, Santiago?"

Santiago smiled and slapped his hand hard on the wall of the cell. "These walls are only made of stone, Ibi!" Santiago concluded, "Ibi. You think you fight to defend your faith. You do not. You fight to defend a place, an ideal, your homeland, Spain."

Ibrahim tried to counter Santiago's argument. He weakly objected, "Well, look at you Santiago. You have red hair and green eyes and pale skin. You are not a Spaniard at all."

Santiago countered. "Please, Ibi, you are smarter than that. You know it is not the outward appearance that marks the man. Besides, my people were not from Spain, just as your people are not. She is our adopted home. My ancestor Markus was a legionnaire in the fifth Roman Legion, *Alaudae* or the "Larks." Do you know about them Ibrahim?"

Ibrahim thought for a moment, stroking his goatee. "Yes. Yes I do. My father told me about this. He was fascinated with the Romans and taught me everything he knew about the empire." Ibrahim paused as he pondered what he knew about the *Alaudae.* His mind welcomed the challenge, for it was a pleasant distraction from the conflict within.

Ibrahim said, "This was a legion formed of non-Romans by Julius Caesar. They were Gauls, were sworn enemies of Rome. Yet they became steadfast allies. Their veterans were given homesteads in the *Meritas* cities. The Caesars built them for retired legionnaires, as a reward for their services. I have seen tombstones of these legionnaires from the *Alaudae* in a *Meritas* town to the north and west of here near the border with the Portuguesa."

Santiago nodded. "That is correct! I am impressed! They wore images of wings on their helmets in the tradition of the warriors of Gaul. One of their number, my ancestor Markus, became a favorite of Caesar because of his loyalty and valor on the field. Markus was not his given name. His given name was a name of Gaul, lost to history. But Markus became known not for his birthplace, but for his exploits on the battlefield, serving under the eagle. When Markus received his retirement after twenty-five years of service, he asked Caesar to be re-located to Spain, instead of the *Meritas* city constructed for his legion in Northern Italy. The *Alaudae* campaigned in Spain only once in all the years that Markus served under the eagle. It was that one visit, that one campaign to captivate him. Caesar not only granted Markus' request, but also gave him a tract of land that belonged to his personal estate. This tract of land became the village now known as "Aviles," where my family dwelled for a millennia."

Santiago began to speak excitedly now. "Don't you see what is happening Ibrahim? Even my ancestor, Markus, from a nation composed of sworn enemies of Rome, settled here on Roman land, for he was enslaved by *Espana* herself. You may not understand yet, may not even agree, but you fight not for your religion, nor for a god nor for a human master, but for her . . . for *Espana*."

Ibrahim did not respond verbally, but from underneath his cloak he produced an elongated wineskin. Glancing down the hall to ensure that Yusuf was not watching, he pushed the wineskin through the bars, offering it to Santiago. "It is full of *Tempranillo*, from grapes grown in the Rioja. I know you Spaniards cannot live without it. I do not know of such things," Ibrahim lied, "But from what others tell me this is a particularly good vintage."

Rebecca tended to the bougainvillea that grew up and over the walls of her courtyard. She was bent over at the waist, softly clipping the excess vines. Her long hair fell forward and framed her face the way a picture frame highlights a painting. She was graceful, even while performing such a mundane task as this. She looked up with a start as she heard knocking on the heavy wooden door.

His broad shoulders filled the doorway. He was not wearing his dark cloak with hood, but a green one, for he did not attempt to hide his true identity. He stepped towards her with purpose, grabbed her shoulders and whispered emphatically. "Come with me to Alexandria. Let us leave, now! Nothing awaits us here save suffering and death."

Then Ibrahim Al-Rahim kissed her desperately. Rebecca did not protest. Rebecca finally broke away and said, "You cannot come here and order me to come with you. I am not one of your soldiers whom you can command to go where you wish, on a whim."

"No! Not a command. Please! I beg you to come with me. I must leave Granada. You too must leave or you will die here! Let us go together and escape our fates!"

She would not agree out loud, but she knew the warning to be true. She felt it, as he did, as all in the city did. Violence was about to break upon Granada, like a storm driven wave that is spotted upon the horizon, slowing rolling towards the shore. It swells at first, then rises up to its full height and slams down with full force. Violence was coming, many would die, and all would be changed in the Kingdom forever.

Still, Rebecca was not easily intimidated or ordered about. On the other hand, her growing feelings for this mighty yet desperate man before her confused and frightened her. She strove to put on a brave front and said, "I do not fear what is to come! Granada is my home."

"You do not fear because you do not understand!" he cried. Still gripping her shoulders, his face was flushed, eyes wide. "They will come for you! Men who know not the meaning of mercy! This dance of yours will not save you. God himself cannot save you from this evil; your only salvation is flight! Or this courtyard will be your grave!"

She tried to pull away shaking her head, but his powerful hands locked her in place. He continued. "Why do you insist on performing this dance? What is the point of this? Rebecca, do you truly believe that your fanciful dance will drive us back into the desert? Will it somehow invoke Issa to come again and vanquish us? It will not! It will only lead to more death, and suffering! Listen to me please!"

But Rebecca did not wilt before his questions and warnings. She replied in a most delicate way, attempting to reason with him. "It is you who do not understand, Ibi. You have lived your entire life . . . you are surrounded by men whose every thought and action is motivated by something hidden, by a desire for power or authority or conquest. You cannot see, you will never see, that at times, not often, but at times, someone does a thing for no other reason than the pure love of it."

She had taken command. She whispered to him softly, pointing to the door. "You may take your leave."

Her heart ached as Ibrahim looked away and nodded in agreement, defeated. He said, "As you wish Rebecca, I will leave, and perhaps I will see you again someday, but for a man of my trade, that is certainly not a guarantee."

He turned and strode out, slamming the door behind him so hard she was surprised the walls did not crack.

Chapter 25

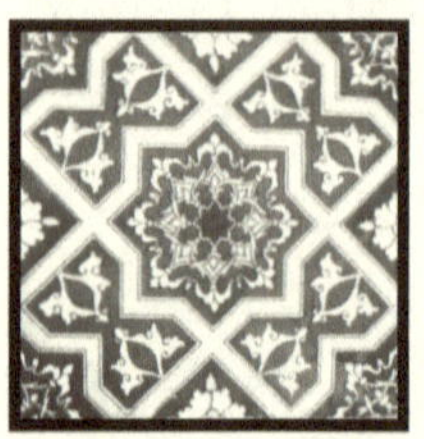

Yawm Ad-Din

"And every man shall know
one day his labors worth,
when his loss or gain
is cast up on the Judgment Day."

Ibrahim was at the foot of the Red Castle. The green and white banners of the Kingdom of Granada that grew like a forest upon the ramparts at the top of the castle hung limp and still in the dead desert air. Far beyond, over the peaks of the grey Sierra Nevada, a black thunderstorm grew by the minute, gathering the force it would soon unleash upon Granada.

He heard a whisper, "Ibi! I have been searching for you!"

Ibrahim turned and saw the Sultan Abdul-Rahkman standing framed by a willow tree along the path that lead up to the Red Castle. The Sultan pulled on his long beard nervously. His eyes darted back and forth as if he were afraid a spy was lurking in the shadows, listening in on their conversation.

Ibrahim responded and bowed. "*As salaam Alaikum*, my Lord!"

The Sultan nodded his head slightly in return. "*Wa Alaikum as salaam!*" He asked Ibrahim warmly, "How goes it with my Captain of the Guard?"

"It is well, my Lord."

Both men knew that this statement was far from the truth. Posturing for the sake of appearances. For years the Sultan had been like a father to Ibrahim. Now they could sense their special relationship changing for the worst. The Sultan, his voice barely more than a whisper, continued. "Ibi. I must ask you to do something for me, for Granada, for the All Powerful One himself. It is not a pleasant task, but it must be done. I ask my most trusted officer, the man with whom I entrust my very life, to do this."

He reached into an inside pocket of his cloak and pulled out a papyrus roll. The roll was sealed with green wax that carried the imprint of his signet ring, confirming that the roll contained as an official order.

The Sultan approached Ibrahim. "This roll carries an order that was ratified by the Mexuar, the law judge of all judicial matters in Granada. Though it pains me, I am forced to give you this order. It must be done, to preserve Islamic rule over the Kingdom. For the *convivencia*."

Ibrahim felt dread. The Sultan looked to the left and to the right as if he were committing a criminal act. He rocked back and forth nervously on slippered feet, and handed Ibrahim the scroll.

Ibrahim realized the Sultan was not in fear of being discovered giving this order. No! The Sultan was being watched by someone, someone who caused nervousness in him that Ibrahim had not seen in all the long years he had known the Sultan. The Sultan spoke quickly, a burst of words, "You will close the churches, Ibi. Arrest the priests. Kill the assassin in my dungeon and eliminate the girls who participate in the blasphemous dance. Target especially the girl who leads them."

Ibrahim felt the strength ebb from his body. His mouth opened in shock, his shoulders sagged, and his hands shook as he attempted to digest the terrible order of his lord.

The Sultan took pity upon Ibrahim. He said softly, "It is God's will, it is the will of Allah."

Ibrahim composed himself. "The will of Allah? Or the will of a Sultan?"

"Ibi. You must do this. If you will not, I will turn to others to fulfill my orders, others who will not carry them out with the mercy that you would."

In the distance Ibrahim heard a deep, low rumble from the approaching thunderstorm. The hot air moved slightly, and Ibrahim saw the hairs of the Sultan's beard ruffle. Ibrahim felt hot rage. His face turned red. His voice rose in intensity with each word. "My Lord, we have always stood for justice for peace. The Kingdom of Granada is the one place in this wicked world where Muslims and Christians and Jew can live together without slaughtering each other like dogs. We do not do this! We do not skulk in the dark of the night and make secret pacts to eliminate our enemies! This is what THEY do! This is why I fight *them*! The infidels in their religious fanaticism crying out to their gods for thanks as they dash babies headfirst onto the rocks! This may be your will but do not blaspheme and say it is Allah's!"

The Sultan put his hands up in an attempt to calm Ibrahim. "Ibi. Please. Lower your voice. We have no choice. You know that. This order will secure Granada and protect the gardens of Heaven for the next hundred years."

Now it was the Sultan's turn to show anger. "Those *Christians!*" He spat the words as if he tasted a piece of rotted fruit. They always plot against us! They will not stop! They will never stop!" He continued. "Now they have their symbols to rally their rebellion! They have their martyrs! That damn dance! We, *YOU* should have stopped it long ago! It was your duty! That dance is an abomination against our prophet and our book! We must not allow Christian assassins to live unpunished in our fortress. Ibrahim Al-Rahim, you know this! You knew it would come to this. Do not be naïve!"

Ibrahim shook his head in protest, his voice rising in anger. "This is murder! This is cowardice! These orders say nothing of James the priest. Why not?"

Maria's accusation rang in Ibrahim's ears, he cried. "What machination did you devise to kill off that frail old man?"

The Sultan's eyes flashed in irritation. He pointed an accusing finger at Ibrahim and repeated. "If you had taken the forceful steps necessary long ago, instead of neglecting your duty, it would not have come to this!"

Ibrahim winced as if hit in the chest by a rock. The performance of his duty had never before been questioned. Both men glared at each other in frustration—the father and the son—long years of friendship and trust now tested by forces spinning out of control, pushing them into the abyss. The Sultan sighed and broke the silence and tenseness with a proverb. He quoted it the way a grandfather would to his grandson when teaching an invaluable life lesson. "Ibi . . . Sad are only those who understand." The Sultan embraced Ibrahim lightly as he pushed the roll into his hand and closed his fingers around it.

Ibrahim made eye contact with the Sultan, a defiant stare, they were close now and Ibrahim whispered, "To please the Divine One, sometimes we must displease mortals."

The Sultan did not respond. He simply shook his head slowly and walked away, leaving Ibrahim alone. In the distance reverberated a low bass tone from the thunderstorm that towered over the plain of the Vega, blowing toward Granada.

The Sultan, now out of sight of Ibrahim, stopped in the middle of the path. He spoke even though it appeared no one was present to hear. "Who gave you permission to spy upon me?"

At those words, appearing as if by magic, the five assassins of Sinan, their grayish cloaks blending in seamlessly with the surrounding vegetation, came into view and formed a close circle around the Sultan.

Their leader stood in front of the Sultan, hood pulled tightly around his gaunt face. The corneas of his eyes were yellow instead of white, the yellow interspersed with swollen red blood vessels, adding to his ominous appearance.

There was the ever-present odor of hashish from the smoke that permeated every fiber of cloth of their cloaks and each hair of their heads.

The lead *Fidai* spoke, his voice raspy, almost a growl, "My dear Sultan, there are many rulers who wish to know what occurs here in Granada. Many rulers more powerful and," he paused, "much richer than you."

The *Fidai* continued, "I think that your puppet, Ibrahim, is not willing to carry out your orders. If you were our master Sinan, our heads would already be on the tips of pikes, planted on the top of the rampart of this fortress, for all to learn what it means to hear, then disobey."

The Sultan rebutted. "No doubt. But the Kingdom of Granada is a more enlightened and tolerant place then your desolate mountains."

The head *Fidai* grinned and said sarcastically, "Any more enlightened, and the infidel would have already overrun you and turned the Alhambra to ash."

The five crowded around the Sultan, almost in contact, menacing. The Sultan knew the Grey Cloaks would have no qualms about striking down a Sultan if it were so ordered by Sinan.

The leader puffed on a hashish cigarette, breathed in the fumes and exhaled slowly, the smoke hanging lazily around his hooded face. "I believe we must aid your puppet in the fulfillment of the will of the Maker. If he stands in our way, he will be disposed of."

The Sultan dejected, waved his hand and said sadly, "Do what must be done."

The lead assassin exhaled a low hissing noise of joy at the thought of the kill. With that, the five *Fidai* disappeared into the bushes as quickly as they appeared, leaving nothing but a faint wisp of smoke on the path.

The Sultan was alone, but only momentarily. The young auditor of the Caliph of Baghdad also watched from a distance, taking mental notes for his own report to the Caliph. He approached the Sultan, and noted his sad countenance.

He asked slyly. "Is there something amiss, my lord?"

The Sultan sighed, then sprang to life. He rammed into the young auditor, pinning him up against the stone wall that lined the path. The Sultan jammed his forearm into the young man's throat until he squeaked in pain and surprise.

The Sultan growled at the young man. "You insignificant worm! You dare spy on me! I have a message you will deliver to the Caliph. Include it in the secret reports you send by night messenger to the coast. Tell the Caliph that the Kingdom of Granada no longer does his bidding."

The round face of the young auditor turned blue as the Sultan pressed his forearm harder into his throat. "If he wants to raise a Jihad against us, I welcome it! I will crush it! Then I will march my army to his palace and slit his throat myself! Is that clear?"

The young man, eyes bulging in fear gasped, "Yes!"

The Sultan removed his forearm from the young man's throat. He fell to his knees and wretched.

In that moment an alarm sounded.

A single high-pitched note from a trumpet on the top of the Alhambra. The note carried over the rooftops and minarets of all of Granada. It was a call to the defenders of the city to arms.

Ibrahim was still. Frozen in a state of shock, staring at the scroll in his hand. Now he burst to life. He raced to the top of the ramparts leaping three steps at a time, his robe flying behind him. Soldiers yelled, signal flags flapped. All was chaos as he reached the top and looked out beyond the walls of the city, to the plain of the Vega below.

They had somehow by-passed the entrenched army of Osmyn at the springs of Moclin! By a forced night march they arrived over the mountains from Loja. They were here, now! The Spanish King's plan had unfolded to perfection.

The armies of Castile and their foreign allies were deploying into battle formation on the plain of the Vega, just a few miles beyond the main gate of Granada.

This was the first time, in all the centuries of Islamic rule an army of Christendom had been sighted this close to Granada. The saying came to Ibrahim's mind that was famous in the Greek city of Sparta, "For eight hundred years the women of Sparta never spotted the smoke of an enemy cook fire."

Osmyn was the cautious one, Ibrahim thought. He was the only one concerned that we were allowing the Castilians to penetrate so deeply into our homeland, "Only one day hard ride from the gates of the Alhambra," Osmyn had said.

Ibrahim scolded himself and whispered. "Osmyn saw it! But I was too arrogant to imagine the possibility. Now the King of Castile is here, arraying his troops in battle formation."

Ibrahim saw them, their thousands, running into position, forming their battle lines into one solid mass of steel and armor. He remembered, as a boy, gazing over the ramparts of Jerusalem at the invincible Crusader army, just as now, slowly rolling towards him.

A massive cloud of dust rose, filling the Vega from horizon to horizon from their maneuvers. Clearly seen, *Beauceant,* the huge Templar flag that flew alongside the banners of the King of Castile, the blood-red lion on yellow field. The battle flag of the Order of Santiago was out in front of the foot soldiers, and masses of individual knights in formation rallied around their own standards.

The King of Castile was riding his huge black charger far in front of the battle lines, bearing the flag of his nation, waving it to and fro as he galloped up and down the lines shouting to his men. They responded with cheers and battle cries. Even the foreign contingents, the high-minded French under their and dark blue banners, cheered with enthusiasm as he rode past, as if he were their own regent.

The numbers in the Castilian army had grown since the initial reconnaissance Ibrahim had performed with Adnan and Osmyn. The King of Castile had by some stratagem added to the numbers of his forces. Perhaps they snuck in across the border, or perhaps they were Christian volunteers from outlying villages that gathered under his banner. In any event, Ibrahim did not have enough men to counter them.

Behind the horde flashed silver bolts of lightning. Then the rain began to fall. It came down slowly as great fat drops, the moisture collecting around thc sand particles high in the atmosphere and falling heavily.

Within the Alhambra, men were shouting, strapping on armor. People ran through the streets of Granada below, scurrying like ants with no apparent purpose other than to find some place, any safe place to hide.

Then a new sound struck Ibrahim's ears, a sound that had not been heard in the Kingdom of Granada for centuries, a sound more ominous than the sharpest peal of thunder. It was the single brass clang of a church bell. That outlawed sound, which the Muslims found so abhorrent. A second church bell answered, then another and another joined in.

All over Granada church bells that were walled up and unused in their steeples, silent, abruptly sounded to life. Smaller bells joined the rising chorus, bells forged for the purpose of adding to the din of judgment day. A cacophony of singing brass filled the air, drowning out the Moors' calls to arms, suffocating even the rumble of thunder from the storm now breaking upon them.

Ibrahim recognized the meaning of the sounds at once. It was the signal to rise.

It was a call to arms for all who professed to be faithful Christians in the city of Granada. All those who were taught, that the time had come to fulfill prophecy. At long last, the end was at hand for the Islamic system that had ruled over their lands all these long, dark centuries.

The clanging continued on unabated. Now adding to the noise of the Castilians out in the plain, the rumble of thunder, and the incessant pounding of brass church bells, was the sound of fighting, as the Christians and Muslims of Granada began a contest, played out on the cobblestone streets, in the main market and in the courtyards of the whitewashed homes, for control of the city.

Ibrahim watched it all with a strange sense of calm as his world disintegrated around him. Both hands on the ramparts of the Red Castle, he stood for a long moment, contemplating, taking it all in.

The maelstrom had begun. The rain fell heavily and the wind began to blow in earnest. This did little to dampen the raging sounds of the battle in the streets below or the incessant clanging of church bells.

Is Yusuf still at his post? I must speak to him.

Ibrahim backed away from the ramparts and glanced down at the scroll still held tightly in his hand. He turned slowly and calmly and walked down the stairway to his quarters. He entered and looked at his weapons, still and peaceful upon the wall. He had laid them down for a few hours, sworn never to use them again, in order to find peace. He shook his head; there would be no peace for him. Only death. His hands had been soaked in blood for too long. There would be no peace for him. Abdul Rahkman was correct. He was naïve.

He calmly strapped on his gold leaved armor, stretching to close each of the bronze clasps in turn behind his back. He put on his black cloak with the gold filigree and clasped it at his throat.

Then he looked out over his rain soaked balcony; the noise of conflict rose to a fever pitch. A flash from a lightning bolt lit up the room, followed by a sharp crack of thunder that rattled the walls of the castle.

Ibrahim continued unhurried. Calm. He reached for his scimitar, grasped it tightly. The hilt felt good in his hand, a natural fit, strangely comforting. He lunged forward, stabbing with the sword, then spun in a tight circle, slashing the air with it. He flipped it back and forth between his large, powerful hands, causing a reassurance to settle over him as he prepared for battle. He slowly sheathed the sword and put on his other weapons.

He strapped on his gladius short sword, tight upon his waist, then the dagger that he kept close to his ankle. He reached for a quiver, filled with a dozen arrows; each tipped with long tri-pointed, razor sharp warheads. He lifted his bow from off the wall and pulled the string back four times, in quick succession, testing the resistance of its fibers. Then he slung the bow over his back.

He glanced at the open Bible on the table, his mother Anna's prayer beads on top of the pages. The Bible was opened to the book of Isaiah, the prophet of the Christians who wrote much about peace and paradise. Ibrahim was reading chapter two verse four: "He will judge disputes between nations; he will settle cases for many peoples. They will beat their swords into plowshares, and their spears into pruning hooks. Nations will not take up the sword against other nations, and they will no longer train for war."

He put his hand over the beads, then closed them tight into his fist.

They tried to attain a lasting peace here in Granada, in the gardens of Allah, but it was not to be. It was never to be. Isaiah wrote of a world that could never be achieved by simple human beings divided by opposing faiths. Isaiah was a dreamer. He was naïve. It was a waste of time to believe anything else.

Islam and Christendom would never live in peace together. Not now. Not ever. If the world last a million years, they would not make peace. They were fools to ever dream of it. The sacred books spoke of love of their fellow man, love of their enemies. Such a thing as wonderful as it sounds when preached by a priest or an Imam in the bowels of a dark church, or a bright, airy Mosque, was nothing but a fool's errand. The idea of a panacea could not survive in the real world outside the walls of the sacred meeting places, where the hatred of men crushes all good will.

Ibrahim took a good look around his chambers, knowing he would not see it again. Outside, the din of battle was rising, men and woman yelling, the church bells clanging, and in the far distance was the low bass call of the Castilians battle horns. Thunder cracked as the storm opened up directly over the Alhambra, blowing wind and rain sideways into his chamber.

He strode out of his quarters, face hard, and into the storm.

Yusuf is key.

The streets were choked with people, some fighting each other, others running with their belongings. Streets were blocked with burning, overturned carts. The white-washed brick walls that lined the streets were torn down to allow attackers to strike the occupants inside of their homes. Streets were choked with debris and bodies.

I must get a message to Yusuf.

The avenue that led up to the gates of the Alhambra was a mass of burning barricades, rubble, and people. This was not by accident, it was by design. Part of the enemy's well-laid plans. Obstacles were hastily thrown into the middle of the avenue. Ibrahim could not charge his elite cavalry through Granada and out the main gate onto the Vega where he could check the Castilian advance upon the plain, allowing time for Osmyn and Adnan Al Mansur to come up and strike the enemy in the rear. It would take too much time, time they did not have, to clear the streets sufficiently to allow his cavalry to pass.

No doubt the Christians waited in ambush around every corner and upon every rooftop for such an eventuality.

It would be impossible to get through the carnage on horseback.

He heard over the wall where the stable was located the whining of the mounts of his cavalry. He was certain he could hear Exsecour slamming his flank on the wooden doors of his pen, eager to escape the confines of the stable and join the fray.

It had all been planned very thoroughly, right under his nose. Ibrahim felt a strange surge of admiration for the King of Castile. He was unlike any enemy leader the Moors face in the past. They all realized it, as he and Osmyn and Adnan lay on their bellies on that hill and spied, counting their numbers as he marched his army past. This King was a force to be reckoned with, not to be underestimated. Still, those with the charge to keep the gardens of Heaven from harm from the infidel's designs had been outwitted and outmaneuvered.

They were guilty of the most serious sin of warfare. They underestimated. He underestimated the enemy. This King would be the end of them all.

The invasion of the Kingdom of Granada was a masterstroke. For the first time in all his years of fighting and hating the armies of Christendom, Ibrahim had met his match. No! His superior. Was the Just One punishing them for their arrogance? Was it hubris to believe they were superior to the armies of the infidel? Was it dumb pride that had lead them to this dire moment?

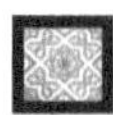

Beyond the walls of the city, through the pouring rain and crash of thunder, the King of Spain brought his charge to a halt and enjoyed the view.

Even through the mist, the King saw the red walls of the Alhambra rising above the trees and crowning the upper most hills of Granada.

The King turned in his saddle to watch his army formed into a perfect battle line, awaiting his orders to advance. They looked to him, thousands of warriors, and he relished it.

He smiled as he thought to himself, *You are mine! The wily old Sultan! Ibrahim Al-Rahim, Osmyn—I have you now! All my preparations have climaxed, led us to this moment. I am in front of Granada at long last! Staring at the walls of the last Muslim Bastion in Europe! Before this day ends it will be mine and bring me everlasting glory!*

The King fixed his attention on the orchards and fields in front of him, hoping for a glimpse of Osmyn. The King yearned to see the great Sudanese warrior charging him, hell-bent to engage in one-on-one combat as was foretold in the tent of truce. But he saw no enemy troops in front of the walls.

He grasped his banner from a waiting squire, lifted it, and waved it back and forth as he cried with all of his might. "Forward! For God and *Espana*!

As the battle lines of the King of Spain approached Granada, Ibrahim, on foot, started out at a slow trot, intent on reaching the main lane of the Alhambra that separated the Red Castle, the Mexuar, the royal palace and gardens on one hill, from the spacious garden-like forest and pathways of the other.

He was close to the main gate of the Alhambra, the keyhole shaped structure that marked the separation between the peaceful gardens, and the riotous maelstrom taking place below in the city. His lame leg was holding him back from running as quickly as he desired. No matter, he must move quickly.

He had to arrive at the main gate of the city and organize the defense. The Christian rioters who placed the barricades in the streets would surely attempt to capture the main gate and allow the enemy hordes to pour through into Granada proper.

In front of him appearing like wraiths, the five charcoal-grey draped assassins of the old man of the mountains, Sinan.

They faced him, arranged in a semi-circle, blocking his path, hoods pulled down tight over their faces. The leader spoke, voice an evil rasp. "In what direction are you heading, puuu-pet? Your master gave you a command, yet you do not seem eager to fulfill it. How do you expect others to respect your orders, when you do not carry out yours?"

Ibrahim felt the hairs on the back of his head rise, not out of fear, but out of anger. "You will remove yourself from my path."

The leader of the assassins wore a sinister tight smile on his cracked and gaunt face. The rain poured down, releasing a damp musty odor from the cloaks of the five who confronted Ibrahim. "Oh look! The puuuuppet has resolve after all."

The *Fidai*, swept back his cloak and reached to unsheathe his sword as his four companions did the same. The *Fidai's* sword had not cleared its scabbard and already the point of Ibrahim's scimitar was at the assassin's throat. Ibrahim drew the blade back, holding it level and steady at the height of the assassin's chest, giving the grey cloak sufficient space to finish drawing his own sword. His four companions, swords in hand, crouched down, ready to spring like a pride of lionesses on an injured animal.

Ibrahim spoke, his voice barely heard above the steady rain. "You would do me a kind service by drawing your weapon. Draw it!"

The assassin put up his hands in a mock gesture of submission. "My! The puuuu-ppet has teeth! You can move quickly when provoked I see. Too bad you were not as quick to counter the army outside your walls, or to eliminate those who blaspheme! Now we must do your work for you. You hesitate to eliminate your subversive girlfriend or the Christian pig you hold in your dungeon."

The lead *Fidai* smiled at the thought of the kill. "Goodbye puppet! Go to the glorious defense of your city and leave the distasteful tasks to us! If you get in our way, we will kill you. We have been patient with you and your Sultan, but no one interferes with the messengers of Sinan, not even the prophet himself!"

As quickly as they appeared the *Fidai* dived into the brush, followed by his four companions.

Ibrahim sprang into the brush, using his scimitar to swish branches and leaves out of his line of sight and give chase to the assassins, but they were gone, leaving nothing in their wake but a few broken palm fronds, hanging down, dripping with water.

Ibrahim returned to the avenue. He ran. A rapid sprint, as quickly as the limp of his left leg and the rain-slicked cobblestones would allow. His sprint was a skip that propelled him forward, out the main gate of the Alhambra and down the avenue toward the market place.

The rain was pouring down in solid grey sheets, slapping the cobblestones and bouncing upwards. Water poured off Ibrahim's face in steady rivulets, his long hair matted to his shoulders and back. Ibrahim grabbed a passing soldier roughly by the shoulders and shouted at him, so as to be heard above the storm. "Saliel! Have your men clear this street, now! If any oppose you, strike them down!"

Saliel nodded and yelled orders and gathered troops to carry out his commander's words.

Ibrahim continued to run, shoving his way through the debris covered avenue, and the masses of people running pell-mell through the streets. He reached the place where the avenue rose to overlook the market place. Five Islamic soldiers rushed past him toward the main gate of the city scimitars drawn, white robes flying. He stopped them and commanded them to follow.

He saw below in the marketplace, that many of the stalls had been overturned. Some were on fire. Through the grey rain he saw people fighting each other. It was too far to discern who was attacking whom, but it was easy to see that the marketplace was being destroyed by the riot.

He squinted through the rain to see what had become of the pomegranate stall of Maria de Alicante. He felt a surge of worry for the safety of the old woman. He knew she would stubbornly attempt to fend off any attacker and probably be killed in the process.

There it was! The mountain of pomegranates that always obscured Maria from view had been upset, small round globes spilled all over the pathway in front of her stall. A man, possibly a Christian but impossible to tell at such a distance, was behind Maria, holding both of her arms tightly. Another man in front of her was grabbing her in an attempt to find the hidden gold coins that Maria always kept on her person.

Ibrahim growled as the rage rose. In spite of the rain his face burned with anger. He reached over his shoulder, grabbed his bow and strung a steel-tipped arrow onto the bowstring, intent upon an almost impossible shot at this distance through the drenching downpour.

Uncle Harun's countless lessons came back to Ibrahim's mind—"Take slow aim my boy, you will only have one good shot. It could mean your life! Deep breaths! Yes, that's it! Clear the air out of your lungs, hold your breath, concentrate only on your target, and ignore all else around you, no matter how terrible the battle . . ."

Ibrahim took three deep slow breaths, slowing his heartbeat, steadying his hand, and lining up the shot.

The man in front of Maria, frustrated for not having found the hidden monies on the old lady, struck her backhanded, hard across the face then raised his dagger to strike . . .

He collapsed to a gasping, gurgling sound, an arrow protruding out of his neck. The second assailant, who held Maria firmly from behind, glanced around frantically for the source of the silent death that had just stricken his comrade. He squinted as he saw the outline of an Islamic soldier on the hillock above the market. The shadowy outline was hard to see through the falling rain, but it appeared as if the soldier was grasping a bow with his hand, and with his right had just let an arrow fly.

This was the attacker's final thought. The arrow found its target square on his forehead, with a thud as the steel point ripped through bone and flesh. Another arrow struck just above his eye-socket a split second later, striking with such force that it exploded out of his head and stuck into a wooden post of the stall, pinning his lifeless body upright.

Ibrahim scanned the scene looking for more threats to his friend. He yelled at two of the soldiers that accompanied him.

"You two! Take her back to the Alhambra. She will not come willingly! Throw her over your shoulder but take care not to harm even a hair on her head. Watch over her until I return."

The pair nodded and immediately set off down the hill towards Maria's stall.

The rain let up slightly, but the ominous grey sky was still split open by flashes of lighting.

The church bells continued to clang unabated.

All around Ibrahim and his escort a flood of people—commoners, soldiers and rioters streamed in every direction. It seemed as if all of Granada had taken to the streets to defend, attack or loot. All order was gone. Up ahead, Ibrahim saw the figure of a man in mid-air, limbs flailing, who had been thrown from the top of a minaret.

Thick smoke hung over the city from the burning fires of the barricades, market stalls and homes. The raging thunderstorm held the smoke low to the ground. It was hard to see.

The rise in the avenue above the market branched off into several different routes. One road lead off to the left, directly toward the main gate of Granada, the very same avenue upon which he had led his cavalry on so many triumphal charges after a victory. Another street led off to the right toward the Christian sections of the city, the Albacin and the caves of the Sacramonte.

Ibrahim knew the Grey Cloaks would head toward the Christian quarter at top speed, anxious to kill. They were hunting her. He could also see, beyond the main gate, the army of Castile fully formed into battle lines. It stirred a memory inside him. It was the same sight he beheld from the ramparts of Jerusalem as a boy, a long line of mounted chivalry filing the horizon, advancing at a slow trot unchecked toward the main gate of his city. The gate was lined with Moorish soldiers, his men and militia arriving at the entrance of the city in droves to defend their home from the invader.

He should go to the gates without the slightest hesitation and take command of the defense of Granada. It was his duty. With his leadership they could hold the walls until Osmyn and Adnan arrived. Together, they would crush the Castilians up against the stone face of Granada the way barley grains are crushed between mortar and pestle.

If the Christians burst through the gate and into the city all would be killed, regardless of religion, in the furious massacre that would surely follow. He must defend Granada and the gardens of the Creator. For this very purpose Allah spared his life at Jerusalem, so that he would live a life dedicated to protecting his gardens, the living testimony to his power and grace.

Yes! It was the only course that he could choose!

Ibrahim ran down the avenue as quickly as his damaged leg would allow. He focused in on his surroundings as he ran, evaluating threats, sword ready to strike. The small entourage of soldiers that accompanied him struggled to keep up; he was so fast, even with his uneven gait.

It was several seconds before he realized he was running down the avenue *away* from the market, not toward the main gate of Granada, but instead in the opposite direction! He was heading toward the Christian quarter, toward the enemy's domain, toward the home of Rebecca, his body ignoring common sense and his mind's will.

He would certainly die this day. In the end, what difference did it make, his manner of death? Was it vital that he run to the gates of the city to take command of the defense? He would go the way of the all mankind, hands soaked in the blood of Christendom's monks, covered in crimson stains and tissue, surrounded by the lifeless bodies of unbelieving men with the red cross emblazoned upon their chests. Or he would go down fighting to preserve the life of an innocent girl whose only crime against the state was a strong will and a love of something that transcended the sword. Something beautiful. Something more powerful than a charge by ten thousand knights.

Besides, everything that Ibrahim had fought for, killed for, and believed in, was now at an end.

The Castilians would overrun them. If somehow by the will of Allah, by divine intervention, Osmyn and Adnan arrived on the field of battle in time to save Granada and the gardens of god from the infidel, the dream would still be lost.

The *convivencia* had come crashing down to the noise of clanging church bells, the peal of thunder and the calls of the battle horns.

Before this day was over, the streets of Granada would shine red, as if Satan himself had decorated the avenues to his own perverted tastes.

For his part, he would meet death gladly. Once the dream was shattered, why continue on as a shell? He thought of the proverb, "There is no greater death, than the death of hope."

Why live to be an old broken down man, speaking in pathetic, wistful tones of days long gone, of a world now past?

Better to die now, accept it. Embrace it. Welcome the peace.

He ran over the slick cobblestones, mind racing, mobs of people rushing past. Many were Christians armed with rudimentary weapons, heading toward the main gate, or struggling with Islamic soldiers and citizens in the street.

Toward him, coming on fast, were two large men with thick-barreled chests. A thought flew through his mind that they wore armor. The underlying armor gave them a wider aspect. But how could that be? It could not be. By law only his men, Moorish soldiers, were allowed the use of armor. It was outlawed for the common citizen. The Christian population was not allowed any type of armor, or sharpened weapons.

The two men singled Ibrahim out as a special target, as the officer in command of the convoy of Moors running toward the Christian quarter. As they drew their gleaming broadswords, their dark brown cloaks opened to reveal bronze colored plate armor, emblazoned with the blood-red lion standing on its hindquarters thrashing at the air.

Ibrahim saw that these were not common Christians of Granada, but professional soldiers in the employ of the King of Castile.

The master plan of the King of Spain continued to unfold.

Before the attack on Granada, Castilian soldiers slipped into the city, unobserved by the Islamic soldiers keeping watch on the walls. They came in during the light of day disguised as poor beggars in rags, hunched over like sick old men, shuffling along through the main gate. They arrived in wagons, curled up inside of empty wine barrels or hidden under wagonloads of corn, cloth and hay. To accomplish the covert missions, the King of Spain had enlisted hundreds of accomplices among the Christian population of Granada. These conspirators were more than willing to aid in the infiltration of the city.

Ibrahim thought of the proverb, "Better a thousand enemies outside the house than one inside."

He sped up. The two Castilians came at him, one on his right the other on his left. Ibrahim's companions were several paces back, fighting through a massed knot of people, pushing and shoving and slashing in order to reach and defend their Captain.

As Ibrahim closed the distance between himself and the two attackers he lunged headfirst into a somersault. The two men slashed at Ibrahim's head and found nothing to mark their sword strokes but empty space. As Ibrahim rolled forward, he unsheathed his Roman gladius with his left hand, while grasping his scimitar with his right.

He finished his roll and landed on his knees, directly behind the two attacking Castilians. He struck backwards with his arms simultaneously with all his might, his two sword points finding the soft, unprotected flesh of the lower back of the Castilians. The strokes were swift but lethal, an in-and-out motion that did not penetrate deeply, but allowed Ibrahim to withdraw his weapons, jump to his feet and continue on his course.

He moved on and did not look back to see the astonished expression on the faces of his attackers as they collapsed and died, nor the wide-eyed looks of his Islamic escort as they witnessed firsthand the agility and speed of their commander.

The noise of battle was all around. Moors and Christians were locked in a mortal struggle for supremacy of streets and town. Ibrahim plowed through, heedless of friend or foe, hell bent on arriving at Rebecca's home before the Grey Cloaks could accomplish their lethal mission.

Ibrahim's escort was now down to two men. A brick launched from an unknown rooftop, crashed down upon one of the Moorish soldier's head, slamming him to the pavement, his body immediately lost from view as the fighting mob closed over it.

They were in the Albacin, the Christian quarter that led up to the caves of the Sacramonte. Enemy territory.

Christians poured down the streets armed with scythes, pitchforks, handmade spears and the occasional sword, eager for combat.

Ibrahim ran through them, ignoring those that did not take heed of him, slashing with his scimitar at those who posed a threat, his sword flashing back and forth striking men down to the left and the right.

Most of the Christians passed, ignoring him in their rush to invade the Muslim sectors of Granada, reach the gates, and aid the King of Castile. The soldiers of Castile who infiltrated the city targeted Ibrahim as a man of import among the Moors and lunged forward to engage him.

The two soldiers following Ibrahim were now down to one. An infiltrating soldier of Castile struck him down with a blow to the abdomen. Ibrahim in turn slew the attacker, dropped to one knee and attended to his fallen comrade. Ibrahim recognized him, a young man, a native of the Kingdom of Granada from one of the villages that dotted the Alpujarra Mountains to the south.

Ibrahim had met the young man's parents when he was accepted into the elite cavalry of the Alhambra. They were very proud that their son would serve Allah thus. The young man had a reputation for taking in the occasional stray dog or cat that wandered the streets of Granada. Ibrahim could not recall his name, only that he had garnered the sarcastic nickname from his fellow soldiers; "*The Veterinarian.*" Ibrahim recalled that the soldier was disciplined by an officer for housing the wayward animals in his quarters.

Ibrahim watched helplessly as the young man's eyes glazed over and the last soft exhalation of breath marked his passing. He gently closed the eyelids of the still wide-eyed but lifeless soldier.

As he did so, something stirred then broke open, deep in Ibrahim's being, in the same manner that an earthen dam, hastily built, and outwardly appearing stout and strong masks inherent imperfections.

Without warning, with the sound of a thousand peals of thunder, the dam bursts open. The vast pool of water explodes in freedom down the valley below, draining itself of pent up energy and releasing an unstoppable fury of churning destruction, leaving in its wake a land bare, scraped clean, having borne away all structure and vegetation. Finally the pent up energy expends itself, and in the earthen dam's place nothing remains but a gapping muddy gap.

Ibrahim spent a lifetime controlling his emotions, keeping himself in balance. Not acting on impulse. Setting the proper example. The men looked to him. He had to keep his mind clear at all times in order to command his men properly. He could not be reckless.

Now, finally, his deepest emotions broke forth. From deep in his bowels, Ibrahim let forth a cry that could be heard above all the other competing sounds in the city, a primal yell of pain and anger that sounded as if hell itself erupted through a crack in the earth and would devour humanity.

Ibrahim leapt up, at his full height, *gladius* in one hand, scimitar in the other. Coming toward him was a crowd of common men armed with farming implements, scythes, axes, handmade spears and crude swords.

Ibrahim saw, not the commoners before him, but Templars in the form of demons. Each creature ten feet tall, tunics drenched in blood and all manner of human tissue, decorated in human ears that were shorn from their owners, emblazoned with crimson crosses that belched fire and acrid smoke. Their faces took on an evil aspect, fangs instead of teeth dripping in rivulets of blood. The specters were Ibrahim's nightmares come to life in the light of day.

Ibrahim did not turn and run as one might expect when one's worst nightmare leaves the subconscious and takes living form. Fear did not come up into his heart. Instead he sprinted towards them borne along by manic rage. His well-tended veneer of calm, logic and self-control was stripped away. He charged, screaming holy terror, with murderous intent.

Many men caught sight of Ibrahim Al-Rahim and rushed in to kill him to cries of, "Devil! The Moor! Kill Him!"

Isolated and alone, he looked to be an easy target, easily overwhelmed by their superior numbers.

As the unearthly figures came into striking distance, Ibrahim leveled a vicious blow at the closest. The "Templar" flew into the air as if launched by a spring.

Next, in spite of his damaged leg, Ibrahim leapt high, spinning in a tight half-circle, striking two of his attackers while still airborne, one after the other with a single lethal blow. Their chests exploded open in a spray of crimson. They died while still upright, even before Ibrahim's feet lighted once again upon the cobblestones.

Ibrahim went down on one knee, ducking his head to avoid a series of counter-blows. He thrust upward with the gladius. The Roman-inspired sword sunk deeply into the gut of the nearest attacker, another mortal blow.

Rage unabated, Ibrahim continued to drive the sword deeper with both hands lifting his victim off the ground. Then Ibrahim jumped into the air, lunged forward, and landed with all of his weight onto the now dead man as if he could kill him twice.

He jumped to his feet, withdrawing his sword from the dead man. His face and hair was sprayed with blood. He cried out and slashed at the other men who were nearby, but they thought it best to avoid his blows.

Ibrahim was one man, a tiny island in a river of enemies that flowed out of the Christian quarter to the battle raging around the main gates of the city. He screamed and slashed wildly, yearning to feel flesh being torn asunder by his two flashing swords.

They would not oblige him.

Dozens of armed men ran by, steering clear of the crazed, furious Moor. No one, not even the professional soldiers of Castile who were smuggled into the city to engage the Moors in battle, dared to engage this one maniac in combat.

He swore at them, screaming in Spanish and Arabic and challenged them, to stand and fight like men. None obliged him.

He spotted the door to the courtyard of the home of Rebecca, and sprinted towards it. He pounded on the door with the pommel of his scimitar. No one answered. He stepped back, raised his leg and kicked with all of his might, aiming the blow at the point where the brass hinges of the door met the whitewashed wall. The door exploded inward in a cloud of dust and splintered wood. He charged inside.

There were no Grey Cloaks. Only Fortino. Ibrahim grasped him by the collar and lifted him off the ground while yelling.

"Where is she? Where is she?"

Suddenly, she appeared in the courtyard, unharmed, her expression an astonished look of horror.

The terrible rage that filled Ibrahim at once subsided as he watched her walk toward him, dressed in a sleek white silk dress that was even more revealing because of the rain.

At the sight of her, Ibrahim's world came back into focus. His body and mind relaxed. Reason once again took control of his mind, replacing murderous anger. The ghosts dissipated like the morning mist.

He became self-conscious as he realized how he must appear to Rebecca. He still grasped a terrified Fortino by the collar holding him up high. Fontino's feet dangled as if he were a child sitting on the edge of a cliff. Ibrahim's long black hair was matted to his face from the rain and blood that had splattered it. His cloak was torn and covered with splotches of brown mud and sprays of red blood of a dozen different men. It looked as if a mad artist had used his robe as a canvass in an expression of unchecked dementia.

He let out an audible exhalation of breath and slowly lowered Fortino to the ground.

Rebecca approached him with a confident stride, scolding him like a schoolteacher. "Leave my brother alone!"

He turned to her and pleaded, "Rebecca. You must come with me now. I do not have time to explain, but they are coming for you. They will be here in minutes. Not even I can stop them."

Rebecca began to protest. "Why? Of whom do you speak?"

Ibrahim screamed at her in his mind, but the words came out softly, almost a whisper. "Please. No questions. You will understand in time."

Rebecca perceived from the desperation on Ibrahim's face that she was in mortal danger. Still she could not help but ask, "Of whom do you speak?"

In his mind he grabbed her, in order to silence her questions, hoisted her up over his shoulder and strode out of the courtyard.

In reality he softly grasped her wrist as if it were the fragile wing of a butterfly and said softly, but urgently, pulling her close, "You knew it would come to this. I warned you. Powerful men who hate what your dance represents. They have hired men. Nay, they are not men! They are evil beings in the form of men who do not know mercy. They live for the thrill of shedding blood. Once ordered to kill, they always carry out their orders. There is no safe shelter from them in Granada. Not even in the Alhambra, not even the very quarters of the Sultan himself are beyond their reach."

His eyes darted back and forth, sweeping the courtyard, expecting at any second to see five grey shapes vault over the whitewashed wall in deadly silence.

He tugged at Rebecca's arm. There would be no more discussion. "You are coming! Now!"

He pulled her out into the empty street. The Christian mobs had evacuated the Christian quarter in their rush to wrest control of the main gates from the rulers of the town. The rain subsided.

The pair moved swiftly down a long, back alley, Ibrahim in front, scimitar leading on alert, attuned to every movement and sound. He led Rebecca onward. She came willingly, finally without protest. At last, almost too late, she sensed the danger of the situation.

Ibrahim stopped. He tilted his head in order to hear more clearly. He heard a sound in the distance. The rain had at last stopped, the thunder too. It was replaced with this new sound.

Rebecca questioned, "What is it, Ibi?"

Ibrahim motioned with his hand for her to be silent. There it was! The sound of a battle horn.

He heard it again faintly, coming from far away over the walls originating somewhere on the plain of the Vega below. It was not the note of a horn of Castile. It must be Adnan Al-Mansur and Osmyn!

They had arrived on the field of battle! Granada could still be saved!

He heard the sounding of the battle horn again!

Then Ibrahim realized the battle horn was not that of the Moors. The distinct, unique call must belong to one of the foreign contingents in the host of Castile. Perhaps it was the Franks calling out to one another. Whatever the case, it was not the army of Granada arriving to save the city.

He cursed himself for his stupidity, for giving in to false hope. There was no hope. He knew there was no hope. Today would be a day of death and defeat, not a day of salvation and sudden victory. They emerged from the alleyway close to a small gate on a lonely portion of the fortified wall of Granada.

Standing there was his beloved mount Exsecour. Holding the reins of the charger was Yusuf, the loyal sentry who kept watch over Santiago de Aviles in the dungeon of the Alhambra.

Exsecour bore a rider. A sack was over his head and his hands bound behind him. Ibrahim approached, and with a quick flick of his scimitar slit the ropes open that bound the man's hands. He said, "Yusuf. You have done well!"

He grasped the soldier by the side of his face in a gentle, paternal way. "You have always served Allah, and me well."

Yusuf smiled, his round face beamed, grateful of the praise, like a young child commended by his father.

"Now go! Fight with your brothers at the gates and save Granada from the infidel."

Yusuf bowed, a deep respectful motion, asked, "Are you not coming to lead us, my Lord?"

"No. Not this time, my friend."

"I do not understand, my Lord."

"Nor do I Yusuf, nor do I. I am no longer of assistance to you and your brothers. Now go."

Yusuf bowed once again then ran off, puzzled, but determined to fight. He drew his sword and sprinted as fast as his weight allowed toward the ever-increasing sounds of the battle raging around the main gates. Yusuf stopped and turned back toward Ibrahim, catching his breath, "Emir Rahim!" he shouted, "It has been a privilege serving under your hand!"

Ibrahim raised his hand in objection and called, "No, my brother, no! The privilege is mine, and mine alone."

With that, Ibrahim bowed to Yusuf, a deeper and longer bow than any gesture of respect he ever offered to Sultan, King or Imam.

Ibrahim turned his attention to Rebecca. "You will ride out to the King of Castile. He will give you shelter and protection."

Ibrahim withdrew from under his robe a papyrus scroll, with his personal red wax seal upon it. "Give him this. It is my personal request that he grant you safe passage to Christian lands under guard. I have met this king. He is an honorable man, and he will watch over you until you are safe."

Ibrahim thrust the scroll into Rebecca's hand, then turned and lifted the sack from off of the head of the rider on the horse to reveal the face of Santiago de Aviles.

Rebecca gasped! Ibrahim turned in alarm to face her but she was looking up at Santiago. She exclaimed in delight, "Santiago! What are you doing in Granada?"

Santiago's brows furrowed, then his eyes widened as he beheld the girl standing before him. He stammered, "Rebecca?"

Santiago swung down off the horse and Rebecca leapt into his arms the way a child leaps into the arms of a beloved parent. They hugged, a deeply intense embrace. Tears streamed down Rebecca's cheeks, and Santiago laughed as he spun her around over and over again.

Ibrahim did not know how Santiago and Rebecca had met each other. Perhaps they were related. He did not care. He scanned the alley behind them, the wall in front of them and all around, knowing that the *Fidai* could appear at any moment. This was no time for a family reunion.

Ibrahim interrupted. "Enough! You have to go now! Get on the horse and ride!"

Santiago stopped spinning Rebecca and placed her back on the ground. "Don't you understand, Ibi? This is the girl! This is the girl that I told you about! Rebecca is the little girl that I saved from the Bishop!"

With those words, the weight of Ibrahim's life came crashing down upon his shoulders. His entire body went limp. He fell to his knees, his scimitar clanged on the cobblestones. Ibrahim began to sob. It could not be. This was all some terrible joke played upon him by the Divine One. He had been played like a marionette, led about on a string his entire life, up to this exact moment. He finally felt the full gravity of his sins, the consequence of all of the men he killed. He could see them all now, in his minds eye, faces gliding across the face of the scimitar, whether in heaven or hell he was not sure, laughing at him, mocking him, all he had slain over the decades. God himself must be laughing at the cruel twist of fate that was played upon him.

He could not speak as the thought flashed over and over in his mind—*I killed the man who saved the girl I love! I killed the man who saved the girl I love!*

They had all enacted upon him a profound and deep vengeance. A swift death from a sword or spear point would have been much easier to bear than the pain that tore through Ibrahim's heart. He killed the brother of the man who saved the girl whom he loved. It was too much for him. He closed his eyes and his mind went blank. Overwhelmed. It was too much for any honorable man to bear.

Rebecca fell to her knees beside him and threw her arms about his neck. "You poor, tortured, beautiful man! Come with us! Ride with us! Leave this place. You were right, only death awaits you here. Leave it now, Ibi! This is your chance. Do not sacrifice your life as compensation. Enough blood has been spilled. He is opening the door for you, walk through it and live a life of peace and joy, with me, together. You will become the man Anna and Musa wanted you to become."

Ibrahim looked into her dark eyes, long lashes encased in tears. He saw before him the life he could have, the life that his parents wanted for him. Didn't he deserve a life such as this? A life of peace? No. He did not.

He shook his head. "No Rebecca! My sins have amassed to the heavens. I do not deserve to live such a life. The only thing that I deserve is death. The only thing that will bring me true peace is death."

Rebecca began to contradict him, to argue, when he sprang to his feet and grasped his scimitar, transformed to warrior once again, for five grey shapes emerged from the narrow alleyway, hooded beings with swords drawn, walking slowly, shoulder to shoulder, moving in for the kill. Ibrahim hoisted Rebecca up onto the back of Exsecour. He pressed Anna's string of wooden beads into her hand, then closed her fingers over it. He looked into her beautiful dark eyes one last time and simply said, "Remember."

Rebecca replied, "You remember this. That I love you, Ibrahim Al-Rahim."

Overcome, tears streaming down his cheeks, he replied, "I promise I will see you again, Rebecca. If not in this life, then in eternity."

Ibrahim turned his attention to his beloved charger, and whispered, "It has been an honor, my friend. Now I ask of you only one more thing. I need you to take her to safety, run like the wind, like you have never run before."

Exsecour's eyes carried a sadness. He neighed, and tossed his mane. Could the beast perceive he would never see his beloved master again?

Ibrahim motioned for Santiago to climb onto Exsecour. Then he said to Santiago a few final words, softly, as if the words were too sacred to be said out loud, "I grant you life. Do with it what you will. My prayer is that henceforth you will use it wisely, so that one day, when you go the way of all mankind, all will say that they were the better for knowing you."

Ibrahim slapped Santiago on the leg and added, "You know more than anyone else what you must do with the time you have left, the time I have granted to you."

The assassins approached slowly, cautiously, the way a big cat stalks its prey, taking its time, to ensure the kill is successful.

He turned and yelled, "Take her to safety! GO!"

Santiago grasped Exsecour by the reigns and galloped toward the open gate that meant salvation to them both.

Alone now, Ibrahim turned to face the *Fidai* no more than twenty paces away. He grasped the gladius in one hand and gripped his scimitar tightly in the other. The lead assassin, in the middle of the line, rasped the words, "Puuuu-pet, come to me. It is time for you to die, puuuu-pet."

Ibrahim cleared his mind of the confusion, guilt and sadness in order to concentrate on the impossible task at hand. Five against one. Five professionals. He weighed which of the five to strike first. If he could kill the leader, then strike down another with the same blow, he may have a chance . . .

Someone came up behind him. He whirled, sword raised to strike.

It was Santiago.

Santiago looked at the five and then at Ibrahim. "I think you will need a bit of help!"

Ibrahim was angered to see Santiago still present.

"Damn you! Get Rebecca out of here! Take her to safety! This is not your fight! Return to Aviles!"

Santiago reached for the gladius. "She is gone, Ibi. I don't know what you said to that horse, but Exsecour is riding straight for the Christian lines at a full gallop as if the Fourth Horseman was in pursuit! She is safe, Ibi. I promise you! Now let us see to these bastard *Fidai* shall we?" He grinned as he declared, "I HATE assassins!"

Ibrahim saw that Santiago was determined to fight and if need be, die by his side. An undeserved honor. Ibrahim held the gladius in the air, then flipped it to him. Santiago snatched the hilt in mid-air.

Ibrahim asked, "Does the son of a legionnaire know how to use one of these?"

Santiago grasped the hilt of the short, wide sword and sliced the air in front of him. It was a natural movement, as if the gladius were an extension of his very arm.

Ibrahim remarked. "Markus would be proud!"

He turned his attention to the Grey Cloaks.

They stood in a line, resolute, evil, yellow-stained eyes peering out from under grey hoods, a wall of grey, certain death.

Ibrahim looked at Santiago. Then something occurred that had not occurred since he was a child running through the narrow alleys of Jerusalem with his playmates, when his life was an unencumbered joy. Ibrahim Al-Rahim, the Captain of the Guard, the scourge of the Templars, the hammer of Allah, the Sword of the Alhambra, smiled broadly, wide, even child-like, a gladness in his eyes, a relief, for a huge burden had finally been lifted from his shoulders. He appeared to stand more erect and gain height as the terrible weight of his life was at last borne away. He smiled broadly as he nodded to Santiago.

"For Abran."

Santiago smiled too, eyes moistening, nodding his head in accord and repeated, the words barely coming forth, his voice choking up.

"For Abran."

With that, Ibrahim spun and charged. He ran at a full sprint. Wide smile. One man gloriously charging fearlessly into hell itself.

As he charged, he screamed, "ABRAN DE AVILES!"

A high-pitched, terrifying war cry that caused the hair on the assassin's necks to rise. The cry echoed off the cobblestones, down the alleyway and over the city of Granada, and for a brief moment rose above the din of battle at the main gates. He ran. Long elegant strides, like a runner from the ancient games of Greece, feet barely brushing the cobblestones, for his limiting limp had at last completely disappeared.

The resolute *Fidai*, fearless and wicked in their altered fanatical state, who eagerly anticipated killing the outnumbered captain of the guard of the Alhambra, to a man involuntarily winced in the face of the awe-inspiring charge . . .

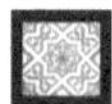

For decades henceforth the story was passed from guard to guard of the Red Castle, that stalwart fortress of the Alhambra, that on certain cold dark nights, during the late night watches when all Granada slept, upon the ramparts, could be heard a soft whisper carried upon the night breezes, words, barely discernible, a mere exhalation of breath, powered with all the intensity of the most bone-chilling battle cry: "*Abran de Aviles.*"

The End.

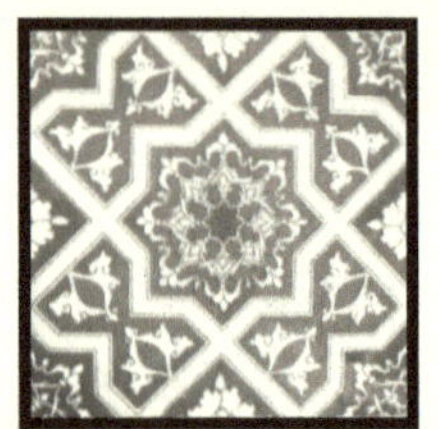

Acknowledgments

I am indebted to Marsha Ziff, my tough and persistent editor, who aided me in my unfinished quest to become a competent writer.

My gratitude also goes to the Ortegas, our friends from Sevilla who personally guided us through Granada and the Alhambra.

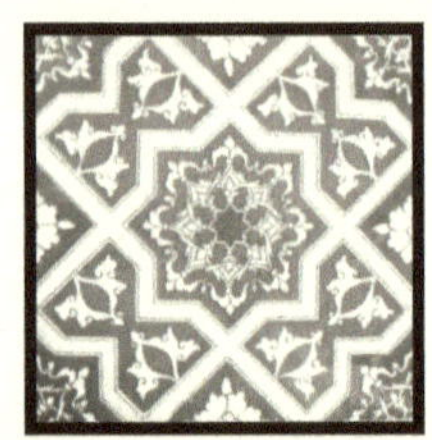

About the Author

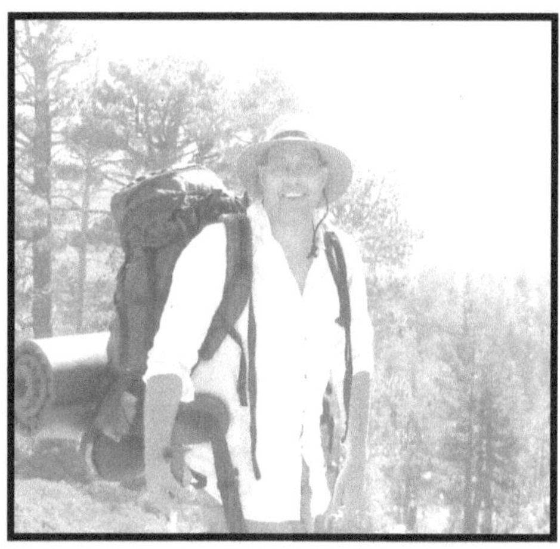

Joseph Anthony, born and raised in the North Bay Area of San Francisco, began writing at age nine. He founded, produced and edited his elementary school's first school paper, the "McKinley Sting" and wrote for his high school newspaper, winning numerous local writing contests.

He is a two-book-at-time reader of all things historical; especially the great authors, both ancient and modern, such as Josephus and Tuchman. Joseph also finds inspiration in works by Hemingway, London, and Poe.

He has traveled extensively with his wife Jessica. For seven years they lived in the remote Andean provinces of Peru, working as volunteer teachers and missionaries.

Joseph currently works as an Investment Advisor and enjoys backpacking the wilderness areas of his home state of California. This is his first novel.

Contact:

Joseph Anthony
Author
joseph.advisor@gmail.com

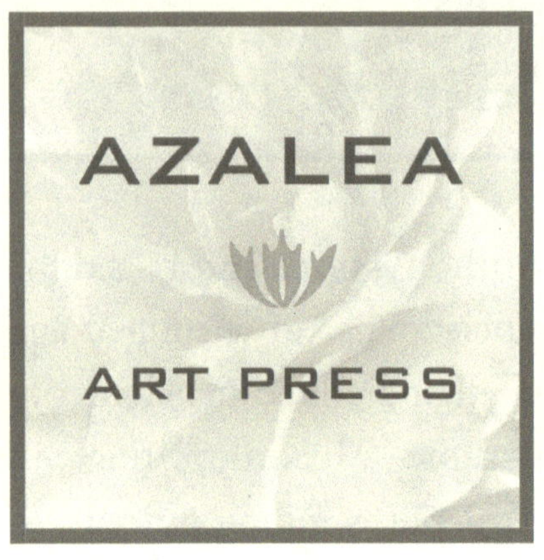

Karen Mireau
Publisher
Azalea Art Press
azaleaartpress@gmail.com

Book Orders
www.lulu.com

www.ingramcontent.com/pod-product-compliance
Lightning Source LLC
LaVergne TN
LVHW050923080826
845145LV00001B/186

* 9 7 8 0 9 8 4 6 9 7 7 2 4 *